Edgar Rice Burroughs (1875–1950) was born in Chicago, Illinois. After serving a short time in the Seventh U.S. Cavalry, Burroughs was a shopkeeper, gold miner, cowboy, and policeman before becoming a full-time writer. His first novel, *Tarzan of the Apes*, was published in 1914, and along with its twenty-two sequels has sold more than thirty million copies in fifty-eight languages. Author of numerous other jungle and science fiction novels and novellas, including *The Land That Time Forgot*, Burroughs had a writing career that spanned almost thirty years, with his last novel, *The Land of Terror*, being published in 1941. He died at his ranch near Tarzana, the California town named for his legendary hero.

Gore Vidal (1925–2012) was born Eugene Vidal and later adopted the surname of his grandfather, Senator Thomas Gore, as his first name. He wrote numerous novels—the first, *Williwaw*, written when he was twenty-one—as well as scripts for film, television and the stage, including the extremely successful *The Best Man* and *Visit to a Small Planet*. He is perhaps best known for his historical novels, including *Burr* (1973), *1876* (1976), and *Lincoln* (1984). He won the National Book Award in 1993 for his book *United States—Essays 1952–1992*.

continued . . .

THE PRISONER OF ZENDA

Anthony Hope (1863–1933) is the pseudonym of Anthony Hope Hawkins, a successful and prolific author of fiction and drama. The son of a school headmaster, Hope was born in London in 1863. While practicing law, Hope also experimented with creative writing, and he published his first novel, a political satire entitled *A Man of Mark* (1890), at his own expense. With the publication of his most famous novel, *The Prisoner of Zenda* (1894), Hope abandoned his legal career to write full-time, penning the short story collection *The Heart of Princess Osra* (1896) and the *Zenda* sequel, *Rupert of Hentzau* (1898). Throughout his productive life, Hope published a wide variety of fiction, in areas ranging from the light domestic comedy of *The Dolly Dialogues* (1894) to the more serious fiction of *Simon Dole* (1889).

Justin Kaplan was the author of many critically acclaimed books, including *Mr. Clemens and Mark Twain*, winner of the Pulitzer Prize and the National Book Award, *Mark Twain and His World*, and *Walt Whitman: A Life*. In 1985, he was elected to the American Academy and Institute of Arts and Letters, and he later edited the sixteenth and seventeenth editions of *Bartlett's Familiar Quotations*. He died in 2014.

TARZAN OF THE APES

Edgar Rice Burroughs

With an Introduction by
Gore Vidal

THE PRISONER OF ZENDA

Anthony Hope

With an Introduction by
Justin Kaplan

SIGNET CLASSICS

SIGNET CLASSICS
Published by the Penguin Group
Penguin Group (USA) LLC, 375 Hudson Street,
New York, New York 10014

USA | Canada | UK | Ireland | Australia | New Zealand | India | South Africa | China
penguin.com
A Penguin Random House Company

Published by Signet Classics, an imprint of New American Library,
a division of Penguin Group (USA) LLC

First Signet Classics Printing, June 2006

 REGISTERED TRADEMARK—MARCA REGISTRADA

ISBN 978-0-451-53018-9

Printed in the United States of America
10 9 8 7 6 5 4 3 2

TARZAN OF
THE APES

To Emma Hulbert Burroughs

Contents

6   *Contents*

Tarzan Revisited

THERE are so many things that people who take polls never get around to asking. Fascinated as we all are to know what our countrymen think of great issues (approving, disapproving, don't-knowing, with that native shrewdness which made a primeval wilderness bloom with Howard Johnson signs), the pollsters never get around to asking the sort of interesting personal questions our new Romans might be able to answer knowledgeably. For instance, how many adults have an adventure serial running in their heads? How many consciously daydream, turning on a story in which the dreamer ceases to be an employee of IBM and becomes a handsome demigod moving through splendid palaces, saving maidens from monsters (or monsters from maidens: this is a jaded time). Most children tell themselves stories in which they figure as powerful figures, enjoying the pleasures not only of the adult world as they conceive it but of a world of wonders unlike dull reality. Although this sort of Mittyesque daydreaming is supposed to cease in maturity, I suggest that more adults than we suspect are dazedly wandering about with a full Technicolor extravaganza going on in their heads. Clad in tights, rapier in hand, the daydreamers drive their Jaguars at fantastic speeds through a glittering world of

7

adoring love objects, mingling anachronistic historic
worlds with science fiction. "Captain, the time-warp's
been closed! We are now trapped in a parallel world, inhabited entirely by women with three breasts!" Though
from what we can gather about these imaginary worlds,
they tend to be more Adlerian than Freudian: the motor
drive is the desire not for sex (other briefer fantasies
take care of that) but for power, for the ability to dominate one's environment through physical strength, best
demonstrated in the works of Edgar Rice Burroughs.

When I was growing up, I read all twenty-three
Tarzan books, as well as the ten Mars books. My own
inner storytelling mechanism was vivid. At any one
time, I had at least three serials going as well as a number of tried and true reruns. I mined Burroughs largely
for source material. When he went to the center of the
earth à la Jules Verne (much too fancy a writer for one's
taste), I immediately worked up a thirteen-part series,
with myself as lead and various friends as guest stars.
Sometimes I used the master's material, but more often
I adapted it freely to suit myself. One's daydreams
tended to be Tarzanish pre-puberty (physical strength
and freedom) and Martian post-puberty (exotic worlds
and subtle *combinazione* to be worked out). After ado-
lescence, if one's life is sufficiently interesting, the desire
to tell oneself stories diminishes. My last serial ran into
sponsor trouble when I was in the Second World War,
and it was never renewed.

Until recently I assumed that most people were like
myself: daydreaming ceases when the real world becomes interesting and reasonably manageable. Now I
am not so certain. Pondering the life and success of Burroughs leads one to believe that a good many people
find their lives so unsatisfactory that they go right on
year after year telling themselves stories in which they
are able to dominate their environment in a way that is
not possible in the overorganized society.

According to Edgar Rice Burroughs, "Most of the
stories I wrote were the stories I told myself just before

I went to sleep." He is a fascinating figure to contemplate, an archetypal American dreamer. Born in 1875 in Chicago, he was a drifter until he was thirty-six. He served briefly in the U.S. Cavalry; then he was a gold miner in Oregon, a cowboy in Idaho, a railroad policeman in Salt Lake City; he attempted several businesses that failed. He was perfectly in the old-American grain: the man who could take on almost any job, who liked to keep moving, who tried to get rich quick but could never pull it off. And while he was drifting through the unsatisfactory real world, he consoled himself with an inner world where he was strong and handsome, adored by beautiful women and worshiped by exotic races. His principal source of fantasy was Rider Haggard. But even that rich field was limited, and so, searching for new veins to tap, he took to reading the pulp magazines, only to find that none of the stories could compare for excitement with his own imaginings. Since the magazine writers could not please him, he had no choice but to please himself, and the public. He composed a serial about Mars and sold it to *Munsey's*. The rest was easy, for his fellow daydreamers recognized at once a master dreamer.

In 1914 Burroughs published *Tarzan of the Apes* (Rousseau's noble savage reborn in Africa), and history was made. To date the Tarzan books have sold over twenty-five million copies in fifty-six languages. There is hardly an American male of my generation who has not at one time or another tried to master the victory cry of the great ape as it issued from the androgynous chest of Johnny Weissmuller, to the accompaniment of thousands of arms and legs snapping during attempts to swing from tree to tree in the backyards of the Republic. Between 1914 and his death in 1950, the squire of Tarzana, California (a prophet more than honored in his own land), produced over sixty books, while enjoying the unique status of being the first American writer to be a corporation. Burroughs is said to have been a pleasant, unpretentious man who liked to ride and play golf. Not one to compromise a vivid unconscious with dim reality, he never set foot in Africa.

With a sense of recapturing childhood, I recently reread several Tarzan books. It is fascinating to see how much one recalls after a quarter century. At times the sense of *déjà vu* is overpowering. It is equally interesting to discover that one's memories of Tarzan of the Apes are mostly action scenes. The plot had slipped one's mind ... and a lot of plot there is. The beginning is worthy of Conrad. "I had this story from one who had no business to tell it to me, or to any other. I may credit the seductive influence of an old vintage upon the narrator for the beginning of it, and my own skeptical incredulity during the days that followed for the balance of the strange tale." It is 1888. The young Lord and Lady Greystoke are involved in a ship mutiny ("There was in the whole atmosphere of the craft that undefinable something which presages disaster"). The peer and peeress are put ashore on the west coast of Africa, where they promptly build a tree house. Here Burroughs is at his best. He tells you the size of the logs, the way to hang a door when you have no hinges, the problems of roofing. One of the best things about his books is the descriptions of making things. The Greystokes have a child, and conveniently die. The "man-child" is discovered by Kala, a Great Ape, who brings him up as a member of her tribe. As anthropologist, Burroughs is pleasantly vague. His apes are carnivorous, and they are able, he darkly suspects, to mate with human beings.

Tarzan grows up as an ape, kills his first lion (with a full nelson), teaches himself to read and write English by studying some books found in the cabin. The method he used, sad to say, is the currently fashionable "look-see." Though he can read and write, he cannot speak any language except that of the apes. He also gets on well with other members of the animal kingdom, with Tantor the elephant, Ska the vulture, Numa the lion (Kipling was also grist for the Burroughs dream mill). Then white folks arrive: Professor Archimedes Q. Porter and his daughter Jane. Also, a Frenchman named D'Arnot who teaches Tarzan to speak French, which is confusing. By an extraordinary coincidence, Jane's suitor is the current Lord Greystoke, who thinks the Greystoke baby is dead. Tarzan saves Jane from an ape. Then he puts on clothes and goes to Paris. Next stop, America. In Wisconsin, he saves Jane Porter from a forest fire: only to give her up nobly to Lord Greystoke, not revealing the fact that *he* is the real Lord Greystoke. Fortunately in the next volume, *The Return of Tarzan,* he marries Jane and they live happily ever after in Africa, raising a son John, who in turn grows up and has a son. Yet even as a grandfather, Tarzan continues to have adventures with people a foot high, with descendants of Atlantis, with the heirs of a Roman legion who think that Rome is still a success. All through these stories one gets the sense that one is daydreaming, too. Episode follows episode with no particular urgency. Tarzan is always knocked on the head and taken captive; he always escapes; there is always a beautiful princess or high priestess who loves him and assists him; there is always a loyal friend who fights beside him, very much in that Queequeg tradition which, Professor Leslie Fiedler assures us, is the urning in the fuel supply of the American psyche. But no matter how difficult the adventure, Tarzan, clad only in a loincloth with no weapon save a knife (the style is comforting to imitate), wins against all odds and returns to his shadowy wife.

Stylistically, Burroughs is—how shall I put it?—uneven. He has moments of ornate pomp, when the darkness is "Cimmerian"; of redundancy, "she was hideous and ugly"; of extraordinary dialogue: "Name of a name," shrieked Rokoff. "Pig, but you shall die for this!" Or Lady Greystoke to Lord G.: "Duty is duty, my husband, and no amount of sophistries may change it. I would be a poor wife for an English lord were I to be responsible for his shirking a plain duty." Or the grandchild: "Muvver," he cried, "Dackie doe? Dackie doe?" "Let him come along," urged Tarzan. "Dare!" exclaimed the boy, turning triumphantly upon the governess, "Dackie do doe yalk!" Burroughs' use of coincidence is shameless even for a pulp writer. In one book he has three sets of characters shipwrecked at exactly the same point on the shore of Africa. Even Burroughs finds this a bit much. "Could it be possible [muses Tarzan] that fate had thrown him up at the very threshold of his own beloved jungle?" It was possible since anything can happen in a daydream. Though Burroughs is innocent of literature and cannot reproduce human speech, he does have a gift very few writers of any kind possess: he can describe action vividly. I give away no trade secrets when I say that this is as difficult for a Tolstoi as it is for a Burroughs (even William). Because it is so hard, the craftier contemporary novelists usually prefer to tell their stories in the first person, which is simply writing dialogue. In character, as it were, the writer settles for an impression of what happened rather than creating the sense of the thing happening. In action Tarzan is excellent.

   There is something basic in the appeal of the 1914 Tarzan which makes me think that he can still hold his own as a daydream figure, despite the sophisticated challenge of his two young competitors, James Bond and Mike Hammer. For most adults, Tarzan (and John Carter of Mars) can hardly compete with the conspicuous consumer consumption of James Bond or the sickly violence of Mike Hammer, but for children and adolescents the old appeal continues. All of us need the idea of a world alternative to this one. From Plato's Republic to Opar to Bondland, at every level, the human imagination has tried to imagine something better for itself than the existing society. Man left Eden when he got up off all fours, endowing his descendants with nostalgia as well as chronic backache. In its naïve way, the Tarzan legend returns us to that Eden where, free of clothes and the inhibitions of an oppressive society, a man is able, as William Faulkner put it in his high Confederate style, to prevail as well as endure. The current obsession with drugs—not to mention alcohol—is all a result of a general sense of boredom. Since the individual's desire to dominate his environment is not a desirable trait in a society that every day grows more and more confining, the average person is apt to take to daydreaming. Tarzan is a classic dream-self, able to give the dreamer a spacious sense of mastery over a world that, more and more, diminishes the individual. Tarzan lives! even if we do not.

—Gore Vidal

CHAPTER I

Out to Sea

I HAD this story from one who had no business to tell it to me, or to any other. I may credit the seductive influence of an old vintage upon the narrator for the beginning of it, and my own skeptical incredulity during the days that followed for the balance of the strange tale.

When my convivial host discovered that he had told me so much, and that I was prone to doubtfulness, his foolish pride assumed the task the old vintage had commenced, and so he unearthed written evidence in the form of musty manuscript, and dry official records of the British Colonial Office to support many of the salient features of his remarkable narrative.

I do not say the story is true, for I did not witness the happenings which it portrays, but the fact that in the telling of it to you I have taken fictitious names for the principal characters quite sufficiently evidences the sincerity of my own belief that it *may* be true.

The yellow, mildewed pages of the diary of a man long dead, and the records of the Colonial Office dovetail perfectly with the narrative of my convivial host, and so I give you the story as I painstakingly pieced it out from these several various agencies.

If you do not find it credible you will at least be as

one with me in acknowledging that it is unique, remarkable, and interesting.

From the records of the Colonial Office and from the dead man's diary we learn that a certain young English nobleman, whom we shall call John Clayton, Lord Greystoke, was commissioned to make a peculiarly delicate investigation of conditions in a British West Coast African Colony from whose simple native inhabitants another European power was known to be recruiting soldiers for its native army, which it used solely for the forcible collection of rubber and ivory from the savage tribes along the Congo and the Aruwimi.

The natives of the British Colony complained that many of their young men were enticed away through the medium of fair and glowing promises, but that few if any ever returned to their families.

The Englishmen in Africa went even further: saying that these poor blacks were held in virtual slavery, since when their terms of enlistment expired their ignorance was imposed upon by their white officers, and they were told that they had yet several years to serve.

And so the Colonial Office appointed John Clayton to a new post in British West Africa, but his confidential instructions centered on a thorough investigation of the unfair treatment of black British subjects by the officers of a friendly European power. Why he was sent, is, however, of little moment to this story, for he never made an investigation, nor, in fact, did he ever reach his destination.

Clayton was the type of Englishman that one likes best to associate with the noblest monuments of historic achievement upon a thousand victorious battlefields—a strong, virile man—mentally, morally, and physically.

In stature he was above the average height; his eyes were gray, his features regular and strong; his carriage that of perfect, robust health influenced by his years of army training.

Political ambition had caused him to seek transference from the army to the Colonial Office and so we find him, still young, intrusted with a delicate and important commission in the service of the Queen.

When he received this appointment he was both elated and appalled. The preferment seemed to him in the nature of a well-merited reward for painstaking and intelligent service, and as a stepping-stone to posts of greater importance and responsibility; but, on the other hand, he had been married to the Hon. Alice Rutherford for scarce a three months, and it was the thought of taking this fair young girl into the dangers and isolation of tropical Africa that dismayed and appalled him.

For her sake he would have refused the appointment; but she would not have it so. Instead she insisted that he accept, and, indeed, take her with him.

There were mothers and brothers and sisters, and aunts and cousins to express various opinions on the subject, but as to what they severally advised history is silent.

We know only that on a bright May morning in 1888, John, Lord Greystoke, and Lady Alice sailed from Dover on their way to Africa.

A month later they arrived at Freetown where they chartered a small sailing vessel, the *Fuwalda*, which was to bear them to their final destination.

And here John, Lord Greystoke, and Lady Alice, his wife, vanished from the eyes and from the knowledge of men.

Two months after they weighed anchor and cleared from the port of Freetown a half dozen British war vessels were scouring the south Atlantic for trace of them or their little vessel, and it was almost immediately that the wreckage was found upon the shores of St. Helena which convinced the world that the *Fuwalda* had gone down with all on board, and hence the search was stopped ere it had scarce begun; though hope lingered in longing hearts for many years.

The *Fuwalda,* a barkantine of about one hundred tons, was a vessel of the type often seen in coastwise trade in the far southern Atlantic, their crews composed of the offscourings of the sea—unhanged murderers and cutthroats of every race and every nation.

The *Fuwalda* was no exception to the rule. Her officers were swarthy bullies, hating and hated by their crew. The captain, while a competent seaman, was a brute in his treatment of his men. He knew, or at least he used, but two arguments in his dealings with them— a belaying pin and a revolver—nor is it likely that the motley aggregation he signed would have understood aught else.

So it was that from the second day out from Freetown John Clayton and his young wife witnessed scenes upon the deck of the *Fuwalda* such as they had believed were never enacted outside the covers of printed stories of the sea.

It was on the morning of the second day that the first link was forged of what was destined to form a chain of circumstances ending in a life for one then unborn such as has probably never been paralleled in the history of man.

Two sailors were washing down the decks of the *Fuwalda,* the first mate was on duty, and the captain had stopped to speak with John Clayton and Lady Alice.

The men were working backwards toward the little party who were facing away from the sailors. Closer and closer they came, until one of them was directly behind the captain. In another moment he would have passed by and this strange narrative had never been recorded.

But just that instant the officer turned to leave Lord and Lady Greystoke, and, as he did so, tripped against the sailor and sprawled headlong upon the deck, overturning the waterpail so that he was drenched in its dirty contents.

For an instant the scene was ludicrous; but only for an instant. With a volley of awful oaths, his face suffused with the scarlet of mortification and rage, the captain regained his feet, and with a terrific blow felled the sailor to the deck.

The man was small and rather old, so that the brutality of the act was thus accentuated. The other seaman, however, was neither old nor small—a huge bear of a man, with fierce black mustachios, and a great bull neck set between massive shoulders.

As he saw his mate go down he crouched, and, with a low snarl, sprang upon the captain crushing him to his knees with a single mighty blow.

From scarlet the officer's face went white, for this was mutiny; and mutiny he had met and subdued before in his brutal career. Without waiting to rise he whipped a revolver from his pocket, firing point blank at the great mountain of muscle towering before him; but, quick as he was, John Clayton was almost as quick, so that the bullet which was intended for the sailor's heart lodged in the sailor's leg instead, for Lord Greystoke had struck down the captain's arm as he had seen the weapon flash in the sun.

Words passed between Clayton and the captain, the former making it plain that he was disgusted with the brutality displayed toward the crew, nor would he countenance anything further of the kind while he and Lady Greystoke remained passengers.

The captain was on the point of making an angry reply, but, thinking better of it, turned on his heel and black and scowling, strode aft.

He did not care to antagonize an English official, for the Queen's mighty arm wielded a punitive instrument which he could appreciate, and which he feared—England's far-reaching navy.

The two sailors picked themselves up, the older man assisting his wounded comrade to rise. The big fellow, who was known among his mates as Black Michael, tried his leg gingerly, and finding that it bore his weight, turned to Clayton with a word of gruff thanks.

Though the fellow's tone was surly, his words were evidently well meant. Ere he had scarce finished his little speech he had turned and was limping off toward the forecastle with the very apparent intention of forestalling any further conversation.

They did not see him again for several days, nor did the captain vouchsafe them more than the surliest of grunts when he was forced to speak to them.

They messed in his cabin, as they had before the unfortunate occurrence; but the captain was careful to see that his duties never permitted him to eat at the same time.

The other officers were coarse, illiterate fellows, but little above the villainous crew they bullied, and were only too glad to avoid social intercourse with the polished English noble and his lady, so that the Claytons were left very much to themselves.

This in itself accorded perfectly with their desires, but it also rather isolated them from the life of the little ship so that they were unable to keep in touch with the daily happenings which were to culminate so soon in bloody tragedy.

There was in the whole atmosphere of the craft that undefinable something which presages disaster. Outwardly, to the knowledge of the Claytons, all went on as before upon the little vessel, but that there was an undertow leading them toward some unknown danger both felt, though they did not speak of it to each other.

On the second day after the wounding of Black Michael, Clayton came on deck just in time to see the limp body of one of the crew being carried below by four of his fellows while the first mate, a heavy belaying pin in his hand, stood glowering at the little party of sullen sailors.

Clayton asked no questions—he did not need to—and the following day, as the great lines of a British battleship grew out of the distant horizon, he half determined to demand that he and Lady Alice be put aboard her, for his fears were steadily increasing that nothing but harm could result from remaining on the lowering, sullen *Fuwalda*.

Toward noon they were within speaking distance of the British vessel, but when Clayton had about decided to ask the captain to put them aboard her, the obvious ridiculousness of such a request became suddenly apparent. What reason could he give the officer commanding her majesty's ship for desiring to go back in the direction from which he had just come!

Faith, what if he told them that two insubordinate seamen had been roughly handled by their officers. They would but laugh in their sleeves and attribute his reason for wishing to leave the ship to but one thing—cowardice.

John Clayton, Lord Greystoke, did not ask to be transferred to the British man-of-war, and late in the afternoon he saw her upper works fade below the far horizon, but not before he learned that which confirmed his greatest fears, and caused him to curse the false pride which had restrained him from seeking safety for his young wife a few short hours before, when safety was within reach—a safety which was now gone forever.

It was mid-afternoon that brought the little old sailor, who had been felled by the captain a few days before, to where Clayton and his wife stood by the ship's side watching the ever diminishing outlines of the great battleship. The old fellow was polishing brasses, and as he came edging along until close to Clayton he said, in an undertone:

" 'Ell's to pay, sir, on this 'ere craft, an' mark my word for it, sir. 'Ell's to pay."

"What do you mean, my good fellow?" asked Clayton.

"Wy, hasn't ye seen wats goin' on? Hasn't ye 'eard that devil's spawn of a capting an' 'is mates knockin' the bloomin' lights outen 'arf the crew?

"Two busted 'eads yeste'day, an' three to-day. Black Michael's as good as new agin an' 'e's not the bully to stand fer it, not 'e; an' mark my word for it, sir."

"You mean, my man, that the crew contemplates mutiny?" asked Clayton.

"Mutiny!" exclaimed the old fellow. "Mutiny! They means murder, sir, an' mark my word for it, sir."

"When?"

"Hit's comin', sir; hit's comin' but I'm not a-sayin' wen, an' I've said too damned much now, but ye was a good sort t'other day an' I thought it no more'n right to warn ye. But keep a still tongue in yer 'ead an' when ye hear shootin' git below an' stay there.

"That's all, only keep a still tongue in yer 'ead, or they'll put a pill between yer ribs, an' mark my word for it, sir," and the old fellow went on with his polishing, which carried him away from where the Claytons were standing.

"Deuced cheerful outlook, Alice," said Clayton.

"You should warn the captain at once, John. Possibly the trouble may yet be averted," she said.

"I suppose I should, but yet from purely selfish motives I am almost prompted to 'keep a still tongue in my 'ead.' Whatever they do now they will spare us in recognition of my stand for this fellow Black Michael, but should they find that I had betrayed them there would be no mercy shown us, Alice."

"You have but one duty, John, and that lies in the interest of vested authority. If you do not warn the captain you are as much a party to whatever follows as though you had helped to plot and carry it out with your own head and hands."

"You do not understand, dear," replied Clayton. "It is of you I am thinking—there lies my first duty. The captain has brought this condition upon himself, so why then should I risk subjecting my wife to unthinkable horrors in probably futile attempt to save him from his own brutal folly? You have no conception, dear, of what would follow were this pack of cutthroats to gain control of the *Fuwalda*."

"Duty is duty, my husband, and no amount of sophistries may change it. I would be a poor wife for an English lord were I to be responsible for his shirking a plain duty. I realize the danger which must follow, but I can face it with you—face it much more bravely than I could face the dishonor of always knowing that you might have averted a tragedy had you not neglected your duty."

"Have it as you will then, Alice," he answered, smiling. "Maybe we are borrowing trouble. While I do not like the looks of things on board this ship, they may not be so bad after all, for it is possible that the 'Ancient Mariner' was but voicing the desires of his wicked old heart rather than speaking of real facts.

"Mutiny on the high sea may have been common a hundred years ago, but in this good year 1888 it is the least likely of happenings.

"But there goes the captain to his cabin now. If I am going to warn him I might as well get the beastly job over for I have little stomach to talk with the brute at all."

So saying he strolled carelessly in the direction of the companionway through which the captain had passed, and a moment later was knocking at his door.

"Come in," growled the deep tones of that surly officer.

And when Clayton had entered, and closed the door behind him:

"Well?"

"I have come to report the gist of a conversation I heard to-day, because I feel that, while there may be nothing to it, it is as well that you be forearmed. In short, the men contemplate mutiny and murder."

"It's a lie!" roared the captain. "And if you have been interfering again with the discipline of this ship, or meddling in affairs that don't concern you you can take the consequences, and be damned. I don't care whether you are an English lord or not. I'm captain of this here ship, and from now on you keep your meddling nose out of my business."

As he reached this peroration, the captain had worked himself up to such a frenzy of rage that he was fairly purple of face, and shrieked the last words at the top of his voice; emphasizing his remarks by a loud thumping of the table with one huge fist, shaking the other in Clayton's face.

Greystoke never turned a hair, but stood eyeing the excited man with level gaze.

"Captain Billings," he drawled finally, "if you will pardon my candor, I might remark that you are something of an ass, don't you know."

Whereupon he turned and left the captain with the same indifferent ease that was habitual with him, and which was more surely calculated to raise the ire of a man of Billings' class than a torrent of invective.

So, whereas the captain might easily have been brought to regret his hasty speech had Clayton attempted to conciliate him, his temper was now irrevocably set in the mold in which Clayton had left it, and the last chance of their working together for their common good and preservation of life was gone.

"Well, Alice," said Clayton, as he rejoined his wife, "if I had saved my breath I should likewise have saved myself a bit of a calling. The fellow proved most ungrateful. Fairly jumped at me like a mad dog.

"He and his blasted old ship may go hang, for aught I care; and until we are safe off the thing I shall spend my energies in looking after our own welfare. And I rather fancy the first step to that end should be to go to our cabin and look over my revolvers. I am sorry now that we packed the larger guns and the ammunition with the stuff below."

They found their quarters in a bad state of disorder. Clothing from their open boxes and bags strewed the little apartment, and even their beds had been torn to pieces.

"Evidently some one was more anxious about our belongings than we," said Clayton. "By jove, I wonder what the bounder was after. Let's have a look around, Alice, and see what's missing."

A thorough search revealed the fact that nothing had been taken but Clayton's two revolvers and the small supply of ammunition he had saved out for them.

"Those are the very things I most wish they had left

us," said Clayton, "and the fact that they wished for them and them alone is the most sinister circumstance of all that have transpired to endanger us since we set foot on this miserable hulk."

"What are we to do, John?" asked his wife. "I shall not urge you to go again to the captain for I cannot see you affronted further. Possibly our best chance for salvation lies in maintaining a neutral position.

"If the officers are able to prevent a mutiny, we have nothing to fear, while if the mutineers are victorious our one slim hope lies in not having attempted to thwart or antagonize them."

"Right you are, Alice. We'll keep in the middle of the road."

As they fell to in an effort to straighten up their cabin, Clayton and his wife simultaneously noticed the corner of a piece of paper protruding from beneath the door of their quarters. As Clayton stooped to reach for it he was amazed to see it move further into the room, and then he realized that it was being pushed inward by some one from without.

Quickly and silently he stepped toward the door, but, as he reached for the knob to throw it open, his wife's hand fell upon his wrist.

"No, John," she whispered. "They do not wish to be seen, and so we cannot afford to see them. Do not forget that we are keeping the middle of the road."

Clayton smiled and dropped his hand to his side. Thus they stood watching the little bit of white paper until it finally remained at rest upon the floor just inside the door.

Then Clayton stooped and picked it up. It was a bit of grimy, white paper roughly folded into a ragged square. Opening it they found a crude message printed in uncouth letters, with many evidences of an unaccustomed task.

Translated, it was a warning to the Claytons to refrain from reporting the loss of the revolvers, or from repeating what the old sailor had told them—to refrain on pain of death.

"I rather imagine we'll be good," said Clayton with a rueful smile. "About all we can do is to sit tight and wait for whatever may come."

CHAPTER II

❧❧

The Savage Home

NOR did they have long to wait, for the next morning as Clayton was emerging on deck for his accustomed walk before breakfast, a shot rang out, and then another, and another.

The sight which met his eyes confirmed his worst fears. Facing the little knot of officers was the entire motley crew of the *Fuwalda*, and at their head stood Black Michael.

At the first volley from the officers the men ran for shelter, and from points of vantage behind masts, wheelhouse and cabin they returned the fire of the five men who represented the hated authority of the ship.

Two of their number had gone down before the captain's revolver. They lay where they had fallen between the combatants.

Presently the first mate lunged forward upon his face, and at a cry of command from Black Michael the bloodthirsty ruffians charged the remaining four. The crew had been able to muster but six firearms, so most of them were armed with boat hooks, axes, hatchets and crowbars.

The captain had emptied his revolver and was reloading as the charge was made. The second mate's gun had jammed, and so there were but two weapons op-

posed to the mutineers as they rapidly approached the
officers, who now started to give back before the infuriated rush of their men.

Both sides were cursing and swearing in a frightful
manner, which, together with the reports of the firearms
and the screams and groans of the wounded, turned the
deck of the *Fuwalda* to the likeness of a madhouse.

Before the officers had taken a dozen backward steps
the men were upon them. An ax in the hands of a burly
negro cleft the captain from forehead to chin, and an instant later the others were down; dead or wounded from
dozens of blows and bullet wounds.

Short and grisly had been the work of the mutineers
of the *Fuwalda,* and through it all John Clayton had
stood leaning carelessly beside the companionway puffing meditatively upon his pipe as though he had been
but watching an indifferent cricket match.

As the last officer went down he bethought him that
it was time that he returned to his wife lest some members of the crew find her alone below.

Though outwardly calm and indifferent, Clayton was
inwardly apprehensive and wrought up, for he feared
for his wife's safety at the hands of these ignorant, half-
brutes into whose hands fate had so remorselessly
thrown them.

As he turned to descend the ladder he was surprised
to see his wife standing on the steps almost at his side.

"How long have you been here, Alice?"

"Since the beginning," she replied. "How awful, John.
Oh, how awful! What can we hope for at the hands of
such as those?"

"Breakfast, I hope," he answered, smiling bravely in
an attempt to allay her fears.

"At least," he added, "I'm going to ask them. Come
with me, Alice. We must not let them think we expect
any but courteous treatment."

The men had by this time surrounded the dead and
wounded officers, and without either partiality or compassion proceeded to throw both living and dead over

the sides of the vessel. With equal heartlessness they disposed of their own wounded and the bodies of the three sailors to whom a merciful Providence had vouchsafed instant death before the bullets of the officers.

Presently one of the crew spied the approaching Claytons, and with a cry of: "Here's two more for the fishes," rushed toward them with uplifted ax.

But Black Michael was even quicker, so that the fellow went down with a bullet in his back before he had taken a half dozen steps.

With a loud roar, Black Michael attracted the attention of the others, and, pointing to Lord and Lady Greystoke, cried:

"These here are my friends, and they are to be left alone. D'ye understand?

"I'm captain of this ship now, an' what I says goes," he added, turning to Clayton. "Just keep to yourselves, and nobody'll harm ye," and he looked threateningly on his fellows.

The Claytons heeded Black Michael's instructions so well that they saw but little of the crew and knew nothing of the plans the men were making.

Occasionally they heard faint echoes of brawls and quarreling among the mutineers, and on two occasions the vicious bark of firearms rang out on the still air. But Black Michael was a fit leader for this heterogeneous band of cutthroats, and, withal, held them in fair subjection to his rule.

On the fifth day following the murder of the ship's officers, land was sighted by the lookout. Whether island or mainland, Black Michael did not know, but he announced to Clayton that if investigation showed that the place was habitable he and Lady Greystoke were to be put ashore with their belongings.

"You'll be all right there for a few months," he explained, "and by that time we'll have been able to make an inhabited coast somewheres and scatter a bit. Then I'll see that yer gover'ment's notified where you be an' they'll soon send a man-o'war to fetch ye off.

"You may be all right, but it would be a hard matter to land you in civilization without a lot o' questions being asked, an' none o' us here has any very convincin' answers up our sleeves."

Clayton remonstrated against the inhumanity of landing them upon an unknown shore to be left to the mercies of savage beasts, and, possibly, still more savage men.

But his words were of no avail, and only tended to anger Black Michael, so he was forced to desist and make the best he could of a bad situation.

About three o'clock in the afternoon they came about off a beautiful wooded shore opposite the mouth of what appeared to be a land-locked harbor.

Black Michael sent a small boat filled with men to sound the entrance in an effort to determine if the *Fuwalda* could be safely worked through the entrance.

In about an hour they returned and reported deep water through the passage as well as far into the little basin.

Before dark the barkantine lay peacefully at anchor upon the bosom of the still, mirrorlike surface of the harbor.

The surrounding shores were beautiful with semi-tropical verdure, while in the distance the country rose from the ocean in hill and tableland, almost uniformly clothed by primeval forest.

No signs of habitation were visible, but that the land might easily support human life was evidenced by the abundant bird and animal life of which the watchers on the *Fuwalda*'s deck caught occasional glimpses, as well as by the shimmer of a little river which emptied into the harbor, insuring fresh water in plentitude.

As darkness settled upon the earth, Clayton and Lady Alice still stood by the ship's rail in silent contemplation of their future abode. From the dark shadows of the mighty forest came the wild calls of savage beasts—the deep roar of the lion, and, occasionally, the shrill scream of a panther.

The woman shrank closer to the man in terror-stricken anticipation of the horrors lying in wait for them in the awful blackness of the nights to come, when they two should be alone upon that wild and lonely shore.

Later in the evening Black Michael joined them long enough to instruct them to make their preparations for landing on the morrow. They tried to persuade him to take them to some more hospitable coast near enough to civilization so that they might hope to fall into friendly hands. But no pleas, or threats, or promises of reward could move him.

"I am the only man aboard who would not rather see you both safely dead, and, while I know that that's the sensible way to make sure of our own necks, yet Black Michael's not the man to forget a favor. You saved my life once, and in return I'm goin' to spare yours, but that's all I can do.

"The men won't stand for any more, and if we don't get you landed pretty quick they may even change their minds about giving you that much show. I'll put all your stuff ashore with you as well as cookin' utensils an' some old sails for tents, an' enough grub to last you until you can find fruit and game.

"So that with your guns for protection, you ought to be able to live here easy enough until help comes. When I get safely hid away I'll see to it that the British gover'ment learns about where you be; for the life of me I couldn't tell 'em exactly where, for I don't know myself. But they'll find you all right."

After he had left them they went silently below, each wrapped in gloomy forebodings.

Clayton did not believe that Black Michael had the slightest intention of notifying the British government of their whereabouts, nor was he any too sure but that some treachery was contemplated for the following day when they should be on shore with the sailors who would have to accompany them with their belongings.

Once out of Black Michael's sight any of the men

might strike them down, and still leave Black Michael's conscience clear.

And even should they escape that fate was it not but to be faced with far graver dangers? Alone, he might hope to survive for years; for he was a strong, athletic man.

But what of Alice, and that other little life so soon to be launched amidst the hardships and grave dangers of a primeval world?

The man shuddered as he meditated upon the awful gravity, the fearful helplessness, of their situation. But it was a merciful Providence which prevented him from foreseeing the hideous reality which awaited them in the grim depths of that gloomy wood.

Early next morning their numerous chests and boxes were hoisted on deck and lowered to waiting small boats for transportation to shore.

There was a great quantity and variety of stuff, as the Claytons had expected a possible five to eight years' residence in their new home, so that, in addition to the many necessities they had brought, were also many luxuries.

Black Michael was determined that nothing belonging to the Claytons should be left on board. Whether out of compassion for them, or in furtherance of his own self-interests, it were difficult to say.

There is no question but that the presence of property of a missing British official upon a suspicious vessel would have been a difficult thing to explain in any civilized port in the world.

So zealous was he in his efforts to carry out his intentions that he insisted upon the return of Clayton's revolvers to him by the sailors in whose possession they were.

Into the small boats were also loaded salt meats and biscuit, with a small supply of potatoes and beans, matches, and cooking vessels, a chest of tools, and the old sails which Black Michael had promised them.

As though himself fearing the very thing which Clayton had suspected, Black Michael accompanied them to shore, and was the last to leave them when the small boats, having filled the ship's casks with fresh water, were pushed out toward the waiting *Fuwalda*.

As the boats moved slowly over the smooth water of the bay, Clayton and his wife stood silently watching their departure—in the breasts of both a feeling of impending disaster and utter hopelessness.

And behind them, over the edge of a low ridge, other eyes watched—close-set, wicked eyes, gleaming beneath shaggy brows.

As the *Fuwalda* passed through the narrow entrance to the harbor and out of sight behind a projecting point, Lady Alice threw her arms about Clayton's neck and burst into uncontrolled sobs.

Bravely had she faced the dangers of the mutiny; with heroic fortitude she had looked into the terrible future; but now that the horror of absolute solitude was upon them, her overwrought nerves gave way, and the reaction came.

He did not attempt to check her tears. It were better that nature have her way in relieving these long-pent emotions, and it was many minutes before the girl—little more than a child she was—could again gain mastery of herself.

"Oh, John," she cried at last, "the horror of it. What are we to do? What are we to do?"

"There is but one thing to do, Alice," and he spoke as quietly as though they were sitting in their snug living room at home, "and that is work. Work must be our salvation. We must not give ourselves time to think, for in that direction lies madness.

"We must work and wait. I am sure that relief will come, and come quickly, when once it is apparent that the *Fuwalda* has been lost, even though Black Michael does not keep his word to us."

"But John, if it were only you and I," she sobbed, "we could endure it I know; but—"

"Yes, dear," he answered, gently, "I have been thinking of that, also; but we must face it, as we must face whatever comes, bravely and with the utmost confidence in our ability to cope with circumstances whatever they may be.

"Hundreds of thousands of years ago our ancestors of the dim and distant past faced the same problems which we must face, possibly in these same primeval forests. That we are here to-day evidences their victory.

"What they did may we not do? And even better, for are we not armed with ages of superior knowledge, and have we not the means of protection, defense, and sustenance which science has given us, but of which they were totally ignorant? What they accomplished, Alice, with instruments and weapons of stone and bone, surely that may we accomplish also."

"Ah, John, I wish that I might be a man with a man's philosophy, but I am but a woman, seeing with my heart rather than my head, and all that I can see is too horrible, too unthinkable to put into words.

"I only hope you are right, John. I will do my best to be a brave primeval woman, a fit mate for the primeval man."

Clayton's first thought was to arrange a sleeping shelter for the night; something which might serve to protect them from prowling beasts of prey.

He opened the box containing his rifles and ammunition, that they might both be armed against possible attack while at work, and then together they sought a location for their first night's sleeping place.

A hundred yards from the beach was a little level spot, fairly free of trees and here they decided eventually to build a permanent house, but, for the time being, they both thought it best to construct a little platform in the trees out of reach of the larger of the savage beasts in whose realm they were.

To this end Clayton selected four trees which formed a rectangle about eight feet square, and cutting long branches from other trees he constructed a framework around them, about ten feet from the ground, fastening the ends of the branches securely to the trees by means of rope, a quantity of which Black Michael had furnished him from the hold of the *Fuwalda*.

Across his framework Clayton placed other smaller branches quite close together. This platform he paved with the huge fronds of elephant's ear which grew in profusion about them, and over the fronds he laid a great sail folded into several thicknesses.

Seven feet higher he constructed a similar, though lighter platform to serve as roof, and from the sides of this he suspended the balance of his sailcloth for walls.

When completed he had a rather snug little nest, to which he carried their blankets and some of the lighter luggage.

It was now late in the afternoon, and the balance of the daylight hours were devoted to the building of a rude ladder by means of which Lady Alice could mount to her new home.

All during the day the forest about them had been filled with excited birds of brilliant plumage, and dancing, chattering monkeys, who watched these new arrivals and their wonderful nest-building operations with every mark of keenest interest and fascination.

Notwithstanding that both Clayton and his wife kept a sharp lookout they saw nothing of larger animals, though on two occasions they had seen their little simian neighbors come screaming and chattering from the near-by ridge, casting affrighted glances back over their little shoulders, and evincing as plainly as though by speech that they were fleeing some terrible thing which lay concealed there.

Just before dusk Clayton finished his ladder, and, filling a great basin with water from the near-by stream, the two mounted to the comparative safety of their aërial chamber.

As it was quite warm, Clayton had left the side curtains thrown back over the roof, and as they squatted, like Turks, upon their blankets, Lady Alice, straining her eyes into the darkening shadows of the wood, suddenly reached out and grasped Clayton's arm.

"John," she whispered, "look! What is it, a man?"

As Clayton turned his eyes in the direction she indicated, he saw silhouetted dimly against the shadows beyond, a great figure standing upright upon the ridge.

For a moment it stood as though listening and then turned slowly, and melted into the shadows of the jungle.

"What is it, John?"

"I do not know, Alice," he answered gravely, "it is too dark to see so far, and it may have been but a shadow cast by the rising moon."

"No, John, if it was not a man it was some huge and grotesque mockery of man. Oh, I am afraid."

He gathered her in his arms, whispering words of courage and love into her ears, for the greatest pain of their misfortunes, to Clayton, was the mental anguish of his young wife. Himself brave and fearless, yet was he able to appreciate the awful suffering which fear entails—a rare gift, though but one of many which had made the young Lord Greystoke respected and loved by all who knew him.

Soon after, he lowered the curtain walls, tying them securely to the trees so that, except for a little opening toward the beach, they were entirely enclosed.

As it was now pitch dark within their tiny aërie they lay down upon their blankets to try to wrest, through sleep, a brief respite of forgetfulness.

Clayton lay facing the opening at the front, a rifle and a brace of revolvers at his hand.

Scarcely had they closed their eyes than the terrifying cry of a panther rang out from the jungle behind them. Closer and closer it came until they could hear the great beast directly beneath them. For an hour or more they heard it sniffing and clawing at the trees which supported their platform, but at last it roamed away across the beach, where Clayton could see it clearly in the brilliant moonlight—a great, handsome beast; the largest he had ever seen.

During the long hours of darkness they caught but fitful snatches of sleep, for the night noises of a great jungle teeming with myriad animal life kept their overwrought nerves on edge, so that a hundred times they were startled to wakefulness by piercing screams, or the stealthy moving of great bodies beneath them.

CHAPTER III

Life and Death

MORNING found them but little, if at all refreshed, though it was with a feeling of intense relief that they saw the day dawn.

As soon as they had made their meager breakfast of salt pork, coffee, and biscuit, Clayton commenced work upon their house, for he realized that they could hope for no safety and no peace of mind at night until four strong walls effectually barred the jungle life from them.

The task was an arduous one and required the better part of a month, though he built but one small room. He constructed his cabin of small logs about six inches in diameter, stopping the chinks with clay which he found at the depth of a few feet beneath the surface soil.

At one end he built a fireplace of small stones from the beach. These also he set in clay and when the house had been entirely completed he applied a coating of the clay to the entire outside surface to the thickness of four inches.

In the window opening he set small branches about an inch in diameter both vertically and horizontally, and so woven that they formed a substantial grating that could withstand the strength of a powerful animal. Thus they obtained air and proper ventilation without fear of lessening the safety of their cabin.

The A-shaped roof was thatched with small branches laid close together and over these long jungle grass and palm fronds, with a final coating of clay.

The door he built of pieces of the packing-boxes which had held their belongings; nailing one piece upon another, the grain of contiguous layers running transversely, until he had a solid body some three inches thick and of such great strength that they were both moved to laughter as they gazed upon it.

Here the greatest difficulty confronted Clayton, for he had no means whereby to hang his massive door now that he had built it. After two days' work, however, he succeeded in fashioning two massive hardwood hinges, and with these he hung the door so that it opened and closed easily.

The stuccoing and other final touches were added after they moved into the house, which they had done as soon as the roof was on, piling their boxes before the door at night and thus having a comparatively safe and comfortable habitation.

The building of a bed, chairs, table, and shelves was a relatively easy matter, so that by the end of the second month they were well settled, and, but for the constant dread of attack by wild beasts and the ever growing loneliness, they were not uncomfortable or unhappy.

At night great beasts snarled and roared about their tiny cabin, but, so accustomed may one become to oft repeated noises, that soon they paid little attention to them, sleeping soundly the whole night through.

Thrice had they caught fleeting glimpses of great manlike figures like that of the first night, but never at sufficiently close range to know positively whether the half-seen forms were those of man or brute.

The brilliant birds and the little monkeys had become accustomed to their new acquaintances, and as they had evidently never seen human beings before they presently, after their first fright had worn off, approached closer and closer, impelled by that strange curiosity which dominates the wild creatures of the forest and the jungle and the plain, so that within the first month several of the birds had gone so far as even to accept morsels of food from the friendly hands of the Claytons.

One afternoon, while Clayton was working upon an addition to their cabin, for he contemplated building several more rooms, a number of their grotesque little friends came shrieking and scolding through the trees from the direction of the ridge. Ever as they fled they cast fearful glances back of them, and finally they stopped near Clayton jabbering excitedly to him as though to warn him of approaching danger.

At last he saw it, the thing the little monkeys so feared—the man-brute of which the Claytons had caught occasional fleeting glimpses.

It was approaching through the jungle in a semi-erect position, now and then placing the backs of its closed fists upon the ground—a great anthropoid ape, and, as it advanced, it emitted deep guttural growls and an occasional low barking sound.

Clayton was at some distance from the cabin, having come to fell a particularly perfect tree, for his building operations. Grown careless from months of continued safety, during which time they had seen no dangerous animals during the daylight hours, he had left his rifles and revolvers all within the little cabin, and now that he saw the great ape crashing through the underbrush directly toward him, and from a direction which practically cut him off from escape, he felt a vague little shiver play up and down his spine.

He knew that, armed only with an ax, his chances with this ferocious monster were small indeed—and Alice; O God, he thought, what will become of Alice?

There was yet a slight chance of reaching the cabin. He turned and ran toward it, shouting an alarm to his wife to run in and close the great door in case the ape cut off his retreat.

Lady Greystoke had been sitting a little way from the cabin, and when she heard his cry she looked up to see the ape springing with almost incredible swiftness, for so large and awkward an animal, in an effort to head off Clayton.

With a low cry she sprang toward the cabin, and, as she entered, gave a backward glance which filled her soul with terror, for the brute had intercepted her husband, who now stood at bay grasping his ax with both hands ready to swing it upon the infuriated animal when he should make his final charge.

"Close and bolt the door, Alice," cried Clayton. "I can finish this fellow with my ax."

But he knew he was facing a horrible death, and so did she.

The ape was a great bull, weighing probably three hundred pounds. His nasty, close-set eyes gleamed hatred from beneath his shaggy brows, while his great canine fangs were bared in a horrid snarl as he paused a moment before his prey.

Over the brute's shoulder Clayton could see the doorway of his cabin, not twenty paces distant, and a great wave of horror and fear swept over him as he saw his young wife emerge, armed with one of his rifles.

She had always been afraid of firearms, and would never touch them, but now she rushed toward the ape with the fearlessness of a lioness protecting its young.

"Back, Alice," shouted Clayton, "for God's sake, go back."

But she would not heed, and just then the ape charged, so that Clayton could say no more.

The man swung his ax with all his mighty strength, but the powerful brute seized it in those terrible hands, and tearing it from Clayton's grasp hurled it far to one side.

With an ugly snarl he closed upon his defenseless victim, but ere his fangs had reached the throat they thirsted for, there was a sharp report and a bullet entered the ape's back between his shoulders.

Throwing Clayton to the ground the beast turned upon his new enemy. There before him stood the terrified girl vainly trying to fire another bullet into the animal's body; but she did not understand the mechanism of the firearm, and the hammer fell futilely upon an empty cartridge.

Almost simultaneously Clayton regained his feet, and without thought of the utter hopelessness of it, he rushed forward to drag the ape from his wife's prostrate form.

With little or no effort he succeeded, and the great bulk rolled inertly upon the turf before him—the ape was dead. The bullet had done its work.

A hasty examination of his wife revealed no marks upon her, and Clayton decided that the huge brute had died the instant he had sprung toward Alice.

Gently he lifted his wife's still unconscious form, and bore her to the little cabin, but it was fully two hours before she regained consciousness.

Her first words filled Clayton with vague apprehension. For some time after regaining her senses, Alice gazed wonderingly about the interior of the little cabin, and then, with a satisfied sigh, said:

"O John, it is so good to be really home! I have had an awful dream, dear. I thought we were no longer in London, but in some horrible place where great beasts attacked us."

"There, there, Alice," he said, stroking her forehead, "try to sleep again, and do not worry your head about bad dreams."

That night a little son was born in the tiny cabin beside the primeval forest, while a leopard screamed before the door, and the deep notes of a lion's roar sounded from beyond the ridge.

Lady Greystoke never recovered from the shock of the great ape's attack, and, though she lived for a year after her baby was born, she was never again outside the cabin, nor did she ever fully realize that she was not in England.

Sometimes she would question Clayton as to the strange noises of the nights; the absence of servants and friends, and the strange rudeness of the furnishings within her room, but, though he made no effort to deceive her, never could she grasp the meaning of it all.

In other ways she was quite rational, and the joy and happiness she took in the possession of her little son and the constant attentions of her husband made that year a very happy one for her, the happiest of her young life.

That it would have been beset by worries and apprehension had she been in full command of her mental faculties Clayton well knew; so that while he suffered terribly to see her so, there were times when he was almost glad, for her sake, that she could not understand.

Long since had he given up any hope of rescue, except through accident. With unremitting zeal he had worked to beautify the interior of the cabin.

Skins of lion and panther covered the floor. Cupboards and bookcases lined the walls. Odd vases made by his own hand from the clay of the region held beautiful tropical flowers. Curtains of grass and bamboo covered the windows, and, most arduous task of all, with his meager assortment of tools he had fashioned lumber to neatly seal the walls and ceiling and lay a smooth floor within the cabin.

That he had been able to turn his hands at all to such unaccustomed labor was a source of mild wonder to him. But he loved the work because it was for her and the tiny life that had come to cheer them, though adding a hundredfold to his responsibilities and to the terribleness of their situation.

During the year that followed, Clayton was several times attacked by the great apes which now seemed to continually infest the vicinity of the cabin; but as he never again ventured outside without both rifle and revolvers he had little fear of the huge beasts.

He had strengthened the window protections and fitted a unique wooden lock to the cabin door, so that when he hunted for game and fruits, as it was constantly necessary for him to do to insure sustenance, he had no fear that any animal could break into the little home.

At first he shot much of the game from the cabin windows, but toward the end the animals learned to fear the strange lair from whence issued the terrifying thunder of his rifle.

In his leisure Clayton read, often aloud to his wife, from the store of books he had brought for their new home. Among these were many for little children—picture books, primers, readers—for they had known that their little child would be old enough for such before they might hope to return to England.

At other times Clayton wrote in his diary, which he had always been accustomed to keep in French, and in which he recorded the details of their strange life. This book he kept locked in a little metal box.

A year from the day her little son was born Lady Alice passed quietly away in the night. So peaceful was her end that it was hours before Clayton could awake to a realization that his wife was dead.

The horror of the situation came to him very slowly, and it is doubtful that he ever fully realized the enormity of his sorrow and the fearful responsibility that had devolved upon him with the care of that wee thing, his son, still a nursing babe.

The last entry in his diary was made the morning following her death, and there he recites the sad details in a matter-of-fact way that adds to the pathos of it; for it breathes a tired apathy born of long sorrow and hopelessness, which even this cruel blow could scarcely awake to further suffering:

My little son is crying for nourishment—O Alice, Alice, what shall I do?

And as John Clayton wrote the last words his hand was destined ever to pen, he dropped his head wearily upon his outstretched arms where they rested upon the table he had built for her who lay still and cold in the bed beside him.

For a long time no sound broke the deathlike stillness of the jungle midday save the piteous wailing of the tiny man-child.

CHAPTER IV

The Apes

IN the forest of the table-land a mile back from the ocean old Kerchak the Ape was on a rampage of rage among his people.

The younger and lighter members of his tribe scampered to the higher branches of the great trees to escape his wrath; risking their lives upon branches that scarce supported their weight rather than face old Kerchak in one of his fits of uncontrolled anger.

The other males scattered in all directions, but not before the infuriated brute had felt the vertebrae of one snap between his great, foaming jaws.

A luckless young female slipped from an insecure hold upon a high branch and came crashing to the ground almost at Kerchak's feet.

With a wild scream he was upon her, tearing a great piece from her side with his mighty teeth, and striking her viciously upon her head and shoulders with a broken tree limb until her skull was crushed to a jelly.

And then he spied Kala, who, returning from a search for food with her young babe, was ignorant of the state of the mighty male's temper until suddenly the shrill warnings of her fellows caused her to scamper madly for safety.

But Kerchak was close upon her, so close that he had

almost grasped her ankle had she not made a furious leap far into space from one tree to another—a perilous chance which apes seldom if ever take, unless so closely pursued by danger that there is no alternative.

She made the leap successfully, but as she grasped the limb of the further tree the sudden jar loosened the hold of the tiny babe where it clung frantically to her neck, and she saw the little thing hurled, turning and twisting, to the ground thirty feet below.

With a low cry of dismay Kala rushed headlong to its side, thoughtless now of the danger from Kerchak; but when she gathered the wee, mangled form to her bosom life had left it.

With low moans, she sat cuddling the body to her; nor did Kerchak attempt to molest her. With the death of the babe his fit of demoniacal rage passed as suddenly as it had seized him.

Kerchak was a huge king ape, weighing perhaps three hundred and fifty pounds. His forehead was extremely low and receding, his eyes bloodshot, small and close set to his coarse, flat nose; his ears large and thin, but smaller than most of his kind.

His awful temper and his mighty strength made him supreme among the little tribe into which he had been born some twenty years before.

Now that he was in his prime, there was no simian in all the mighty forest through which he roved that dared contest his right to rule, nor did the other and larger animals molest him.

Old Tantor, the elephant, alone of all the wild savage life, feared him not—and he alone did Kerchak fear. When Tantor trumpeted, the great ape scurried with his fellows high among the trees of the second terrace.

The tribe of anthropoids over which Kerchak ruled with an iron hand and bared fangs, numbered some six or eight families, each family consisting of an adult male with his wives and their young, numbering in all some sixty or seventy apes.

Kala was the youngest wife of a male called Tublat,

meaning broken nose, and the child she had seen dashed to death was her first; for she was but nine or ten years old.

Notwithstanding her youth, she was large and powerful—a splendid, clean-limbed animal, with a round, high forehead, which denoted more intelligence than most of her kind possessed. So, also, she had a greater capacity for mother love and mother sorrow.

But she was still an ape, a huge, fierce, terrible beast of a species closely allied to the gorilla, yet more intelligent; which, with the strength of their cousin, made her kind the most fearsome of those awe-inspiring progenitors of man.

When the tribe saw that Kerchak's rage had ceased they came slowly down from their arboreal retreats and pursued again the various occupations which he had interrupted.

The young played and frolicked about among the trees and bushes. Some of the adults lay prone upon the soft mat of dead and decaying vegetation which covered the ground, while others turned over pieces of fallen branches and clods of earth in search of the small bugs and reptiles which formed a part of their food.

Others, again, searched the surrounding trees for fruits, nuts, small birds, and eggs.

They had passed an hour or so thus when Kerchak called them together, and with a word of command to them to follow him, set off toward the sea.

They traveled for the most part upon the ground, where it was open, following the path of the great elephants whose comings and goings break the only roads through those tangled mazes of bush, vine, creeper, and tree. When they walked it was with a rolling, awkward motion, placing the knuckles of their closed hands upon the ground and swinging their ungainly bodies forward.

But when the way was through the lower trees they moved more swiftly, swinging from branch to branch with the agility of their smaller cousins, the monkeys.

And all the way Kala carried her little dead baby hugged closely to her breast.

It was shortly after noon when they reached a ridge overlooking the beach where below them lay the tiny cottage which was Kerchak's goal.

He had seen many of his kind go to their deaths before the loud noise made by the little black stick in the hands of the strange white ape who lived in that wonderful lair, and Kerchak had made up his brute mind to own that death-dealing contrivance, and to explore the interior of the mysterious den.

He wanted, very, very much, to feel his teeth sink into the neck of the queer animal that he had learned to hate and fear, and because of this, he came often with his tribe to reconnoiter, waiting for a time when the white ape should be off his guard.

Of late they had quit attacking, or even showing themselves; for every time they had done so in the past the little stick had roared out its terrible message of death to some member of the tribe.

To-day there was no sign of the man about, and from where they watched they could see that the cabin door was open. Slowly, cautiously, and noiselessly they crept through the jungle toward the little cabin.

There were no growls, no fierce screams of rage—the little black stick had taught them to come quietly lest they awaken it.

On, on they came until Kerchak himself slunk stealthily to the very door and peered within. Behind him were two males, and then Kala, closely straining the little dead form to her breast.

Inside the den they saw the strange white ape lying half across a table, his head buried in his arms; and on the bed lay a figure covered by a sailcloth, while from a tiny rustic cradle came the plaintive wailing of a babe.

Noiselessly Kerchak entered, crouching for the charge; and then John Clayton rose with a sudden start and faced them.

The sight that met his eyes must have frozen him with

horror, for there, within the door, stood three great bull apes, while behind them crowded many more; how many he never knew, for his revolvers were hanging on the far wall beside his rifle, and Kerchak was charging.

When the king ape released the limp form which had been John Clayton, Lord Greystoke, he turned his attention toward the little cradle; but Kala was there before him, and when he would have grasped the child she snatched it herself, and before he could intercept her she had bolted through the door and taken refuge in a high tree.

As she took up the little live baby of Alice Clayton she dropped the dead body of her own into the empty cradle; for the wail of the living had answered the call of universal motherhood within her wild breast which the dead could not still.

High up among the branches of a mighty tree she hugged the shrieking infant to her bosom, and soon the instinct that was as dominant in this fierce female as it had been in the breast of his tender and beautiful mother—the instinct of mother love—reached out to the tiny man-child's half-formed understanding, and he became quiet.

Then hunger closed the gap between them, and the son of an English lord and an English lady nursed at the breast of Kala, the great ape.

In the meantime the beasts within the cabin were warily examining the contents of this strange lair.

Once satisfied that Clayton was dead, Kerchak turned his attention to the thing which lay upon the bed, covered by a piece of sailcloth.

Gingerly he lifted one corner of the shroud, but when he saw the body of the woman beneath he tore the cloth roughly from her form and seized the still, white throat in his huge, hairy hands.

A moment he let his fingers sink deep into the cold flesh, and then, realizing that she was already dead, he turned from her, to examine the contents of the room; nor did he again molest the body of either Lady Alice or Sir John.

The rifle hanging upon the wall caught his first attention; it was for this strange, death-dealing thunder-stick that he had yearned for months; but now that it was within his grasp he scarcely had the temerity to seize it.

Cautiously he approached the thing, ready to flee precipitately should it speak in its deep roaring tones, as he had heard it speak before, the last words to those of his kind who, through ignorance or rashness, had attacked the wonderful white ape that had borne it.

Deep in the beast's intelligence was something which assured him that the thunder-stick was only dangerous when in the hands of one who could manipulate it, but yet it was several minutes ere he could bring himself to touch it.

Instead, he walked back and forth along the floor before it, turning his head so that never once did his eyes leave the object of his desire.

Using his long arms as a man uses crutches, and rolling his huge carcass from side to side with each stride, the great king ape paced to and fro, uttering deep growls, occasionally punctuated with the ear-piercing scream, than which there is no more terrifying noise in all the jungle.

Presently he halted before the rifle. Slowly he raised a huge hand until it almost touched the shining barrel, only to withdraw it once more and continue his hurried pacing.

It was as though the great brute by this show of fearlessness, and through the medium of his wild voice, were endeavoring to bolster up his courage to the point which would permit him to take the rifle in his hand.

Again he stopped, and this time succeeded in forcing his reluctant hand to the cold steel, only to snatch it away almost immediately and resume his restless beat.

Time after time this strange ceremony was repeated, but on each occasion with increased confidence, until, finally, the rifle was torn from its hook and lay in the grasp of the great brute.

Finding that it harmed him not, Kerchak began to examine it closely. He felt of it from end to end, peered down the black depths of the muzzle, fingered the sights, the breech, the stock, and finally the trigger.

During all these operations the apes who had entered sat huddled near the door watching their chief, while those outside strained and crowded to catch a glimpse of what transpired within.

Suddenly Kerchak's finger closed upon the trigger. There was a deafening roar in the little room and the apes at and beyond the door fell over one another in their wild anxiety to escape.

Kerchak was equally frightened, so frightened, in fact, that he quite forgot to throw aside the author of that fearful noise, but bolted for the door with it tightly clutched in one hand.

As he passed through the opening, the front sight of the rifle caught upon the edge of the in-swung door with sufficient force to close it tightly after the fleeing ape.

When Kerchak came to a halt a short distance from the cabin and discovered that he still held the rifle, he dropped it as he might have dropped a red-hot iron, nor did he again essay to recover it—the noise was too much for his brute nerves; but he was now quite convinced that the terrible stick was quite harmless by itself if left alone.

It was an hour before the apes could again bring themselves to approach the cabin to continue their investigations, and when they finally did so, they found to their chagrin that the door was closed and so securely fastened that they could not force it.

The cleverly constructed latch which Clayton had made for the door had sprung as Kerchak passed out; nor could the apes find means of ingress through the heavily barred windows.

After roaming about the vicinity for a short time, they started back for the deeper forests and the higher land from whence they had come.

Kala had not once come to earth with her little adopted babe, but now Kerchak called to her to descend with the rest, and as there was no note of anger in his voice she dropped lightly from branch to branch and joined the others on their homeward march.

Those of the apes who attempted to examine Kala's strange baby were repulsed with bared fangs and low menacing growls, accompanied by words of warning from Kala.

When they assured her that they meant the child no harm she permitted them to come close, but would not allow them to touch her charge.

It was as though she knew that her baby was frail and delicate and feared lest the rough hands of her fellows might injure the little thing.

Another thing she did, and which made traveling an onerous trial for her. Remembering the death of her own little one, she clung desperately to the new babe, with one hand, whenever they were upon the march.

The other young rode upon their mothers' backs; their little arms tightly clasping the hairy necks before them, while their legs were locked beneath their mothers' armpits.

Not so with Kala; she held the small form of the little Lord Greystoke tightly to her breast, where the dainty hands clutched the long black hair which covered that portion of her body. She had seen one child fall from her back to a terrible death, and she would take no further chances with this.

CHAPTER V

The White Ape

TENDERLY Kala nursed her little waif, wondering silently why it did not gain strength and agility as did the little apes of other mothers. It was nearly a year from the time the little fellow came into her possession before he would walk alone, and as for climbing—my, but how stupid he was!

Kala sometimes talked with the older females about her young hopeful, but none of them could understand how a child could be so slow and backward in learning to care for itself. Why, it could not even find food alone, and more than twelve moons had passed since Kala had come upon it.

Had they known that the child had seen thirteen moons before it had come into Kala's possession they would have considered its case as absolutely hopeless, for the little apes of their own tribe were as far advanced in two or three moons as was this little stranger after twenty-five.

Tublat, Kala's husband, was sorely vexed, and but for the female's careful watching would have put the child out of the way.

"He will never be a great ape," he argued. "Always will you have to carry him and protect him. What good will he be to the tribe? None; only a burden.

"Let us leave him quietly sleeping among the tall grasses, that you may bear other and stronger apes to guard us in our old age."

"Never, Broken Nose," replied Kala. "If I must carry him forever, so be it."

And then Tublat went to Kerchak to urge him to use his authority with Kala, and force her to give up little Tarzan, which was the name they had given to the tiny Lord Greystoke, and which meant "White-Skin."

But when Kerchak spoke to her about it Kala threatened to run away from the tribe if they did not leave her in peace with the child; and as this is one of the inalienable rights of the jungle folk, if they be dissatisfied among their own people, they bothered her no more, for Kala was a fine clean-limbed young female, and they did not wish to lose her.

As Tarzan grew he made more rapid strides, so that by the time he was ten years old he was an excellent climber, and on the ground could do many wonderful things which were beyond the powers of his little brothers and sisters.

In many ways did he differ from them, and they often marveled at his superior cunning, but in strength and size he was deficient; for at ten the great anthropoids were fully grown, some of them towering over six feet in height, while little Tarzan was still but a half-grown boy.

Yet such a boy!

From early infancy he had used his hands to swing from branch to branch after the manner of his giant mother, and as he grew older he spent hour upon hour daily speeding through the tree tops with his brothers and sisters.

He could spring twenty feet across space at the dizzy heights of the forest top, and grasp with unerring precision, and without apparent jar, a limb waving wildly in the path of an approaching tornado.

He could drop twenty feet at a stretch from limb to limb in rapid descent to the ground, or he could gain the utmost pinnacle of the loftiest tropical giant with the ease and swiftness of a squirrel.

Though but ten years old he was fully as strong as the average man of thirty, and far more agile than the most practiced athlete ever becomes. And day by day his strength was increasing.

His life among these fierce apes had been happy; for his recollection held no other life, nor did he know that there existed within the universe aught else than his little forest and the wild jungle animals with which he was familiar.

He was nearly ten before he commenced to realize that a great difference existed between himself and his fellows. His little body, burned brown by exposure, suddenly caused him feelings of intense shame, for he realized that it was entirely hairless, like some low snake, or other reptile.

He attempted to obviate this by plastering himself from head to foot with mud, but this dried and fell off. Besides it felt so uncomfortable that he quickly decided that he preferred the shame to the discomfort.

In the higher land which his tribe frequented was a little lake, and it was here that Tarzan first saw his face in the clear, still waters of its bosom.

It was on a sultry day of the dry season that he and one of his cousins had gone down to the bank to drink. As they leaned over, both little faces were mirrored on the placid pool; the fierce and terrible features of the ape beside those of the aristocratic scion of an old English house.

Tarzan was appalled. It had been bad enough to be hairless, but to own such a countenance! He wondered that the other apes could look at him at all.

That tiny slit of a mouth and those puny white teeth! How they looked beside the mighty lips and powerful fangs of his more fortunate brothers!

And the little pinched nose of his; so thin was it that it looked half starved. He turned red as he compared it with the beautiful broad nostrils of his companion. Such a generous nose! Why it spread half across his face! It certainly must be fine to be so handsome, thought poor little Tarzan.

But when he saw his own eyes; ah, that was the final blow—a brown spot, a gray circle and then blank whiteness! Frightful! not even the snakes had such hideous eyes as he.

So intent was he upon this personal appraisement of his features that he did not hear the parting of the tall grass behind him as a great body pushed itself stealthily through the jungle; nor did his companion, the ape, hear either, for he was drinking and the noise of his sucking lips and gurgles of satisfaction drowned the quiet approach of the intruder.

Not thirty paces behind the two she crouched— Sabor, the huge lioness—lashing her tail. Cautiously she moved a great padded paw forward, noiselessly placing it before she lifted the next. Thus she advanced; her belly low, almost touching the surface of the ground—a great cat preparing to spring upon its prey.

Now she was within ten feet of the two unsuspecting little playfellows—carefully she drew her hind feet well up beneath her body, the great muscles rolling under the beautiful skin.

So low she was crouching now that she seemed to be flattened to the earth except for the upward bend of the glossy back as it gathered for the spring.

No longer the tail lashed—quiet and straight behind her it lay.

An instant she paused thus as though turned to stone, and then, with an awful scream, she sprang.

Sabor, the lioness, was a wise hunter. To one less wise the wild alarm of her fierce cry as she sprang would have seemed a foolish thing, for could she not more surely have fallen upon her victims had she but quietly leaped without that loud shriek?

But Sabor knew well the wondrous quickness of the jungle folk and their almost unbelievable powers of hearing. To them the sudden scraping of one blade of grass across another was as effectual a warning as her loudest cry, and Sabor knew that she could not make that mighty leap without a little noise.

Her wild scream was not a warning. It was voiced to freeze her poor victims in a paralysis of terror for the tiny fraction of an instant which would suffice for her mighty claws to sink into their soft flesh and hold them beyond peradventure of escape.

In so far as the ape was concerned, Sabor reasoned correctly. The little fellow crouched trembling just an instant, but that instant was quite long enough to prove his undoing.

Not so, however, with Tarzan, the man-child. His life amidst the dangers of the jungle had taught him to meet emergencies with self-confidence, and his higher intelligence resulted in a quickness of mental action far beyond the powers of the apes.

So the scream of Sabor, the lioness, galvanized the brain and muscles of little Tarzan into instant action.

Before him lay the deep waters of the little lake, behind him certain death; a cruel death beneath tearing claws and rending fangs.

Tarzan had always hated water except as a medium for quenching his thirst. He hated it because he connected it with the chill and discomfort of the torrential rains, and he feared it for the thunder and lightning and wind which accompanied them.

The deep waters of the lake he had been taught by his wild mother to avoid, and further, had he not seen little Neeta sink beneath its quiet surface only a few short weeks before never to return to the tribe?

But of the two evils his quick mind chose the lesser ere the first note of Sabor's scream had scarce broken the quiet of the jungle, and before the great beast had covered half her leap Tarzan felt the chill waters close above his head.

He could not swim, and the water was very deep; but still he lost no particle of that self-confidence and resourcefulness which were the badges of his superior being.

Rapidly he moved his hands and feet in an attempt to scramble upward, and, possibly more by chance than design, he fell into the stroke that a dog uses when swimming, so that within a few seconds his nose was above water and he found that he could keep it there by continuing his strokes, and also make progress through the water.

He was much surprised and pleased with this new acquirement which had been so suddenly thrust upon him, but he had no time for thinking much upon it.

He was now swimming parallel to the bank and there he saw the cruel beast that would have seized him crouching upon the still form of his little playmate.

The lioness was intently watching Tarzan, evidently expecting him to return to shore, but this the boy had no intention of doing.

Instead he raised his voice in the call of distress common to his tribe, adding to it the warning which would prevent would-be rescuers from running into the clutches of Sabor.

Almost immediately there came an answer from the distance, and presently forty or fifty great apes swung rapidly and majestically through the trees toward the scene of tragedy.

In the van was Kala, for she had recognized the tones of her best beloved, and with her was the mother of the little ape who lay dead beneath cruel Sabor.

Though more powerful and better equipped for fighting than the apes, the lioness had no desire to meet these enraged adults, and with a snarl of hatred she sprang quickly into the brush and disappeared.

Tarzan now swam to shore and clambered quickly upon dry land. The feeling of freshness and exhilaration which the cool waters had imparted to him, filled his little being with grateful surprise, and ever after he lost no opportunity to take a daily plunge in lake or stream or ocean when it was possible to do so.

For a long time Kala could not accustom herself to the sight; for though her people could swim when forced to it, they did not like to enter water, and never did so voluntarily.

The adventure with the lioness gave Tarzan food for pleasurable memories, for it was such affairs which broke the monotony of his daily life—otherwise but a dull round of searching for food, eating, and sleeping.

The tribe to which he belonged roamed a tract extending, roughly, twenty-five miles along the seacoast and some fifty miles inland. This they traversed almost continually, occasionally remaining for months in one locality; but as they moved through the trees with great speed they often covered the territory in a very few days.

Much depended upon food supply, climatic conditions, and the prevalence of animals of the more dangerous species; though Kerchak often led them on long marches for no other reason than that he had tired of remaining in the same place.

At night they slept where darkness overtook them, lying upon the ground, and sometimes covering their heads, and more seldom their bodies, with the great leaves of the elephant's ear. Two or three might lie cuddled in each other's arms for additional warmth if the night were chill, and thus Tarzan had slept in Kala's arms nightly for all these years.

That the huge, fierce brute loved this child of another race is beyond question, and he, too, gave to the great, hairy beast all the affection that would have belonged to his fair young mother had she lived.

When he was disobedient she cuffed him, it is true, but she was never cruel to him, and was more often caressing him than chastising him.

Tublat, her husband, always hated Tarzan, and on several occasions had come near ending his youthful career.

Tarzan on his part never lost an opportunity to show that he fully reciprocated his foster father's sentiments, and whenever he could safely annoy him or make faces at him or hurl insults upon him from the safety of his mother's arms, or the slender branches of the higher trees, he did so.

His superior intelligence and cunning permitted him to invent a thousand diabolical tricks to add to the burdens of Tublat's life.

Early in his boyhood he had learned to form ropes by twisting and tying long grasses together, and with these he was forever tripping Tublat or attempting to hang him from some overhanging branch.

By constant playing and experimenting with these he learned to tie rude knots, and make sliding nooses; and with these he and the younger apes amused themselves. What Tarzan did they tried to do also, but he alone originated and became proficient.

One day while playing thus Tarzan had thrown his rope at one of his fleeing companions, retaining the other end in his grasp. By accident the noose fell squarely about the running ape's neck, bringing him to a sudden and surprising halt.

Ah, here was a new game, a fine game, thought Tarzan, and immediately he attempted to repeat the trick. And thus, by painstaking and continued practice, he learned the art of roping.

Now, indeed, was the life of Tublat a living nightmare. In sleep, upon the march, night or day, he never knew when that quiet noose would slip about his neck and nearly choke the life out of him.

Kala punished, Tublat swore dire vengeance, and old Kerchak took notice and warned and threatened; but all to no avail.

Tarzan defied them all, and the thin, strong noose continued to settle about Tublat's neck whenever he least expected it.

The other apes derived unlimited amusement from Tublat's discomfiture, for Broken Nose was a disagreeable old fellow, whom no one liked, anyway.

In Tarzan's clever little mind many thoughts revolved, and back of these was his divine power of reason.

If he could catch his fellow apes with his long arm of many grasses, why not Sabor, the lioness?

It was the germ of a thought, which, however, was

destined to mull around in his conscious and subconscious mind until it resulted in magnificent achievement.

But that came in later years.

CHAPTER VI

⟨decoration⟩

Jungle Battles

T HE wanderings of the tribe brought them often near the closed and silent cabin by the little land-locked harbor. To Tarzan this was always a source of never-ending mystery and pleasure.

He would peek into the curtained windows, or, climbing upon the roof, peer down the black depths of the chimney in vain endeavor to solve the unknown wonders that lay within those strong walls.

His little childish imagination pictured wonderful creatures within, and the very impossibility of forcing entrance added a thousandfold to his desire to do so.

He would clamber about the roof and windows for hours attempting to discover means of ingress, but to the door he paid little attention, for this was apparently as solid as the walls.

It was in the next visit to the vicinity, following the adventure with old Sabor, that, as he approached the cabin, Tarzan noticed that from a distance the door appeared as though an independent part of the wall in which it was set, and for the first time it occurred to him that this might prove the means of entrance which had so long eluded him.

He was alone, as was often the case when he visited the cabin, for the apes had no love for it; the story of the thunder-stick having lost nothing in the telling during these ten years had quite surrounded the white man's deserted abode with an atmosphere of weirdness and terror for the simians.

The story of his own connection with the cabin had never been told him. The language of the apes has so few words that they could talk but little of what they had seen in the cabin, having no words to accurately describe either the strange people or their belongings, and so, long before Tarzan was old enough to understand, the subject had been forgotten by the tribe.

Only in a dim, vague way had Kala explained to him that his father had been a strange white ape, but he did not know that Kala was not his own mother.

On this day, then, he went directly to the door and spent hours examining it and fussing with the hinges, the knob and the latch. Finally he stumbled upon the right combination, and the door swung creakingly open before his astonished eyes.

For some minutes he did not dare venture within, but finally, as his eyes became accustomed to the dim light of the interior he slowly and cautiously entered.

In the middle of the floor lay a skeleton, every vestige of flesh gone from the bones to which still clung the mildewed and moldered remnants of what had once been clothing. Upon the bed lay a similar gruesome thing, but smaller, while in a tiny cradle near-by was a third, a wee mite of a skeleton.

To none of these evidences of a fearful tragedy of a long-dead day did little Tarzan give but passing heed. His wild jungle life had inured him to the sight of dead and dying animals, and had he known that he was looking upon the remains of his own father and mother he would have been no more greatly moved.

The furnishings and other contents of the room it was which riveted his attention. He examined many things minutely—strange tools and weapons, books, papers, clothing—what little had withstood the ravages of time in the humid atmosphere of the jungle coast.

He opened chests and cupboards, such as did not baffle his small experience, and in these he found the contents much better preserved.

Among other things he found a sharp hunting knife, on the keen blade of which he immediately proceeded to cut his finger. Nothing daunted he continued his experiments, finding that he could hack and hew splinters of wood from the table and chairs with this new toy.

For a long time this amused him, but finally tiring he continued his explorations. In a cupboard filled with books he came across one with brightly colored pictures—it was a child's illustrated alphabet—

> A is for Archer
> Who shoots with a bow.
> B is for Boy,
> His first name is Joe.

The pictures interested him greatly.

There were many apes with faces similar to his own, and further over in the book he found, under "M," some little monkeys such as he saw daily flitting through the trees of his primeval forest. But nowhere was pictured any of his own people; in all the book was none that resembled Kerchak, or Tublat, or Kala.

At first he tried to pick the little figures from the leaves, but he soon saw that they were not real, though he knew not what they might be, nor had he any words to describe them.

The boats, and trains, and cows and horses were quite meaningless to him, but not quite so baffling as the odd little figures which appeared beneath and between the colored pictures—some strange kind of bug he thought they might be, for many of them had legs though nowhere could he find one with eyes and a mouth. It was his first introduction to the letters of the alphabet, and he was over ten years old.

Of course he had never seen print, or never had spoken with any living thing which had the remotest idea that such a thing as a written language existed, nor ever had he seen anyone reading.

So what wonder that the little boy was quite at a loss to guess the meaning of these strange figures.

Near the middle of the book he found his old enemy, Sabor, the lioness, and, further on, coiled Histah, the snake.

Oh, it was most engrossing! Never before in all his ten years had he enjoyed anything so much. So absorbed was he that he did not note the approaching dusk, until it was quite upon him and the figures were blurred.

He put the book back in the cupboard and closed the door, for he did not wish anyone else to find and destroy his treasure, and as he went out into the gathering darkness he closed the great door of the cabin behind him as it had been before he discovered the secret of its lock, but before he left he had noticed the hunting knife lying where he had thrown it upon the floor, and this he picked up and took with him to show to his fellows.

He had taken scarce a dozen steps toward the jungle when a great form rose up before him from the shadows of a low bush. At first he thought it was one of his own people but in another instant he realized that it was Bolgani, the huge gorilla.

So close was he that there was no chance for flight and little Tarzan knew that he must stand and fight for his life; for these great beasts were the deadly enemies of his tribe, and neither one or the other ever asked or gave quarter.

Had Tarzan been a full-grown bull ape of the species of his tribe he had been more than a match for the gorilla, but being only a little English boy, though enormously muscular for such, he stood no show against his cruel antagonist. In his veins, though, flowed the blood of the best of a race of mighty fighters, and back of this was the training of his short lifetime among the fierce brutes of the jungle.

He knew no fear, as we know it; his little heart beat the faster but from the excitement and exhilaration of adventure. Had the opportunity presented itself he would have escaped, but solely because his judgment told him he was no match for the great thing which confronted him. And since reason showed him that successful flight was impossible he met the gorilla squarely and bravely without a tremor of a single muscle, or any sign of panic.

In fact he met the brute midway in its charge, striking its huge body with his closed fists and as futilely as he had been a fly attacking an elephant. But in one hand he still clutched the knife he had found in the cabin of his father, and as the brute, striking and biting, closed upon him the boy accidentally turned the point toward the hairy beast. As it sank deep into the body of him the gorilla shrieked in pain and rage.

But the boy had learned in that brief second a use for his sharp and shining toy, so that, as the tearing, striking beast dragged him to earth he plunged the blade repeatedly and to the hilt into its breast.

The gorilla, fighting after the manner of its kind, struck terrific blows with its open hand, and tore the flesh at the boy's throat and chest with its mighty tusks.

For a moment they rolled upon the ground in the fierce frenzy of combat. More and more weakly the torn and bleeding arm struck home with the long sharp blade, then the little figure stiffened with a spasmodic jerk, and Tarzan, the young Lord Greystoke, rolled lifeless upon the dead and decaying vegetation which carpeted his jungle home.

A mile back in the forest the tribe had heard the fierce challenge of the gorilla, and, as was his custom when any danger threatened, Kerchak called his people together, partly for mutual protection against a common enemy, since this gorilla might be but one of a party of several, and also to see that all members of the tribe were accounted for.

It was soon discovered that Tarzan was missing, and

Tublat was strongly opposed to sending assistance. Kerchak himself had no liking for the strange little waif, so he listened to Tublat, and, finally, with a shrug of his shoulders, turned back to the pile of leaves on which he had made his bed.

But Kala was of a different mind; in fact, she had not waited but to learn that Tarzan was absent ere she was fairly flying through the matted branches toward the point from which the cries of the gorilla were still plainly audible.

Darkness had now fallen, and an early moon was sending its faint light to cast strange, grotesque shadows among the dense foliage of the forest.

Here and there the brilliant rays penetrated to earth, but for the most part they only served to accentuate the Stygian blackness of the jungle's depths.

Like some huge phantom, Kala swung noiselessly from tree to tree; now running nimbly along a great branch, now swinging through space at the end of another, only to grasp that of a further tree in her rapid progress toward the scene of the tragedy her knowledge of jungle life told her was being enacted a short distance before her.

The cries of the gorilla proclaimed that it was in mortal combat with some other denizen of the fierce wood. Suddenly these cries ceased, and the silence of death reigned throughout the jungle.

Kala could not understand, for the voice of Bolgani had at the last been raised in the agony of suffering and death, but no sound had come to her by which she possibly could determine the nature of his antagonist.

That her little Tarzan could destroy a great bull gorilla she knew to be improbable, and so, as she neared the spot from which the sounds of the struggle had come, she moved more warily and at last slowly and with extreme caution she traversed the lowest branches, peering eagerly into the moon-splashed blackness for a sign of the combatants.

Presently she came upon them, lying in a little open

space full under the brilliant light of the moon—little Tarzan's torn and bloody form, and beside it a great bull gorilla, stone dead.

With a low cry Kala rushed to Tarzan's side, and gathering the poor, blood-covered body to her breast, listened for a sign of life. Faintly she heard it—the weak beating of the little heart.

Tenderly she bore him back through the inky jungle to where the tribe lay, and for many days and nights she sat guard beside him, bringing him food and water, brushing the flies and other insects from his cruel wounds.

Of medicine or surgery the poor thing knew nothing. She could but lick the wounds, and thus she kept them cleansed, that healing nature might the more quickly do her work.

At first Tarzan would eat nothing, but rolled and tossed in a wild delirium of fever. All he craved was water, and this she brought him in the only way she could, bearing it in her own mouth.

No human mother could have shown more unselfish and sacrificing devotion than did this poor, wild brute for the little orphaned waif whom fate had thrown into her keeping.

At last the fever abated and the boy commenced to mend. No word of complaint passed his tight set lips, though the pain of his wounds was excruciating.

A portion of his chest was laid bare to the ribs, three of which had been broken by the mighty blows of the gorilla. One arm was nearly severed by the giant fangs, and a great piece had been torn from his neck, exposing his jugular vein, which the cruel jaws had missed but by a miracle.

With the stoicism of the brutes who had raised him he endured his suffering quietly, preferring to crawl away from the others and lie huddled in some clump of tall grasses rather than to show his misery before their eyes.

Kala, alone, he was glad to have with him, but now

that he was better she was gone longer at a time, in search of food; for the devoted animal had scarcely eaten enough to support her own life while Tarzan had been so low, and was in consequence, reduced to a mere shadow of her former self.

CHAPTER VII

The Light of Knowledge

AFTER what seemed an eternity to the little sufferer he was able to walk once more, and from then on his recovery was rapid, so that in another month he was as strong and active as ever.

During his convalescence he had gone over in his mind many times the battle with the gorilla, and his first thought was to recover the wonderful little weapon which had transformed him from a hopelessly outclassed weakling to the superior of the mighty terror of the jungle.

Also, he was anxious to return to the cabin and continue his investigations of its wondrous contents.

So, early one morning, he set forth alone upon his quest. After a little search he located the clean-picked bones of his late adversary, and close by, partly buried beneath the fallen leaves, he found the knife, now red with rust from its exposure to the dampness of the ground and from the dried blood of the gorilla.

He did not like the change in its former bright and gleaming surface; but it was still a formidable weapon, and one which he meant to use to advantage whenever the opportunity presented itself. He had in mind that no more would he run from the wanton attacks of old Tublat.

In another moment he was at the cabin, and after a short time had again thrown the latch and entered. His first concern was to learn the mechanism of the lock, and this he did by examining it closely while the door was open, so that he could learn precisely what caused it to hold the door, and by what means it released at his touch.

He found that he could close and lock the door from within, and this he did so that there would be no chance of his being molested while at his investigations.

He commenced a systematic search of the cabin; but his attention was soon riveted by the books which seemed to exert a strange and powerful influence over him, so that he could scarce attend to aught else for the lure of the wondrous puzzle which their purpose presented to him.

Among the other books were a primer, some child's readers, numerous picture books, and a great dictionary. All of these he examined, but the pictures caught his fancy most, though the strange little bugs which covered the pages where there were no pictures excited his wonder and deepest thought.

Squatting upon his haunches on the table top in the cabin his father had built—his smooth, brown, naked little body bent over the book which rested in his strong slender hands, and his great shock of long, black hair falling about his well-shaped head and bright, intelligent eyes—Tarzan of the Apes, little primitive man, presented a picture filled, at once, with pathos and with promise—an allegorical figure of the primordial groping through the black night of ignorance toward the light of learning.

His little face was tense in study, for he had partially grasped, in a hazy, nebulous way, the rudiments of a thought which was destined to prove the key and the solution to the puzzling problem of the strange little bugs.

In his hands was a primer opened at a picture of a little ape similar to himself, but covered, except for hands and face, with strange, colored fur, for such he thought the jacket and trousers to be. Beneath the picture were three little bugs—

BOY.

And now he had discovered in the text upon the page that these three were repeated many times in the same sequence.

Another fact he learned—that there were comparatively few individual bugs; but these were repeated many times, occasionally alone, but more often in company with others.

Slowly he turned the pages, scanning the pictures and the text for a repetition of the combination *b-o-y*. Presently he found it beneath a picture of another little ape and a strange animal which went upon four legs like the jackal and resembled him not a little. Beneath this picture the bugs appeared as:

A BOY AND A DOG.

There they were, the three little bugs which always accompanied the little ape.

And so he progressed very, very slowly, for it was a hard and laborious task which he had set himself without knowing it—a task which might seem to you or me impossible—learning to read without having the slightest knowledge of letters or written language, or the faintest idea that such things existed.

He did not accomplish it in a day, or in a week or in a month, or in a year; but slowly, very slowly, he learned after he had grasped the possibilities which lay in those little bugs, so that by the time he was fifteen he knew the various combinations of letters which stood for every pictured figure in the little primer and in one or two of the picture books.

Of the meaning and use of the articles and conjunctions, verbs and adverbs and pronouns he had but the faintest and haziest conception.

One day when he was about twelve he found a number of lead pencils in a hitherto undiscovered drawer beneath the table, and in scratching upon the table top with one of them he was delighted to discover the black line it left behind it.

He worked so assiduously with this new toy that the table top was soon a mass of scrawly loops and irregular lines and his pencil-point worn down to the wood. Then he took another pencil, but this time he had a definite object in view.

He would attempt to reproduce some of the little bugs that scrambled over the pages of his books.

It was a difficult task, for he held the pencil as one would grasp the hilt of a dagger, which does not add greatly to ease in writing nor to the legibility of the results.

But he persevered for months, at such times as he was able to come to the cabin, until at last by repeated experimenting he found a position in which to hold the pencil that best permitted him to guide and control it, so that at last he could roughly reproduce any of the little bugs.

Thus he made a beginning at writing.

Copying the bugs taught him another thing, their number; and though he could not count as we understand it yet he had an idea of quantity, the base of his calculations being the number of fingers upon one of his hands.

His search through the various books convinced him that he had discovered all the different kinds of bugs most often repeated in combination, and these he arranged in proper order with great ease because of the frequency with which he had perused the fascinating alphabet picture book.

His education progressed; but his greatest finds were in the inexhaustible storehouse of the huge illustrated dictionary, for he learned more through the medium of pictures than text, even after he had grasped the significance of the bugs.

When he discovered the arrangement of words in alphabetical order he delighted in searching for and finding the combinations with which he was familiar, and the words which followed them, their definitions, led him still further into the mazes of erudition.

By the time he was seventeen he had learned to read the simple, child's primer and had fully realized the true and wonderful purpose of the little bugs.

No longer did he feel shame for his hairless body or his human features, for now his reason told him that he was of a different race from his wild and hairy companions. He was a M-A-N, they were A-P-E-S, and the little apes which scurried through the forest top were M-O-N-K-E-Y-S. He knew, too, that old Sabor was a L-I-O-N-E-S-S, and Histah a S-N-A-K-E, and Tantor an E-L-E-P-H-A-N-T. And so he learned to read.

From then on his progress was rapid. With the help of the great dictionary and the active intelligence of a healthy mind endowed by inheritance with more than ordinary reasoning powers he shrewdly guessed at much which he could not really understand, and more often than not his guesses were close to the mark of truth.

There were many breaks in his education, caused by the migratory habits of his tribe, but even when removed from recourse to his books his active brain continued to search out the mysteries of his fascinating avocation.

Pieces of bark and flat leaves and even smooth stretches of bare earth provided him with copy books whereon to scratch with the point of his hunting knife the lessons he was learning.

Nor did he neglect the sterner duties of life while following the bent of his inclination toward the solving of the mystery of his library.

He practiced with his rope and played with his sharp knife, which he had learned to keep keen by whetting upon flat stones.

The tribe had grown larger since Tarzan had come

among them, for under the leadership of Kerchak they had been able to frighten the other tribes from their part of the jungle so that they had plenty to eat and little or no loss from predatory incursions of neighbors.

Hence the younger males as they became adult found it more comfortable to take wives from their own tribe, or if they captured one of another tribe to bring her back to Kerchak's band and live in amity with him rather than attempt to set up a new establishment of their own, or fight with the redoubtable Kerchak for supremacy at home.

Occasionally one more ferocious than his fellows would attempt this latter alternative, but none had come yet who could wrest the palm of victory from the fierce and brutal ape.

Tarzan held a peculiar position in the tribe. They seemed to consider him one of them and yet in some way different. The older males either ignored him entirely or else hated him so vindictively that but for his wondrous agility and speed and the fierce protection of the huge Kala he would have been dispatched at an early age.

Tublat was his most consistent enemy, but it was through Tublat that, when he was about thirteen, the persecution of his enemies suddenly ceased and he was left severely alone, except on the occasions when one of them ran amuck in the throes of one of those strange, wild fits of insane rage which attacks the males of many of the fiercer animals of the jungle. Then none was safe.

On the day that Tarzan established his right to respect, the tribe was gathered about a small natural amphitheater which the jungle had left free from its entangling vines and creepers in a hollow amongst some low hills.

The open space was almost circular in shape. Upon every hand rose the mighty giants of the untouched forest, with the matted undergrowth banked so closely between the huge trunks that the only opening into the little, level arena was through the upper branches of the trees.

Here, safe from interruption, the tribe often gathered. In the center of the amphitheater was one of those strange earthen drums which the anthropoids build for the queer rites the sounds of which men have heard in the fastnesses of the jungle, but which none has ever witnessed.

Many travelers have seen the drums of the great apes, and some have heard the sounds of their beating and the noise of the wild, weird revelry of these first lords of the jungle, but Tarzan, Lord Greystoke, is, doubtless, the only human being who ever joined in the fierce, mad, intoxicating revel of the Dum-Dum.

From this primitive function has arisen, unquestionably, all the forms and ceremonials of modern church and state, for through all the countless ages, back beyond the last, uttermost ramparts of a dawning humanity our fierce, hairy forebears danced out the rites of the Dum-Dum to the sound of their earthen drums, beneath the bright light of a tropical moon in the depth of a mighty jungle which stands unchanged to-day as it stood on that long forgotten night in the dim, unthinkable vistas of the long dead past when our first shaggy ancestor swung from a swaying bough and dropped lightly upon the soft turf of the first meeting place.

On the day that Tarzan won his emancipation from the persecution that had followed him remorselessly for twelve of his thirteen years of life, the tribe, now a full hundred strong, trooped silently through the lower terrace of the jungle trees and dropped noiselessly upon the floor of the amphitheater.

The rites of the Dum-Dum marked important events in the life of the tribe—a victory, the capture of a prisoner, the killing of some large fierce denizen of the jungle, the death or accession of a king, and were conducted with set ceremonialism.

To-day it was the killing of a giant ape, a member of another tribe, and as the people of Kerchak entered the

arena two mighty bulls might have been seen bearing
the body of the vanquished between them.

They laid their burden before the earthen drum and
then squatted there beside it as guards, while the other
members of the community curled themselves in grassy
nooks to sleep until the rising moon should give the signal for the commencement of their savage orgy.

For hours absolute quiet reigned in the little clearing,
except as it was broken by the discordant notes of brilliantly feathered parrots, or the screeching and twitter-
ing of the thousand jungle birds flitting ceaselessly
amongst the vivid orchids and flamboyant blossoms
which festooned the myriad, moss-covered branches of
the forest kings.

At length as darkness settled upon the jungle the
apes commenced to bestir themselves, and soon they
formed a great circle about the earthen drum. The females and young squatted in a thin line at the outer pe-
riphery of the circle, while just in front of them ranged
the adult males. Before the drum sat three old females,
each armed with a knotted branch fifteen or eighteen
inches in length.

Slowly and softly they began tapping upon the re-
sounding surface of the drum as the first faint rays of
the ascending moon silvered the encircling tree tops.

As the light in the amphitheater increased the females augmented the frequency and force of their
blows until presently a wild, rhythmic din pervaded the
great jungle for miles in every direction. Huge, fierce
brutes stopped in their hunting, with up-pricked ears
and raised heads, to listen to the dull booming that betokened the Dum-Dum of the apes.

Occasionally one would raise his shrill scream or
thunderous roar in answering challenge to the savage
din of the anthropoids, but none came near to investi-
gate or attack, for the great apes, assembled in all the
power of their numbers, filled the breasts of their jungle
neighbors with deep respect.

As the din of the drum rose to almost deafening volume Kerchak sprang into the open space between the squatting males and the drummers.

Standing erect he threw his head far back and looking full into the eye of the rising moon he beat upon his breast with his great hairy paws and emitted his fearful roaring shriek.

One—twice—thrice that terrifying cry rang out across the teeming solitude of that unspeakable quick, yet unthinkably dead, world.

Then, crouching, Kerchak slunk noiselessly around the open circle, veering far away from the dead body lying before the altar-drum, but, as he passed, keeping his little, fierce, wicked, red eyes upon the corpse.

Another male then sprang into the arena, and, repeating the horrid cries of the king, followed stealthily in his wake. Another and another followed in quick succession until the jungle reverberated with the now almost ceaseless notes of their bloodthirsty screams.

It was the challenge and the hunt.

When all the adult males had joined in the thin line of circling dancers the attack commenced.

Kerchak, seizing a huge club from the pile which lay at hand for the purpose, rushed furiously upon the dead ape, dealing the corpse a terrific blow, at the same time emitting the growls and snarls of combat. The din of the drum was now increased, as well as the frequency of the blows, and the warriors, as each approached the victim of the hunt and delivered his bludgeon blow, joined in the mad whirl of the Death Dance.

Tarzan was one of the wild, leaping horde. His brown, sweat-streaked, muscular body, glistening in the moonlight, shone supple and graceful among the uncouth, awkward, hairy brutes about him.

None more craftily stealthy in the mimic hunt, none more ferocious than he in the wild ferocity of the attack, nor none who leaped so high into the air in the Dance of Death.

As the noise and rapidity of the drum beats increased the dancers apparently became intoxicated with the

wild rhythm and the savage yells. Their leaps and
bounds increased, their bared fangs dripped saliva, and
their lips and breasts were flecked with foam.

For half an hour the weird dance went on, until, at a
sign from Kerchak, the noise of the drums ceased, the
female drummers scampering hurriedly through the
line of dancers toward the outer rim of squatting spec-
tators. Then, as one man, the males rushed headlong
upon the thing which their terrific blows had reduced to
a mass of hairy pulp.

Flesh seldom came to their jaws in satisfying quanti-
ties, so a fit finale to their wild revel was a taste of fresh-
killed meat, and it was to the purpose of devouring their
late enemy that they now turned their attention.

Great fangs sunk into the carcass tearing away huge
hunks, the mightiest of the apes obtaining the choicest
morsels, while the weaker circled the outer edge of the
fighting, snarling pack awaiting their chance to dodge in
and snatch a dropped titbit or filch a remaining bone
before all was gone.

Tarzan, more than the apes, craved and needed flesh.
Descended from a race of meat eaters, never in his life,
he thought, had he once satisfied his appetite for animal
food, and so now his agile little body wormed its way far
into the mass of struggling, rending apes in an endeavor
to obtain a share which his strength would have been
unequal to the task of winning for him.

At his side hung the hunting knife of his unknown father in a sheath self-fashioned in copy of one he had
seen among the pictures of his treasure-books.

At last he reached the fast disappearing feast and
with his sharp knife slashed off a more generous portion
than he had hoped for, an entire hairy forearm, where it
protruded from beneath the feet of the mighty Kerchak,
who was so busily engaged in perpetuating the royal
prerogative of hogging that he failed to note the act of
lèse-majesté.

So little Tarzan wriggled out from beneath the struggling mass, clutching his grisly prize close to his breast.

Among those circling futilely the outskirts of the banqueters was old Tublat. He had been among the first at the feast, but had retreated with a goodly share to eat in quiet, and was now forcing his way back for more.

So it was that he spied Tarzan as the boy emerged from the clawing, pushing throng with that hairy forearm hugged firmly to his body.

Tublat's little, close-set, bloodshot, pig eyes shot wicked gleams of hate as they fell upon the object of his loathing. In them, too, was greed for the toothsome dainty the boy carried.

But Tarzan saw his archenemy as quickly, and divining what the great beast would do he leaped nimbly away toward the women and children, hoping to hide himself among them. Tublat, however, was close upon his heels, so that he had no opportunity to seek a place of concealment, but saw that he would be put to it to escape at all.

Swiftly he sped toward the surrounding trees and with an agile bound gained a lower limb with one hand, and then, transferring his burden to his teeth, he climbed rapidly upward, closely followed by Tublat.

Up, up he went to the waving pinnacle of a lofty monarch of the forest where his heavy pursuer dared not follow him. There he perched, hurling taunts and insults at the raging, foaming beast fifty feet below him.

And then Tublat went mad.

With horrifying screams and roars he rushed to the ground, among the females and young, sinking his great fangs into a dozen tiny necks and tearing great pieces from the backs and breasts of the females who fell into his clutches.

In the brilliant moonlight Tarzan witnessed the whole mad carnival of rage. He saw the females and the young scamper to the safety of the trees. Then the great bulls in the center of the arena felt the mighty fangs of their demented fellow, and with one accord they melted into the black shadows of the overhanging forest.

There was but one in the amphitheater besides Tublat,

a belated female running swiftly toward the tree where Tarzan perched, and close behind her came the awful Tublat.

It was Kala, and as quickly as Tarzan saw that Tublat was gaining on her he dropped with the rapidity of a falling stone, from branch to branch, toward his foster mother.

Now she was beneath the overhanging limbs and close above her crouched Tarzan, waiting the outcome of the race.

She leaped into the air grasping a low-hanging branch, but almost over the head of Tublat, so nearly had he distanced her. She should have been safe now but there was a rending, tearing sound, the branch broke and precipitated her full upon the head of Tublat, knocking him to the ground.

Both were up in an instant, but as quick as they had been Tarzan had been quicker, so that the infuriated bull found himself facing the man-child who stood between him and Kala.

Nothing could have suited the fierce beast better, and with a roar of triumph he leaped upon the little Lord Greystoke. But his fangs never closed in that nut brown flesh.

A muscular hand shot out and grasped the hairy throat, and another plunged a keen hunting knife a dozen times into the broad breast. Like lightning the blows fell, and only ceased when Tarzan felt the limp form crumple beneath him.

As the body rolled to the ground Tarzan of the Apes placed his foot upon the neck of his lifelong enemy and raising his eyes to the full moon threw back his fierce young head and voiced the wild and terrible cry of his people.

One by one the tribe swung down from their arboreal retreats and formed a circle about Tarzan and his vanquished foe. When they had all come Tarzan turned toward them.

"I am Tarzan," he cried. "I am a great killer. Let all respect Tarzan of the Apes and Kala, his mother. There be none among you as mighty as Tarzan. Let his enemies beware."

Looking full into the wicked, red eyes of Kerchak, the young Lord Greystoke beat upon his mighty breast and screamed out once more his shrill cry of defiance.

CHAPTER VIII

The Tree-Top Hunter

THE morning after the Dum-Dum the tribe started slowly back through the forest toward the coast.

The body of Tublat lay where it had fallen, for the people of Kerchak do not eat their own dead.

The march was but a leisurely search for food. Cabbage palm and gray plum, pisang and scitamine they found in abundance, with wild pineapple, and occasionally small mammals, birds, eggs, reptiles, and insects. The nuts they cracked between their powerful jaws, or, if too hard, broke by pounding between stones.

Once old Sabor, crossing their path, sent them scurrying to the safety of the higher branches, for if she respected their number and their sharp fangs, they on their part held her cruel and mighty ferocity in equal esteem.

Upon a low-hanging branch sat Tarzan directly above the majestic, supple body as it forged silently through the thick jungle. He hurled a pineapple at the ancient enemy of his people. The great beast stopped and, turning, eyed the taunting figure above her.

With an angry lash of her tail she bared her yellow fangs, curling her great lips in a hideous snarl that wrinkled her bristling snout in serried ridges and closed her wicked eyes to two narrow slits of rage and hatred.

With back-laid ears she looked straight into the eyes of Tarzan of the Apes and sounded her fierce, shrill challenge.

And from the safety of his overhanging limb the ape-child sent back the fearsome answer of his kind.

For a moment the two eyed each other in silence, and then the great cat turned into the jungle, which swallowed her as the ocean engulfs a tossed pebble.

But into the mind of Tarzan a great plan sprang. He had killed the fierce Tublat, so was he not therefore a mighty fighter? Now would he track down the crafty Sabor and slay her likewise. He would be a mighty hunter, also.

At the bottom of his little English heart beat the great desire to cover his nakedness with *clothes* for he had learned from his picture books that all *men* were so covered, while *monkeys* and *apes* and every other living thing went naked.

Clothes therefore, must be truly a badge of greatness; the insignia of the superiority of *man* over all other animals, for surely there could be no other reason for wearing the hideous things.

Many moons ago, when he had been much smaller, he had desired the skin of Sabor, the lioness, or Numa, the lion, or Sheeta, the leopard to cover his hairless body that he might no longer resemble hideous Histah, the snake; but now he was proud of his sleek skin for it betokened his descent from a mighty race, and the conflicting desires to go naked in prideful proof of his ancestry, or to conform to the customs of his own kind and wear hideous and uncomfortable apparel found first one and then the other in the ascendency.

As the tribe continued their slow way through the forest after the passing of Sabor, Tarzan's head was filled with his great scheme for slaying his enemy, and for many days thereafter he thought of little else.

On this day, however, he presently had other and more immediate interests to attract his attention.

Of a sudden it became as midnight; the noises of the

jungle ceased; the trees stood motionless as though in paralyzed expectancy of some great and imminent disaster. All nature waited—but not for long.

Faintly, from a distance, came a low, sad moaning. Nearer and nearer it approached, mounting louder and louder in volume.

The great trees bent in unison as though pressed earthward by a mighty hand. Further and further toward the ground they inclined, and still there was no sound save the deep and awesome moaning of the wind.

Then, suddenly, the jungle giants whipped back, lashing their mighty tops in angry and deafening protest. A vivid and blinding light flashed from the whirling, inky clouds above. The deep cannonade of roaring thunder belched forth its fearsome challenge. The deluge came—and hell broke loose upon the jungle.

The tribe huddled, shivering from the cold rain, at the bases of the great trees. The lightning darting and flashing through the blackness, showed wildly waving branches, whipping streamers and bending trunks.

Now and again some ancient patriarch of the woods, rent by a flashing bolt, would crash in a thousand pieces among the surrounding trees, carrying down numberless branches and many smaller neighbors to add to the tangled confusion of the tropical jungle.

Branches, great and small, torn away by the ferocity of the tornado, hurtled through the wildly waving verdure, carrying death and destruction to countless unhappy denizens of the thickly peopled world below.

For hours the fury of the storm continued without surcease, and still the tribe huddled close in shivering fear. In constant danger from falling trunks and branches and paralyzed by the vivid flashing of lightning and the bellowing of thunder they crouched in pitiful misery until the storm passed.

The end was as sudden as the beginning. The wind ceased, the sun shone forth—nature smiled once more.

The dripping leaves and branches, and the moist petals of gorgeous flowers glistened in the splendor of the returning day. And, so—as Nature forgot, her children forgot also. Busy life went on as it had been before the darkness and the fright.

But to Tarzan a dawning light had come to explain the mystery of *clothes*. How snug he would have been beneath the heavy coat of Sabor! And so was added a further incentive to the adventure.

For several months the tribe hovered near the beach where stood Tarzan's cabin, and his studies took up the greater portion of his time, but always when journeying through the forest he kept his rope in readiness, and many were the smaller animals that fell into the snare of the quick-thrown noose.

Once it fell about the short neck of Horta, the boar, and his mad lunge for freedom toppled Tarzan from the overhanging limb where he had lain in wait and from whence he had launched his sinuous coil.

The mighty tusker turned at the sound of his falling body, and, seeing only the easy prey of a young ape, he lowered his head and charged madly at the surprised youth.

Tarzan, happily, was uninjured by the fall, alighting catlike upon all fours far outspread to take up the shock. He was on his feet in an instant and, leaping with the agility of the monkey he was, he gained the safety of a low limb as Horta, the boar, rushed futilely beneath.

Thus it was that Tarzan learned by experience the limitations as well as the possibilities of his strange weapon.

He lost a long rope on this occasion, but he knew that had it been Sabor, who had thus dragged him from his perch the outcome might have been very different, for he would have lost his life, doubtless, into the bargain.

It took him many days to braid a new rope, but when, finally, it was done he went forth purposely to hunt, and lie in wait among the dense foliage of a great branch right above the well-beaten trail that led to water.

Several small animals passed unharmed beneath him. He did not want such insignificant game. It would take a strong animal to test the efficacy of his new scheme.

At last came she whom Tarzan sought, with lithe sinews rolling beneath shimmering hide; fat and glossy came Sabor, the lioness.

Her great padded feet fell soft and noiseless on the narrow trail. Her head was high in ever alert attention; her long tail moved slowly in sinuous and graceful undulations.

Nearer and nearer she came to where Tarzan of the Apes crouched upon his limb, the coils of his long rope poised ready in his hand.

Like a thing of bronze, motionless as death, sat Tarzan. Sabor passed beneath. One stride beyond she took—a second, a third, and then the silent coil shot out above her.

For an instant the spreading noose hung above her head like a great snake, and then, as she looked upward to detect the origin of the swishing sound of the rope, it settled about her neck. With a quick jerk Tarzan snapped the noose tight about the glossy throat, and then he dropped the rope and clung to his support with both hands.

Sabor was trapped.

With a bound the startled beast turned into the jungle, but Tarzan was not to lose another rope through the same cause as the first. He had learned from experience. The lioness had taken but half her second bound when she felt the rope tighten about her neck; her body turned completely over in the air and she fell with a heavy crash upon her back. Tarzan had fastened the end of the rope securely to the trunk of the great tree on which he sat.

Thus far his plan had worked to perfection, but when he grasped the rope, bracing himself behind a crotch of two mighty branches, he found that dragging the mighty, struggling, clawing, biting, screaming mass of iron-muscled fury up to the tree and hanging her was a very different proposition.

The weight of old Sabor was immense, and when she braced her huge paws nothing less than Tantor, the elephant, himself, could have budged her.

The lioness was now back in the path where she could see the author of the indignity which had been placed upon her. Screaming with rage she suddenly charged, leaping high into the air toward Tarzan, but when her huge body struck the limb on which Tarzan had been, Tarzan was no longer there.

Instead he perched lightly upon a smaller branch twenty feet above the raging captive. For a moment Sabor hung half across the branch, while Tarzan mocked, and hurled twigs and branches at her unprotected face.

Presently the beast dropped to the earth again and Tarzan came quickly to seize the rope, but Sabor had now found that it was only a slender cord that held her, and grasping it in her huge jaws severed it before Tarzan could tighten the strangling noose a second time.

Tarzan was much hurt. His well-laid plan had come to naught, so he sat there screaming at the roaring creature beneath him and making mocking grimaces at it.

Sabor paced back and forth beneath the tree for hours; four times she crouched and sprang at the dancing sprite above her, but as well have clutched at the elusive wind that murmured through the tree tops.

At last Tarzan tired of the sport, and with a parting roar of challenge and a well-aimed ripe fruit that spread soft and sticky over the snarling face of his enemy, he swung rapidly through the trees, a hundred feet above the ground, and in a short time was among the members of his tribe.

Here he recounted the details of his adventure, with swelling chest and so considerable swagger that he quite impressed even his bitterest enemies, while Kala fairly danced for joy and pride.

CHAPTER IX

❧❧

Man and Man

TARZAN of the Apes lived on in his wild jungle existence with little change for several years, only that he grew stronger and wiser, and learned from his books more and more of the strange worlds which lay somewhere outside his primeval forest.

To him life was never monotonous or stale. There was always Pisah the fish, to be caught in the many streams and the little lakes, and Sabor, with her ferocious cousins to keep one ever on the alert and give zest to every instant that one spent upon the ground.

Often they hunted him, and more often he hunted them, but though they never quite reached him with those cruel, sharp claws of theirs, yet there were times when one could scarce have passed a thick leaf between their talons and his smooth hide.

Quick was Sabor, the lioness, and quick were Numa and Sheeta, but Tarzan of the Apes was lightning.

With Tantor, the elephant, he made friends. How? Ask me not. But this is known to the denizens of the jungle, that on many moonlit nights Tarzan of the Apes and Tantor, the elephant, walked together, and where the way was clear Tarzan rode, perched high upon Tantor's mighty back.

All else of the jungle were his enemies, except his own tribe, among whom he now had many friends.

Many days during these years he spent in the cabin of his father, where still lay, untouched, the bones of his parents and the little skeleton of Kala's baby. At eighteen he read fluently and understood nearly all he read in the many and varied volumes on the shelves.

Also could he write, with printed letters, rapidly and plainly, but script he had not mastered, for though there were several copy books among his treasure, there was so little written English in the cabin that he saw no use for bothering with this other form of writing, though he could read it, laboriously.

Thus, at eighteen, we find him, an English lordling, who could speak no English, and yet who could read and write his native language. Never had he seen a human being other than himself, for the little area traversed by his tribe was watered by no great river to bring down the savage natives of the interior.

High hills shut it off on three sides, the ocean on the fourth. It was alive with lions and leopards and poisonous snakes. Its untouched mazes of matted jungle had as yet invited no hardy pioneer from the human beasts beyond its frontier.

But as Tarzan of the Apes sat one day in the cabin of his father delving into the mysteries of a new book, the ancient security of his jungle was broken forever.

At the far eastern confine a strange cavalcade strung, in single file, over the brow of a low hill.

In advance were fifty black warriors armed with slender wooden spears with ends hard baked over slow fires, and long bows and poisoned arrows. On their backs were oval shields, in their noses huge rings, while from the kinky wool of their heads protruded tufts of gay feathers.

Across their foreheads were tattooed three parallel

lines of color, and on each breast three concentric circles. Their yellow teeth were filed to sharp points, and their great protruding lips added still further to the low and bestial brutishness of their appearance.

Following them were several hundred women and children, the former bearing upon their heads great burdens of cooking pots, household utensils and ivory. In the rear were a hundred warriors, similar in all respects to the advance guard.

That they more greatly feared an attack from the rear than whatever unknown enemies lurked in their advance was evidenced by the formation of the column; and such was the fact, for they were fleeing from the white man's soldiers who had so harassed them for rubber and ivory that they had turned upon their conquerors one day and massacred a white officer and a small detachment of his black troops.

For many days they had gorged themselves on meat, but eventually a stronger body of troops had come and fallen upon their village by night to revenge the death of their comrades.

That night the black soldiers of the white man had had meat a-plenty, and this little remnant of a once powerful tribe had slunk off into the gloomy jungle toward the unknown, and freedom.

But what meant freedom and the pursuit of happiness to these savage blacks meant consternation and death to many of the wild denizens of their new home.

For three days the little cavalcade marched slowly through the heart of this unknown and untracked forest, until finally, early in the fourth day, they came upon a little spot, near the banks of a small river, which seemed less thickly overgrown than any ground they had yet encountered.

Here they set to work to build a new village, and in a month a great clearing had been made, huts and palisades erected, plantains, yams and maize planted, and they had taken up their old life in their new home. Here there were no white men, no soldiers; nor any rubber or ivory to be gathered for cruel and thankless taskmasters.

Several moons passed by ere the blacks ventured far into the territory surrounding their new village. Several had already fallen prey to old Sabor, and because the jungle was so infested with these fierce and bloodthirsty cats, and with lions and leopards, the ebony warriors hesitated to trust themselves far from the safety of their palisades.

But one day, Kulonga, a son of the old king, Mbonga, wandered far into the dense mazes to the west. Warily he stepped, his slender lance ever ready, his long oval shield firm grasped in his left hand close to his sleek ebony body.

At his back his bow, and in the quiver upon his shield many slim, straight arrows, well smeared with the thick, dark, tarry substance that rendered deadly their tiniest needle prick.

Night found Kulonga far from the palisades of his father's village, but still headed westward, and climbing into the fork of a great tree he fashioned a rude platform and curled himself for sleep.

Three miles to the west of him slept the tribe of Kerchak.

Early the next morning the apes were astir, moving through the jungle in search of food. Tarzan, as was his custom, prosecuted his search in the direction of the cabin so that by leisurely hunting on the way his stomach was filled by the time he reached the beach.

The apes scattered by ones, and twos, and threes in all directions, but ever within sound of a signal of alarm.

Kala had moved slowly along an elephant track toward the east, and was busily engaged in turning over rotted limbs and logs in search of esculent bugs and fungi, when the faintest shadow of a strange noise brought her to startled attention.

For fifty yards before her the trail was straight, and down this leafy tunnel she saw the stealthy advancing figure of a strange and fearful creature.

It was Kulonga.

Kala did not wait to see more, but, turning, moved rapidly back along the trail. She did not run; but, after the manner of her kind when not aroused, sought rather to avoid than to escape.

Close after her came Kulonga. Here was meat. He could make a killing and feast well this day. On he hurried, his spear poised for the throw.

At a turning of the trail he came in sight of her again upon another straight stretch. His spear hand went far back, the muscles rolled, lightninglike, beneath the sleek hide. Out shot the arm, and the spear sped toward Kala.

A poor cast. It but grazed her side.

With a cry of rage and pain the she-ape turned upon her tormentor. In an instant the trees were crashing beneath the weight of her hurrying fellows, swinging rapidly toward the scene of trouble in answer to Kala's scream.

As she charged, Kulonga unslung his bow and fitted an arrow with almost unthinkable quickness. Drawing the shaft far back he drove the poisoned missile straight into the heart of the great anthropoid.

With a horrid scream Kala plunged forward upon her face before the astonished members of her tribe.

Roaring and shrieking the apes dashed toward Kulonga, but the wary savage was fleeing down the trail like a frightened antelope.

He knew something of the ferocity of these wild, hairy men, and his one desire was to put as many miles between himself and them as he possibly could.

They followed him, racing through the trees, for a long distance, but finally one by one they abandoned the chase and returned to the scene of the tragedy.

None of them had ever seen a man before, other than Tarzan, and so they wondered vaguely what strange manner of creature it might be that had invaded their jungle.

On the far beach, by the little cabin Tarzan heard the faint echoes of the conflict and knowing that something was seriously amiss among the tribe he hastened rapidly toward the direction of the sound.

When he arrived he found the entire tribe gathered jabbering about the dead body of his slain mother.

Tarzan's grief and anger were unbounded. He roared out his hideous challenge time and again. He beat upon his great chest with his clenched fists, and then he fell upon the body of Kala and sobbed out the pitiful sorrowing of his lonely heart.

To lose the only creature in all one's world who ever had manifested love and affection for one, is a great bereavement indeed.

What though Kala was a fierce and hideous ape! To Tarzan she had been kind, she had been beautiful.

Upon her he had lavished, unknown to himself, all the reverence and respect and love that a normal English boy feels for his own mother. He had never known another, and so to Kala was given, though mutely, all that would have belonged to the fair and lovely Lady Alice had she lived.

After the first outburst of grief Tarzan controlled himself, and questioning the members of the tribe who had witnessed the killing of Kala he learned all that their meager vocabulary could vouchsafe him.

It was enough, however, for his needs. It told him of a strange, hairless, black ape with feathers growing upon its head, who launched death from a slender branch, and then ran, with the fleetness of Bara, the deer, toward the rising sun.

Tarzan waited no longer, but leaping into the branches of the trees sped rapidly through the forest. He knew the windings of the elephant trail along which Kala's murderer had flown, and so he cut straight through the jungle to intercept the black warrior who was evidently following the tortuous detours of the trail.

At his side was the hunting knife of his unknown sire, and across his shoulders the coils of his own long rope. In an hour he struck the trail again, and coming to earth examined the soil minutely.

In the soft mud on the bank of a tiny rivulet he found footprints such as he alone in all the jungle had ever made, but much larger than his. His heart beat fast. Could it be that he was trailing a MAN—one of his own race?

There were two sets of imprints pointing in opposite directions. So his quarry had already passed on his return along the trail. As he examined the newer spoor a tiny particle of earth toppled from the outer edge of one of the footprints to the bottom of its shallow depression— ah, the trail was very fresh, his prey must have but scarcely passed.

Tarzan swung himself to the trees once more, and with swift noiselessness sped along high above the trail.

He had covered barely a mile when he came upon the black warrior standing in a little open space. In his hand was his slender bow to which he had fitted one of his death-dealing arrows.

Opposite him across the little clearing stood Horta, the boar, with lowered head and foam-flecked tusks, ready to charge.

Tarzan looked with wonder upon the strange creature beneath him—so like him in form and yet so different in face and color. His books had portrayed the *negro,* but how different had been the dull, dead print to this sleek and hideous thing of ebony, pulsing with life.

As the man stood there with taut drawn bow Tarzan recognized in him not so much the *negro* as the *Archer* of his picture book—

A stands for Archer

How wonderful! Tarzan almost betrayed his presence in the deep excitement of his discovery.

But things were commencing to happen below him. The sinewy black arm had drawn the shaft far back;

Horta, the boar, was charging, and then the black released the little poisoned arrow, and Tarzan saw it fly with the quickness of thought and lodge in the bristling neck of the boar.

Scarcely had the shaft left his bow ere Kulonga had fitted another to it, but Horta, the boar, was upon him so quickly that he had no time to discharge it. With a bound the black leaped entirely over the rushing beast and turning with incredible swiftness planted a second arrow in Horta's back.

Then Kulonga sprang into a near-by tree.

Horta wheeled to charge his enemy once more, a dozen steps he took, then he staggered and fell upon his side. For a moment his muscles stiffened and relaxed convulsively, then he lay still.

Kulonga came down from his tree.

With a knife that hung at his side he cut several large pieces from the boar's body, and in the center of the trail he built a fire, cooking and eating as much as he wanted. The rest he left where it had fallen.

Tarzan was an interested spectator. His desire to kill burned fiercely in his wild breast, but his desire to learn was even greater. He would follow this savage creature for a while and know from whence he came. He could kill him at his leisure later, when the bow and deadly arrows were laid aside.

When Kulonga had finished his repast and disappeared beyond a near turning of the path, Tarzan dropped quietly to the ground. With his knife he severed many strips of meat from Horta's carcass, but he did not cook them.

He had seen fire, but only when Ara, the lightning, had destroyed some great tree. That any creature of the jungle could produce the red-and-yellow fangs which devoured wood and left nothing but fine dust surprised Tarzan greatly, and why the black warrior had ruined his delicious repast by plunging it into the blighting heat was quite beyond him. Possibly Ara was a friend with whom the Archer was sharing his food.

But, be that as it may, Tarzan would not ruin good meat in any such foolish manner, so he gobbled down a great quantity of the raw flesh, burying the balance of the carcass beside the trail where he could find it upon his return.

And then Lord Greystoke wiped his greasy fingers upon his naked thighs and took up the trail of Kulonga, the son of Mbonga, the king; while in far-off London another Lord Greystoke, the younger brother of the real Lord Greystoke's father, sent back his chops to the club's *chef* because they were underdone, and when he had finished his repast he dipped his finger-ends into a silver bowl of scented water and dried them upon a piece of snowy damask.

All day Tarzan followed Kulonga, hovering above him in the trees like some malign spirit. Twice more he saw him hurl his arrows of destruction—once at Dango, the hyena, and again at Manu, the monkey. In each instance the animal died almost instantly, for Kulonga's poison was very fresh and very deadly.

Tarzan thought much on this wondrous method of slaying as he swung slowly along at a safe distance behind his quarry. He knew that alone the tiny prick of the arrow could not so quickly dispatch these wild things of the jungle, who were often torn and scratched and gored in a frightful manner as they fought with their jungle neighbors, yet as often recovered as not.

No, there was something mysterious connected with these tiny slivers of wood which could bring death by a mere scratch. He must look into the matter.

That night Kulonga slept in the crotch of a mighty tree and far above him crouched Tarzan of the Apes. When Kulonga awoke he found that his bow and arrows had disappeared. The black warrior was furious and frightened, but more frightened than furious. He searched the ground below the tree, and he searched the tree above the ground; but there was no sign of either bow or arrows or of the nocturnal marauder.

Kulonga was panic-stricken. His spear he had hurled at Kala and had not recovered; and, now that his bow and arrows were gone, he was defenseless except for a single knife. His only hope lay in reaching the village of Mbonga as quickly as his legs would carry him.

That he was not far from home he was certain, so he took the trail at a rapid trot.

From a great mass of impenetrable foliage a few yards away emerged Tarzan of the Apes to swing quietly in his wake.

Kulonga's bow and arrows were securely tied high in the top of a giant tree from which a patch of bark had been removed by a sharp knife near to the ground, and a branch half cut through and left hanging about fifty feet higher up. Thus Tarzan blazed the forest trails and marked his caches.

As Kulonga continued his journey Tarzan closed up on him until he traveled almost over the black's head. His rope he now held coiled in his right hand; he was almost ready for the kill.

The moment was delayed only because Tarzan was anxious to ascertain the black warrior's destination, and presently he was rewarded, for they came suddenly in view of a great clearing, at one end of which lay many strange lairs.

Tarzan was directly over Kulonga, as he made his discovery. The forest ended abruptly and beyond lay two hundred yards of planted fields between the jungle and the village.

Tarzan must act quickly or his prey would be gone; but Tarzan's life training left so little space between decision and action when an emergency confronted him that there was not even room for the shadow of a thought between.

So it was that as Kulonga emerged from the shadow of the jungle a slender coil of rope sped sinuously above him from the lowest branch of a mighty tree directly upon the edge of the fields of Mbonga, and ere the king's son had taken a half dozen steps into the clearing a quick noose tightened about his neck.

So quickly did Tarzan of the Apes drag back his prey that Kulonga's cry of alarm was throttled in his windpipe. Hand over hand Tarzan drew the struggling black until he had him hanging by his neck in midair; then Tarzan climbed to a larger branch drawing the still threshing victim well up into the sheltering verdure of the tree.

Here he fastened the rope securely to a stout branch, and then, descending, plunged his hunting knife into Kulonga's heart. Kala was avenged.

Tarzan examined the black minutely, never had he seen any other human being. The knife with its sheath and belt caught his eye; he appropriated them. A copper anklet also took his fancy, and this he transferred to his own leg.

He examined and admired the tattooing on the forehead and the breast. He marveled at the sharp filed teeth. He investigated and appropriated the feathered headdress, and then he prepared to get down to business, for Tarzan of the Apes was hungry, and here was meat; meat of the kill, which jungle ethics permitted him to eat.

How may we judge him, by what standards, this apeman with the heart and body of an English gentleman, and the training of a wild beast?

Tublat, whom he had hated and who had hated him, he had killed in fair fight, and yet never had the thought of eating Tublat's flesh entered his head. It would have been as revolting to him as is cannibalism to us.

But who was Kulonga that he might not be eaten as fairly as Horta, the boar, or Bara, the deer? Was he not simply another of the countless wild things of the jungle who preyed upon one another to satisfy the cravings of hunger?

Of a sudden, a strange doubt stayed his hand. Had

not his books taught him that he was a man? And was not The Archer a man, also?

Did men eat men? Alas, he did not know. Why, then, this hesitancy! Once more he essayed the effort, but of a sudden a qualm of nausea overwhelmed him. He did not understand.

All he knew was that he could not eat the flesh of this black man, and thus hereditary instinct, ages old, usurped the functions of his untaught mind and saved him from transgressing a worldwide law of whose very existence he was ignorant.

Quickly he lowered Kulonga's body to the ground, removed the noose, and took to the trees again.

CHAPTER X

The Fear-Phantom

FROM a lofty perch Tarzan viewed the village of thatched huts across the intervening plantation.

He saw that at one point the forest touched the village, and to this spot he made his way, lured by a fever of curiosity to behold animals of his own kind, and to learn more of their ways and view the strange lairs in which they lived.

His savage life among the fierce wild brutes of the jungle left no opening for any thought that these could be aught else than enemies. Similarity of form led him into no erroneous conception of the welcome that would be accorded him should he be discovered by these, the first of his own kind he had ever seen.

Tarzan of the Apes was no sentimentalist. He knew nothing of the brotherhood of man. All things outside his own tribe were his deadly enemies, with the few exceptions of which Tantor, the elephant, was a marked example.

And he realized all this without malice or hatred. To kill was the law of the wild world he knew. Few were his primitive pleasures, but the greatest of these was to hunt and kill, and so he accorded to others the right to cherish the same desires as he, even though he himself might be the object of their hunt.

His strange life had left him neither morose nor bloodthirsty. That he joyed in killing, and that he killed with a joyous laugh upon his handsome lips betokened no innate cruelty. He killed for food most often, but, being a man, he sometimes killed for pleasure, a thing which no other animal does; for it has remained for man alone among all creatures to kill senselessly and wantonly for the mere pleasure of inflicting suffering and death.

And when he killed for revenge, or in self-defense, he did that also without hysteria, but it was a very businesslike proceeding which admitted of no levity.

So it was that now, as he cautiously approached the village of Mbonga, he was quite prepared either to kill or be killed should he be discovered. He proceeded with unwonted stealth, for Kulonga had taught him great respect for the little sharp splinters of wood which dealt death so swiftly and unerringly.

At length he came to a great tree, heavy laden with thick foliage and loaded with pendant loops of giant creepers. From this almost impenetrable bower above the village he crouched, looking down upon the scene below him, wondering over every feature of this new, strange life.

There were naked children running and playing in the village street. There were women grinding dried plantain in crude stone mortars, while others were fashioning cakes from the powdered flour. Out in the fields he could see still other women hoeing, weeding, or gathering.

All wore strange protruding girdles of dried grass about their hips and many were loaded with brass and copper anklets, armlets and bracelets. Around many a dusky neck hung curiously coiled strands of wire, while several were further ornamented by huge nose rings.

Tarzan of the Apes looked with growing wonder at these strange creatures. Dozing in the shade he saw several men, while at the extreme outskirts of the clearing he occasionally caught glimpses of armed warriors apparently guarding the village against surprise from an attacking enemy.

He noticed that the women alone worked. Nowhere was there evidence of a man tilling the fields or performing any of the homely duties of the village.

Finally his eyes rested upon a woman directly beneath him.

Before her was a small caldron standing over a low fire and in it bubbled a thick, reddish, tarry mass. On one side of her lay a quantity of wooden arrows the points of which she dipped into the seething substance, then laying them upon a narrow rack of boughs which stood upon her other side.

Tarzan of the Apes was fascinated. Here was the secret of the terrible destructiveness of The Archer's tiny missiles. He noted the extreme care which the woman took that none of the matter should touch her hands, and once when a particle spattered upon one of her fingers he saw her plunge the member into a vessel of water and quickly rub the tiny stain away with a handful of leaves.

Tarzan of the Apes knew nothing of poison, but his shrewd reasoning told him that it was this deadly stuff that killed, and not the little arrow, which was merely the messenger that carried it into the body of its victim.

How he should like to have more of those little death-dealing slivers. If the woman would only leave her work for an instant he could drop down, gather up a handful, and be back in the tree again before she drew three breaths.

As he was trying to think out some plan to distract her attention he heard a wild cry from across the clearing. He looked and saw a black warrior standing beneath the very tree in which he had killed the murderer of Kala an hour before.

The fellow was shouting and waving his spear above his head. Now and again he would point to something on the ground before him.

The village was in an uproar instantly. Armed men

rushed from the interior of many a hut and raced madly across the clearing toward the excited sentry. After them trooped the old men, and the women and children until, in a moment, the village was deserted.

Tarzan of the Apes knew that they had found the body of his victim, but that interested him far less than the fact that no one remained in the village to prevent his taking a supply of the arrows which lay below him.

Quickly and noiselessly he dropped to the ground beside the caldron of poison. For a moment he stood motionless, his quick, bright eyes scanning the interior of the palisade.

No one was in sight. His eyes rested upon the open doorway of a near-by hut. He would take a look within, thought Tarzan, and so, cautiously, he approached the low thatched building.

For a moment he stood without, listening intently. There was no sound, and he glided into the semi-darkness of the interior.

Weapons hung against the walls—long spears, strangely shaped knives, a couple of narrow shields. In the center of the room was a cooking pot, and at the far end a litter of dry grasses covered by woven mats which evidently served the owners as beds and bedding. Several human skulls lay upon the floor.

Tarzan of the Apes felt of each article, hefted the spears, smelled of them, for he "saw" largely through his sensitive and highly trained nostrils. He determined to own one of these long, pointed sticks, but he could not take one on this trip because of the arrows he meant to carry.

One by one, as he took each article from the walls, he placed them in a pile in the center of the room, and on top of all he placed the cooking pot, inverted, and on top of this he laid one of the grinning skulls, upon which he fastened the headdress of the dead Kulonga.

Then he stood back and surveyed his work, and grinned. Tarzan of the Apes was a joker.

But now he heard, without, the sounds of many

voices, and long mournful howls, and mighty wailing. He
was startled. Had he remained too long? Quickly he
reached the doorway and peered down the village street
toward the village gate.

The natives were not yet in sight, though he could
plainly hear them approaching across the plantation.
They must be very near.

Like a flash he sprang across the opening to the pile
of arrows. Gathering up all he could carry under one
arm, he overturned the seething caldron with a kick,
and disappeared into the foliage above just as the first
of the returning natives entered the gate at the far end
of the village street. Then he turned to watch the proceeding below, poised like some wild bird ready to take
swift wing at the first sign of danger.

The natives filed up the street, four of them bearing
the dead body of Kulonga. Behind trailed the women,
uttering strange cries and weird lamentation. On they
came to the portals of Kulonga's hut, the very one in
which Tarzan had wrought his depredations.

Scarcely had half a dozen entered the building ere
they came rushing out in wild, jabbering confusion. The
others hastened to gather about. There was much excited gesticulating, pointing, and chattering; then several
of the warriors approached and peered within.

Finally an old fellow with many ornaments of metal
about his arms and legs, and a necklace of dried human
hands depending upon his chest, entered the hut.

It was Mbonga, the king, father of Kulonga.

For a few moments all were silent. Then Mbonga
emerged, a look of mingled wrath and superstitious
fear writ upon his hideous countenance. He spoke a
few words to the assembled warriors, and in an instant the men were flying through the little village
searching minutely every hut and corner within the
palisades.

Scarcely had the search commenced than the overturned caldron was discovered, and with it the theft of
the poisoned arrows. Nothing more they found, and it

was a thoroughly awed and frightened group of savages which huddled around their king a few moments later.

Mbonga could explain nothing of the strange events that had taken place. The finding of the still warm body of Kulonga—on the very verge of their fields and within easy earshot of the village—knifed and stripped at the door of his father's home, was in itself sufficiently mysterious, but these last awesome discoveries within the village, within the dead Kulonga's own hut, filled their hearts with dismay, and conjured in their poor brains only the most frightful of superstitious explanations.

They stood in little groups, talking in low tones, and ever casting affrighted glances behind them from their great rolling eyes.

Tarzan of the Apes watched them for a while from his lofty perch in the great tree. There was much in their demeanor which he could not understand, for of superstition he was ignorant, and of fear of any kind he had but a vague conception.

The sun was high in the heavens. Tarzan had not broken fast this day, and it was many miles to where lay the toothsome remains of Horta the boar.

So he turned his back upon the village of Mbonga and melted away into the leafy fastness of the forest.

CHAPTER XI

"King of the Apes"

IT was not yet dark when he reached the tribe, though he stopped to exhume and devour the remains of the wild boar he had cached the preceding day, and again to take Kulonga's bow and arrows from the tree top in which he had hidden them.

It was a well-laden Tarzan who dropped from the branches into the midst of the tribe of Kerchak.

With swelling chest he narrated the glories of his adventure and exhibited the spoils of conquest.

Kerchak grunted and turned away, for he was jealous of this strange member of his band. In his little evil brain he sought for some excuse to wreak his hatred upon Tarzan.

The next day Tarzan was practicing with his bow and arrows at the first gleam of dawn. At first he lost nearly every bolt he shot, but finally he learned to guide the little shafts with fair accuracy, and ere a month had passed he was no mean shot; but his proficiency had cost him nearly his entire supply of arrows.

The tribe continued to find the hunting good in the vicinity of the beach, and so Tarzan of the Apes varied his archery practice with further investigation of his father's choice though little store of books.

It was during this period that the young English lord

found hidden in the back of one of the cupboards in the cabin a small metal box. The key was in the lock, and in a few moments investigation and experimentation were rewarded with the successful opening of the receptacle.

In it he found a faded photograph of a smooth-faced young man, a golden locket studded with diamonds, linked to a small gold chain, a few letters and a small book.

Tarzan examined these all minutely.

The photograph he liked most of all, for the eyes were smiling, and the face was open and frank. It was his father.

The locket, too, took his fancy, and he placed the chain about his neck in imitation of the ornamentation he had seen to be so common among the black men he had visited. The brilliant stones gleamed strangely against his smooth, brown hide.

The letters he could scarcely decipher for he had learned little or nothing of script, so he put them back in the box with the photograph and turned his attention to the book.

This was almost entirely filled with fine script, but while the little bugs were all familiar to him, their arrangement and the combinations in which they occurred were strange, and entirely incomprehensible.

Tarzan had long since learned the use of the dictionary, but much to his sorrow and perplexity it proved of no avail to him in this emergency. Not a word of all that was writ in the book could he find, so he put it back in the metal box, but with a determination to work out the mysteries of it later on.

Poor little ape-man! Had he but known it that tiny, baffling mystery held between its seal covers the key to his origin; the answer to the strange riddle of his strange life.

It was the diary of John Clayton, Lord Greystoke— kept in French, as had always been his custom.

Tarzan replaced the box in the cupboard, but always thereafter he carried the features of the strong, smiling face of his father in his heart, and in his head a fixed determination to solve the mystery of the strange words in the little black book.

At present he had more important business in hand, for his supply of arrows was exhausted, and he must needs journey to the black men's village and renew it.

Early the following morning he set out, and, traveling rapidly, he came before midday to the clearing. Once more he took up his position in the great tree, and, as before, he saw the women in the fields and the village street, and the caldron of bubbling poison directly beneath him.

For hours he lay awaiting his opportunity to drop down unseen and gather up the arrows for which he had come; but nothing now occurred to call the villagers away from their homes. The day wore on, and still Tarzan of the Apes crouched above the unsuspecting woman at the caldron.

Presently the workers in the fields returned. The hunting warriors emerged from the forest, and when all were within the palisade the gates were closed and barred.

Many cooking pots were now in evidence about the village. Before each hut a woman presided over a boiling stew, while little cakes of plantain, and cassava puddings were to be seen on every hand.

Suddenly there came a hail from the edge of the clearing.

Tarzan looked.

It was a party of belated hunters returning from the north, and among them they half led, half carried a struggling animal.

As they approached the village the gates were thrown open to admit them, and then, as the people saw the victim of the chase, a savage cry rose to the heavens, for the quarry was a man.

As he was dragged, still resisting, into the village street, the women and children set upon him with sticks and stones, and Tarzan of the Apes, young and savage beast of the jungle, wondered at the cruel brutality of his own kind.

Sheeta, the leopard, alone of all the jungle folk, tortured his prey. The ethics of all the others meted a quick and merciful death to their victims.

Tarzan had learned from his books but scattered fragments of the ways of human beings.

When he had followed Kulonga through the forest he had expected to come to a city of strange houses on wheels, puffing clouds of black smoke from a huge tree stuck in the roof of one of them—or to a sea covered with mighty floating buildings which he had learned were called, variously, ships and boats and steamers and craft.

He had been sorely disappointed with the poor little village of the blacks, hidden away in his own jungle, and with not a single house as large as his own cabin upon the distant beach.

He saw that these people were more wicked than his own apes, and as savage and cruel as Sabor, herself. Tarzan began to hold his own kind in but low esteem.

Now they had tied their poor victim to a great post near the center of the village, directly before Mbonga's hut, and here they formed a dancing, yelling circle of warriors about him, alive with flashing knives and menacing spears.

In a larger circle squatted women, yelling and beating upon drums. It reminded Tarzan of the Dum-Dum, and so he knew what to expect. He wondered if they would spring upon their meat while it was still alive. The Apes did not do such things as that.

The circle of warriors about the cringing captive drew closer and closer to their prey as they danced in wild and savage abandon to the maddening music of the drums. Presently a spear reached out and pricked the victim. It was the signal for fifty others.

Eyes, ears, arms and legs were pierced; every inch of the poor writhing body that did not cover a vital organ became the target of the cruel lancers.

The women and children shrieked their delight.

The warriors licked their hideous lips in anticipation of the feast to come, and vied with one another in the savagery and loathsomeness of the cruel indignities with which they tortured the still conscious prisoner.

Then it was that Tarzan of the Apes saw his chance. All eyes were fixed upon the thrilling spectacle at the stake. The light of day had given place to the darkness of a moonless night, and only the fires of the immediate vicinity of the orgy had been kept alight to cast a restless glow upon the restless scene.

Gently the lithe boy dropped to the soft earth at the end of the village street. Quickly he gathered up the arrows—all of them this time, for he had brought a number of long fibers to bind them into a bundle.

Without haste he wrapped them securely, and then, ere he turned to leave, the devil of capriciousness entered his heart. He looked about for some hint of a wild prank to play upon these strange, grotesque creatures that they might be again aware of his presence among them.

Dropping his bundle of arrows at the foot of the tree, Tarzan crept among the shadows at the side of the street until he came to the same hut he had entered on the occasion of his first visit.

Inside all was darkness, but his groping hands soon found the object for which he sought, and without further delay he turned again toward the door.

He had taken but a step, however, ere his quick ear caught the sound of approaching footsteps immediately without. In another instant the figure of a woman darkened the entrance of the hut.

Tarzan drew back silently to the far wall, and his hand sought the long, keen hunting knife of his father. The woman came quickly to the center of the hut. There she paused for an instant feeling about with her hands for the thing she sought. Evidently it was not in its accustomed place, for she explored ever nearer and nearer the wall where Tarzan stood.

So close was she now that the ape-man felt the animal warmth of her naked body. Up went the hunting knife, and then the woman turned to one side and soon a guttural "ah" proclaimed that her search had at last been successful.

Immediately she turned and left the hut, and as she passed through the doorway Tarzan saw that she carried a cooking pot in her hand.

He followed closely after her, and as he reconnoitered from the shadows of the doorway he saw that all the women of the village were hastening to and from the various huts with pots and kettles. These they were filling with water and placing over a number of fires near the stake where the dying victim now hung, an inert and bloody mass of suffering.

Choosing a moment when none seemed near, Tarzan hastened to his bundle of arrows beneath the great tree at the end of the village street. As on the former occasion he overthrew the caldron before leaping, sinuous and catlike, into the lower branches of the forest giant.

Silently he climbed to a great height until he found a point where he could look through a leafy opening upon the scene beneath him.

The women were now preparing the prisoner for their cooking pots, while the men stood about resting after the fatigue of their mad revel. Comparative quiet reigned in the village.

Tarzan raised aloft the thing he had pilfered from the hut, and, with aim made true by years of fruit and coconut throwing, launched it toward the group of savages.

Squarely among them it fell, striking one of the warriors full upon the head and felling him to the ground. Then it rolled among the women and stopped beside the half-butchered thing they were preparing to feast upon.

All gazed in consternation at it for an instant, and then, with one accord, broke and ran for their huts.

It was a grinning human skull which looked up at them from the ground. The dropping of the thing out of the open sky was a miracle well aimed to work upon their superstitious fears.

Thus Tarzan of the Apes left them filled with terror at this new manifestation of the presence of some unseen and unearthly evil power which lurked in the forest about their village.

Later, when they discovered the overturned caldron, and that once more their arrows had been pilfered, it commenced to dawn upon them that they had offended some great god who ruled this part of the jungle by placing their village there without propitiating him. From then on an offering of food was daily placed below the great tree from whence the arrows had disappeared, in an effort to conciliate the mighty one.

But the seed of fear was deep sown, and had he but known it, Tarzan of the Apes had laid the foundation for much future misery for himself and his tribe.

That night he slept in the forest not far from the village, and early the next morning set out slowly on his homeward march, hunting as he traveled. Only a few berries and an occasional grub worm rewarded his search, and he was half famished when, looking up from a log he had been rooting beneath, he saw Sabor, the lioness, standing in the center of the trail not twenty paces from him.

The great yellow eyes were fixed upon him with a wicked and baleful gleam, and the red tongue licked the longing lips as Sabor crouched, worming her stealthy way with belly flattened against the earth.

Tarzan did not attempt to escape. He welcomed the opportunity for which, in fact, he had been searching for days past, now armed only with a rope of grass.

Quickly he unslung his bow and fitted a well-daubed arrow, and as Sabor sprang, the tiny missile leaped to meet her in midair. At the same instant Tarzan of the Apes jumped to one side, and as the great cat struck the ground beyond him another death-tipped arrow sunk deep into Sabor's loin.

With a mighty roar the beast turned and charged

once more, only to be met with a third arrow full in one eye; but this time she was too close to the ape-man for the latter to sidestep the onrushing body.

Tarzan of the Apes went down beneath the great body of his enemy, but with gleaming knife drawn and striking home. For a moment they lay there, and then Tarzan realized that the inert mass lying upon him was beyond power ever again to injure man or ape.

With difficulty he wriggled from beneath the great weight, and as he stood erect and gazed down upon the trophy of his skill, a mighty wave of exultation swept over him.

With swelling breast, he placed a foot upon the body of his powerful enemy, and throwing back his fine young head, roared out the awful challenge of the victorious bull ape.

The forest echoed to the savage and triumphant paean. Birds fell still, and the larger animals and beasts of prey slunk stealthily away, for few there were of all the jungle who sought for trouble with the great anthropoids.

And in London another Lord Greystoke was speaking to *his* kind in the House of Lords, but none trembled at the sound of his soft voice.

Sabor proved unsavory eating even to Tarzan of the Apes, but hunger served as a most efficacious disguise to toughness and rank taste, and ere long, with well-filled stomach, the ape-man was ready to sleep again. First, however, he must remove the hide, for it was as much for this as for any other purpose that he had desired to encompass the destruction of Sabor.

Deftly he removed the great pelt, for he had practiced often on smaller animals. When the task was finished he carried his trophy to the fork of a high tree, and there, curling himself securely in a crotch, he fell into deep and dreamless slumber.

What with loss of sleep, arduous exercise, and a full belly, Tarzan of the Apes slept the sun around, awakening about noon of the following day. He straightaway repaired to the carcass of Sabor, but was angered to find the bones picked clean by other hungry denizens of the jungle.

Half an hour's leisurely progress through the forest brought to sight a young deer, and before ever the little creature knew that an enemy was near a tiny arrow had lodged in its neck.

So quickly the virus worked that at the end of a dozen leaps the deer plunged headlong into the undergrowth, dead. Again did Tarzan feast well, but this time he did not sleep.

Instead, he hastened on toward the point where he had left the tribe, and when he had found them proudly exhibited the skin of Sabor, the lioness.

"Look!" he cried, "Apes of Kerchak. See what Tarzan, the mighty killer, has done. Who else among you has ever killed one of Numa's people? Tarzan is mightiest amongst you for Tarzan is no ape. Tarzan is—" But here he stopped, for in the language of the anthropoids there was no word for man, and Tarzan could only write the word in English; he could not pronounce it.

The tribe had gathered about to look upon the proof of his wondrous prowess, and to listen to his words.

Only Kerchak hung back, nursing his hatred and his rage.

Suddenly something snapped in the wicked little brain of the anthropoid. With a frightful roar the great beast sprang among the assemblage.

Biting, and striking with his huge hands, he killed and maimed a dozen ere the balance could escape to the upper terraces of the forest.

Frothing and shrieking in the insanity of his fury, Kerchak looked about for the object of his greatest hatred, and there, upon a near-by limb, he saw him sitting.

"Come down, Tarzan, great killer," cried Kerchak. "Come down and feel the fangs of a greater! Do mighty fighters fly to the trees at the first approach of danger?" And then Kerchak emitted the volleying challenge of his kind.

Quietly Tarzan dropped to the ground. Breathlessly the tribe watched from their lofty perches as Kerchak, still roaring, charged the relatively puny figure.

Nearly seven feet stood Kerchak on his short legs. His enormous shoulders were bunched and rounded with huge muscles. The back of his short neck was a single lump of iron sinew which bulged beyond the base of his skull, so that his head seemed like a small ball protruding from a huge mountain of flesh.

His back-drawn, snarling lips exposed his great fighting fangs, and his little, wicked, bloodshot eyes gleamed in horrid reflection of his madness.

Awaiting him stood Tarzan, himself a mighty muscled animal, but his six feet of height and his great rolling sinews seemed pitifully inadequate to the ordeal which awaited them.

His bow and arrows lay some distance away where he had dropped them while showing Sabor's hide to his fellow apes, so that he confronted Kerchak now with only his hunting knife and his superior intellect to offset the ferocious strength of his enemy.

As his antagonist came roaring toward him, Lord Greystoke tore his long knife from its sheath, and with an answering challenge as horrid and bloodcurdling as that of the beast he faced, rushed swiftly to meet the attack. He was too shrewd to allow those long hairy arms to encircle him, and just as their bodies were about to crash together, Tarzan of the Apes grasped one of the huge wrists of his assailant, and, springing lightly to one side, drove his knife to the hilt into Kerchak's body, below the heart.

Before he could wrench the blade free again, the bull's quick lunge to seize him in those awful arms had torn the weapon from Tarzan's grasp.

Kerchak aimed a terrific blow at the ape-man's head with the flat of his hand, a blow which, had it landed, might easily have crushed in the side of Tarzan's skull.

The man was too quick, and, ducking beneath it, himself delivered a mighty one, with clenched fist, in the pit of Kerchak's stomach.

The ape was staggered, and what with the mortal wound in his side had almost collapsed, when, with one mighty effort he rallied for an instant—just long enough to enable him to wrest his arm free from Tarzan's grasp and close in a terrific clinch with his wiry opponent.

Straining the ape-man close to him, his great jaws sought Tarzan's throat, but the young lord's sinewy fingers were at Kerchak's own before the cruel fangs could close on the sleek brown skin.

Thus they struggled, the one to crush out his opponent's life with those awful teeth, the other to close forever the windpipe beneath his strong grasp, the while he held the snarling mouth from him.

The greater strength of the ape was slowly prevailing, and the teeth of the straining beast were scarce an inch from Tarzan's throat when, with a shuddering tremor, the great body stiffened for an instant and then sank limply to the ground.

Kerchak was dead.

Withdrawing the knife that had so often rendered him master of far mightier muscles than his own, Tarzan of the Apes placed his foot upon the neck of his vanquished enemy, and once again, loud through the forest rang the fierce, wild cry of the conqueror.

And thus came the young Lord Greystoke into the kingship of the Apes.

CHAPTER XII

Man's Reason

THERE was one of the tribe of Tarzan who questioned his authority, and that was Terkoz, the son of Tublat, but he so feared the keen knife and the deadly arrows of his new lord that he confined the manifestation of his objections to petty disobediences and irritating mannerisms; Tarzan knew, however, that he but waited his opportunity to wrest the kingship from him by some sudden stroke of treachery, and so he was ever on his guard against surprise.

For months the life of the little band went on much as it had before, except that Tarzan's greater intelligence and his ability as a hunter were the means of providing for them more bountifully than ever before. Most of them, therefore, were more than content with the change in rulers.

Tarzan led them by night to the fields of the black men, and there, warned by their chief's superior wisdom, they ate only what they required, nor ever did they destroy what they could not eat, as is the way of Manu, the monkey, and of most apes.

So, while the blacks were wroth at the continued pilfering of their fields, they were not discouraged in their efforts to cultivate the land, as would have been the case had Tarzan permitted his people to lay waste the plantation wantonly.

During this period Tarzan paid many nocturnal visits to the village, where he often renewed his supply of arrows. He soon noticed the food always standing at the foot of the tree which was his avenue into the palisade, and after a little, he commenced to eat whatever the blacks put there.

When the awestruck savages saw that the food disappeared over night they were filled with consternation and awe, for it was one thing to put food out to propitiate a god or a devil, but quite another thing to have the spirit really come into the village and eat it. Such a thing was unheard of, and it filled their superstitious minds with all manner of vague fears.

Nor was this all. The periodic disappearance of their arrows, and the strange pranks perpetrated by unseen hands, had wrought them to such a state that life had become a veritable burden in their new home, and now it was that Mbonga and his head men began to talk of abandoning the village and seeking a site further on in the jungle.

Presently the black warriors began to strike further south into the heart of the forest when they went to hunt, looking for a site for a new village.

More often was the tribe of Tarzan disturbed by these wandering huntsmen. Now was the quiet, fierce solitude of the primeval forest broken by new, strange cries. No longer was there safety for bird or beast. Man had come.

Other animals passed up and down the jungle by day and by night—fierce, cruel beasts—but their weaker neighbors only fled from their immediate vicinity to return again when the danger was past.

With man it is different. When he comes many of the larger animals instinctively leave the district entirely, seldom if ever to return; and thus it has always been with the great anthropoids. They flee man as man flees a pestilence.

For a short time the tribe of Tarzan lingered in the vicinity of the beach because their new chief hated the thought of leaving the treasured contents of the little cabin forever. But when one day a member of the tribe discovered the blacks in great numbers on the banks of a little stream that had been their watering place for generations, and in the act of clearing a space in the jungle and erecting many huts, the apes would remain no longer, and so Tarzan led them inland for many marches to a spot as yet undefiled by the foot of a human being.

Once every moon Tarzan would go swinging rapidly back through the swaying branches to have a day with his books, and to replenish his supply of arrows. This latter task was becoming more and more difficult, for the blacks had taken to hiding their supply away at night in granaries and living huts.

This necessitated watching by day on Tarzan's part to discover where the arrows were being concealed.

Twice had he entered huts at night while the inmates lay sleeping upon their mats, and stolen the arrows from the very sides of the warriors. But this method he realized to be too fraught with danger, and so he commenced picking up solitary hunters with his long, deadly noose, stripping them of weapons and ornaments and dropping their bodies from a high tree into the village street during the still watches of the night.

These various escapades again so terrorized the blacks that, had it not been for the monthly respite between Tarzan's visits, in which they had opportunity to renew hope that each fresh incursion would prove the last, they soon would have abandoned their new village.

The blacks had not as yet come upon Tarzan's cabin on the distant beach, but the ape-man lived in constant dread that, while he was away with the tribe, they would discover and despoil his treasure. So it came that he spent more and more time in the vicinity of his father's last home, and less and less with the tribe. Presently the members of his little community began to suffer on account of his neglect, for disputes and quarrels constantly arose which only the king might settle peaceably.

At last some of the older apes spoke to Tarzan on the

subject, and for a month thereafter he remained constantly with the tribe.

The duties of kingship among the anthropoids are not many or arduous.

In the afternoon comes Thaka, possibly, to complain that old Mungo has stolen his new wife. Then must Tarzan summon all before him, and if he finds that the wife prefers her new lord he commands that matters remain as they are, or possibly that Mungo give Thaka one of his daughters in exchange.

Whatever his decision, the apes accept it as final, and return to their occupations satisfied.

Then comes Tana, shrieking and holding tight her side from which blood is streaming. Gunto, her husband, has cruelly bitten her! And Gunto, summoned, says that Tana is lazy and will not bring him nuts and beetles, or scratch his back for him.

So Tarzan scolds them both and threatens Gunto with a taste of the death-bearing slivers if he abuses Tana further, and Tana, for her part, is compelled to promise better attention to her wifely duties.

And so it goes, little family differences for the most part, which, if left unsettled would result finally in greater factional strife, and the eventual dismemberment of the tribe.

But Tarzan tired of it as he found that kingship meant the curtailment of his liberty. He longed for the little cabin and the sun-kissed sea—for the cool interior of the well-built house, and for the never-ending wonders of the many books.

As he had grown older, he found that he had grown away from his people. Their interests and his were far removed. They had not kept pace with him, nor could they understand aught of the many strange and wonderful dreams that passed through the active brain of their human king. So limited was their vocabulary that Tarzan could not even talk with them of the many new truths, and the great fields of thought that his reading had opened up before his longing eyes, or make known ambitions which stirred his soul.

Among the tribe he no longer had friends and cronies as of old. A little child may find companionship in many strange and simple creatures, but to a grown man there must be some semblance of equality in intellect as the basis for agreeable consociation.

Had Kala lived, Tarzan would have sacrificed all else to remain near her, but now that she was dead, and the playful friends of his childhood grown into fierce and surly brutes, he felt that he much preferred the peace and solitude of his cabin to the irksome duties of leadership amongst a horde of wild beasts.

The hatred and jealousy of Terkoz, son of Tublat, did much to counteract the effect of Tarzan's desire to renounce his kingship among the apes, for, stubborn young Englishman that he was, he could not bring himself to retreat in the face of so malignant an enemy.

That Terkoz would be chosen leader in his stead he knew full well, for time and again the ferocious brute had established his claim to physical supremacy over the few bull apes who had dared resent his savage bullying.

Tarzan would have liked to subdue the ugly beast without recourse to knife or arrows. So much had his great strength and agility increased in the period following his maturity that he had come to believe that he might master the redoubtable Terkoz in a hand-to-hand fight were it not for the terrible advantage the anthropoid's huge fighting fangs gave him over the poorly armed Tarzan.

The entire matter was taken out of Tarzan's hands one day by force of circumstances, and his future left open to him, so that he might go or stay without any stain upon his savage escutcheon.

It happened thus:

The tribe was feeding quietly, spread over a considerable area, when a great screaming arose some distance east of where Tarzan lay upon his belly beside a limpid brook, attempting to catch an elusive fish in his quick, brown hands.

With one accord the tribe swung rapidly toward the frightened cries, and there found Terkoz holding an old female by the hair and beating her unmercifully with his great hands.

As Tarzan approached he raised his hand aloft for Terkoz to desist, for the female was not his, but belonged to a poor old ape whose fighting days were long over, and who, therefore, could not protect his family.

Terkoz knew that it was against the laws of his kind to strike the woman of another, but being a bully, he had taken advantage of the weakness of the female's husband to chastise her because she had refused to give up to him a tender young rodent she had captured.

When Terkoz saw Tarzan approaching without his arrows, he continued to belabor the poor woman in a studied effort to affront his hated chieftain.

Tarzan did not repeat his warning signal, but instead rushed bodily upon the waiting Terkoz.

Never had the ape-man fought so terrible a battle since that long-gone day when Bolgani, the great king gorilla, had so horribly manhandled him ere the new-found knife had, by accident, pricked the savage heart.

Tarzan's knife on the present occasion but barely offset the gleaming fangs of Terkoz, and what little advantage the ape had over the man in brute strength was almost balanced by the latter's wonderful quickness and agility.

In the sum total of their point, however, the anthropoid had a shade the better of the battle, and had there been no other personal attribute to influence the final outcome, Tarzan of the Apes, the young Lord Greystoke, had died as he had lived—an unknown savage beast in equatorial Africa.

But there was that which had raised him far above his fellows of the jungle—that little spark which spells the whole vast difference between man and brute—Reason. This it was which saved him from death beneath the iron muscles and tearing fangs of Terkoz.

Scarcely had they fought a dozen seconds ere they

were rolling upon the ground, striking, tearing and rending—two great savage beasts battling to the death.

Terkoz had a dozen knife wounds on head and breast, and Tarzan was torn and bleeding—his scalp in one place half torn from his head so that a great piece hung down over one eye, obstructing his vision.

But so far the young Englishman had been able to keep those horrible fangs from his jugular and now, as they fought less fiercely for a moment, to regain their breath, Tarzan formed a cunning plan. He would work his way to the other's back and, clinging there with tooth and nail, drive his knife home until Terkoz was no more.

The maneuver was accomplished more easily than he had hoped, for the stupid beast, not knowing what Tarzan was attempting, made no particular effort to prevent the accomplishment of the design.

But when, finally, he realized that his antagonist was fastened to him where his teeth and fists alike were useless against him, Terkoz hurled himself about upon the ground so violently that Tarzan could but cling desperately to the leaping, turning, twisting body, and ere he had struck a blow the knife was hurled from his hand by a heavy impact against the earth, and Tarzan found himself defenseless.

During the rollings and squirmings of the next few minutes, Tarzan's hold was loosened a dozen times until finally an accidental circumstance of those swift and ever-changing evolutions gave him a new hold with his right hand, which he realized was absolutely unassailable.

His arm was passed beneath Terkoz's arm from behind and his hand and forearm encircled the back of Terkoz's neck. It was the half-Nelson of modern wrestling which the untaught ape-man had stumbled upon, but divine reason showed him in an instant the value of the thing he had discovered. It was the difference to him between life and death.

And so he struggled to encompass a similar hold with

the left hand, and in a few moments Terkoz's bull neck was creaking beneath a full-Nelson.

There was no more lunging about now. The two lay perfectly still upon the ground, Tarzan upon Terkoz's back. Slowly the bullet head of the ape was being forced lower and lower upon his chest.

Tarzan knew what the result would be. In an instant the neck would break. Then there came to Terkoz's rescue the same thing that had put him in these sore straits—a man's reasoning power.

"If I kill him," thought Tarzan, "what advantage will it be to me? Will it not but rob the tribe of a great fighter? And if Terkoz be dead, he will know nothing of my supremacy, while alive he will ever be an example to the other apes."

"Ka-goda?" hissed Tarzan in Terkoz's ear, which, in ape tongue, means, freely translated: "Do you surrender?"

For a moment there was no reply, and Tarzan added a few more ounces of pressure, which elicited a horrified shriek of pain from the great beast.

"Ka-goda?" repeated Tarzan.

"Ka-goda!" cried Terkoz.

"Listen," said Tarzan, easing up a trifle, but not releasing his hold. "I am Tarzan, King of the Apes, mighty hunter, mighty fighter. In all the jungle there is none so great.

"You have said: *'Ka-goda'* to me. All the tribe have heard. Quarrel no more with your king or your people, for next time I shall kill you. Do you understand?"

"Huh," assented Terkoz.

"And you are satisfied?"

"Huh," said the ape.

Tarzan let him up, and in a few minutes all were back at their vocations, as though naught had occurred to mar the tranquillity of their primeval forest haunts.

But deep in the minds of the apes was rooted the conviction that Tarzan was a mighty fighter and a strange creature. Strange because he had had it in his power to kill his enemy, but had allowed him to live—unharmed.

That afternoon as the tribe came together, as was their wont before darkness settled on the jungle, Tarzan, his wounds washed in the waters of the stream, called the old males about him.

"You have seen again to-day that Tarzan of the Apes is the greatest among you," he said.

"*Huh,*" they replied with one voice, "Tarzan is great."

"Tarzan," he continued, "is not an ape. He is not like his people. His ways are not their ways, and so Tarzan is going back to the lair of his own kind by the waters of the great lake which has no further shore. You must choose another to rule you, for Tarzan will not return."

And thus young Lord Greystoke took the first step toward the goal which he had set—the finding of other white men like himself.

CHAPTER XIII

His Own Kind

THE following morning Tarzan, lame and sore from the wounds of his battle with Terkoz, set out toward the west and the seacoast.

He traveled very slowly, sleeping in the jungle at night, and reaching his cabin late the following morning.

For several days he moved about but little, only enough to gather what fruit and nuts he required to satisfy the demands of hunger.

In ten days he was quite sound again, except for a terrible, half-healed scar, which, starting above his left eye ran across the top of his head, ending at the right ear. It was the mark left by Terkoz when he had torn the scalp away.

During his convalescence Tarzan tried to fashion a mantle from the skin of Sabor, which had lain all this time in the cabin. But he found the hide had dried as stiff as a board, and as he knew naught of tanning, he was forced to abandon his cherished plan.

Then he determined to filch what few garments he could from one of the black men of Mbonga's village, for Tarzan of the Apes had decided to mark his evolution from the lower orders in every possible manner, and nothing seemed to him a more distinguishing badge of manhood than ornaments and clothing.

To this end, therefore, he collected the various arm and leg ornaments he had taken from the black warriors who had succumbed to his swift and silent noose, and donned them all after the way he had seen them worn.

About his neck hung the golden chain from which depended the diamond-encrusted locket of his mother, the Lady Alice. At his back was a quiver of arrows slung from a leathern shoulder belt, another piece of loot from some vanquished black.

About his waist was a belt of tiny strips of rawhide fashioned by himself as a support for the homemade scabbard in which hung his father's hunting knife. The long bow which had been Kulonga's hung over his left shoulder.

The young Lord Greystoke was indeed a strange and warlike figure, his mass of black hair falling to his shoulders behind and cut with his hunting knife to a rude bang upon his forehead, that it might not fall before his eyes.

His straight and perfect figure, muscled as the best of the ancient Roman gladiators must have been muscled, and yet with the soft and sinuous curves of a Greek god, told at a glance the wondrous combination of enormous strength with suppleness and speed.

A personification, was Tarzan of the Apes, of the primitive man, the hunter, the warrior.

With the noble poise of his handsome head upon those broad shoulders, and the fire of life and intelligence in those fine, clear eyes, he might readily have typified some demigod of a wild and warlike bygone people of his ancient forest.

But of these things Tarzan did not think. He was worried because he had not clothing to indicate to all the jungle folks that he was a man and not an ape, and grave doubt often entered his mind as to whether he might not yet become an ape.

Was not hair commencing to grow upon his face? All the apes had hair upon theirs, but the black men were entirely hairless, with very few exceptions.

True, he had seen pictures in his books of men with great masses of hair upon lip and cheek and chin, but, nevertheless, Tarzan was afraid. Almost daily he whetted his keen knife and scraped and whittled at his young beard to eradicate this degrading emblem of apehood.

And so he learned to shave—rudely and painfully, it is true—but, nevertheless, effectively.

When he felt quite strong again, after his bloody battle with Terkoz, Tarzan set off one morning toward Mbonga's village. He was moving carelessly along a winding jungle trail, instead of making his progress through the trees, when suddenly he came face-to-face with a black warrior.

The look of surprise on the savage face was almost comical, and before Tarzan could unsling his bow the fellow had turned and fled down the path crying out in alarm as though to others before him.

Tarzan took to the trees in pursuit, and in a few moments came in view of the men desperately striving to escape.

There were three of them, and they were racing madly in single file through the dense undergrowth.

Tarzan easily distanced them, nor did they see his silent passage above their heads, nor note the crouching figure squatted upon a low branch ahead of them beneath which the trail led them.

Tarzan let the first two pass beneath him, but as the third came swiftly on, the quiet noose dropped about the black throat. A quick jerk drew it taut.

There was an agonized scream from the victim, and his fellows turned to see his struggling body rise as by magic slowly into the dense foliage of the trees above.

With affrighted shrieks they wheeled once more and plunged on in their efforts to escape.

Tarzan dispatched his prisoner quickly and silently; removed the weapons and ornaments, and—oh, the greatest joy of all—a handsome doeskin breechcloth, which he quickly transferred to his own person.

Now indeed was he dressed as a man should be. None

there was who could now doubt his high origin. How he should liked to have returned to the tribe to parade before their envious gaze this wondrous finery.

Taking the body across his shoulder, he moved more slowly through the trees toward the little palisaded village, for he again needed arrows.

As he approached quite close to the enclosure he saw an excited group surrounding the two fugitives, who, trembling with fright and exhaustion, were scarce able to recount the uncanny details of their adventure.

Mirando, they said, who had been ahead of them a short distance, had suddenly come screaming toward them, crying that a terrible white and naked warrior was pursuing him. The three of them had hurried toward the village as rapidly as their legs would carry them.

Again Mirando's shrill cry of mortal terror had caused them to look back, and there they had seen the most horrible sight—their companion's body flying upwards into the trees, his arms and legs beating the air and his tongue protruding from his open mouth. No other sound did he utter nor was there any creature in sight about him.

The villagers were worked up into a state of fear bordering on panic, but wise old Mbonga affected to feel considerable skepticism regarding the tale, and attributed the whole fabrication to their fright in the face of some real danger.

"You tell us this great story," he said, "because you do not dare to speak the truth. You do not dare admit that when the lion sprang upon Mirando you ran away and left him. You are cowards."

Scarcely had Mbonga ceased speaking when a great crashing of branches in the trees above them caused the blacks to look up in renewed terror. The sight that met their eyes made even wise old Mbonga shudder, for there, turning and twisting in the air, came the dead body of Mirando, to sprawl with a sickening reverberation upon the ground at their feet.

With one accord the blacks took to their heels; nor

did they stop until the last of them was lost in the dense shadows of the surrounding jungle.

Again Tarzan came down into the village and renewed his supply of arrows, and ate of the offering of food which the blacks had made to appease his wrath.

Before he left he carried the body of Mirando to the gate of the village, and propped it up against the palisade in such a way that the dead face seemed to be peering around the edge of the gatepost down the path which led to the jungle.

Then Tarzan returned, hunting, always hunting, to the cabin by the beach.

It took a dozen attempts on the part of the thoroughly frightened blacks to reenter their village, past the horrible, grinning face of their dead fellow, and when they found the food and arrows gone they knew what they had only too well feared, that Mirando had seen the evil spirit of the jungle.

That now seemed to them the logical explanation. Only those who saw this terrible god of the jungle died; for was it not true that none left alive in the village had ever seen him? Therefore, those who had died at his hands must have seen him and paid the penalty with their lives.

As long as they supplied him with arrows and food he would not harm them unless they looked upon him, so it was ordered by Mbonga that in addition to the food offering there should also be laid out an offering of arrows for this Munango-Keewati, and this was done from then on.

If you ever chance to pass that far-off African village you will still see before a tiny thatched hut, built just without the village, a little iron pot in which is a quantity of food, and beside it a quiver of well-daubed arrows.

When Tarzan came in sight of the beach where stood his cabin, a strange and unusual spectacle met his vision.

On the placid waters of the landlocked harbor floated a great ship, and on the beach a small boat was drawn up.

But, most wonderful of all, a number of white men like himself were moving about between the beach and his cabin.

Tarzan saw that in many ways they were like the men of his picture books. He crept closer through the trees until he was quite close above them.

There were ten men. Swarthy, suntanned, villainous looking fellows. Now they had congregated by the boat and were talking in loud, angry tones, with much gesticulating and shaking of fists.

Presently one of them, a little, mean-faced, black-bearded fellow with a countenance which reminded Tarzan of Pamba, the rat, laid his hand upon the shoulder of a giant who stood next him, and with whom all the others had been arguing and quarreling.

The little man pointed inland, so that the giant was forced to turn away from the others to look in the direction indicated. As he turned, the little, mean-faced man drew a revolver from his belt and shot the giant in the back.

The big fellow threw his hands above his head, his knees bent beneath him, and without a sound he tumbled forward upon the beach, dead.

The report of the weapon, the first that Tarzan had ever heard, filled him with wonderment, but even this unaccustomed sound could not startle his healthy nerves into even a semblance of panic.

The conduct of the white strangers it was that caused him the greatest perturbation. He puckered his brows into a frown of deep thought. It was well, thought he, that he had not given way to his first impulse to rush forward and greet these white men as brothers.

They were evidently no different from the black men—no more civilized than the apes—no less cruel than Sabor.

For a moment the others stood looking at the little, mean-faced man and the giant lying dead upon the beach.

Then one of them laughed and slapped the little man

upon the back. There was much more talk and gesticulating, but less quarreling.

Presently they launched the boat and all jumped into it and rowed away toward the great ship, where Tarzan could see other figures moving about upon the deck.

When they had clambered aboard, Tarzan dropped to earth behind a great tree and crept to his cabin, keeping it always between himself and the ship.

Slipping in at the door he found that everything had been ransacked. His books and pencils strewed the floor. His weapons and shields and other little store of treasures were littered about.

As he saw what had been done a great wave of anger surged through him, and the new-made scar upon his forehead stood suddenly out, a bar of inflamed crimson against his tawny hide.

Quickly he ran to the cupboard and searched in the far recess of the lower shelf. Ah! He breathed a sigh of relief as he drew out the little tin box, and, opening it, found his greatest treasures undisturbed.

The photograph of the smiling, strong-faced young man, and the little black puzzle book were safe.

What was that?

His quick ear had caught a faint but unfamiliar sound.

Running to the window Tarzan looked toward the harbor, and there he saw that a boat was being lowered from the great ship beside the one already in the water. Soon he saw many people clambering over the sides of the larger vessel and dropping into the boats. They were coming back in full force.

For a moment longer Tarzan watched while a number of boxes and bundles were lowered into the waiting boats, then, as they shoved off from the ship's side, the ape-man snatched up a piece of paper, and with a pencil printed on it for a few moments until it bore several lines of strong, well-made, almost letter-perfect characters.

This notice he stuck upon the door with a small sharp splinter of wood. Then gathering up his precious tin box, his arrows, and as many bows and spears as he could carry, he hastened through the door and disappeared into the forest.

When the two boats were beached upon the silvery sand it was a strange assortment of humanity that clambered ashore.

Some twenty souls in all there were, if the fifteen rough and villainous-appearing seamen could have been said to possess that immortal spark, since they were, forsooth, a most filthy and bloodthirsty-looking aggregation.

The others of the party were of different stamp.

One was an elderly man, with white hair and large rimmed spectacles. His slightly stooped shoulders were draped in an ill-fitting, though immaculate, frock coat; a shiny silk hat added to the incongruity of his garb in an African jungle.

The second member of the party to land was a tall young man in white ducks, while directly behind came another elderly man with a very high forehead and a fussy, excitable manner.

After these came a huge negress clothed like Solomon as to colors. Her great eyes rolling in evident terror first toward the jungle and then toward the cursing band of sailors who were removing the bales and boxes from the boats.

The last member of the party to disembark was a girl of about nineteen, and it was the young man who stood at the boat's bow to lift her high and dry upon the land. She gave him a brave and pretty smile of thanks, but no words passed between them.

In silence the party advanced toward the cabin. It was evident that whatever their intentions, all had been decided upon before they left the ship; and so they came to the door, the sailors carrying the boxes and bales, followed by the five who were of so different a class. The men put down their burdens, and then one caught sight of the notice which Tarzan had posted.

"Ho, mates!" he cried. "What's here? This sign was not posted an hour ago or I'll eat the cook."

The others gathered about, craning their necks over the shoulders of those before them, but as few of them could read at all, and then only after the most laborious fashion, one finally turned to the little old man of the top hat and frock coat.

"Hi, perfesser," he called, "step for'rd and read the bloomin' notis."

Thus addressed, the old man came slowly to where the sailors stood, followed by the other members of his party. Adjusting his spectacles he looked for a moment at the placard and then, turning away, strolled off muttering to himself: "Most remarkable—most remarkable!"

"Hi, old fossil," cried the man who had first called on him for assistance, "did je think we wanted of you to read the bloomin' notis to yourself? Come back here and read it out loud, you old barnacle."

The old man stopped and, turning back, said: "Oh, yes, my dear sir, a thousand pardons. It was quite thoughtless of me, yes—very thoughtless. Most remarkable—most remarkable!"

Again he faced the notice and read it through, and doubtless would have turned off again to ruminate upon it had not the sailor grasped him roughly by the collar and howled into his ear.

"Read it out loud, you blithering, old idiot."

"Ah, yes indeed, yes indeed," replied the professor softly, and adjusting his spectacles once more he read aloud:

THIS IS THE HOUSE OF TARZAN, THE KILLER OF BEASTS AND MANY BLACK MEN. DO NOT HARM THE THINGS WHICH ARE TARZAN'S. TARZAN WATCHES.
    TARZAN OF THE APES.

"Who the devil is Tarzan?" cried the sailor who had before spoken.

"He evidently speaks English," said the young man.

"But what does 'Tarzan of the Apes' mean?" cried the girl.

"I do not know, Miss Porter," replied the young man, "unless we have discovered a runaway simian from the London Zoo who has brought back a European education to his jungle home. What do you make of it, Professor Porter?" he added, turning to the old man.

Professor Archimedes Q. Porter adjusted his spectacles.

"Ah, yes, indeed; yes indeed—most remarkable, most remarkable!" said the professor; "but I can add nothing further to what I have already remarked in elucidation of this truly momentous occurrence," and the professor turned slowly in the direction of the jungle.

"But, Papa," cried the girl, "you haven't said anything about it yet."

"Tut, tut, child; tut, tut," responded Professor Porter, in a kindly and indulgent tone, "do not trouble your pretty head with such weighty and abstruse problems," and again he wandered slowly off in still another direction, his eyes bent upon the ground at his feet, his hands clasped behind him beneath the flowing tails of his coat.

"I reckon the daffy old bounder don't know no more'n we do about it," growled the rat-faced sailor.

"Keep a civil tongue in your head," cried the young man, his face paling in anger, at the insulting tone of the sailor. "You've murdered our officers, and robbed us. We are absolutely in your power, but you'll treat Professor Porter and Miss Porter with respect or I'll break that vile neck of yours with my bare hands—guns or no guns," and the young fellow stepped so close to the rat-faced sailor that the latter, though he bore two revolvers and a villainous-looking knife in his belt, slunk back abashed.

"You damned coward," cried the young man. "You'd never dare shoot a man until his back was turned. You don't dare shoot me even then," and he deliberately turned his back full upon the sailor and walked nonchalantly away as if to put him to the test.

The sailor's hand crept slyly to the butt of one of his revolvers; his wicked eyes glared vengefully at the retreating form of the young Englishman. The gaze of his fellows was upon him, but still he hesitated. At heart he was even a greater coward than Mr. William Cecil Clayton had imagined.

What he would have done will never be known, for there was another factor abroad which none of the party had yet guessed would enter so largely into the problems of their life on this inhospitable African shore.

Two keen eyes had watched every move of the party from the foliage of a near-by tree. Tarzan had seen the surprise caused by his notice, and while he could understand nothing of the spoken language of these strange people their gestures and facial expressions told him much.

The act of the little rat-faced sailor in killing one of his comrades had aroused a strong dislike in Tarzan, and now that he saw him quarreling with the fine-looking young man his animosity was still further stirred.

Tarzan had never seen the effects of a firearm before, though his books had taught him something of them, but when he saw the rat-faced one fingering the butt of his revolver he thought of the scene he had witnessed so short a time before, and naturally expected to see the young man murdered as had been the huge sailor earlier in the day.

So Tarzan fitted a poisoned arrow to his bow and drew a bead upon the rat-faced sailor, but the foliage was so thick that he soon saw the arrow would be deflected by the leaves or some small branch, and instead he launched a heavy spear from his lofty perch.

Clayton had taken but a dozen steps. The rat-faced sailor had half drawn his revolver; the other sailors stood watching the scene intently.

Professor Porter had already disappeared into the jungle, whither he was being followed by the fussy Samuel T. Philander, his secretary and assistant.

Esmeralda, the negress, was busy sorting her mistress' baggage from the pile of bales and boxes beside the cabin, and Miss Porter had turned away to follow Clayton, when something caused her to turn again toward the sailor.

And then three things happened almost simultaneously—the sailor jerked out his weapon and leveled it at Clayton's back, Miss Porter screamed a warning, and a long, metal-shod spear shot like a bolt from above and passed entirely through the right shoulder of the rat-faced man.

The revolver exploded harmlessly in the air, and the seaman crumpled up with a scream of pain and terror.

Clayton turned and rushed back toward the scene. The sailors stood in a frightened group, with drawn weapons, peering into the jungle. The wounded man writhed and shrieked upon the ground.

Clayton, unseen by any, picked up the fallen revolver and slipped it inside his shirt, then he joined the sailors in gazing, mystified, into the jungle.

"Who could it have been?" whispered Jane Porter, and the young man turned to see her standing, wide-eyed and wondering, close beside him.

"I dare say Tarzan of the Apes is watching us all right," he answered, in a dubious tone. "I wonder, now, who that spear was intended for. If for Snipes, then our ape friend is a friend indeed.

"By jove, where are your father and Mr. Philander? There's some one or something in that jungle, and it's armed, whatever it is. Ho! Professor! Mr. Philander!" young Clayton shouted. There was no response.

"What's to be done, Miss Porter?" continued the young man, his face clouded by a frown of worry and indecision.

"I can't leave you here alone with these cutthroats, and you certainly can't venture into the jungle with me; yet some one must go in search of your father. He is more than apt to wandering off aimlessly, regardless of danger or direction, and Mr. Philander is only a trifle less impractical than he. You will pardon my bluntness, but our lives are all in jeopardy here, and when we get your father back something must be done to impress upon him the dangers to which he exposes you as well as himself by his absentmindedness."

"I quite agree with you," replied the girl, "and I am not offended at all. Dear old Papa would sacrifice his life for me without an instant's hesitation, provided one could keep his mind on so frivolous a matter for an entire instant. There is only one way to keep him in safety, and that is to chain him to a tree. The poor dear is *so* impractical."

"I have it!" suddenly exclaimed Clayton. "You can use a revolver, can't you?"

"Yes. Why?"

"I have one. With it you and Esmeralda will be comparatively safe in this cabin while I am searching for your father and Mr. Philander. Come, call the woman and I will hurry on. They can't have gone far."

Jane Porter did as he suggested and when he saw the door close safely behind them Clayton turned toward the jungle.

Some of the sailors were drawing the spear from their wounded comrade and, as Clayton approached, he asked if he could borrow a revolver from one of them while he searched the jungle for the professor.

The rat-faced one, finding he was not dead, had regained his composure, and with a volley of oaths directed at Clayton refused in the name of his fellows to allow the young man any firearms.

This man, Snipes, had assumed the rôle of chief since he had killed their former leader, and so little time had elapsed that none of his companions had as yet questioned his authority.

Clayton's only response was a shrug of the shoulders, but as he left them he picked up the spear which had transfixed Snipes, and thus primitively armed, the son of the then Lord Greystoke strode into the dense jungle.

Every few moments he called aloud the names of the wanderers. The watchers in the cabin by the beach heard the sound of his voice growing even fainter and fainter, until at last it was swallowed up by the myriad noises of the primeval wood.

When Professor Archimedes Q. Porter and his assistant, Samuel T. Philander, after much insistence on the part of the latter, had finally turned their steps toward camp, they were as completely lost in the wild and tangled labyrinth of the matted jungle as two human beings well could be, though they did not know it.

It was by the merest caprice of fortune that they headed toward the west coast of Africa, instead of toward Zanzibar on the opposite side of the dark continent.

When in a short time they reached the beach, only to find no camp in sight, Philander was positive that they were north of their proper destination, while, as a matter of fact they were about two hundred yards south of it.

It never occurred to either of these impractical theorists to call aloud on the chance of attracting their friends' attention. Instead, with all the assurance that deductive reasoning from a wrong premise induces in one, Mr. Samuel T. Philander grasped Professor Archimedes Q. Porter firmly by the arm and hurried the weakly protesting old gentleman off in the direction of Cape Town, fifteen hundred miles to the south.

When Jane Porter and Esmeralda found themselves safely behind the cabin door the negress' first thought was to barricade the portal from the inside. With this idea in mind she turned to search for some means of putting it into execution; but her first view of the interior of the cabin brought a shriek of terror to her lips, and like a frightened child the huge black ran to bury her face on her mistress' shoulder.

Jane Porter, turning at the cry, saw the cause of it lying prone upon the floor before them—the whitened skeleton of a man. A further glance revealed a second skeleton upon the bed.

"What horrible place are we in?" murmured the awestruck girl. But there was no panic in her fright.

At last, disengaging herself from the frantic clutch of

the still shrieking Esmeralda, Jane Porter crossed the room to look into the little cradle, knowing what she should see there before ever the tiny skeleton disclosed itself in all its pitiful and pathetic frailty.

What an awful tragedy these poor mute bones proclaimed! The girl shuddered at the thought of the eventualities which might lie before herself and her friends in this ill-fated cabin; the haunt of mysterious, perhaps hostile, beings.

Quickly, with an impatient stamp of her little foot, she endeavored to shake off the gloomy forebodings, and turning to Esmeralda bade her cease her wailing.

"Stop, Esmeralda; stop it this minute!" she cried. "You are only making it worse. Why, I never saw such a big baby."

She ended lamely, a little quiver in her own voice as she thought of the three men, upon whom she depended for protection, wandering in the depth of that awful forest.

Soon the girl found that the door was equipped with a heavy wooden bar upon the inside, and after several efforts the combined strength of the two enabled them to slip it into place, the first time in twenty years.

Then they sat down upon a bench with their arms about one another, and waited.

CHAPTER XIV

At the Mercy of the Jungle

AFTER Clayton had plunged into the jungle, the sailors—mutineers of the *Arrow*—fell into a discussion of their next step; but on one point all were agreed—that they should hasten to put off to the anchored *Arrow,* where they could at least be safe from the spears of their unseen foe. And so, while Jane Porter and Esmeralda were barricading themselves within the cabin, the cowardly crew of cutthroats were pulling rapidly for their ship in the two boats that had brought them ashore.

So much had Tarzan seen that day that his head was in a whirl of wonder. But the most wonderful sight of all, to him, was the face of the beautiful white girl.

Here at last was one of his own kind; of that he was positive. And the young man and the two old men; they, too, were much as he had pictured his own people to be.

But doubtless they were as ferocious and cruel as other men he had seen. The fact that they alone of all the party were unarmed might account for the fact that they had killed no one. They might be very different if provided with weapons.

Tarzan had seen the young man pick up the fallen revolver of the wounded Snipes and hide it away in his breast; and he had also seen him slip it cautiously to the girl as she entered the cabin door.

He did not understand anything of the motives behind all that he had seen; but, somehow, intuitively he liked the young man and the two old men, and for the girl he had a strange longing which he scarcely understood. As for the big black woman, she was evidently connected in some way to the girl, and so he liked her, also.

For the sailors, and especially Snipes, he had developed a great hatred. He knew by their threatening gestures and by the expressions upon their evil faces that they were enemies of the others of the party, and so he decided to watch them closely.

Tarzan wondered why the men had gone into the jungle, nor did it ever occur to him that one could become lost in that maze of undergrowth which to him was as simple as is the main street of your own hometown to you.

When he saw the sailors row away toward the ship, and knew that the girl and her companion were safe in his cabin, Tarzan decided to follow the young man into the jungle and learn what his errand might be. He swung off rapidly in the direction taken by Clayton, and in a short time heard faintly in the distance the now only occasional calls of the Englishman to his friends.

Presently Tarzan came up with the white man, who, almost fagged, was leaning against a tree wiping the perspiration from his forehead. The ape-man, hiding safe behind a screen of foliage, sat watching this new specimen of his own race intently.

At intervals Clayton called aloud and finally it came to Tarzan that he was searching for the old man.

Tarzan was on the point of going off to look for them himself, when he caught the yellow glint of a sleek hide moving cautiously through the jungle toward Clayton.

It was Sheeta, the leopard. Now, Tarzan heard the soft bending of grasses and wondered why the young white man was not warned. Could it be he had failed to note the loud warning? Never before had Tarzan known Sheeta to be so clumsy.

No, the white man did not hear. Sheeta was crouching for the spring, and then, shrill and horrible, there rose upon the stillness of the jungle the awful cry of the challenging ape, and Sheeta turned, crashing into the underbrush.

Clayton came to his feet with a start. His blood ran cold. Never in all his life had so fearful a sound smote upon his ears. He was no coward; but if ever man felt the icy fingers of fear upon his heart, William Cecil Clayton, eldest son of Lord Greystoke of England, did that day in the fastness of the African jungle.

The noise of some great body crashing through the underbrush so close beside him, and the sound of that bloodcurdling shriek from above, tested Clayton's courage to the limit; but he could not know that it was to that very voice he owed his life; nor that the creature who hurled it forth was his own cousin—the real Lord Greystoke.

The afternoon was drawing to a close, and Clayton, disheartened and discouraged, was in a terrible quandary as to the proper course to pursue; whether to keep on in search of Professor Porter, at the almost certain risk of his own death in the jungle by night, or to return to the cabin where he might at least serve to protect Jane Porter from the perils which confronted her on all sides.

He disliked to return to camp without her father; still more, he shrank from the thought of leaving her alone and unprotected in the hands of the mutineers of the *Arrow,* or to the hundred unknown dangers of the jungle.

Possibly, too, he thought, ere this the professor and Philander had returned to camp. Yes, that was more than likely. At least he would return and see, before he continued what bade fair to be a most fruitless quest. And so he started, stumbling back through the thick and matted underbrush in the direction that he thought the cabin lay.

To Tarzan's surprise the young man was heading further into the jungle in the general direction of Mbonga's village, and the shrewd young ape-man was convinced that he was lost.

To Tarzan this was scarcely comprehensible; but his judgment told him that no man would venture toward the village of the cruel blacks armed only with a spear which, from the awkward way in which he carried it, was evidently an unaccustomed weapon to this white man. Nor was he following the trail of the old men. That, they had crossed and left long since, though it had been fresh and plain before Tarzan's eyes.

Tarzan was perplexed. The fierce jungle would make easy prey of this unprotected stranger in a very short time if he were not guided quickly to the beach.

Yes, there was Numa, the lion, even now, stalking the white man a dozen paces to the right.

Clayton heard the great body paralleling his course, and now there rose upon the evening air the beast's thunderous roar. The man stopped with upraised spear and faced the brush from which issued the awful sound. The shadows were deepening, darkness was settling in.

God! To die here alone, beneath the fangs of wild beasts; to be torn and rended; to feel the hot breath of the brute on his face as the great paw crushed down upon his breast!

For a moment all was still. Clayton stood rigid, with raised spear. Presently a faint rustling of the bush apprised him of the stealthy creeping of the thing behind. It was gathering for the spring. At last he saw it, not twenty feet away—the long, lithe, muscular body and tawny head of a huge black-maned lion.

The beast was upon its belly, moving forward very slowly. As its eyes met Clayton's it stopped, and deliberately, cautiously gathered its hind quarters beneath it.

In agony the man watched; fearful to launch his spear; powerless to fly.

He heard a noise in the tree above him. Some new danger, he thought, but he dared not take his eyes from the yellow-green orbs before him. There was a sharp twang as of a broken banjo-string, and at the same instant an arrow appeared in the yellow hide of the crouching lion.

With a roar of pain and anger the beast sprang; but, somehow, Clayton stumbled to one side, and as he turned again to face the infuriated king of beasts, he was appalled at the sight which confronted him. Almost simultaneously with the lion's turning to renew the attack a naked giant dropped from the tree above squarely on the brute's back.

With lightning speed an arm that was banded layers of iron muscle encircled the huge neck, and the great beast was raised from behind, roaring and pawing the air—raised as easily as Clayton would have lifted a pet dog.

The scene he witnessed there in the twilight depths of the African jungle was burned forever into the Englishman's brain.

The man before him was the embodiment of physical perfection and giant strength, yet it was not upon these he depended in his battle with the great cat, for, mighty as were his muscles, they were as nothing by comparison with Numa's. To his agility, to his brain and to his long keen knife he owed his supremacy.

His right arm encircled the lion's neck, while the left hand plunged the knife time and again into the unprotected side behind the left shoulder. The infuriated beast, pulled up and backwards until he stood upon his hind legs, struggled impotently in this unnatural position.

Had the battle been of a few seconds' longer duration the outcome might have been different, but it was all accomplished so quickly that the lion had scarce time to recover from the confusion of its surprise ere it sank lifeless to the ground.

Then the strange figure which had vanquished it stood erect upon the carcass, and throwing back the wild and handsome head, gave out the fearsome cry which a few moments earlier had so startled Clayton.

Before him he saw the figure of a young man, naked except for a loin cloth and a few barbaric ornaments about arms and legs; on the breast a priceless diamond locket gleaming against a smooth brown skin.

The hunting knife had been returned to its homely sheath, and the man was gathering up his bow and quiver from where he had tossed them, when he leaped to attack the lion.

Clayton spoke to the stranger in English, thanking him for his brave rescue and complimenting him on the wondrous strength and dexterity he had displayed, but the only answer was a steady stare and a faint shrug of the mighty shoulders, which might betoken either disparagement of the service rendered, or ignorance of Clayton's language.

When the bow and quiver had been slung to his back the wild man, for such Clayton now thought him, once more drew his knife and deftly carved a dozen large strips of meat from the lion's carcass. Then, squatting upon his haunches, he proceeded to eat, first motioning Clayton to join him.

The strong white teeth sank into the raw and dripping flesh in apparent relish of the meal, but Clayton could not bring himself to share the uncooked meat with his strange host; instead he watched him, and presently there dawned upon him the conviction that this was Tarzan of the Apes, whose notice he had seen posted upon the cabin door that morning.

If so he must speak English.

Again Clayton essayed speech with the ape-man; but the replies, now vocal, were in a strange tongue, which resembled the chattering of monkeys mingled with the growling of some wild beast.

No, this could not be Tarzan of the Apes, for it was very evident that he was an utter stranger to English.

When Tarzan had completed his repast he rose and, pointing in a very different direction from that which Clayton had been pursuing, started off through the jungle toward the point he had indicated.

Clayton, bewildered and confused, hesitated to follow him, for he thought he was but being led more deeply into the mazes of the forest; but the ape-man, seeing him disinclined to follow, returned, and, grasping him by the coat, dragged him along until he was convinced that Clayton understood what was required of him. Then he left him to follow voluntarily.

The Englishman, finally concluding that he was a prisoner, saw no alternative open but to accompany his captor, and thus they traveled slowly through the jungle while the sable mantle of the impenetrable forest night fell about them, and the stealthy footfalls of padded paws mingled with the breaking of twigs and the wild calls of the savage life that Clayton felt closing in upon him.

Suddenly Clayton heard the faint report of a firearm—a single shot, and then silence.

In the cabin by the beach two thoroughly terrified women clung to each other as they crouched upon the low bench in the gathering darkness.

The negress sobbed hysterically, bemoaning the evil day that had witnessed her departure from her dear Maryland, while the white girl, dry eyed and outwardly calm, was torn by inward fears and forebodings. She feared not more for herself than for the three men whom she knew to be wandering in the abysmal depths of the savage jungle, from which she now heard issuing the almost incessant shrieks and roars, barkings and growlings of its terrifying and fearsome denizens as they sought their prey.

And now there came the sound of a heavy body brushing against the side of the cabin. She could hear the great padded paws upon the ground without. Then, for an instant, all was silence; even the bedlam of the forest died to a faint murmur; then she distinctly heard the beast without sniffing at the door, not two feet from where she crouched. Instinctively the girl shuddered, and shrank closer to the black woman.

"Hush!" she whispered. "Hush, Esmeralda," for the

woman's sobs and groans seemed to have attracted the thing that stalked there just beyond the thin wall.

A gentle scratching sound was heard on the door. The brute tried to force an entrance; but presently this ceased, and again she heard the great pads creeping stealthily around the cabin. Again they stopped—beneath the window on which the terrified eyes of the girl now glued themselves.

"God!" she murmured, for now, silhouetted against the moonlit sky beyond, she saw framed in the tiny square of the latticed window the head of a huge lioness. The gleaming eyes were fixed upon her in intent ferocity.

"Look, Esmeralda!" she whispered. "For God's sake, what shall we do? Look! Quick! The window!"

Esmeralda, cowering still closer to her mistress, took one affrighted glance toward the little square of moonlight, just as the lioness emitted a low, savage snarl.

The sight that met the poor black's eyes was too much for the already overstrung nerves.

"Oh, Gaberelle!" she shrieked, and slid to the floor an inert and senseless mass.

For what seemed an eternity the great brute stood with its forepaws upon the sill, glaring into the little room. Presently it tried the strength of the lattice with its great talons.

The girl had almost ceased to breathe, when, to her relief, the head disappeared and she heard the brute's footsteps leaving the window. But now they came to the door again, and once more the scratching commenced; this time with increasing force until the great beast was tearing at the massive panels in a perfect frenzy of eagerness to seize its defenseless victims.

Could Jane Porter have known the immense strength of that door, builded piece by piece, she would have felt less fear of the lioness reaching her by this avenue.

Little did John Clayton imagine when he fashioned that crude but mighty portal that one day, twenty years later, it would shield a fair American girl, then unborn, from the teeth and talons of a man-eater.

For full twenty minutes the brute alternately sniffed and tore at the door, occasionally giving voice to a wild, savage cry of baffled rage. At length, however, she gave up the attempt, and Jane Porter heard her returning toward the window, beneath which she paused for an instant, and then launched her great weight against the timeworn lattice.

The girl heard the wooden rods groan beneath the impact; but they held, and the huge body dropped back to the ground below.

Again and again the lioness repeated these tactics, until finally the horrified prisoner within saw a portion of the lattice give way, and in an instant one great paw and the head of the animal were thrust within the room.

Slowly the powerful neck and shoulders spread the bars apart, and the lithe body protruded further and further into the room.

As in a trance, the girl rose, her hand upon her breast, wide eyes staring horror-stricken into the snarling face of the beast scarce ten feet from her. At her feet lay the prostrate form of the negress. If she could but arouse her, their combined efforts might possibly avail to beat back the fierce and bloodthirsty intruder.

Jane Porter stooped to grasp the black woman by the shoulder. Roughly she shook her.

"Esmeralda! Esmeralda!" she cried. "Help me, or we are lost."

Esmeralda slowly opened her eyes. The first object they encountered was the dripping fangs of the hungry lioness.

With a horrible scream the poor woman rose to her hands and knees, and in this position scurried across the room, shrieking: "O Gaberelle! O Gaberelle!" at the top of her lungs.

Esmeralda weighed some two hundred and eighty pounds, which enhanced nothing the gazellelike grace of her carriage when walking erect, and her extreme haste, added to her extreme corpulency, produced a most amazing result when Esmeralda elected to travel on all fours.

For a moment the lioness remained quiet with intense gaze directed upon the flitting Esmeralda, whose goal appeared to be the cupboard, into which she attempted to propel her huge bulk; but, as the shelves were but nine or ten inches apart, she only succeeded in getting her head in, whereupon, with a final screech, which paled the jungle noises into insignificance, she fainted once again.

With the subsidence of Esmeralda the lioness renewed her efforts to wriggle her huge bulk through the weakening lattice.

The girl, standing pale and rigid against the further wall, sought with ever-increasing terror for some loophole of escape. Suddenly her hand, tight-pressed against her bosom, felt the hard outline of the revolver that Clayton had left with her earlier in the day.

Quickly she snatched it from its hiding-place, and, leveling it full at the lioness' face, pulled the trigger.

There was a flash of flame, the roar of the discharge, and an answering roar of pain and anger from the beast.

Jane Porter saw the great form disappear from the window, and then she, too, fainted, the revolver falling at her side.

But Sabor was not killed. The bullet had but inflicted a painful wound in one of the great shoulders. It was the surprise at the blinding flash and the deafening roar that had caused her hasty, though but temporary, retreat.

In another instant she was back at the lattice, and with renewed fury was clawing at the aperture, but with lessened effect, since the wounded member was almost useless.

She saw her prey—the two women—lying senseless upon the floor; there was no longer any resistance to be overcome. Her meat lay before her, and Sabor had only to worm her way through the lattice to claim it.

Slowly she forced her great bulk, inch by inch, through the opening. Now her head was through, now one great forearm and shoulder.

Carefully she drew up the wounded member to insinuate it gently beyond the tight-pressing bars.

A moment more and both shoulders through, the long, sinuous body and the narrow hips would glide quickly after.

It was on this sight that Jane Porter again opened her eyes.

CHAPTER XV

❦

The Forest God

WHEN Clayton heard the report of the firearm he fell into an agony of fear and apprehension. He knew that one of the sailors might be the author of it; but the fact that he had left the revolver with Jane Porter, together with the overwrought conditions of his nerves, made him morbidly positive that she was threatened with some great danger; perhaps even now attempting to defend herself against some savage man or beast.

What were the thoughts of his strange captor or guide Clayton could only vaguely conjecture; but that he had heard the shot, and was in some matter affected by it was quite evident, for he quickened his pace so appreciably that Clayton, stumbling blindly in his wake, was down a dozen times in as many minutes in a vain effort to keep pace with him, and soon was left hopelessly behind.

Fearing that he would again be irretrievably lost, he called aloud to the wild man ahead of him, and in a moment had the satisfaction of seeing him drop lightly to his side from the branches above.

For a moment Tarzan looked at the young man closely, as though undecided as to just what was best to do; then, stooping down before Clayton, he motioned him to grasp him about the neck, and, with the white man upon his back, Tarzan took to the trees.

The next few minutes were such as the young Englishman never forgot. High into bending and swaying branches he was borne with what seemed to him incredible swiftness, while Tarzan chafed at the slowness of his progress.

From one lofty branch the agile creature swung with Clayton through a dizzy arc to a neighboring tree; then for a hundred yards maybe the sure feet threaded a maze of interwoven limbs, balancing like a tightrope walker high above the black depths of verdure beneath.

From the first sensation of chilling fear Clayton passed to one of keen admiration and envy of those giant muscles and that wondrous instinct or knowledge which guided this forest god through the inky blackness of the night as easily and safely as Clayton could have strolled a London street at high noon.

Occasionally they would enter a spot where the foliage above was less dense, and the bright rays of the moon lit up before Clayton's wondering eyes the strange path they were traversing.

At such times the man fairly caught his breath at sight of the horrid depths below them, for Tarzan took the easiest way, which often led over a hundred feet above the earth.

And yet with all his seeming speed, Tarzan was in reality feeling his way with comparative slowness, searching constantly for limbs of adequate strength for the maintenance of this double weight.

Presently they came to the clearing before the beach. Tarzan's quick ears had heard the strange sounds of Sabor's efforts to force her way through the lattice, and it seemed to Clayton that they dropped a straight hundred feet to earth, so quickly did Tarzan descend. Yet when they struck the ground it was with scarce a jar; and as Clayton released his hold on the ape-man he saw him dart like a squirrel for the opposite side of the cabin.

The Englishman sprang quickly after him just in time to see the hind quarters of some huge animal about to disappear through the window of the cabin.

As Jane Porter opened her eyes to a realization of the again imminent peril which threatened her, her brave young heart gave up at last its final vestige of hope, and she turned to grope for the fallen weapon that she might mete to herself a merciful death ere the cruel fangs tore into her fair flesh.

The lioness was almost through the opening before Jane found the weapon, and she raised it quickly to her temple to shut out forever the hideous jaws gaping for their prey.

An instant she hesitated, to breathe a short and silent prayer to her Maker, and as she did so her eyes fell upon her poor Esmeralda lying inert, but alive, beside the cupboard.

How could she leave the poor, faithful thing to those merciless, yellow fangs? No, she must use one cartridge on the senseless woman ere she turned the cold muzzle toward herself again.

How she shrank from the ordeal! But it had been cruelty a thousand times less justifiable to have left the loving black woman who had reared her from infancy with all a mother's care and solicitude, to regain consciousness beneath the rending claws of the great cat.

Quickly Jane Porter sprang to her feet and ran to the side of the black. She pressed the muzzle of the revolver tight against that devoted heart, closed her eyes, and—

Sabor emitted a frightful shriek.

The girl, startled, pulled the trigger and turned to face the beast, and with the same movement raised the weapon against her own temple.

She did not fire a second time, for to her surprise she saw the huge animal being slowly drawn back through the window, and in the moonlight beyond she saw the heads and shoulders of two men.

As Clayton rounded the corner of the cabin to behold the animal disappearing within, it was also to see the ape-man seize the long tail in both hands, and, bracing himself with his feet against the side of the cabin, throw all his mighty strength into the effort to draw the beast out of the interior.

Clayton was quick to lend a hand, but the ape-man jabbered to him in a commanding and peremptory tone something which Clayton knew to be orders, though he could not understand them.

At last, under their combined efforts, the great body commenced to appear farther and farther without the window, and then there came to Clayton's mind a dawning conception of the rash bravery of his companion's act.

For a naked man to drag a shrieking, clawing man-eater forth from a window by the tail to save a strange white girl, was indeed the last word in heroism.

In so far as Clayton was concerned it was a very different matter, since the girl was not only of his own kind and race, but was the one woman in all the world whom he loved.

Though he knew that the lioness would make short work of both of them, he pulled with a will to keep it from Jane Porter. And then he recalled the battle between this man and the great, black-maned lion which he had witnessed a short time before, and he commenced to feel more assurance.

Tarzan was still issuing orders which Clayton could not understand.

He was trying to tell the stupid white man to plunge his poisoned arrows into Sabor's back and sides, and to reach the savage heart with the long, thin hunting knife that hung at Tarzan's hip; but the man would not understand, and Tarzan did not dare release his hold to do the things himself, for he knew that the puny white man never could hold mighty Sabor alone, for an instant.

Slowly the lioness was emerging from the window. At last her shoulders were out.

And then Clayton saw a thing done which not even the eternal heavens had ever seen before. Tarzan, racking his brains for some means to cope single-handed with the infuriated beast, had suddenly recalled his battle with Terkoz; and as the great shoulders came clear of the window, so that the lioness hung upon the sill only by her fore-paws, Tarzan suddenly released his hold upon the brute.

With the quickness of a striking rattler he launched himself full upon Sabor's back, his strong young arms seeking and gaining a full-Nelson upon the beast, as he had learned it that other day during his bloody, wrestling victory over Terkoz.

With a shriek the lioness turned completely over upon her back, falling full upon her enemy; but the black-haired giant only closed tighter his hold.

Pawing and tearing at earth and air, Sabor rolled and threw herself this way and that in an effort to dislodge this strange antagonist; but ever tighter and tighter drew the iron bands that were forcing her head lower and lower upon her tawny breast.

Higher crept the steel forearms of the ape-man about the back of Sabor's neck. Weaker and weaker became the lioness' efforts.

At last Clayton saw the immense muscles of Tarzan's shoulders and biceps leap into corded knots beneath the silver moonlight. There was a long sustained and supreme effort on the ape-man's part—and the vertebrae of Sabor's neck parted with a sharp snap.

In an instant Tarzan was upon his feet, and for the second time that day Clayton heard the bull ape's savage roar of victory. Then he heard Jane Porter's agonized cry:

"Cecil—Mr. Clayton! Oh, what is it? What is it?"

Running quickly to the cabin door, Clayton called out that all was right, and bade her open. As quickly as she could she raised the great bar and fairly dragged Clayton within.

"What was that awful noise?" she whispered, shrinking close to him.

"It was the cry of the kill from the throat of the man who has just saved your life, Miss Porter. Wait, I will fetch him that you may thank him."

The frightened girl would not be left alone, so she accompanied Clayton to the side of the cabin where lay the dead body of the lioness.

Tarzan of the Apes was gone.

Clayton called several times, but there was no reply, and so the two returned to the greater safety of the interior.

"What a frightful sound!" cried Jane Porter. "I shudder at the mere thought of it. Do not tell me that human throat voiced that hideous and fearsome shriek."

"But it did, Miss Porter," replied Clayton; "or at least if not a human throat that of a forest god."

And then he told her of his experiences with this strange creature—of how twice the wild man had saved his life—of the wondrous strength, and agility, and bravery—of the brown skin and the handsome face.

"I cannot make it out at all," he concluded. "At first I thought he might be Tarzan of the Apes; but he neither speaks nor understands English, so that theory is untenable."

"Well, whatever he may be," cried the girl, "we owe him our lives, and may God bless him and keep him in safety in his wild and savage jungle!"

"Amen," said Clayton, fervently.

"Fo' de good Lawd's sake, ain' Ah daid?"

The two turned to see Esmeralda sitting upright upon the floor, her great eyes rolling from side to side as though she could not believe their testimony to her whereabouts.

The lioness' shriek as Jane Porter had been about to put a bullet into poor Esmeralda, had saved the black's life, for the little start the girl gave had turned the muzzle of the revolver to one side, and the bullet had passed harmlessly into the floor.

And now, for Jane Porter, the reaction came, and she threw herself upon the bench, screaming with hysterical laughter.

CHAPTER XVI

"Most Remarkable"

SEVERAL miles south of the cabin, upon a strip of sandy beach, stood two old men, arguing.

Before them stretched the broad Atlantic; at their backs the Dark Continent; close around them loomed the impenetrable blackness of the jungle.

Savage beasts roared and growled; noises, hideous and weird, assailed their ears. They had wandered for miles in search of their camp; but always in the wrong direction. They were as hopelessly lost as though they suddenly had been transported to another world.

At such a time indeed must every fiber of their combined intellects have been concentrated upon the vital question of the minute—the life-and-death question to them of retracing their steps to camp.

Samuel T. Philander was speaking.

"But, my dear professor," he was saying, "I still maintain that but for the victories of Ferdinand and Isabella over the fifteenth-century Moors in Spain the world would be today a thousand years in advance of where we now find ourselves.

"The Moors were essentially a tolerant, broad-minded, liberal race of agriculturists, artisans and merchants—the very type of people that has made possible such civilization as we find to-day in America and Europe—while the Spaniards—"

160

"Tut, tut, dear Mr. Philander," interrupted Professor Porter; "their religion positively precluded the possibilities you suggest. Moslemism was, is, and always will be, a blight on that scientific progress which has marked—"

"Bless me! Professor," interjected Mr. Philander, who had turned his gaze toward the jungle, "there seems to be some one approaching."

Professor Archimedes Q. Porter turned in the direction indicated by the nearsighted Mr. Philander.

"Tut, tut, Mr. Philander," he chided. "How often must I urge you to seek that absolute concentration of your mental faculties which alone may permit you to bring to bear the highest powers of intellectuality upon the momentous problems which naturally fall to the lot of great minds? And now I find you guilty of a most flagrant breach of courtesy in interrupting my learned discourse to call attention to a mere quadruped of the genus *Felis*. As I was saying, Mr.—"

"Heavens, Professor, a lion?" cried Mr. Philander, straining his weak eyes toward the dim figure outlined against the dark tropical underbrush.

"Yes, yes, Mr. Philander, if you insist upon employing slang in your discourse, a 'lion.' But as I was saying—"

"Bless me, Professor," again interrupted Mr. Philander; "permit me to suggest that doubtless the Moors who were conquered in the fifteenth century will continue in that most regrettable condition for the time being at least, even though we postpone discussion of that world calamity until we may attain the enchanting view of yon *Felis carnivora* which distance proverbially is credited with lending."

In the meantime the lion had approached with quiet dignity to within ten paces of the two men, where he stood curiously watching them.

The moonlight flooded the beach, and the strange group stood out in bold relief against the yellow sand.

"Most reprehensible, most reprehensible," exclaimed Professor Porter, with a faint trace of irritation in his voice.

"Never, Mr. Philander, never before in my life have I known one of these animals to be permitted to roam at large from its cage. I shall most certainly report this outrageous breach of ethics to the directors of the adjacent zoölogical garden."

"Quite right, Professor," agreed Mr. Philander, "and the sooner it is done the better. Let us start now."

Seizing the professor by the arm, Mr. Philander set off in the direction that would put the greatest distance between themselves and the lion.

They had proceeded but a short distance when a backward glance revealed to the horrified gaze of Mr. Philander that the lion was following them. He tightened his grip upon the protesting professor and increased his speed.

"As I was saying, Mr. Philander," repeated Professor Porter.

Mr. Philander took another hasty glance rearward. The lion also had quickened his gait, and was doggedly maintaining an unvarying distance behind them.

"He is following us!" gasped Mr. Philander, breaking into a run.

"Tut, tut, Mr. Philander," remonstrated the professor, "this unseemly haste is most unbecoming men of letters.

"What will our friends think of us, who may chance to be upon the street and witness our frivolous antics? Pray let us proceed with more decorum."

Mr. Philander stole another observation astern.

Horrors! The lion was bounding along in easy leaps scarce five paces behind.

Mr. Philander dropped the professor's arm, and broke into a mad orgy of speed that would have done credit to any varsity track team.

"As I was saying, Mr. Philander—" screamed Professor Porter, as, metaphorically speaking, he himself "threw her into high." He, too, had caught a fleeting backward glimpse of cruel yellow eyes and half-open mouth within startling proximity of his person.

With streaming coat tails and shiny silk hat Professor

Archimedes Q. Porter fled through the moonlight close upon the heels of Mr. Samuel T. Philander.

Before them a point of the jungle ran out toward a narrow promontory, and it was for the haven of the trees he saw there that Mr. Samuel T. Philander directed his prodigious leaps and bounds; while from the shadows of this same spot peered two keen eyes in interested appreciation of the race.

It was Tarzan of the Apes who watched, with face a-grin, this odd game of follow-the-leader.

He knew the two men were safe enough from attack in so far as the lion was concerned. The very fact that Numa had foregone such easy prey at all convinced the wise forest craft of Tarzan that Numa's belly already was full.

The lion might stalk them until hungry again; but the chances were that if not angered he would soon tire of the sport, and slink away to his jungle lair.

Really, the one great danger was that one of the men might stumble and fall, and then the yellow devil would be upon him in a moment and the joy of the kill would be too great a temptation to withstand.

So Tarzan swung quickly to a lower limb in line with the approaching fugitives; and as Mr. Samuel T. Philander came panting and blowing beneath him, already too spent to struggle up to the safety of the limb, Tarzan reached down and, grasping him by the collar of his coat, yanked him to the limb by his side.

Another moment brought the professor within the sphere of the friendly grip, and he, too, was drawn upward to safety just as the baffled Numa, with a roar, leaped to recover his vanishing quarry.

For a moment the two men clung panting to the great branch, while Tarzan squatted with his back to the stem of the tree, watching them with mingled curiosity and amusement.

It was the professor who first broke the silence.

"I am deeply pained, Mr. Philander, that you should have evinced such a paucity of manly courage in the presence of one of the lower orders, and by your crass timidity have caused me to exert myself to such an unaccustomed degree in order that I might resume my discourse.

"As I was saying, Mr. Philander, when you interrupted me, the Moors—"

"Professor Archimedes Q. Porter," broke in Mr. Philander, in icy tones, "the time has arrived when patience becomes a crime and mayhem appears garbed in the mantle of virtue. You have accused me of cowardice. You have insinuated that you ran only to overtake me, not to escape the clutches of the lion.

"Have a care, Professor Achimedes Q. Porter! I am a desperate man. Goaded by long-suffering patience the worm will turn."

"Tut, tut, Mr. Philander, tut, tut!" cautioned Professor Porter; "you forget yourself."

"I forget nothing as yet, Professor Archimedes Q. Porter; but, believe me, sir, I am tottering on the verge of forgetfulness as to your exalted position in the world of science, and your gray hairs."

The professor sat in silence for a few minutes, and in the darkness hid the grim smile that wreathed his wrinkled countenance. Presently he spoke.

"Look here, Skinny Philander," he said, in belligerent tones, "if you are lookin' for a scrap, peel off your coat and come on down on the ground, and I'll punch your head just as I did sixty years ago in the alley back of Porky Evans' barn."

"Ark!" gasped the astonished Mr. Philander. "Lordy, how good that sounds! When you're human, Ark, I love you; but somehow it seems as though you had forgotten how to be human for the last twenty years."

The professor reached out a thin, trembling old hand through the darkness until it found his old friend's shoulder.

"Forgive me, Skinny," he said, softly. "It hasn't been quite twenty years, and God alone knows how hard I have tried to be 'human' for Jane's sake, and yours, too, since He took my other Jane away."

Another old hand stole up from Mr. Philander's side to clasp the one that lay upon his shoulder, and no other message could better have translated the one heart to the other.

They did not speak for some minutes. The lion below them paced nervously back and forth. The third figure in the tree was hidden by the dense shadows near the stem. He, too, was silent—motionless as a graven image.

"You certainly pulled me up into this tree just in time," said the professor at last. "I want to thank you. You saved my life."

"But I didn't pull you up here, Professor," said Mr. Philander. "Bless me! The excitement of the moment quite caused me to forget that I myself was drawn up here by some outside agency—there must be some one or something in this tree with us."

"Eh?" ejaculated Professor Porter. "Are you quite positive, Mr. Philander?"

"Most positive, Professor," replied Mr. Philander, "and," he added, "I think we should thank the party. He may be sitting right next to you now, Professor."

"Eh? What's that? Tut, tut, Mr. Philander, tut, tut!" said Professor Porter, edging cautiously nearer to Mr. Philander.

Just then it occurred to Tarzan of the Apes that Numa had loitered beneath the tree for a sufficient length of time, so he raised his young head toward the heavens, and there rang out upon the terrified ears of the two old men the awful warning challenge of the anthropoid.

The two friends, huddled trembling in their precarious position on the limb, saw the great lion halt in his restless pacing as the bloodcurdling cry smote his ears, and then slink quickly into the jungle, to be instantly lost to view.

"Even the lion trembles in fear," whispered Mr. Philander.

"Most remarkable, most remarkable," murmured Professor Porter, clutching frantically at Mr. Philander to regain the balance which the sudden fright had so perilously endangered. Unfortunately for them both, Mr. Philander's center of equilibrium was at that very moment hanging upon the ragged edge of nothing, so that it needed but the gentle impetus supplied by the additional weight of Professor Porter's body to topple the devoted secretary from the limb.

For a moment they swayed uncertainly, and then, with mingled and most unscholarly shrieks, they pitched headlong from the tree, locked in frenzied embrace.

It was quite some moments ere either moved, for both were positive that any such attempt would reveal so many breaks and fractures as to make further progress impossible.

At length Professor Porter essayed an attempt to move one leg. To his surprise, it responded to his will as in days gone by. He now drew up its mate and stretched it forth again.

"Most remarkable, most remarkable," he murmured.

"Thank God, Professor," whispered Mr. Philander, fervently, "you are not dead, then?"

"Tut, tut, Mr. Philander, tut, tut," cautioned Professor Porter, "I do not know with accuracy as yet."

With infinite solicitude Professor Porter wiggled his right arm—joy! It was intact. Breathlessly he waved his left arm above his prostrate body—it waved!

"Most remarkable, most remarkable," he said.

"To whom are you signaling, Professor?" asked Mr. Philander, in an excited tone.

Professor Porter deigned to make no response to this puerile inquiry. Instead he raised his head gently from the ground, nodding it back and forth a half dozen times.

"Most remarkable," he breathed. "It remains intact."

Mr. Philander had not moved from where he had fallen; he had not dared the attempt. How indeed could one move when one's arms and legs and back were broken?

One eye was buried in the soft loam; the other, rolling sidewise, was fixed in awe upon the strange gyrations of Professor Porter.

"How sad!" exclaimed Mr. Philander, half aloud. "Concussion of the brain, superinducing total mental aberration. How very sad indeed! and for one still so young!"

Professor Porter rolled over upon his stomach; gingerly he bowed his back until he resembled a huge cat in proximity to a yelping dog. Then he sat up and felt of various portions of his anatomy.

"They are all here," he ejaculated. "Most remarkable!"

Whereupon he arose, and, bending a scathing glance upon the still prostrate form of Mr. Samuel T. Philander, he said:

"Tut, tut, Mr. Philander; this is no time to indulge in slothful ease. We must be up and doing."

Mr. Philander lifted his other eye out of the mud, and gazed in speechless rage at Professor Porter. Then he attempted to rise; nor could there have been any more surprised than he when his efforts were immediately crowned with marked success.

He was still bursting with rage, however, at the cruel injustice of Professor Porter's insinuation, and was on the point of rendering a tart rejoinder when his eyes fell upon a strange figure standing a few paces away, scrutinizing them intently.

Professor Porter had recovered his shiny silk hat, which he had brushed carefully upon the sleeve of his coat and replaced upon his head. When he saw Mr. Philander pointing to something behind him he turned to behold a giant, naked but for a loin cloth and a few metal ornaments, standing motionless before him.

"Good evening, sir!" said the professor, lifting his hat. For reply the giant motioned them to follow him, and set off up the beach in the direction from which they had recently come.

"I think it the part of discretion to follow him," said Mr. Philander.

"Tut, tut, Mr. Philander," returned the professor. "A short time since you were advancing most logical argument in substantiation of your theory that camp lay directly south of us. I was skeptical, but you finally convinced me; so now I am positive that toward the south we must travel to reach our friends. Therefore I shall continue south."

"But, Professor Porter, this man may know better than either of us. He seems to be indigenous to this part of the world. Let us at least follow him for a short distance."

"Tut, tut, Mr. Philander," repeated the professor. "I am a difficult man to convince, but when once convinced my decision is unalterable. I shall continue in the proper direction, if I have to circumnambulate the continent of Africa to reach my destination."

Further argument was interrupted by Tarzan, who, seeing that these strange men were not following him, had returned to their side.

Again he beckoned to them; but still they stood in argument.

Presently the ape-man lost patience with their stupid ignorance. He grasped the frightened Mr. Philander by the shoulder, and before that worthy gentleman knew whether he was being killed or merely maimed for life, Tarzan had tied one end of his rope securely about Mr. Philander's neck.

"Tut, tut, Mr. Philander," remonstrated Professor Porter; "it is most unbeseeming in you to submit to such indignities."

But scarcely were the words out of his mouth ere he, too, had been seized and securely bound by the neck with the same rope. Then Tarzan set off toward the north, leading the now thoroughly frightened professor and his secretary.

In deathly silence they proceeded for what seemed hours to the two tired and hopeless old men; but presently as they topped a little rise of ground they were overjoyed to see the cabin lying before them, not a hundred yards distant.

Here Tarzan released them, and, pointing toward the little building, vanished into the jungle beside them.

"Most remarkable, most remarkable!" gasped the professor. "But you see, Mr. Philander, that I was quite right, as usual; and but for your stubborn willfulness we should have escaped a series of most humiliating, not to say dangerous accidents. Pray allow yourself to be guided by a more mature and practical mind hereafter when in need of wise counsel."

Mr. Samuel T. Philander was too much relieved at the happy outcome to their adventure to take umbrage at the professor's cruel fling. Instead he grasped his friend's arm and hastened him forward in the direction of the cabin.

It was a much-relieved party of castaways that found itself recounting their various adventures, and speculating upon the identity of the strange guardian and protector they had found on this savage shore.

Esmeralda was positive that it was none other than an angel of the Lord, sent down especially to watch over them.

"Had you seen him devour the raw meat of the lion, Esmeralda," laughed Clayton, "you would have thought him a very material angel."

"Ah doan know nuffin' 'bout dat, Marse Clayton," rejoined Esmeralda; "but Ah 'specs de Lawd clean fergot to gib him any matches, He sent him down in sech a hurry to look after we-all. An' he suttinly cain't cook nuffin' 'thout matches—no, sah."

"There was nothing heavenly about his voice," said Jane Porter, with a little shudder at recollection of the awful roar which had followed the killing of the lioness.

"Nor did it precisely comport with my preconceived ideas of the dignity of divine messengers," remarked

Professor Porter, "when the—ah—gentleman tied two highly respectable and erudite scholars neck to neck and dragged them through the jungle as though they had been cows."

CHAPTER XVII

❦

Burials

AS it was not quite light, the party, none of whom had eaten or slept since the previous morning, began to bestir themselves to prepare food.

The mutineers of the *Arrow* had landed a small supply of dried meats, canned soups and vegetables, crackers, flour, tea, and coffee for the five they had marooned, and these were hurriedly drawn upon to satisfy the craving of long-famished appetites.

The next task was to make the cabin habitable, and to this end it was decided to at once remove the gruesome relics of the tragedy which had taken place there on some bygone day.

Professor Porter and Mr. Philander were deeply interested in examining the skeletons. The two larger, they stated, had belonged to a male and female of one of the higher white races.

The smallest skeleton was given but passing attention, as its location, in the crib, left no doubt as to its having been the infant offspring of this unhappy couple.

As they were preparing the skeleton of the man for burial, Clayton discovered a massive ring which had evidently encircled the man's finger at the time of his death, for one of the slender bones of the hand still lay within the golden bauble.

Picking it up to examine it, Clayton gave a cry of astonishment, for the ring bore the crest of the house of Greystoke.

At the same time, Jane Porter discovered the books in the cupboard, and on opening to the flyleaf of one of them saw the name, *John Clayton, London.* In a second book which she hurriedly examined was the single name, *Greystoke.*

"Why, Mr. Clayton," she cried, "what does this mean? Here are the names of some of your own people in these books."

"And here," he replied gravely, "is the great ring of the house of Greystoke which has been lost since my uncle, John Clayton, the former Lord Greystoke, disappeared, presumably lost at sea."

"But how do you account for these things being here, in this savage African jungle?" exclaimed the girl.

"There is but one way to account for it, Miss Porter," said Clayton. "The late Lord Greystoke was not drowned. He died here in this cabin and this poor thing upon the floor is all that is mortal of him."

"Then this must have been Lady Greystoke," said Jane Porter reverently, indicating the poor mass of bones upon the bed.

"The beautiful Lady Alice," replied Clayton, "of whose many virtues and remarkable personal charms I often have heard my mother and father speak. Poor, unhappy lady," he murmured sadly.

With deep reverence and solemnity the bodies of the late Lord and Lady Greystoke were buried beside their little African cabin, and between them was placed the tiny skeleton of the baby of Kala, the ape.

As Mr. Philander was placing the frail bones of the infant in a bit of sail cloth, he examined the skull minutely. Then he called Professor Porter to his side, and the two argued in low tones for several minutes.

"Most remarkable, most remarkable," said Professor Porter.

"Bless me," said Mr. Philander, "we must acquaint Mr. Clayton with our discovery at once."

"Tut, tut, Mr. Philander, tut, tut!" remonstrated Professor Archimedes Q. Porter. " 'Let the dead past bury its dead.' "

And so the white-haired old man repeated the burial service over this strange grave, while his four companions stood with bowed and uncovered heads about him.

From the trees Tarzan of the Apes watched the solemn ceremony; but most of all he watched the sweet face and graceful figure of Jane Porter.

In his savage, untutored breast new emotions were stirring. He could not fathom them. He wondered why he felt so great an interest in these people—why he had gone to such pains to save the three men. But he did not wonder why he had torn Sabor from the tender flesh of the strange girl.

Surely the men were stupid and ridiculous and cowardly. Even Manu, the monkey, was more intelligent than they. If these were creatures of his own kind he was doubtful if his past pride in blood was warranted.

But the girl, ah—that was a different matter. He did not reason here. He knew that she was created to be protected, and that he was created to protect her.

He wondered why they had dug a great hole in the ground merely to bury dry bones. Surely there was no sense in that; no one wanted to steal dry bones.

Had there been meat upon them he could have understood, for thus alone might one keep his meat from Dango, the hyena, and the other robbers of the jungle.

When the grave had been filled with earth the little party turned back toward the cabin, and Esmeralda, still weeping copiously for the two she had never heard of before to-day, and who had been dead twenty years, chanced to glance toward the harbor. Instantly her tears ceased.

"Look at dem low-down white trash out dere!" she shrilled, pointing toward the *Arrow*. "They-all's a desecretin' us, right yere on dis yere perverted islan'."

And, sure enough, the *Arrow* was being worked toward the open sea, slowly, through the harbor's entrance.

"They promised to leave us firearms and ammunition," said Clayton. "The merciless beasts!"

"It is the work of that fellow they call Snipes, I am sure," said Jane Porter. "King was a scoundrel, but he had a little sense of humanity. If they had not killed him I know that he would have seen that we were properly provided for before they left us to our fate."

"I regret that they did not visit us before sailing," said Professor Porter. "I had purposed requesting them to leave the treasure with us, as I shall be a ruined man if that is lost."

Jane Porter looked at her father sadly.

"Never mind, dear," she said. "It wouldn't have done any good, because it is solely for the treasure that they killed their officers and landed us upon this awful shore."

"Tut, tut, child, tut, tut!" replied Professor Porter. "You are a good child, but inexperienced in practical matters," and Professor Porter turned and walked slowly away toward the jungle, his hands clasped beneath his long coat tails and his eyes bent upon the ground.

His daughter watched him with a pathetic smile upon her lips, and then turning to Mr. Philander, she whispered:

"Please don't let him wander off again as he did yesterday. We depend upon you, you know, to keep a close watch upon him."

"He becomes more difficult to handle each day," replied Mr. Philander, with a sigh and a shake of his head. "I presume he is now off to report to the directors of the zoo that one of their lions was at large last night. Oh, Miss Jane, you don't know what I have to contend with."

"Yes, I do, Mr. Philander; but while we all love him, you alone are best fitted to manage him; for, regardless of what he may say to you, he respects your great learning, and, therefore, has immense confidence in your judgment. The poor dear cannot differentiate between erudition and wisdom."

Mr. Philander, with a mildly puzzled expression on his face, turned to pursue Professor Porter, and in his mind he was revolving the question of whether he should feel complimented or aggrieved at Miss Porter's rather backhanded compliment.

Tarzan had seen the consternation depicted upon the faces of the little group as they witnessed the departure of the *Arrow*; so, as the ship was a wonderful novelty to him in addition, he determined to hasten out to the point of land at the north of the harbor's mouth and obtain a nearer view of the boat, as well as to learn, if possible, the direction of its flight.

Swinging through the trees with great speed, he reached the point but a moment after the ship had passed out of the harbor, so that he obtained an excellent view of the wonders of this strange, floating house.

There were some twenty men running hither and thither about the deck, pulling and hauling on ropes.

A light land breeze was blowing, and the ship had been worked through the harbor's mouth under scant sail, but now that they had cleared the point every available shred of canvas was being spread that she might stand out to sea as handily as possible.

Tarzan watched the graceful movements of the ship in rapt admiration, and longed to be aboard her. Presently his keen eyes caught the faintest suspicion of smoke on the far northern horizon, and he wondered over the cause of such a thing out on the great water.

At about the same time the lookout on the *Arrow* must have discerned it, for in a few minutes Tarzan saw the sails being shifted and shortened. The ship came about, and presently he knew that she was beating back toward land.

A man at the bows was constantly heaving into the sea a rope to the end of which a small object was fastened. Tarzan wondered what the purpose of this action might be.

At last the ship came up directly into the wind; the anchor was lowered; down came the sails. There was great scurrying about on deck.

A boat was lowered, and in it a great chest was placed. Then a dozen sailors bent to the oars and pulled rapidly toward the point where Tarzan crouched in the branches of a tree.

In the stern of the boat, as it drew nearer, Tarzan saw the rat-faced man.

It was but a few minutes later that the boat touched the beach. The men jumped out and lifted the great chest to the sand. They were on the north side of the point so that their presence was concealed from those at the cabin.

The men argued angrily for a moment. Then the rat-faced one, with several companions, ascended the low bluff on which stood the tree that concealed Tarzan. They looked about for several minutes.

"Here is a good place," said the rat-faced sailor, indicating a spot beneath Tarzan's tree.

"It is as good as any," replied one of his companions. "If they catch us with the treasure aboard it will all be confiscated anyway. We might as well bury it here on the chance that some of us will escape the gallows to come back and enjoy it later."

The rat-faced one now called to the men who had remained at the boat, and they came slowly up the bank carrying picks and shovels.

"Hurry, —— you!" cried Snipes.

"Stow it!" retorted one of the men, in a surly tone. "You're no admiral, you —— —— shrimp."

"I'm Cap'n here, though, I'll have you to understand, you swab," shrieked Snipes, with a volley of frightful oaths.

"Steady, boys," cautioned one of the men who had not spoken before. "It ain't goin' to get us nothing by fightin' amongst ourselves."

"Right enough," replied the sailor who had resented Snipes' autocratic tones; "but by the same token it ain't a-goin' to get nobody nothin' to put on airs in this bloomin' company neither."

"You fellows dig here," said Snipes, indicating a spot beneath the tree. "And while you're diggin', Peter kin be a-makin' of a map of the location, so's we kin find it again. You, Tom, and Bill, take a couple more down and fetch up the chest."

"Wot are you a-goin' to do?" asked he of the previous altercation. "Just boss?"

"Git busy there," growled Snipes. "You didn't think your Cap'n was a-goin' to dig with a shovel, did you?"

The men all looked up angrily. None of them liked Snipes, and his disagreeable show of authority since he had murdered King, the real head and ringleader of the mutineers, had only added fuel to the flames of their hatred.

"Do you mean to say that you don't intend to take a shovel, and lend a hand with this work? Your shoulder's not hurted so all-fired bad as that," said Tarrant, the sailor who had before spoken.

"Not by a——sight," replied Snipes, fingering the butt of his revolver nervously.

"Then, by God," replied Tarrant, "if you won't take a shovel you'll take a pickax."

With the words he raised his pick above his head, and, with a mighty blow, buried the point in Snipes' brain.

For a moment the men stood silently looking at the result of their fellow's grim humor. Then one of them spoke.

"Served the skunk jolly well right," he said.

One of the others commenced to ply his pick to the ground. The soil was soft and he threw aside the pick and grasped a shovel; then the others joined him. There was no further comment on the killing, but the men worked in a better frame of mind than they had since Snipes had assumed command.

When they had a trench of ample size to bury the

chest, Tarrant suggested that they enlarge it and inter Snipes' body on top of the chest.

"It might 'elp fool any as 'appened to be diggin' 'ere-abouts," he explained.

The others saw the cunning of the suggestion, and so the trench was lengthened to accommodate the corpse, and in the center a deeper hole was excavated for the box, which was first wrapped in sailcloth and then low-ered to its place, which brought its top about a foot below the bottom of the grave. Earth was shoveled in and tramped down about the chest until the bottom of the grave showed level and uniform.

Two of the men rolled the rat-faced corpse uncere-moniously into the grave, after first stripping it of its weapons and various other articles which the several members of the party coveted for their own.

They then filled the grave with earth and tramped upon it until it would hold no more.

The balance of the loose earth was thrown far and wide, and a mass of dead undergrowth spread in as nat-ural a manner as possible over the new-made grave to obliterate all signs of the ground having been disturbed.

Their work done the sailors returned to the small boat, and pulled off rapidly toward the *Arrow*.

The breeze had increased considerably, and as the smoke upon the horizon was now plainly discernible in considerable volume, the mutineers lost no time in getting under full sail and bearing away toward the southwest.

Tarzan, an interested spectator of all that had taken place, sat speculating on the strange actions of these pe-culiar creatures.

Men were indeed more foolish and more cruel than the beasts of the jungle! How fortunate was he who lived in the peace and security of the great forest!

Tarzan wondered what the chest they had buried con-tained. If they did not want it why did they not merely throw it into the water? That would have been much easier.

Ah, he thought, but they do want it. They have hidden it here because they intend returning for it later.

Tarzan dropped to the ground and commenced to examine the earth about the excavation. He was looking to see if these creatures had dropped anything which he might like to own. Soon he discovered a spade hidden by the underbrush which they had laid upon the grave.

He seized it and attempted to use it as he had seen the sailors do. It was awkward work and hurt his bare feet, but he persevered until he had partially uncovered the body. This he dragged from the grave and laid to one side.

Then he continued digging until he had unearthed the chest. This also he dragged to the side of the corpse. Then he filled in the smaller hole below the grave, replaced the body and the earth around and above it; covered it over with underbrush and returned to the chest.

Four sailors had sweated beneath the burden of its weight—Tarzan of the Apes picked it up as though it had been an empty packing case, and with the spade slung to his back by a piece of rope, carried it off into the densest part of the jungle.

He could not well negotiate the trees with his awkward burden, but he kept to the trails, and so made fairly good time.

For several hours he traveled a little north of east until he came to an impenetrable wall of matted and tangled vegetation. Then he took to the lower branches, and in another fifteen minutes he emerged into the amphitheater of the apes, where they met in council, or to celebrate the rites of the Dum-Dum.

Near the center of the clearing, and not far from the drum, or altar, he commenced to dig. This was harder work than turning up the freshly excavated earth at the grave, but Tarzan of the Apes was persevering and so he kept at his labor until he was rewarded by seeing a hole sufficiently deep to receive the chest and effectually hide it from view.

Why had he gone to all this labor without knowing the value of the contents of the chest?

Tarzan of the Apes had a man's figure and a man's brain, but he was an ape by training and environment. His brain told him that the chest contained something valuable, or the men would not have hidden it; his training had taught him to imitate whatever was new and unusual, and now the natural curiosity, which is as common to men as to apes, prompted him to open the chest and examine its contents.

But the heavy lock and massive iron bands baffled both his cunning and his immense strength, so that he was compelled to bury the chest without having his curiosity satisfied.

By the time Tarzan had hunted his way back to the vicinity of the cabin, feeding as he went, it was quite dark.

Within the little building a light was burning, for Clayton had found an unopened tin of oil which had stood intact for twenty years; a part of the supplies left with the Claytons by Black Michael. The lamps also were still usable, and thus the interior of the cabin appeared as bright as day to the astonished Tarzan.

He had often wondered at the exact purpose of the lamps. His reading and the pictures had told him what they were, but he had no idea of how they could be made to produce the wondrous sunlight that some of his pictures had portrayed them as diffusing upon all surrounding objects.

As he approached the window nearest the door he saw that the cabin had been divided into two rooms by a rough partition of boughs and sailcloth.

In the front room were the three men; the two older deep in argument, while the younger, tilted back against the wall on an improvised stool, was deeply engrossed in reading one of Tarzan's books.

Tarzan was not particularly interested in the men, however, so he sought the other window. There was the girl. How beautiful her features! How delicate her snowy skin!

She was writing at Tarzan's own table beneath the

window. Upon a pile of grasses at the far side of the
room lay the negress, asleep.

For an hour Tarzan feasted his eyes upon her while
she wrote. How he longed to speak to her, but he dared
not attempt it, for he was convinced that, like the young
man, she would not understand him, and he feared, too,
that he might frighten her away.

At length she arose, leaving her manuscript upon the
table. She went to the bed upon which had been spread
several layers of soft grasses. These she rearranged.

Then she loosened the soft mass of golden hair which
crowned her head. Like a shimmering waterfall turned
to burnished metal by a dying sun it fell about her oval
face; in waving lines, below her waist it tumbled.

Tarzan was spellbound. Then she extinguished the
lamp and all within the cabin was wrapped in Cimmerian darkness.

Still Tarzan watched without. Creeping close beneath
the window he waited, listening, for half an hour. At last
he was rewarded by the sounds of the regular breathing
within which denotes sleep.

Cautiously he intruded his hand between the meshes
of the lattice until his whole arm was within the cabin.
Carefully he felt upon the desk. At last he grasped the
manuscript upon which Jane Porter had been writing,
and as cautiously withdrew his arm and hand, holding
the precious treasure.

Tarzan folded the sheets into a small parcel which he
tucked into the quiver with his arrows. Then he melted
away into the jungle as softly and as noiselessly as a
shadow.

CHAPTER XVIII

❧❧

The Jungle Toll

EARLY the following morning Tarzan awoke, and the first thought of the new day, as the last of yesterday, was of the wonderful writing which lay hidden in his quiver.

Hurriedly he brought it forth, hoping against hope that he could read what the beautiful white girl had written there the preceding evening.

At the first glance he suffered the bitterest disappointment of his whole life; never before had he so yearned for anything as now he did for the ability to interpret a message from that golden-haired divinity who had come so suddenly and so unexpectedly into his life.

What if the message were not intended for him? It was an expression of her thoughts, and that was all sufficient for Tarzan of the Apes.

And now to be baffled by strange, uncouth characters the like of which he had never seen before! Why, they even tipped in the opposite direction from all that he had ever examined either in printed books or the difficult script of the few letters he had found.

Even the little bugs of the black book were familiar friends, though their arrangement meant nothing to him; but these bugs were new and unheard of.

For twenty minutes he pored over them, when suddenly they commenced to take familiar though distorted shapes. Ah, they were his old friends, but badly crippled.

Then he began to make out a word here and a word there. His heart leaped for joy. He could read it, and he would.

In another half hour he was progressing rapidly, and, but for an exceptional word now and again, he found it very plain sailing.

Here is what he read:

WEST COAST OF AFRICA, ABOUT 10° DEGREES
SOUTH LATITUDE. (SO MR. CLAYTON SAYS.)

February 3(?), 1909.

DEAREST HAZEL:

It seems foolish to write you a letter that you may never see, but I simply must tell somebody of our awful experiences since we sailed from Europe on the ill-fated Arrow.

If we never return to civilization, as now seems only too likely, this will at least prove a brief record of the events which led up to our final fate, whatever it may be.

As you know, we are supposed to have set out upon a scientific expedition to the Congo. Papa was presumed to entertain some wonderous theory of an unthinkably ancient civilization, the remains of which lay buried somewhere in the Congo valley. But after we were well under sail the truth came out.

It seems that an old bookworm who has a book and curio shop in Baltimore discovered between the leaves of a very old Spanish manuscript a letter written in 1550 detailing the adventures of a crew of mutineers of a Spanish galleon bound from Spain to South America with a vast treasure of "doubloons" and "pieces of eight," I suppose, for they certainly sound weird and piraty.

The writer had been one of the crew, and the letter was to his son, who was, at the very time the letter was written, master of a Spanish merchantman.

Many years had elapsed since the events the letter narrated had transpired, and the old man had become a respected citizen of an obscure Spanish town, but the love of gold was still so strong upon him that he risked all to acquaint his son with the means of attaining fabulous wealth for them both.

The writer told how when but a week out from Spain the crew had mutinied and murdered every officer and man who opposed them; but they defeated their own ends by this very act, for there was none left competent to navigate a ship at sea.

They were blown hither and thither for two months, until sick and dying of scurvy, starvation, and thirst, they had been wrecked on a small islet.

The galleon was washed high upon the beach where she went to pieces; but not before the survivors, who numbered but ten souls, had rescued one of the great chests of treasure.

This they buried well up on the island, and for three years they lived there in constant hope of being rescued.

One by one they sickened and died, until only one man was left, the writer of the letter.

The men had built a boat from the wreckage of the galleon, but having no idea where the island was located they had not dared to put to sea.

When all were dead except himself, however, the awful loneliness so weighed upon the mind of the sole survivor that he could endure it no longer, and choosing to risk death upon the open sea rather than madness on the lonely isle, he set sail in his little boat after nearly a year of solitude.

Fortunately he sailed due north, and within a week was in the track of the Spanish merchantmen plying between the West Indies and Spain, and was

*picked up by one of these vessels homeward
bound.*

*The story he told was merely one of shipwreck in
which all but a few had perished, the balance, except himself, dying after they reached the island. He
did not mention the mutiny or the chest of buried
treasure.*

*The master of the merchantman assured him that
from the position at which they had picked him up,
and the prevailing winds for the past week he could
have been on no other island than one of the Cape
Verde group, which lie off the West Coast of Africa
in about 16° or 17° north latitude.*

*His letter described the island minutely, as well as
the location of the treasure, and was accompanied
by the crudest, funniest little old map you ever saw;
with trees and rocks all marked by scrawly X's to
show the exact spot where the treasure had been
buried.*

*When Papa explained the real nature of the expe-
dition, my heart sank, for I know so well how vision-
ary and impractical the poor dear has always been
that I feared he had again been duped; especially
when he told me he had paid a thousand dollars for
the letter and map.*

*To add to my distress, I learned that he had bor-
rowed ten thousand dollars more from Robert
Canler, and had given his notes for the amount.*

*Mr. Canler had asked for no security, and you
know, dearie, what that will mean for me if Papa
cannot meet them. Oh, how I detest that man!*

*We all tried to look on the bright side of things,
but Mr. Philander, and Mr. Clayton—he joined us
in London just for the adventure—both felt as
skeptical as I.*

*Well, to make a long story short, we found the is-
land and the treasure—a great iron-bound oak
chest, wrapped in many layers of oiled sailcloth,*

and as strong and firm as when it had been buried nearly two hundred years ago.

It was simply filled with gold coin, and was so heavy that four men bent beneath its weight.

The horrid thing seems to bring nothing but murder and misfortune to those who have to do with it, for three days after we sailed from the Cape Verde Islands our own crew mutinied and killed every one of their officers.

Oh, it was the most terrifying experience one could imagine—I cannot even write of it.

They were going to kill us too, but one of them, the leader, named King, would not let them, and so they sailed south along the coast to a lonely spot where they found a good harbor, and here they landed and have left us.

They sailed away with the treasure to-day, but Mr. Clayton says they will meet with a fate similar to the mutineers of the ancient galleon, because King, the only man aboard who knew aught of navigation, was murdered on the beach by one of the men the day we landed.

I wish you could know Mr. Clayton; he is the dearest fellow imaginable, and unless I am mistaken he has fallen very much in love with poor little me.

He is the only son of Lord Greystoke, and some day will inherit the title and estates. In addition, he is wealthy in his own right, but the fact that he is going to be an English Lord makes me very sad— you know what my sentiments have always been relative to American girls who married titled foreigners. Oh, if he were only a plain American gentleman!

But it isn't his fault, poor fellow, and in everything except birth he would do credit to my darling old country, and that is the greatest compliment I know how to pay any man.

We have had the most weird experiences since we

were landed here. Papa and Mr. Philander lost in the jungle, and chased by a real lion.

Mr. Clayton lost, and attacked twice by wild beasts. Esmeralda and I cornered in an old cabin by a perfectly awful man-eating lioness. Oh, it was simply "terrifical," as Esmeralda would say.

But the strangest part of it all is the wonderful creature who rescued us. I have not seen him, but Mr. Clayton and Papa and Mr. Philander have, and they say that he is a perfectly godlike white man tanned to a dusky brown; with the strength of a wild elephant, the agility of a monkey, and the bravery of a lion.

He speaks no English and vanishes as quickly and as mysteriously after he has performed some valorous deed, as though he were a disembodied spirit.

Then we have another weird neighbor, who printed a beautiful sign in English and tacked it on the door of his cabin, which we have preëmpted, warning us to destroy none of his belongings, and signing himself "Tarzan of the Apes."

We have never seen him, though we think he is about, for one of the sailors, who was going to shoot Mr. Clayton in the back, received a spear in his shoulder from some unseen hand in the jungle.

The sailors left us but a meager supply of food, so, as we have only a single revolver with but three cartridges left in it, we do not know how we can procure meat, though Mr. Philander says that we can exist indefinitely on the wild fruit and nuts which abound in the jungle.

I am very tired now, so I shall go to my funny bed of grasses which Mr. Clayton gathered for me, but will add to this from day to day as things happen.

Lovingly,

JANE PORTER.

TO HAZEL STRONG, BALTIMORE, MD.

Tarzan sat in a brown study for a long time after he finished reading the letter. It was filled with so many new and wonderful things that his brain was in a whirl as he attempted to digest them all.

So they did not know that he was Tarzan of the Apes. He would tell them.

In his tree he had constructed a rude shelter of leaves and boughs, beneath which, protected from the rain, he had placed the few treasures brought from the cabin. Among these were some pencils.

He took one, and beneath Jane Porter's signature he wrote:

I am Tarzan of the Apes

He thought that would be sufficient. Later he would return the letter to the cabin.

In the matter of food, thought Tarzan, they had no need to worry—he would provide, and he did.

The next morning Jane Porter found her missing letter in the exact spot from which it had disappeared two nights before. She was mystified; but when she saw the printed words beneath her signature, she felt a cold, clammy chill run up her spine. She showed the letter, or rather the last sheet with the signature, to Clayton.

"And to think," she said, "that uncanny thing was probably watching me all the time that I was writing—oo! It makes me shudder just to think of it."

"But he must be friendly," reassured Clayton, "for he has returned your letter, nor did he offer to harm you, and unless I am mistaken he left a very substantial memento of his friendship outside the cabin door last night, for I just found the carcass of a wild boar there as I came out."

From then on scarcely a day passed that did not bring its offering of game or other food. Sometimes it was a young deer, again a quantity of strange, cooked food—cassava cakes pilfered from the village of Mbonga—or a boar, or leopard, and once a lion.

Tarzan derived the greatest pleasure of his life in hunting meat for these strangers. It seemed to him that no pleasure on earth could compare with laboring for the welfare and protection of the beautiful white girl.

Some day he would venture into the camp in daylight and talk with these people through the medium of the little bugs which were familiar to them and to Tarzan.

But he found it difficult to overcome the timidity of the wild thing of the forest, and so day followed day without seeing a fulfillment of his good intentions.

The party in the camp, emboldened by familiarity, wandered further and yet further into the jungle in search of nuts and fruit.

Scarcely a day passed that did not find Professor Porter straying in his preoccupied indifference toward the jaws of death. Mr. Samuel T. Philander, never what one might call robust, was worn to the shadow of a shadow through the ceaseless worry and mental distraction resultant from his Herculean efforts to safeguard the professor.

A month passed. Tarzan had finally determined to visit the camp by daylight.

It was early afternoon. Clayton had wandered to the point at the harbor's mouth to look for passing vessels. Here he kept a great mass of wood, high piled, ready to be ignited as a signal should a steamer or a sail top the far horizon.

Professor Porter was wandering along the beach south of the camp with Mr. Philander at his elbow, urging him to turn his steps back before the two became again the sport of some savage beast.

The others gone, Jane Porter and Esmeralda had wandered into the jungle to gather fruit, and in their search were led further and further from the cabin.

Tarzan waited in silence before the door of the little house until they should return. His thoughts were of the beautiful white girl. They were always of her now. He wondered if she would fear him, and the thought all but caused him to relinquish his plan.

He was rapidly becoming impatient for her return, that he might feast his eyes upon her and be near her, perhaps touch her. The ape-man knew no god, but he was as near to worshipping his divinity as mortal man ever comes to worship.

While he waited he passed the time printing a message to her; whether he intended giving it to her he himself could not have told, but he took infinite pleasure in seeing his thoughts expressed in print—in which he was not so uncivilized after all. He wrote:

> *I am Tarzan of the Apes. I want you. I am yours. You are mine. We will live here together always in my house. I will bring you the best fruits, the tenderest deer, the finest meats that roam the jungle. I will hunt for you. I am the greatest of the jungle hunters. I will fight for you. I am the mightiest of the jungle fighters. You are Jane Porter, I saw it in your letter. When you see this you will know that it is for you and that Tarzan of the Apes loves you.*

As he stood, straight as a young Indian, by the door, waiting after he had finished the message, there came to his keen ears a familiar sound. It was the passing of a great ape through the lower branches of the forest. For an instant he listened intently, and then from the jungle came the agonized scream of a woman, and Tarzan of the Apes, dropping his first love letter upon the ground, shot like a panther into the forest.

Clayton, also, heard the scream, and Professor Porter and Mr. Philander, and in a few minutes they came panting to the cabin, calling out to each other a volley of excited questions as they approached. A glance within confirmed their worst fears.

Jane Porter and Esmeralda were not there.

Instantly, Clayton, followed by the two old men, plunged into the jungle, calling the girl's name aloud. For half an hour they stumbled on, until Clayton, by merest chance, came upon the prostrate form of Esmeralda.

He stooped beside her, feeling for her pulse and then listening for her heartbeats. She lived. He shook her.

"Esmeralda!" he shrieked in her ear. "Esmeralda! For God's sake, where is Miss Porter? What has happened? Esmeralda!"

Slowly the black opened her eyes. She saw Clayton. She saw the jungle about her.

"Oh, Gaberelle!" she screamed, and fainted again.

By this time Professor Porter and Mr. Philander had come up.

"What shall we do, Mr. Clayton?" asked the old professor. "Where shall we look? God could not have been so cruel as to take my little girl away from me now."

"We must arouse Esmeralda first," replied Clayton. "She can tell us what has happened. Esmeralda!" he cried again, shaking the black woman roughly by the shoulder.

"O Gaberelle, Ah wants to die!" cried the poor woman, but with eyes fast closed. "Lemme die, deah Lawd, but doan lemme see dat awrful face again. Whafer you' sen de devil 'roun' after po ole Esmeralda? She ain't done nuffin' to nobody, Lawd; hones' she ain't. She's puffickly indecent, Lawd; yas'm, 'deed she is."

"Come, come, Esmeralda," cried Clayton.

"The Lord isn't here; it's Mr. Clayton. Open your eyes." Esmeralda did as she was bade.

"O Gaberelle! T'ank de Lawd," she said.

"Where's Miss Porter? What happened?" questioned Clayton.

"Ain' Miss Jane here?" cried Esmeralda, sitting up with wonderful celerity for one of her bulk. "Oh, Lawd, now Ah 'members! It done must have tooked her away," and the negress commenced to sob, and wail her lamentations.

"What took her away?" cried Professor Porter.

"A great big gi'nt all covered with hair."

"A gorilla, Esmeralda?" questioned Mr. Philander, and the three men scarcely breathed as he voiced the horrible thought.

"Ah done thought it was de devil; but Ah guess it mus' a-been one of dem gorilephants. Oh, my po baby, my po li'l honey," and again Esmeralda broke into uncontrollable sobbing.

Clayton immediately began to look about for tracks, but he could find nothing save a confusion of trampled grasses in the close vicinity, and his woodcraft was too meager for the translation of what he did see.

All the balance of the day they sought through the jungle; but as night drew on they were forced to give up in despair and hopelessness, for they did not even know in what direction the thing had borne Jane Porter.

It was long after dark ere they reached the cabin, and a sad and grief-stricken party it was that sat silently within the little structure.

Professor Porter finally broke the silence. His tones were no longer those of the erudite pedant theorizing upon the abstract and the unknowable; but those of the man of action—determined, but tinged also by a note of indescribable hopelessness and grief which wrung an answering pang from Clayton's heart.

"I shall lie down now," said the old man, "and try to sleep. Early to-morrow, so soon as it is light, I shall take what food I can carry and continue the search until I have found Jane. I will not return without her."

His companions did not reply at once. Each was immersed in his own sorrowful thoughts, and each knew, as did the old professor, what the last words meant—Professor Porter would never return from the jungle.

At length Clayton arose and laid his hand gently upon Professor Porter's bent old shoulder.

"I shall go with you, of course," he said. "Do not tell me that I need even have said so."

"I knew that you would offer—that you would wish to go, Mr. Clayton; but you must not. Jane is beyond human assistance now. I simply go that I may face my Maker with her, and know, too, that what was once my dear little girl lies not alone and friendless in the awful jungle.

"The same vines and leaves will cover us, the same rains beat upon us; and when the spirit of her mother is abroad, it will find us together in death, as it has always found us in life.

"No; it is I alone who may go, for she was my daughter—all that was left on earth for me to love."

"I shall go with you," said Clayton simply.

The old man looked up, regarding the strong, handsome face of William Cecil Clayton intently. Perhaps he read there the love that lay in the heart beneath—the love for his daughter.

He had been too preoccupied with his own scholarly thoughts in the past to consider the little occurrences, the chance words, which would have indicated to a more practical man that these young people were being drawn more and more closely to one another. Now they came back to him, one by one.

"As you wish," he said.

"You may count on me, also," said Mr. Philander.

"No, my dear old friend," said Professor Porter. "We may not all go. It would be cruelly wicked to leave poor Esmeralda here alone, and three of us would be no more successful than one.

"There be enough dead things in the cruel forest as it is. Come—let us try to sleep a little."

CHAPTER XIX

The Call of the Primitive

FROM the time Tarzan left the tribe of great anthropoids in which he had been raised, it was torn by continual strife and discord. Terkoz proved a cruel and capricious king, so that, one by one, many of the older and weaker apes, upon whom he was particularly prone to vent his brutish nature, took their families and sought the quiet and safety of the far interior.

But at last those who remained were driven to desperation by the continued truculence of Terkoz, and it so happened that one of them recalled the parting admonition of Tarzan:

"If you have a chief who is cruel, do not do as the other apes do, and attempt, any one of you, to pit yourself against him alone. But, instead, let two or three or four of you attack him together. Then, if you will do this, no chief will dare to be other than he should be, for four of you can kill any chief who may ever be over you."

And the ape who recalled this wise counsel repeated it to several of his fellows, so that when Terkoz returned to the tribe that day he found a warm reception awaiting him.

There were no formalities. As Terkoz reached the group, five huge, hairy beasts sprang upon him.

At heart he was an arrant coward, which is the way

with bullies among apes as well as among men; so he did not remain to fight and die, but tore himself away from them as quickly as he could and fled into the sheltering boughs of the forest.

Two more attempts he made to rejoin the tribe, but on each occasion he was set upon and driven away. At last he gave it up, and turned, foaming with rage and hatred, into the jungle.

For several days he wandered aimlessly, nursing his spite and looking for some weak thing on which to vent his pent anger.

It was in this state of mind that the horrible, manlike beast, swinging from tree to tree, came suddenly upon two women in the jungle.

He was right above them when he discovered them. The first intimation Jane Porter had of his presence was when the great hairy body dropped to the earth beside her, and she saw the awful face and the snarling, hideous mouth thrust within a foot of her.

One piercing scream escaped her lips as the brute hand clutched her arm. Then she was dragged toward those awful fangs which yawned at her throat. But ere they touched that fair skin another mood claimed the anthropoid.

The tribe had kept his women. He must find others to replace them. This hairless white ape would be the first of his new household, and so he threw her roughly across his broad, hairy shoulders and leaped back into the trees, bearing Jane Porter away toward a fate a thousand times worse than death.

Esmeralda's scream of terror had mingled once with that of Jane Porter, and then, as was Esmeralda's manner under stress of emergency which required presence of mind, she swooned.

But Jane Porter did not once lose consciousness. It is true that that awful face, pressing close to hers, and the stench of the foul breath beating upon her nostrils, paralyzed her with terror; but her brain was clear, and she comprehended all that transpired.

With what seemed to her marvelous rapidity the
brute bore her through the forest, but still she did not
cry out or struggle. The sudden advent of the ape had
confused her to such an extent that she thought now
that he was bearing her toward the beach.

For this reason she conserved her energies and her
voice until she could see that they had approached near
enough to the camp to attract the succor she craved.

Poor child! Could she but have known it, she was
being borne farther and farther into the impenetrable
jungle.

The scream that had brought Clayton and the two
older men stumbling through the undergrowth had
led Tarzan of the Apes straight to where Esmeralda
lay, but it was not Esmeralda in whom his interest centered, though pausing over her he saw that she was
unhurt.

For a moment he scrutinized the ground below and
the trees above, until the ape that was in him by virtue
of training and environment, combined with the intelligence that was his by right of birth, told his wondrous
woodcraft the whole story as plainly as though he had
seen the thing happen with his own eyes.

And then he was gone again into the swaying trees,
following the high-flung spoor which no other human
eye could have detected, much less translated.

At boughs' ends, where the anthropoid swings from
one tree to another, there is most to mark the trail,
but least to point the direction of the quarry, for there
the pressure is downward always, toward the small
end of the branch, whether the ape be leaving or entering a tree; but nearer the center of the tree, where
the signs of passage are fainter, the direction is plainly
marked.

Here, on this branch, a caterpillar has been crushed
by the fugitive's great foot, and Tarzan knows instinctively where that same foot would touch in the next
stride. Here he looks to find a tiny particle of the de-

molished larva, ofttimes not more than a speck of moisture.

Again, a minute bit of bark has been upturned by the scraping hand, and the direction of the break indicates the direction of the passage. Or some great limb, or the stem of the tree itself has been brushed by the hairy body, and a tiny shred of hair tells him by the direction from which it is wedged beneath the bark that he is on the right trail.

Nor does he need to check his speed to catch these seemingly faint records of the fleeing beast.

To Tarzan they stand out boldly against all the myriad other scars and bruises and signs upon the leafy way. But strongest of all is the scent, for Tarzan is pursuing up the wind, and his trained nostrils are as sensitive as a hound's.

There are those who believe that the lower orders are specially endowed by nature with better olfactory nerves than man, but it is merely a matter of development.

Man's survival does not hinge so greatly upon the perfection of his senses. His power to reason has relieved them of many of their duties, and so they have, to some extent, atrophied, as have the muscles which move the ears and scalp, merely from disuse.

The muscles are there, about your ears and beneath your scalp, and so are the nerves which transmit sensations to your brain, but they are underdeveloped in you because you do not need them.

Not so with Tarzan of the Apes. From early infancy his survival had depended upon acuteness of eyesight, hearing, smell, touch, and taste far more than upon the more slowly developed organ of reason.

The least developed of all, in Tarzan, was the sense of taste, for he could eat luscious fruits, or raw flesh, long buried, with almost equal appreciation; but in that he differed but slightly from more civilized epicures.

Almost silently the ape-man sped on in the track of

Terkoz and his prey, but the sound of his approach reached the ears of the fleeing beast and spurred it on to greater speed.

Three miles were covered before Tarzan overtook them, and then Terkoz, seeing that further flight was futile, dropped to the ground in a small open glade, that he might turn and fight for his prize, or be free to escape unhampered if he saw that the pursuer was more than a match for him.

He still grasped Jane Porter in one great arm as Tarzan bounded like a leopard into the arena which nature had provided for this primevallike battle.

When Terkoz saw that it was Tarzan who pursued him, he jumped to the conclusion that this was Tarzan's woman, since they were of the same kind—white and hairless—and so he rejoiced at this opportunity for double revenge upon his hated enemy.

To Jane Porter the strange apparition of this godlike man was as wine to sick nerves.

From the description which Clayton and her father and Mr. Philander had given her, she knew that it must be the same wonderful creature who had saved them, and she saw in him only a protector and a friend.

But as Terkoz pushed her roughly aside to meet Tarzan's charge, and she saw the great proportions of the ape and the mighty muscles and the fierce fangs, her heart quailed. How could any animal vanquish such a mighty antagonist?

Like two charging bulls they came together, and like two wolves sought each other's throat. Against the long canines of the ape was pitted the thin blade of the man's knife.

Jane Porter—her lithe, young form flattened against the trunk of a great tree, her hands tight pressed against her rising and falling bosom, and her eyes wide with mingled horror, fascination, fear, and admiration—watched the primordial ape battle with the primeval man for possession of a woman—for her.

As the great muscles of the man's back and shoulders knotted beneath the tension of his efforts, and the huge biceps and forearm held at bay those mighty tusks, the veil of centuries of civilization and culture was swept from the blurred vision of the Baltimore girl.

When the long knife drank deep a dozen times of Terkoz' heart's blood, and the great carcass rolled lifeless upon the ground, it was a primeval woman who sprang forward with outstretched arms toward the primeval man who had fought for her and won her.

And Tarzan?

He did what no red-blooded man needs lessons in doing. He took his woman in his arms and smothered her upturned, panting lips with kisses.

For a moment Jane Porter lay there with half-closed eyes. For a moment—the first in her young life—she knew the meaning of love.

But as suddenly as the veil had been withdrawn it dropped again, and an outraged conscience suffused her face with its scarlet mantle, and a mortified woman thrust Tarzan of the Apes from her and buried her face in her hands.

Tarzan had been surprised when he had found the girl he had learned to love after a vague and abstract manner a willing prisoner in his arms. Now he was surprised that she repulsed him.

He came close to her once more and look hold of her arm. She turned upon him like a tigress, striking his great breast with her tiny hands.

Tarzan could not understand it.

A moment ago and it had been his intention to hasten Jane Porter back to her people, but that little moment was lost now in the dim and distant past of things which were but can never be again, and with it the good intention had gone to join the impossible.

Since then Tarzan of the Apes had felt a warm, lithe form close pressed to his. Hot, sweet breath against his cheek and mouth had fanned a new flame to life within his breast, and perfect lips had clung to his in burning kisses that had seared a deep brand into his soul—a brand which marked a new Tarzan.

Again he laid his hand upon her arm. Again she repulsed him. And then Tarzan of the Apes did just what his first ancestor would have done.

He took his woman in his arms and carried her into the jungle.

Early the following morning the four within the little cabin by the beach were awakened by the booming of a cannon. Clayton was the first to rush out, and there, beyond the harbor's mouth, he saw two vessels lying at anchor.

One was the *Arrow* and the other a small French cruiser. The sides of the latter were crowded with men gazing shoreward, and it was evident to Clayton, as to the others who had now joined him, that the gun which they had heard had been fired to attract their attention if they still remained at the cabin.

Both vessels lay at a considerable distance from shore, and it was doubtful if their glasses would locate the waving hats of the little party far in between the harbor's points.

Esmeralda had removed her red apron and was waving it frantically above her head; but Clayton, still fearing that even this might not be seen, hurried off toward the northern point where lay his signal pyre ready for the match.

It seemed an age to him, as to those who waited breathlessly behind, ere he reached the great pile of dry branches and underbrush.

As he broke from the dense wood and came in sight of the vessels again, he was filled with consternation to see that the *Arrow* was making sail and that the cruiser was already under way.

Quickly lighting the pyre in a dozen places, he hurried to the extreme point of the promontory, where he stripped off his shirt, and, tying it to a fallen branch, stood waving it back and forth above him.

But still the vessels continued to stand out; and he had given up all hope, when the great column of smoke, arising above the forest in one dense vertical shaft, attracted the attention of a lookout aboard the cruiser, and instantly a dozen glasses were leveled on the beach.

Presently Clayton saw the two ships come about again; and while the *Arrow* lay drifting quietly on the ocean, the cruiser steamed slowly back toward shore.

At some distance away she stopped, and a boat was lowered and dispatched toward the beach.

As it was drawn up a young officer stepped out.

"Monsieur Clayton, I presume?" he asked.

"Thank God, you have come!" was Clayton's reply. "And it may be that it is not too late even now."

"What do you mean, Monsieur?" asked the officer.

Clayton told of the abduction of Jane Porter and the need of armed men to aid in the search for her.

"Mon Dieu!" exclaimed the officer, sadly. "Yesterday and it would not have been too late. To-day and it may be better that the poor lady were never found. It is horrible, Monsieur. It is too horrible."

Other boats had now put off from the cruiser, and Clayton, having pointed out the harbor's entrance to the officer, entered the boat with him and its nose was turned toward the little landlocked bay, into which the other craft followed.

Soon the entire party had landed where stood Professor Porter, Mr. Philander and the weeping Esmeralda.

Among the officers in the last boats to put off from the cruiser was the commander of the vessel; and when he had heard the story of Jane Porter's abduction, he generously called for volunteers to accompany Professor Porter and Clayton in their search.

Not an officer or a man was there of those brave and sympathetic Frenchmen who did not quickly beg leave to be one of the expedition.

The commander selected twenty men and two officers, Lieutenant D'Arnot and Lieutenant Charpentier.

A boat was dispatched to the cruiser for provisions, ammunition, and carbines; the men were already armed with revolvers.

Then, to Clayton's inquiries as to how they had happened to anchor offshore and fire a signal gun, the commander, Captain Dufranne, explained that a month before they had sighted the *Arrow* bearing southwest under considerable canvas, and that when they had signaled her to come about she had but crowded on more sail.

They had kept her hull-up until sunset, firing several shots after her, but the next morning she was nowhere to be seen. They had then continued to cruise up and down the coast for several weeks, and had about forgotten the incident of the recent chase, when, early one morning a few days before, the lookout had descried a vessel laboring in the trough of a heavy sea and evidently entirely out of control.

As they steamed nearer to the derelict they were surprised to note that it was the same vessel that had run from them a few weeks earlier. Her forestaysail and mizzen spanker were set as though an effort had been made to hold her head up into the wind, but the sheets had parted, and the sails were tearing to ribbons in the half gale of wind.

In the high sea that was running it was a difficult and dangerous task to attempt to put a prize crew aboard her; and as no signs of life had been seen above deck, it was decided to stand by until the wind and sea abated; but just then a figure was seen clinging to the rail and feebly waving a mute signal of despair toward them.

Immediately a boat's crew was ordered out and an attempt was successfully made to board the *Arrow*. The sight that met the Frenchmen's eyes as they clambered over the ship's side was appalling.

A dozen dead and dying men rolled hither and thither upon the pitching deck, the living intermingled with the dead. Two of the corpses appeared to have been partially devoured as though by wolves.

The prize crew soon had the vessel under proper sail once more and the living members of the ill-starred company carried below to their hammocks.

The dead were wrapped in tarpaulins and lashed on deck to be identified by their comrades before being consigned to the deep.

None of the living was conscious when the Frenchmen reached the *Arrow*'s deck. Even the poor devil who had waved the single despairing signal of distress had lapsed into unconsciousness before he had learned whether it had availed or not.

It did not take the French officer long to learn what had caused the terrible condition aboard; for when water and brandy were sought to restore the men, it was found that not only was there not any of either, but not a vestige of food of any description.

He immediately signaled to the cruiser to send water, medicine, and provisions, and another boat made the perilous trip to the *Arrow*.

When restoratives had been applied several of the men regained consciousness, and then the whole story was told. That part of it we know up to the sailing of the *Arrow* after the murder of Snipes, and the burial of his body above the treasure chest.

It seems that the pursuit by the cruiser had so terrorized the mutineers that they had continued out across the Atlantic for several days after losing her; but on discovering the meager supply of water and provisions aboard, they had turned back toward the east.

With no one on board who understood navigation, discussions soon arose as to their whereabouts; and as three days' sailing to the east did not raise land, they bore off to the north, fearing that the high north winds that had prevailed had driven them south of the southern extremity of Africa. They kept on a north-northeasterly course for two days, when they were overtaken by a calm which lasted for nearly a week. Their water was gone, and in another day they would be without food.

Conditions changed rapidly from bad to worse. One man went mad and leaped overboard. Soon another opened his veins and drank his own blood.

When he died they threw him overboard also, though there were those among them who wanted to keep the corpse on board. Hunger was changing them from human beasts to wild beasts.

Two days before they had been picked up by the cruiser they had become too weak to handle the vessel, and that same day three men died. On the following morning it was seen that one of the corpses had been partially devoured.

All that day the men lay glaring at each other like beasts of prey, and the following morning two of the corpses lay almost entirely stripped of flesh.

The men were but little stronger for their ghoulish repast, for the want of water was by far the greatest agony with which they had to contend. And then the cruiser had come.

When those who could had recovered, the entire story had been told to the French commander, but the men were too ignorant to be able to tell him at just what point on the coast the professor and his party had been marooned, so the cruiser had steamed slowly along within sight of land, firing occasional signal guns and scanning every inch of the beach with glasses.

They had anchored by night so as not to neglect a particle of the shoreline, and it had happened that the preceding night had brought them off the very beach where lay the little camp they sought.

The signal guns of the afternoon before had not been heard by those on shore, it was presumed, because they had doubtless been in the thick of the jungle searching for Jane Porter, where the noise of their own crashing through the underbrush would have drowned the report of a far distant gun.

By the time the two parties had narrated their several adventures, the cruiser's boat had returned with supplies and arms for the expedition.

Within a few minutes the little body of sailors and the two French officers, together with Professor Porter and Clayton, set off upon their hopeless and ill-fated quest into the untracked jungle.

CHAPTER XX

Heredity

WHEN Jane Porter realized that she was being borne away a captive by the strange forest creature who had rescued her from the clutches of the ape, she struggled desperately to escape, but the strong arms, that held her as easily as though she had been but a day-old babe, only pressed a little more tightly.

So presently she gave up the futile effort and lay quietly, looking through half-closed lids at the face of the man who strode easily through the tangled undergrowth with her.

The face above her was one of extraordinary beauty.

A perfect type of the strongly masculine, unmarred by dissipation, or brutal or degrading passions. For, though Tarzan of the Apes was a killer of men and of beasts, he killed as the hunter kills, dispassionately, except on those rare occasions when he had killed for hate—though not the brooding, malevolent hate which marks the features of its own with hideous lines.

When Tarzan killed he more often smiled than scowled, and smiles are the foundation of beauty.

One thing the girl had noticed particularly when she had seen Tarzan rushing upon Terkoz—the vivid scarlet band upon his forehead, from above the left eye to the scalp; but now as she scanned his features she noticed that it was gone, and only a thin white line marked the spot where it had been.

As she lay more quietly in his arms Tarzan slightly relaxed his grip upon her.

Once he looked down into her eyes and smiled and the girl had to close her own to shut out the vision of that handsome, winning face.

Presently Tarzan took to the trees, and Jane Porter, wondering that she felt no fear, began to realize that in many respects she had never felt more secure in her whole life than now as she lay in the arms of this strong, wild creature, being borne, God alone knew where or to what fate, deeper and deeper into the savage fastness of the untamed forest.

When, with closed eyes, she commenced to speculate upon the future, and terrifying fears were conjured by a vivid imagination, she had but to raise her lids and look upon that noble face so close to hers to dissipate the last remnant of apprehension.

No, he could never harm her; of that she was convinced when she translated the fine features and the frank, brave eyes above her into the chivalry which they proclaimed.

On and on they went through what seemed to Jane Porter a solid mass of verdure, yet ever there appeared to open before this forest god a passage, as by magic, which closed behind them as they passed.

Scarce a branch scraped against her, yet above and below, before and behind, the view presented naught but a solid mass of inextricably interwoven branches and creepers.

As Tarzan moved steadily onward his mind was occupied with many strange and new thoughts. Here was a problem the like of which he had never encountered, and he felt rather than reasoned that he must meet it as a man and not as an ape.

The free movement through the middle terrace, which was the route he had followed for the most part, had helped to cool the ardor of the first fierce passion of his newfound love.

Now he discovered himself speculating upon the fate which would have fallen to the girl had he not rescued her from Terkoz.

He knew why the ape had not killed her, and he commenced to compare his intentions with those of Terkoz.

True, it was the order of the jungle for the male to take his mate by force; but could Tarzan be guided by the laws of the beasts? Was not Tarzan a Man? But how did men do? He was puzzled; for he did not know.

He wished that he might ask the girl, and then it came to him that she had already answered him in the futile struggle she had made to escape and to repulse him.

But now they had come to their destination, and Tarzan of the Apes with Jane Porter in his strong arms, swung lightly to the turf of the arena where the great apes held their councils and danced the wild orgy of the Dum-Dum.

Though they had come many miles, it was still but mid-afternoon, and the amphitheater was bathed in the half-light which filtered through the maze of encircling foliage.

The green turf looked soft and cool and inviting. The myriad noises of the jungle seemed far distant and hushed to a mere echo of blurred sounds, rising and falling like the surf upon a remote shore.

A feeling of dreamy peacefulness stole over Jane Porter as she sank down upon the grass where Tarzan had placed her, and as she looked up at his great figure towering above her, there was added a strange sense of perfect security.

As she watched him from beneath half-closed lids, Tarzan crossed the little circular clearing toward the trees upon the further side. She noted the graceful majesty of his carriage, the perfect symmetry of his magnificent figure and the poise of his well-shaped head upon his broad shoulders.

What a perfect creature! There could be naught of

cruelty or baseness beneath that godlike exterior. Never, she thought, had such a man strode the earth since God created the first in his own image.

With a bound Tarzan sprang into the trees and disappeared. Jane Porter wondered where he had gone. Had he left her there to her fate in the lonely jungle?

She glanced nervously about. Every vine and bush seemed but the lurking-place of some huge and horrible beast waiting to bury gleaming fangs into her soft flesh. Every sound she magnified into the stealthy creeping of a sinuous and malignant body.

How different now that he had left her!

For a few minutes, that seemed hours to the frightened girl, she sat with tense nerves waiting for the spring of the crouching thing that was to end her misery of apprehension.

She almost prayed for the cruel teeth that would give her unconsciousness and surcease from the agony of fear.

She heard a sudden, slight sound behind her. With a shriek she sprang to her feet and turned to face her end.

There stood Tarzan, his arms filled with ripe and luscious fruit.

Jane Porter reeled and would have fallen, had not Tarzan, dropping his burden, caught her in his arms. She did not lose consciousness, but she clung tightly to him, shuddering and trembling like a frightened deer.

Tarzan of the Apes stroked her soft hair, and tried to comfort and quiet her as Kala had him, when, as a little ape, he had been frightened by Sabor, the lioness, or Histah, the snake.

Once he pressed his lips lightly upon her forehead, and she did not move, but closed her eyes and sighed.

She could not analyze her feelings, nor did she wish to attempt it. She was satisfied to feel the safety of those strong arms, and to leave her future to fate; for the last few hours had taught her to trust this strange wild creature of the forest as she would have trusted but few of the men of her acquaintance.

As she thought of the strangeness of it, there commenced to dawn upon her the realization that she had, possibly, learned something else which she had never really known before—love. She wondered and then she smiled.

And still smiling, she pushed Tarzan gently away; and looking at him with a half-smiling, half-quizzical expression that made her face wholly entrancing, she pointed to the fruit upon the ground, and seated herself upon the edge of the earthen drum of the anthropoids, for hunger was asserting itself.

Tarzan quickly gathered up the fruit, and, bringing it, laid it at her feet; and then he, too, sat upon the drum beside her, and with his knife opened and prepared the various viands for her meal.

Together and in silence they ate, occasionally stealing sly glances at one another, until finally Jane Porter broke into a merry laugh in which Tarzan joined.

"I wish you spoke English," said the girl.

Tarzan shook his head, and an expression of wistful and pathetic longing sobered his laughing eyes.

Then Jane Porter tried speaking to him in French, and then in German; but she had to laugh at her own blundering attempt at the latter tongue.

"Anyway," she said to him in English, "you understand my German as well as they did in Berlin."

Tarzan had long since reached a decision as to what his future procedure should be. He had had time to recollect all that he had read of the ways of men and women in the books at the cabin. He would act as he imagined the men in the books would have acted were they in his place.

Again he arose and went into the trees, but first he tried to explain by means of signs that he would return shortly, and he did so well that Jane Porter understood and was not afraid when he had gone.

Only a feeling of loneliness came over her and she watched the point where he had disappeared, with longing eyes, awaiting his return. As before, she was apprised of his presence by a soft sound behind her, and turned to see him coming across the turf with a great armful of branches.

Then he went back again into the jungle and in a few minutes reappeared with a quantity of soft grasses and ferns. Two more trips he made until he had quite a pile of material at hand.

Then he spread the ferns and grasses upon the ground in a soft flat bed, and above it he leaned many branches together so that they met a few feet over its center. Upon these he spread layers of huge leaves of the great elephant's ear, and with more branches and more leaves he closed one end of the little shelter he had built.

Then they sat down together again upon the edge of the drum and tried to talk by signs.

The magnificent diamond locket which hung about Tarzan's neck, had been a source of much wonderment to Jane Porter. She pointed to it now, and Tarzan removed it and handed the pretty bauble to her.

She saw that it was the work of a skilled artisan and that the diamonds were of great brilliancy and superbly set, but the cutting of them denoted that they were of a former day.

She noticed too that the locket opened, and, pressing the hidden clasp, she saw the two halves spring apart to reveal in either section an ivory miniature.

One was of a beautiful woman and the other might have been a likeness of the man who sat beside her, except for a subtle difference of expression that was scarcely definable.

She looked up at Tarzan to find him leaning toward her gazing on the miniatures with an expression of astonishment. He reached out his hand for the locket and took it away from her, examining the likenesses within with unmistakable signs of surprise and new interest. His manner clearly denoted that he had never before seen them, nor imagined that the locket opened.

This fact caused Jane Porter to indulge in further

speculation, and it taxed her imagination to picture how this beautiful ornament came into the possession of a wild and savage creature of the unexplored jungles of Africa.

Still more wonderful, how it contained the likeness of one who might be a brother, or, more likely, the father of this woodland demigod who was even ignorant of the fact that the locket opened.

Tarzan was still gazing with fixity at the two faces. Presently he removed the quiver from his shoulder, and emptying the arrows upon the ground reached into the bottom of the baglike receptacle and drew forth a flat object wrapped in many soft leaves and tied with bits of long grass.

Carefully he unwrapped it, removing layer after layer of leaves until at length he held a photograph in his hand.

Pointing to the miniature of the man within the locket he handed the photograph to Jane Porter, holding the open locket beside it.

The photograph only served to puzzle the girl still more, for it was evidently another likeness of the same man whose picture rested in the locket beside that of the beautiful young woman.

Tarzan was looking at her with an expression of puzzled bewilderment in his eyes as she glanced up at him. He seemed to be framing a question with his lips.

The girl pointed to the photograph and then to the miniature and then to him, as though to indicate that she thought the likenesses were of him, but he only shook his head, and then shrugging his great shoulders, he took the photograph from her and having carefully rewrapped it, placed it again in the bottom of his quiver.

For a few moments he sat in silence, his eyes bent upon the ground, while Jane Porter held the little locket in her hand, turning it over and over in an endeavor to find some further clue that might lead to the identity of its original owner.

At length a simple explanation occurred to her.

The locket had belonged to Lord Greystoke, and the likenesses were of himself and Lady Alice.

This wild creature had simply found it in the cabin by the beach. How stupid of her not to have thought of that solution before.

But to account for the strange likeness between Lord Greystoke and this forest god—that was quite beyond her, and it is not strange that she did not imagine that this naked savage was indeed an English nobleman.

At length Tarzan looked up to watch the girl as she examined the locket. He could not fathom the meaning of the faces within, but he could read the interest and fascination upon the face of the live young creature by his side.

She noticed that he was watching her and thinking that he wished his ornament again she held it out to him. He took it from her and taking the chain in his two hands he placed it about her neck, smiling at her expression of surprise at his unexpected gift.

Jane Porter shook her head vehemently and would have removed the golden links from about her throat, but Tarzan would not let her. Taking her hands in his, when she insisted upon it, he held them tightly to prevent her.

At last she desisted and with a little laugh raised the locket to her lips, and, rising, dropped him a little curtsey.

Tarzan did not know precisely what she meant, but he guessed correctly that it was her way of acknowledging the gift, and so he rose, too, and taking the locket in his hand, stooped gravely like some courtier of old, and pressed his lips upon it where hers had rested.

It was a stately and gallant little compliment performed with the grace and dignity of utter unconsciousness of self. It was the hall-mark of his aristocratic birth, the natural outcropping of many generations of fine breeding, an hereditary instinct of graciousness which a lifetime of uncouth and savage training and environment could not eradicate.

It was growing dark now, and so they ate again of the

fruit which was both food and drink for them, and then Tarzan rose and leading Jane Porter to the little bower he had erected, motioned her to go within.

For the first time in hours a feeling of fear swept over her, and Tarzan felt her draw away as though shrinking from him.

Contact with this girl for half a day had left a very different Tarzan from the one on whom the morning's sun had risen.

Now, in every fiber of his being, heredity spoke louder than training.

He had not in one swift transition become a polished gentleman from a savage ape-man, but at last the instincts of the former predominated, and over all was the desire to please the woman he loved, and to appear well in her eyes.

So Tarzan of the Apes did the only thing he knew to assure Jane Porter of her safety. He removed his hunting knife from its sheath and handed it to her hilt first, again motioning her into the bower.

The girl understood, and taking the long knife she entered and lay down upon the soft grasses while Tarzan of the Apes stretched himself upon the ground across the entrance.

And thus the rising sun found them in the morning.

When Jane Porter awoke, she did not at first recall the strange events of the preceding day, and so she wondered at her odd surroundings—the little leafy bower, the soft grasses of her bed, the unfamiliar prospect from the opening at her feet.

Slowly the circumstances of her position crept one by one into her mind. And then a great wonderment arose in her heart—a mighty wave of thankfulness and gratitude that though she had been in such terrible danger, yet she was unharmed.

She moved to the entrance of the shelter to look for Tarzan. He was gone; but this time no fear assailed her for she knew that he would return.

In the grass at the entrance to her bower she saw the

imprint of his body where he had lain all night to guard her. She knew that the fact that he had been there was all that had permitted her to sleep in such peaceful security.

With him near, who could entertain fear? She wondered if there was another man on earth with whom a girl could feel so safe in the heart of this savage African jungle. Why even the lions and panthers had no fears for her now.

She looked up to see his lithe form drop softly from a near-by tree. As he caught her eyes upon him his face lighted with that frank and radiant smile that had won her confidence the day before.

As he approached her Jane Porter's heart beat faster and her eyes brightened as they had never done before at the approach of any man.

He had again been gathering fruit and this he laid at the entrance of her bower. Once more they sat down together to eat.

Jane Porter commenced to wonder what his plans were. Would he take her back to the beach or would he keep her here? Suddenly she realized that the matter did not seem to give her much concern. Could it be that she did not care!

She began to comprehend, also, that she was entirely contented sitting here by the side of this smiling giant eating delicious fruit in a sylvan paradise far within the remote depths of an African jungle—that she was contented and very happy.

She could not understand it. Her reason told her that she should be torn by wild anxieties, weighted by dread fears, cast down by gloomy forebodings; but instead, her heart was singing and she was smiling into the answering face of the man beside her.

When they had finished their breakfast Tarzan went to her bower and recovered his knife. The girl had entirely forgotten it. She realized that it was because she had forgotten the fear that prompted her to accept it.

Motioning her to follow, Tarzan walked toward the

trees at the edge of the arena, and taking her in one strong arm swung to the branches above.

The girl knew that he was taking her back to her people, and she could not understand the sudden feeling of loneliness and sorrow which crept over her.

For hours they swung slowly along.

Tarzan of the Apes did not hurry. He tried to draw out the sweet pleasure of that journey with those dear arms about his neck as long as possible, and so he went far south of the direct route to the beach.

Several times they halted for brief rests, which Tarzan did not need, and at noon they stopped for an hour at a little brook, where they quenched their thirst, and ate.

So it was nearly sunset when they came to the clearing, and Tarzan, dropping to the ground beside a great tree, parted the tall jungle grass and pointed out the little cabin to her.

She took him by the hand to lead him to it, that she might tell her father that this man had saved her from death and worse than death, that he had watched over her as carefully as a mother might have done.

But again the timidity of the wild thing in the face of human habitation swept over Tarzan of the Apes. He drew back, shaking his head.

The girl came close to him, looking up with pleading eyes. Somehow she could not bear the thought of his going back into the terrible jungle alone.

Still he shook his head, and finally he drew her to him very gently and stooped to kiss her, but first he looked into her eyes and waited to learn if she were pleased, or if she would repulse him.

Just an instant the girl hesitated, and then she realized the truth, and throwing her arms about his neck she drew his face to hers and kissed him—unashamed.

"I love you—I love you," she murmured.

From far in the distance came the faint sound of many guns. Tarzan and Jane Porter raised their heads.

From the cabin came Mr. Philander and Esmeralda.

From where Tarzan and the girl stood they could not see the two vessels lying at anchor in the harbor.

Tarzan pointed toward the sounds, touched his breast and pointed again. She understood. He was going, and something told her that it was because he thought her people were in danger.

Again he kissed her.

"Come back to me," she whispered. "I shall wait for you—always."

He was gone—and Jane Porter turned to walk across the clearing to the cabin.

Mr. Philander was the first to see her. It was dusk and Mr. Philander was very nearsighted.

"Quickly, Esmeralda!" he cried. "Let us seek safety within; it is a lioness. Bless me!"

Esmeralda did not bother to verify Mr. Philander's vision. His tone was enough. She was within the cabin and had slammed and bolted the door before he had finished pronouncing her name. The "Bless me" was startled out of Mr. Philander by the discovery that Esmeralda, in the exuberance of her haste, had fastened him upon the same side of the door as was the close-approaching lioness.

He beat furiously upon the heavy portal.

"Esmeralda! Esmeralda!" he shrieked. "Let me in. I am being devoured by a lion."

Esmeralda thought that the noise upon the door was made by the lioness in her attempts to pursue her, so, after her custom, she fainted.

Mr. Philander cast a frightened glance behind him.

Horrors! The thing was quite close now. He tried to scramble up the side of the cabin, and succeeded in catching a fleeting hold upon the thatched roof.

For a moment he hung there, clawing with his feet like a cat on a clothesline, but presently a piece of the thatch came away, and Mr. Philander, preceding it, was precipitated upon his back.

At the instant he fell a remarkable item of natural history leaped to his mind. If one feigns death lions and lionesses are supposed to ignore one, according to Mr. Philander's faulty memory.

So Mr. Philander lay as he had fallen, frozen into the horrid semblance of death. As his arms and legs had been extended stiffly upward as he came to earth upon his back the attitude of death was anything but impressive.

Jane Porter had been watching his antics in mild-eyed surprise. Now she laughed—a little choking, gurgle of a laugh; but it was enough. Mr. Philander rolled over upon his side and peered about. At length he discovered her.

"Jane!" he cried. "Jane Porter. Bless me!"

He scrambled to his feet and rushed toward her. He could not believe that it was she, and alive.

"Bless me! Where did you come from? Where in the world have you been? How—"

"Mercy, Mr. Philander," interrupted the girl, "I never can remember so many questions."

"Well, well," said Mr. Philander. "Bless me! I am so filled with surprise and exuberant delight at seeing you safe and well again that I scarcely know what I am saying, really. But come, tell me all that has happened to you."

CHAPTER XXI

The Village of Torture

A S the little expedition of sailors toiled through the dense jungle searching for signs of Jane Porter, the futility of their venture became more and more apparent, but the grief of the old man and the hopeless eyes of the young Englishman prevented the kindhearted D'Arnot from turning back.

He thought that there might be a bare possibility of finding her body, or the remains of it, for he was positive that she had been devoured by some beast of prey. He deployed his men into a skirmish line from the point where Esmeralda had been found, and in this extended formation they pushed their way, sweating and panting, through the tangled vines and creepers.

It was slow work. Noon found them but a few miles inland. They halted for a brief rest then, and after pushing on for a short distance further one of the men discovered a well-marked trail.

It was an old elephant track, and D'Arnot after consulting with Professor Porter and Clayton decided to follow it.

The path wound through the jungle in a northeasterly direction, and along it the column moved in single file.

Lieutenant D'Arnot was in the lead and moving at a quick pace, for the trail was comparatively open. Immediately behind him came Professor Porter, but as he could not keep pace with the younger man D'Arnot was a hundred yards in advance when suddenly a half dozen black warriors arose about him.

D'Arnot gave a warning shout to his column as the blacks closed on him, but before he could draw his revolver he had been pinioned and dragged into the jungle.

His cry had alarmed the sailors and a dozen of them sprang forward past Professor Porter, running up the trail to their officer's aid.

They did not know the cause of his outcry, only that it was a warning of danger ahead.

They had rushed past the spot where D'Arnot had been seized when a spear hurled from the jungle transfixed one of the men, and then a volley of arrows fell among them.

Raising their rifles they fired into the underbrush in the direction from which the missiles had come.

By this time the balance of the party had come up, and volley after volley was fired toward the concealed foe. It was these shots that Tarzan and Jane Porter had heard.

Lieutenant Charpentier, who had been bringing up the rear of the column, now came running to the scene, and on hearing the details of the ambuscade ordered the men to follow him, and plunged into the tangled vegetation.

In an instant they were in a hand-to-hand fight with some fifty black warriors of Mbonga's village. Arrows and bullets flew thick and fast.

Queer African knives and French gun butts mingled for a moment in savage and bloody duels, but soon the natives fled into the jungle, leaving the Frenchmen to count their losses.

Four of the twenty were dead, a dozen others were wounded, and Lieutenant D'Arnot was missing. Night was falling rapidly, and their predicament was rendered doubly worse through the fact that they could not even find the elephant trail which they had been following.

There was but one thing to do, make camp where they were until daylight. Lieutenant Charpentier ordered a clearing made and a circular abatis of underbrush constructed about the camp.

This work was not completed until long after dark, the men building a huge fire in the center of the clearing to give them light to work by.

When all was safe as could be made from the attack of wild beasts and savage men, Lieutenant Charpentier placed sentries about the little camp and the tired and hungry men threw themselves upon the ground to sleep.

The groans of the wounded, mingled with the roaring and growling of the great beasts which the noise and firelight had attracted, kept sleep, except in its most fitful form, from the tired eyes. It was a sad and hungry party that lay through the long night praying for dawn.

The blacks who had seized D'Arnot, had not waited to participate in the fight which followed, but instead had dragged their prisoner a little way through the jungle and then struck the trail further on beyond the scene of the fighting in which their fellows were engaged.

They hurried him along, the sounds of battle growing fainter and fainter as they drew away from the contestants until there suddenly broke upon D'Arnot's vision a good-sized clearing at one end of which stood a thatched and palisaded village.

It was now dusk, but the watchers at the gate saw the approaching trio and distinguished one as a prisoner ere they reached the portals.

A cry went up within the palisade. A great throng of women and children rushed out to meet the party.

And then began for the French officer the most terrifying experience which man can encounter upon earth—the reception of a white prisoner into a village of African cannibals.

To add to the fiendishness of their cruel savagery was

the poignant memory of still crueler barbarities practiced upon them and theirs by the white officers of that arch hypocrite, Leopold II of Belgium, because of whose atrocities they had fled the Congo Free State—a pitiful remnant of what once had been a mighty tribe.

They fell upon D'Arnot tooth and nail, beating him with sticks and stones and tearing at him with clawlike hands. Every vestige of clothing was torn from him, and the merciless blows fell upon his bare and quivering flesh. But not once did the Frenchman cry out in pain. A silent prayer rose to his Maker that he be quickly delivered from his torture.

But the death he prayed for was not to be so easily had. Soon the warriors beat the women away from their prisoner. He was to be saved for nobler sport than this; and the first wave of their passion having subsided they contented themselves with crying out taunts and insults, and spitting upon him.

Presently they gained the center of the village. There D'Arnot was bound securely to the great post from which no live man had ever been released.

A number of the women scattered to their several huts to fetch pots and water, while others built a row of fires on which portions of the feast were to be boiled while the balance would be slowly dried in strips for future use, as they expected the other warriors to return with many prisoners.

The festivities were delayed awaiting the return of the warriors who had remained to engage in the skirmish with the white men, so that it was quite late when all were in the village, and the dance of death commenced to circle around the doomed officer.

Half fainting from pain and exhaustion, D'Arnot watched from beneath half-closed lids what seemed but the vagary of delirium, or some horrid nightmare from which he must soon awake.

The bestial faces, daubed with color—the huge mouths and flabby hanging lips—the yellow teeth, sharp filed—the rolling, demon eyes—the shining naked bodies—the cruel spears. Surely no such creatures really existed upon earth—he must indeed be dreaming.

The savage, whirling bodies circled nearer. Now a spear sprang forth and touched his arm. The sharp pain and the feel of hot, trickling blood assured him of the awful reality of his hopeless position.

Another spear and then another touched him. He closed his eyes and held his teeth firm set—he would not cry out.

He was a soldier of France, and he would teach these beasts how an officer and a gentleman died.

Tarzan of the Apes needed no interpreter to translate the story of those distant shots. With Jane Porter's kisses still warm upon his lips he was swinging with incredible rapidity through the forest trees straight toward the village of Mbonga.

He was not interested in the location of the encounter, for he judged that that would soon be over. Those who were killed he could not aid; those who escaped would not need his assistance.

It was to those who had neither been killed nor escaped that he hastened. And he knew that he would find them by the great post in the center of Mbonga's village.

Many times had Tarzan seen Mbonga's black raiding parties return from the northward with prisoners, and always were the same scenes enacted about that grim stake, beneath the flaring light of many fires.

He knew, too, that they seldom lost much time before consummating the fiendish purpose of their captures. He doubted that he would arrive in time to do more than avenge.

Tarzan had looked with complacency upon their former orgies, only occasionally interfering for the pleasure of baiting the blacks; but heretofore their victims had been men of their own color.

To-night it was different—white men, men of Tarzan's own race—might be even now suffering the agonies of torture in that grim, jungle fortress.

On he sped. Night had fallen and he traveled high along the upper terrace where the gorgeous tropic moon lighted the dizzy pathway through the gently undulating branches of the tree tops.

Presently he caught the reflection of a distant blaze. It lay to the right of his path. It must be the light from the camp fire the two men had built before they were attacked—Tarzan knew nothing of the presence of the sailors.

So sure was Tarzan of his jungle knowledge that he did not turn from his course, but passed the glare at a distance of a half mile. It was the campfire of the Frenchmen.

In a few minutes more Tarzan swung into the trees above Mbonga's village. Ah, he was not quite too late! Or, was he? He could not tell. The figure at the stake was very still, yet the black warriors were but pricking it.

Tarzan knew their customs. The death blow had not been struck. He could tell almost to a minute how far the dance had gone.

In another instant Mbonga's knife would sever one of the victim's ears—that would mark the beginning of the end, for very shortly after only a writhing mass of mutilated flesh would remain.

There would still be life in it, but death then would be the only charity it craved.

The stake stood forty feet from the nearest tree. Tarzan coiled his rope. Then there rose suddenly above the fiendish cries of the dancing demons the awful challenge of the ape-man.

The dancers halted as though turned to stone.

The rope sped with singing whir high above the heads of the blacks. It was quite invisible in the flaring lights of the campfires.

D'Arnot opened his eyes. A huge black, standing directly before him, lunged backward as though felled by an invisible hand.

Struggling and shrieking, his body, rolling from side to side, moved quickly toward the shadows beneath the trees.

The blacks, their eyes protruding in horror, watched spellbound.

Once beneath the trees, the body rose straight into the air, and as it disappeared into the foliage above, the terrified negroes, screaming with fright, broke into a mad race for the village gate.

D'Arnot was left alone.

He was a brave man, but he had felt the short hairs bristle upon the nape of his neck when that uncanny cry rose upon the air.

As the writhing body of the black soared, as though by unearthly power, into the dense foliage of the forest, D'Arnot felt an icy shiver run along his spine, as though death had risen from a dark grave and laid a cold and clammy finger on his flesh.

As D'Arnot watched the spot where the body had entered the tree he heard the sounds of movement there.

The branches swayed as though under the weight of a man's body—there was a crash and the black came sprawling to earth again—to lie very quietly where he had fallen.

Immediately after him came a white body, but this one alighted erect.

D'Arnot saw a clean-limbed young giant emerge from the shadows into the firelight and come quickly toward him.

What could it mean? Who could it be? Some new creature of torture and destruction, doubtless.

D'Arnot waited. His eyes never left the face of the advancing man. Nor did those frank, clear eyes waver beneath his fixed gaze.

D'Arnot was reassured, but still without much hope, though he felt that that face could not mask a cruel heart.

Without a word Tarzan of the Apes cut the bonds

which held the Frenchman. Weak from suffering and loss of blood, he would have fallen but for the strong arm that caught him.

He felt himself lifted from the ground. There was a sensation as of flying, and then he lost consciousness.

CHAPTER XXII

❧❧

The Search Party

WHEN dawn broke upon the little camp of French-men in the heart of the jungle it found a sad and disheartened group.

As soon as it was light enough to see their surround-ings Lieutenant Charpentier sent men in groups of three in several directions to locate the trail, and in ten minutes it was found and the expedition was hurrying back toward the beach.

It was slow work, for they bore the bodies of six dead men, two more having succumbed during the night, and several of those who were wounded required support to move even very slowly.

Charpentier had decided to return to camp for rein-forcements, and then make an attempt to track down the natives and rescue D'Arnot.

It was late in the afternoon when the exhausted men reached the clearing by the beach, but for two of them the return brought so great a happiness that all their suffering and heartbreaking grief were forgotten on the instant.

As the little party emerged from the jungle the first person that Professor Porter and Cecil Clayton saw was Jane Porter, standing by the cabin door.

With a little cry of joy and relief she ran forward to

greet them, throwing her arms about her father's neck and bursting into tears for the first time since they had been cast upon this hideous and adventurous shore.

Professor Porter strove manfully to suppress his own emotions, but the strain upon his nerves and weakened vitality were too much for him, and at length, burying his old face in the girl's shoulder, he sobbed quietly like a tired child.

Jane Porter led him toward the cabin, and the Frenchmen turned toward the beach from which several of their fellows were advancing to meet them.

Clayton, wishing to leave father and daughter alone, joined the sailors and remained talking with the officers until their boat pulled away toward the cruiser whither Lieutenant Charpentier was bound to report the unhappy outcome of his adventure.

Then Clayton turned back slowly toward the cabin. His heart was filled with happiness. The woman he loved was safe.

He wondered by what manner of miracle she had been spared. To see her alive seemed almost unbelievable.

As he approached the cabin he saw Jane Porter coming out. When she saw him she hurried forward to meet him.

"Jane!" he cried, "God has been good to us, indeed. Tell me how you escaped—what form Providence took to save you for—us."

He had never before called her by her given name. Forty-eight hours before it would have suffused Jane Porter with a soft glow of pleasure to have heard that name from Clayton's lips—now it frightened her.

"Mr. Clayton," she said quietly, extending her hand, "first let me thank you for your chivalrous loyalty to my dear father. He has told me how noble and self-sacrificing you have been. How can we ever repay you!"

Clayton noticed that she did not return his familiar salutation, but he felt no misgivings on that score. She had been through so much. This was no time to force his love upon her, he quickly realized.

"I am already repaid," he said. "Just to see you and Professor Porter both safe, well, and together again. I do not think that I could much longer have endured the pathos of his quiet and uncomplaining grief.

"It was the saddest experience of my life, Miss Porter; and then, added to it, there was my own grief—the greatest I have ever known. But his was so hopeless—it was pitiful. It taught me that no love, not even that of a man for his wife may be so deep and terrible and self-sacrificing as the love of a father for his daughter."

The girl bowed her head. There was a question she wanted to ask, but it seemed almost sacrilegious in the face of the love of these two men, and the terrible suffering they had endured while she sat laughing and happy beside a godlike creature of the forest, eating delicious fruits and looking with eyes of love into answering eyes.

But love is a strange master, and human nature is still stranger, so she asked her question, though she was not coward enough to attempt to justify herself to her own conscience. She felt self-hate, but she asked her question nevertheless.

"Where is the forest man who went to rescue you? Why did he not return?"

"I do not understand," said Clayton. "Whom do you mean?"

"He who has saved each of us—who saved me from the gorilla."

"Oh," cried Clayton, in surprise. "It was he who rescued you? You have not told me anything of your adventure, don't you know; tell me, do."

"But the wood man," she urged. "Have you not seen him? When we heard the shots in the jungle, very faint and far away, he left me. We had just reached the clearing, and he hurried off in the direction of the fighting. I know he went to aid you."

Her tone was almost pleading—her manner tense

with suppressed emotion. Clayton could not but notice it, and he wondered, vaguely, why she was so deeply moved—so anxious to know the whereabouts of this strange creature. He did not suspect the truth, for how could he?

Yet a feeling of apprehension of some impending sorrow haunted him, and in his breast, unknown to himself, was implanted the first germ of jealousy and suspicion of the ape-man to whom he owed his life.

"We did not see him," he replied quietly. "He did not join us." And then after a moment of thoughtful pause: "Possibly he joined his own tribe—the men who attacked us." He did not know why he had said it, for he did not believe it; but love is a strange master.

The girl looked at him wide eyed for a moment.

"No!" she exclaimed vehemently, much too vehemently he thought. "It could not be. They were negroes—he is a white man—and a gentleman."

Clayton looked puzzled. The little green-eyed devil taunted him.

"He is a strange, half-savage creature of the jungle, Miss Porter. We know nothing of him. He neither speaks nor understands any European tongue—and his ornaments and weapons are those of the West Coast savages."

Clayton was speaking rapidly.

"There are no other human beings than savages within hundreds of miles, Miss Porter. He must belong to the tribes which attacked us, or to some other equally savage—he may even be a cannibal."

Jane Porter blanched.

"I will not believe it," she half whispered. "It is not true. You shall see," she said, addressing Clayton, "that he will come back and that he will prove that you are wrong. You do not know him as I do. I tell you that he is a gentleman."

Clayton was a generous and chivalrous man, but something in the girl's breathless defense of the forest man stirred him to unreasoning jealousy, so that for the instant he forgot all that they owed to this wild demigod, and he answered her with a half sneer upon his lip.

"Possibly you are right, Miss Porter," he said, "but I do not think that any of us need worry about our carrion-eating acquaintance. The chances are that he is some half-demented castaway who will forget us more quickly, but no more surely, than we shall forget him. He is only a beast of the jungle, Miss Porter."

The girl did not answer, but she felt her heart shrivel within her. Anger and hate against one we love steels our hearts, but contempt or pity leaves us silent and ashamed.

She knew that Clayton spoke merely what he thought, and for the first time she began to analyze the structure which supported her newfound love, and to subject its object to a critical examination.

Slowly she turned and walked back to the cabin. She tried to imagine her wood-god by her side in the saloon of an ocean liner. She saw him eating with his hands, tearing his food like a beast of prey, and wiping his greasy fingers upon his thighs. She shuddered.

She saw him as she introduced him to her friends—uncouth, illiterate—a boor; and the girl winced.

She had reached her room now, and as she sat upon the edge of her bed of ferns and grasses, with one hand resting upon her rising and falling bosom, she felt the hard outlines of the man's locket beneath her waist.

She drew it out, holding it in the palm of her hand for a moment with tear-blurred eyes bent upon it. Then she raised it to her lips, and crushing it there buried her face in the soft ferns, sobbing.

"Beast?" she murmured. "Then God make me a beast; for, man or beast, I am yours."

She did not see Clayton again that day. Esmeralda brought her supper to her, and she sent word to her father that she was suffering from the reaction following her adventure.

The next morning Clayton left early with the relief expedition in search of Lieutenant D'Arnot. There were two hundred armed men this time, with ten officers and two surgeons, and provisions for a week.

They carried bedding and hammocks, the latter for transporting their sick and wounded.

It was a determined and angry company—a punitive expedition as well as one of relief. They reached the site of the skirmish of the previous expedition shortly after noon, for they were now traveling a known trail and no time was lost in exploring.

From there on the elephant-track led straight to Mbonga's village. It was but two o'clock when the head of the column halted upon the edge of the clearing.

Lieutenant Charpentier, who was in command, immediately sent a portion of his force through the jungle to the opposite side of the village. Another detachment was dispatched to a point before the village gate, while he remained with the balance upon the south side of the clearing.

It was arranged that the party which was to take position to the north, and which would be the last to gain its station should commence the assault, and that their opening volley should be the signal for a concerted rush from all sides in an attempt to carry the village by storm at the first charge.

For half an hour the men with Lieutenant Charpentier crouched in the dense foliage of the jungle, waiting the signal. To them it seemed like hours. They could see natives in the fields, and others moving in and out of the village gate.

At length the signal came—a sharp rattle of musketry, and like one man, an answering volley tore from the jungle to the west and to the south.

The natives in the field dropped their implements and broke madly for the palisade. The French bullets mowed them down, and the French sailors bounded over their prostrate bodies straight for the village gate.

So sudden and unexpected the assault had been that the whites reached the gates before the frightened natives could bar them, and in another minute the village

street was filled with armed men fighting hand to hand
in an inextricable tangle.

For a few moments the blacks held their ground
within the entrance to the street, but the revolvers, rifles
and cutlasses of the Frenchmen crumpled the native
spearmen and struck down the black archers with their
bolts half-drawn.

Soon the battle turned to a wild rout, and then to
grim massacre; for the French sailors had seen bits of
D'Arnot's uniform upon several of the black warriors
who opposed them.

They spared the children and those of the women
whom they were not forced to kill in self-defense, but
when at length they stopped, panting, blood covered
and sweating, it was because there lived to oppose them
no single warrior of all the savage village of Mbonga.

Carefully they ransacked every hut and corner of the
village, but no sign of D'Arnot could they find. They
questioned the prisoners by signs, and finally one of the
sailors who had served in the French Congo found that
he could make them understand the bastard tongue that
passes for language between the whites and the more
degraded tribes of the coast, but even then they could
learn nothing definite regarding the fate of D'Arnot.

Only excited gestures and expressions of fear could
they obtain in response to their inquiries concerning their
fellow; and at last they became convinced that these
were but evidences of the guilt of these demons who
had slaughtered and eaten their comrade two nights before.

At length all hope left them, and they prepared to
camp for the night within the village. The prisoners were
herded into three huts where they were heavily guarded.
Sentries were posted at the barred gates, and finally the
village was wrapped in the silence of slumber, except for
the wailing of the native women for their dead.

The next morning they set out upon the return march.
Their original intention had been to burn the village, but

this idea was abandoned and the prisoners were left behind, weeping and moaning, but with roofs to cover them and a palisade for refuge from the beasts of the jungle.

Slowly the expedition retraced its steps of the preceding day. Ten loaded hammocks retarded its pace. In eight of them lay the more seriously wounded, while two swung beneath the weight of the dead.

Clayton and Lieutenant Charpentier brought up the rear of the column; the Englishman silent in respect for the other's grief, for D'Arnot and Charpentier had been inseparable friends since boyhood.

Clayton could not but realize that the Frenchman felt his grief the more keenly because D'Arnot's sacrifice had been so futile, since Jane Porter had been rescued before D'Arnot had fallen into the hands of the savages, and again because the service in which he had lost his life had been outside his duty and for strangers and aliens; but when he spoke of it to Lieutenant Charpentier, the latter shook his head.

"No, Monsieur," he said, "D'Arnot would have chosen to die thus. I only grieve that I could not have died for him, or at least with him. I wish that you could have known him better, Monsieur. He was indeed an officer and a gentleman—a title conferred on many, but deserved by so few.

"He did not die futilely, for his death in the cause of a strange American girl will make us, his comrades, face our ends the more bravely, however they may come to us."

Clayton did not reply, but within him rose a new respect for Frenchmen which remained undimmed ever after.

It was quite late when they reached the cabin by the beach. A single shot before they emerged from the jungle had announced to those in camp as well as on the ship that the expedition had been too late—for it had been prearranged that when they came within a mile or two of camp one shot was to be fired to denote failure, or three for success, while two would have indicated that they had found no sign of either D'Arnot or his black captors.

So it was a solemn party that awaited their coming, and few words were spoken as the dead and wounded men were tenderly placed in boats and rowed silently toward the cruiser.

Clayton, exhausted from his five days of laborious marching through the jungle and from the effects of his two battles with the blacks, turned toward the cabin to seek a mouthful of food and then the comparative ease of his bed of grasses, after two nights in the jungle.

By the cabin door stood Jane Porter.

"The poor lieutenant?" she asked. "Did you find no trace of him?"

"We were too late, Miss Porter," he replied sadly.

"Tell me. What had happened?" she asked.

"I cannot, Miss Porter, it is too horrible."

"You do not mean that they had tortured him?" she whispered.

"We do not know what they did to him *before* they killed him," he answered, his face drawn with fatigue and the sorrow he felt for poor D'Arnot—and he emphasized the word before.

"*Before* they killed him! What do you mean? They are not—? They are not—?"

She was thinking of what Clayton had said of the forest man's probable relationship to this tribe and she could not frame the awful word.

"Yes, Miss Porter, they were—cannibals," he said, almost bitterly, for to him too had suddenly come the thought of the forest man, and the strange, unaccountable jealousy he had felt two days before swept over him once more.

And then in sudden brutality that was as unlike Clayton as courteous consideration is unlike an ape, he blurted out:

"When your forest god left you he was doubtless hurrying to the feast."

He was sorry ere the words were spoken though he did not know how cruelly they had cut the girl. His regret was for his baseless disloyalty to one who had saved the lives of every member of his party, nor ever offered harm to one.

The girl's head went high.

"There could be but one suitable reply to your assertion, Mr. Clayton," she said icily, "and I regret that I am not a man, that I might make it." She turned quickly and entered the cabin.

Clayton was an Englishman, so the girl had passed quite out of sight before he deduced what reply a man would have made.

"Upon my word," he said ruefully, "she called me a liar. And I fancy I jolly well deserved it," he added thoughtfully. "Clayton, my boy, I know you are tired out and unstrung, but that's no reason why you should make an ass of yourself. You'd better go to bed."

But before he did so he called gently to Jane Porter upon the opposite side of the sailcloth partition, for he wished to apologize, but he might as well have addressed the Sphinx. Then he wrote upon a piece of paper and shoved it beneath the partition.

Jane Porter saw the little note and ignored it, for she was very angry and hurt and mortified, but—she was a woman, and so eventually she picked it up and read it.

> *MY DEAR MISS PORTER:*
>
> *I had no reason to insinuate what I did. My only excuse is that my nerves must be unstrung—which is no excuse at all.*
>
> *Please try and think that I did not say it. I am very sorry. I would not have hurt* you, *above all others in the world. Say that you forgive me.*
> *WM. CECIL CLAYTON.*

"He did think it or he never would have said it," reasoned the girl, "but it cannot be true—oh, I know it is not true!"

One sentence in the letter frightened her: "I would not have hurt *you*, above all others in the world."

A week ago that sentence would have filled her with delight, now it depressed her.

She wished she had never met Clayton. She was sorry that she had ever seen the forest god—no, she was glad. And there was that other note she had found in the grass before the cabin the day after her return from the jungle, the love note signed by Tarzan of the Apes.

Who could be this new suitor? If he were another of the wild denizens of this terrible forest what might he not do to claim her?

"Esmeralda! Wake up," she cried.

"You make me so irritable, sleeping there peacefully when you know perfectly well that the world is filled with sorrow."

"Gaberelle!" screamed Esmeralda, sitting up. "What am it now? A hipponocerous? Where am he, Miss Jane?"

"Nonsense, Esmeralda, there is nothing. Go back to sleep. You are bad enough asleep, but you are infinitely worse awake."

"Yasm, honey, but what's de matter wif you-all, precious? You acts sorter kinder disgranulated dis ebenin'."

"Oh, Esmeralda, I'm just plain ugly to-night," said the girl. "Don't pay any attention to me—that's a dear."

"Yasm, honey; now you-all go right to sleep. Yo' nerves am all on aidge. What wif all dese ripotamuses an' man-eaten geniuses dat Marse Philander been a tellin' about—laws, it ain't no wonder we all get nervous prosecution."

Jane Porter crossed the little room, laughing, and kissing the faithful old black cheek, bid Esmeralda good night.

CHAPTER XXIII

Brother Men

WHEN D'Arnot regained consciousness, he found himself lying upon a bed of soft ferns and grasses beneath a little "A"-shaped shelter of boughs.

At his feet an opening looked out upon a green sward, and at a little distance beyond was the dense wall of jungle and forest.

He was very lame and sore and weak, and as full consciousness returned he felt the sharp torture of many cruel wounds, and the dull aching of every bone and muscle in his body as a result of the hideous beating he had received.

Even the turning of his head caused him such excruciating agony that he lay still with closed eyes for a long time.

He tried to piece out the details of his adventure prior to the time he lost consciousness to see if they would explain his present whereabouts—he wondered if he were among friends or foes.

At length he recollected the whole hideous scene at the stake, and finally recalled the strange white figure in whose arms he had sunk into oblivion.

D'Arnot wondered what fate lay in store for him now. He could neither see nor hear any signs of life about him.

The incessant hum of the jungle—the rustling of millions of leaves—the buzz of insects—the voices of the birds and monkeys seemed blended into a strangely soothing purr, as though he lay apart, far from the myriad life whose sounds came to him only as a blurred echo.

At length he fell in a quiet slumber, nor did he awake again until afternoon.

Once more he experienced the strange sense of utter bewilderment that had marked his earlier awakening, but soon he recalled the recent past, and looking through the opening at his feet he saw the figure of a man squatting on his haunches.

The broad, muscular back was turned toward him, but, tanned though it was, D'Arnot saw that it was the back of a white man, and he thanked his God.

The Frenchman called faintly. The man turned, and, rising, came toward the shelter. His face was very handsome—the handsomest, thought D'Arnot, that he had ever seen.

Stooping, he crawled into the shelter beside the wounded officer, and placed a cool hand upon his forehead.

D'Arnot spoke to him in French, but the man only shook his head—sadly, it seemed to the Frenchman.

Then D'Arnot tried English, but still the man shook his head. Italian, Spanish and German brought similar discouragement.

D'Arnot knew a few words of Norwegian, Russian, Greek, and also had a smattering of the language of one of the West Coast negro tribes—the man denied them all.

After examining D'Arnot's wounds the man left the shelter and disappeared. In half an hour he was back with fruit and a hollow gourdlike vegetable filled with water.

D'Arnot drank and ate a little. He was surprised that he had no fever. Again he tried to converse with his strange nurse, but the attempt was useless.

Suddenly the man hastened from the shelter only to return a few minutes later with several pieces of bark and—wonder of wonders—a lead pencil.

Squatting beside D'Arnot he wrote for a minute on the smooth inner surface of the bark; then he handed it to the Frenchman.

D'Arnot was astonished to see, in plain printlike characters, a message in English:

> *I am Tarzan of the Apes. Who are you? Can you read this language?*

D'Arnot seized the pencil—then he stopped. This strange man wrote English—evidently he was an Englishman.

"Yes," said D'Arnot, "I read English. I speak it also. Now we may talk. First let me thank you for all that you have done for me."

The man only shook his head and pointed to the pencil and the bark.

"Mon Dieu!" cried D'Arnot. "If you are English why is it then that you cannot speak English?"

And then in a flash it came to him—the man was a mute, possibly a deaf mute.

So D'Arnot wrote a message on the bark, in English.

> *I am Paul d'Arnot, Lieutenant in the navy of France. I thank you for what you have done for me. You have saved my life, and all that I have is yours. May I ask how it is that one who writes English does not speak it?*

Tarzan's reply filled D'Arnot with still greater wonder:

> *I speak only the language of my tribe—the great apes who were Kerchak's; and a little of the languages of Tantor, the elephant, and Numa, the lion,*

*and of the other folks of the jungle I understand.
With a human being I have never spoken, except
once with Jane Porter, by signs. This is the first time
I have spoken with another of my kind through
written words.*

D'Arnot was mystified. It seemed incredible that
there lived upon earth a full-grown man who had never
spoken with a fellow man, and still more preposterous
that such a one could read and write.

He looked again at Tarzan's message—"except once
with Jane Porter." That was the American girl who had
been carried into the jungle by a gorilla.

A sudden light commenced to dawn on D'Arnot—this
then was the "gorilla." He seized the pencil and wrote:

Where is Jane Porter?

And Tarzan replied, below:

*Back with her people in the cabin of Tarzan of
the Apes.*

*She is not dead then? Where was she? What hap-
pened to her?*

*She is not dead. She was taken by Terkoz to be
his wife; but Tarzan of the Apes took her away
from Terkoz and killed him before he could harm
her.*
*None in all the jungle may face Tarzan of the
Apes in battle, and live. I am Tarzan of the Apes—
mighty fighter.*

D'Arnot wrote:

*I am glad she is safe. It pains me to write, I will
rest a while.*

And then Tarzan:

> *Yes, rest. When you are well I shall take you back to your people.*

For many days D'Arnot lay upon his bed of soft ferns. The second day a fever had come and D'Arnot thought that it meant infection and he knew that he would die.

An idea came to him. He wondered why he had not thought of it before.

He called Tarzan and indicated by signs that he would write, and when Tarzan had fetched the bark and pencil, D'Arnot wrote:

> *Can you go to my people and lead them here? I will write a message that you may take to them, and they will follow you.*

Tarzan shook his head and taking the bark, wrote:

> *I had thought of that—the first day; but I dared not. The great apes come often to this spot, and if they found you here, wounded and alone, they would kill you.*

D'Arnot turned on his side and closed his eyes. He did not wish to die; but he felt that he was going, for the fever was mounting higher and higher. That night he lost consciousness.

For three days he was in delirium, and Tarzan sat beside him and bathed his head and hands and washed his wounds.

On the fourth day the fever broke as suddenly as it had come, but it left D'Arnot a shadow of his former self, and very weak. Tarzan had to lift him that he might drink from the gourd.

The fever had not been the result of infection as D'Arnot had thought, but one of those that commonly

attack whites in the jungles of Africa, and either kill or
leave them as suddenly as D'Arnot's had left him.

Two days after, D'Arnot was tottering about the amphitheater, Tarzan's strong arm about him to keep him
from falling.

They sat beneath the shade of a great tree, and Tarzan
found some smooth bark that they might converse.

D'Arnot wrote the first message:

> *What can I do to repay you for all that you have
> done for me?*

And Tarzan, in reply:

> *Teach me to speak the language of men.*

And so D'Arnot commenced at once, pointing out familiar objects and repeating their names in French, for
he thought that it would be easier to teach this man his
own language, since he understood it himself best of all.

It meant nothing to Tarzan, of course, for he could not
tell one language from another, so when he pointed to
the word man which he had printed upon a piece of
bark he learned from D'Arnot that it was pronounced
homme, and in the same way he was taught to pronounce ape, *singe,* and tree, *arbre.*

He was a most eager student, and in two more days
had mastered so much French that he could speak little
sentences such as: "That is a tree," "this is grass," "I am
hungry," and the like, but D'Arnot found that it was difficult to teach him the French construction upon a foundation of English.

The Frenchman wrote little lessons for him in English
and had Tarzan repeat them in French, but as a literal
translation was usually very poor French Tarzan was
often confused.

D'Arnot realized now that he had made a mistake,
but it seemed too late to go back and do it all over again
and force Tarzan to unlearn all that he had learned, es-

pecially as they were rapidly approaching a point where they would be able to converse.

On the third day after the fever broke Tarzan wrote a message asking D'Arnot if he felt strong enough to be carried back to the cabin. Tarzan was as anxious to go as D'Arnot, for he longed to see Jane Porter again.

It had been hard for him to remain with the Frenchman all these days for that very reason, and that he had unselfishly done so spoke more glowingly for his nobility of character than even did his rescuing of the French officer from Mbonga's clutches.

D'Arnot, only too willing to attempt the journey, wrote:

> But you cannot carry me all the distance through this tangled forest.

Tarzan laughed.

"*Mais oui,*" he said, and D'Arnot laughed aloud to hear the phrase that he used so often glide from Tarzan's tongue.

So they set out, D'Arnot marveling as had Clayton and Jane Porter at the wondrous strength and agility of the ape-man.

Mid-afternoon brought them to the clearing, and as Tarzan dropped to earth from the branches of the last tree his heart leaped and bounded against his ribs in anticipation of seeing Jane Porter so soon again.

No one was in sight without the cabin, and D'Arnot was perplexed to note that neither the cruiser nor the *Arrow* was at anchor in the bay.

An atmosphere of loneliness pervaded the spot, which caught suddenly at both men as they strode toward the cabin.

Neither spoke, yet both knew before they opened the closed door what they would find beyond.

Tarzan lifted the latch and pushed the great door in upon its wooden hinges. It was as they had feared. The cabin was deserted.

The men turned and looked at one another. D'Arnot knew that his people thought him dead; but Tarzan thought only of the woman who had kissed him in love and now had fled from him while he was serving one of her people.

A great bitterness rose in his heart. He would go away, far into the jungle and join his tribe. Never would he see one of his own kind again, nor could he bear the thought of returning to the cabin. He would leave that forever behind him with the great hopes he had nursed there of finding his own race and becoming a man among men.

And the Frenchman? D'Arnot? What of him? He could get along as Tarzan had. Tarzan did not want to see him more. He wanted to get away from everything that might remind him of Jane Porter.

As Tarzan stood upon the threshold brooding, D'Arnot had entered the cabin. Many comforts he saw that had been left behind. He recognized numerous articles from the cruiser—a camp oven, some kitchen utensils, a rifle and many rounds of ammunition, canned foods, blankets, two chairs and a cot—and several books and periodicals, mostly American.

"They must intend returning," thought D'Arnot.

He walked over to the table that John Clayton had built so many years before to serve as a desk, and on it he saw two notes addressed to Tarzan of the Apes.

One was in a strong masculine hand and was unsealed. The other, in a woman's hand, was sealed.

"Here are two messages for you, Tarzan of the Apes," cried D'Arnot, turning toward the door; but his companion was not there.

D'Arnot walked to the door and looked out. Tarzan was nowhere in sight. He called aloud but there was no response.

"*Mon Dieu!*" exclaimed D'Arnot, "he has left me. I feel it. He has gone back into his jungle and left me here alone."

And then he remembered the look on Tarzan's face

when they had discovered that the cabin was empty—such a look as the hunter sees in the eyes of the wounded deer he has wantonly brought down.

The man had been hard hit—D'Arnot realized it now—but why? He could not understand.

The Frenchman looked about him. The loneliness and the horror of the place commenced to get on his nerves—already weakened by the ordeal of suffering and sickness he had passed through.

To be left here alone beside this awful jungle—never to hear a human voice or see a human face—in constant dread of savage beasts and more terribly savage men—a prey to solitude and hopelessness. It was awful.

And far to the east Tarzan of the Apes was speeding through the middle terrace back to his tribe. Never had he traveled with such reckless speed. He felt that he was running away from himself—that by hurtling through the forest like a frightened squirrel he was escaping from his own thoughts. But no matter how fast he went he found them always with him.

He passed above the sinuous body of Sabor, the lioness, going in the opposite direction; toward the cabin, thought Tarzan.

What could D'Arnot do against Sabor—or if Bolgani, the gorilla, should come upon him—or Numa, the lion, or cruel Sheeta?

Tarzan paused in his flight.

"What are you, Tarzan?" he asked aloud. "An ape or a man?

"If you are an ape you will do as the apes would do—leave one of your kind to die in the jungle if it suited your whim to go elsewhere.

"If you are a man, you will return to protect your kind. You will not run away from one of your own people, because one of them has run away from you."

D'Arnot closed the cabin door. He was very nervous. Even brave men, and D'Arnot was a brave man, are sometimes frightened by solitude.

He loaded one of the rifles and placed it within easy reach. Then he went to the desk and took up the unsealed letter addressed to Tarzan.

Possibly it contained word that his people had but left the beach temporarily. He felt that it would be no breach of ethics to read this letter, so he took the enclosure from the envelope and read:

> To Tarzan of the Apes:
>   We thank you for the use of your cabin, and are sorry that you did not permit us the pleasure of seeing and thanking you in person.
>   We have harmed nothing, but have left many things for you which may add to your comfort and safety here in your lonely home.
>   If you know the strange white man who saved our lives so many times, and brought us food, and if you can converse with him, thank him, also, for his kindness.
>   We sail within the hour, never to return; but we wish you and that other jungle friend to know that we shall always thank you for what you did for strangers on your shore, and that we should have done infinitely more to reward you both had you given us the opportunity.
>   Very respectfully,
>   Wm. Cecil Clayton.

" 'Never to return,' " muttered D'Arnot, and threw himself face downward upon the cot.

An hour later he started up, listening. Something was at the door trying to enter.

D'Arnot reached for the loaded rifle and placed it to his shoulder.

Dusk was falling, and the interior of the cabin was very dark; but the man could see the latch moving from its place.

He felt his hair rising upon his scalp.

Gently the door opened until a thin crack showed something standing just without.

D'Arnot sighted along the blue barrel at the crack of the door—and then he pulled the trigger.

CHAPTER XXIV

Lost Treasure

WHEN the expedition returned, following their fruitless endeavor to succor D'Arnot, Captain Dufranne was anxious to steam away as quickly as possible, and all save Jane Porter had acquiesced.

"No," she said, determinedly, "I shall not go, nor should you, for there are two friends in that jungle who will come out of it some day expecting to find us awaiting them.

"Your officer, Captain Dufranne, is one of them, and the forest man who has saved the lives of every member of my father's party is the other.

"He left me at the edge of the jungle two days ago to hasten to the aid of my father and Mr. Clayton, as he thought, and he has stayed to rescue Lieutenant d'Arnot; of that you may be sure.

"Had he been too late to be of service to the lieutenant he would have been back before now—the fact that he is not back is sufficient proof to me that he is delayed because Lieutenant D'Arnot is wounded, or he has had to follow his captors further than the village which your sailors attacked."

"But poor D'Arnot's uniform and all his belongings were found in that village, Miss Porter," argued the captain, "and the natives showed great excitement when questioned as to the white man's fate."

"Yes, Captain, but they did not admit that he was dead, and as for his clothes and accouterments being in their possession—why more civilized peoples than these poor savage negroes strip their prisoners of every article of value whether they intend killing them or not.

"Even the soldiers of my own dear South looted not only the living but the dead. It is strong circumstantial evidence, I will admit, but it is not positive proof."

"Possibly your forest man, himself, was captured or killed by the savages," suggested Captain Dufranne.

The girl laughed.

"You do not know him," she replied, a little thrill of pride setting her nerves a-tingle at the thought that she spoke of her own.

"I admit that he would be worth waiting for, this super-man of yours," laughed the captain. "I most certainly should like to see him."

"Then wait for him, my dear Captain," urged the girl, "for I intend doing so."

The Frenchman would have been a very much surprised man could he have interpreted the true meaning of the girl's words.

They had been walking from the beach toward the cabin as they talked, and now they joined a little group sitting on camp stools in the shade of a great tree beside the cabin.

Professor Porter was there, and Mr. Philander and Clayton, with Lieutenant Charpentier and two of his brother officers, while Esmeralda hovered in the background, ever and anon venturing opinions and comments with the freedom of an old and much-indulged family servant.

The officers arose and saluted as their superior approached, and Clayton surrendered his camp stool to Jane Porter.

"We were just discussing poor Paul's fate," said Captain Dufranne. "Miss Porter insists that we have no absolute proof of his death—nor have we. And on the other hand she maintains that the continued absence of your omnipotent jungle friend indicates that D'Arnot is still in need of his services, either because he is wounded, or still is a prisoner in a more distant native village."

"It has been suggested," ventured Lieutenant Charpentier, "that the wild man may have been a member of the tribe of blacks who attacked our party—that he was hastening to aid *them*—his own people."

Jane Porter shot a quick glance at Clayton.

"It seems vastly more reasonable," said Professor Porter.

"I do not agree with you," objected Mr. Philander. "He had ample opportunity to harm us himself, or to lead his people against us. Instead, during our long residence here, he has been uniformly consistent in his rôle of protector and provider."

"That is true," interjected Clayton, "yet we must not overlook the fact that except for himself the only human beings within hundreds of miles are savage cannibals. He was armed precisely as are they, which indicates that he has maintained relations of some nature with them, and the fact that he is but one against possibly thousands suggests that these relations could scarcely have been other than friendly."

"It seems improbable then that he is not connected with them," remarked the captain; "possibly a member of this tribe."

"Or," added another of the officers, "that otherwise he could even have lived a sufficient length of time among the savage denizens of the jungle, brute and human, to have become proficient in woodcraft, or in the use of African weapons."

"You are judging him according to your own standards, gentlemen," said Jane Porter. "An ordinary white man such as any of you—pardon me, I did not mean just that—rather, a white man above the ordinary in physique and intelligence could never, I grant you, have lived a year alone and naked in this tropical jungle; but this man not only surpasses the average white man in strength and agility, but as far transcends our trained athletes and 'strong men' as they surpass a day-old babe; and his courage and ferocity in battle are those of the wild beast."

"He has certainly won a loyal champion, Miss Porter," said Captain Dufranne, laughing. "I am sure that there be none of us here but would willingly face death a hundred times in its most terrifying forms to deserve the tributes of one even half so loyal—or so beautiful."

"You would not wonder that I defend him," said the girl, "could you have seen him as I saw him, battling in my behalf with that huge hairy brute.

"Could you have seen him charge the monster as a bull might charge a grizzly—absolutely without sign of fear or hesitation—you would have believed him more than human.

"Could you have seen those mighty muscles knotting under the brown skin—could you have seen them force back those awful fangs—you too would have thought him invincible.

"And could you have seen the chivalrous treatment which he accorded a strange girl of a strange race, you would feel the same absolute confidence in him that I feel."

"You have won your suit, my fair pleader," cried the captain. "This court finds the defendant not guilty, and the cruiser shall wait a few days longer that he may have an opportunity to come and thank the divine Portia."

"Fo' da Lawd's sake, honey," cried Esmeralda. "You all doan mean to tell *me* dat youse a-goin' to stay right yere in dis yere lan' of carnivable animals when you-all done got de oppahtunity to escapade on dat crosier? Doan yo' tell me *dat,* honey."

"Why, Esmeralda! You should be ashamed of yourself," cried Jane Porter. "Is this any way to show your gratitude to the man who saved your life twice?"

"Well, Miss Jane, das all jes' as yo' say; but dat dere fores' lawd never did save us to stay yere. He done save

us so we all could get *away* from yere. Ah expec' he be
mighty peevish when he fin' we ain't got no mo' sense
'n to stay right yere after he done give us de chanct to
get away.

"Ah hoped Ah'd never have to sleep in dis yere geo-
logical garden another night and listen to all dem lonesome noises dat come out of dat jumble after dark."

"I don't blame you a bit, Esmeralda," said Clayton,
"and you certainly did hit it off right when you called
them 'lonesome' noises. I never have been able to find
the right word for them but that's it, don't you know,
lonesome noises."

"You and Esmeralda had better go and live on the
cruiser," said Jane Porter, in fine scorn. "What would
you think if you *had* to live all of your life in that jungle
as our forest man has done?"

"I'm afraid I'd be a blooming bounder as a wild man,"
laughed Clayton, ruefully. "Those noises at night make
the hair on my head bristle. I suppose that I should be
ashamed to admit it, but it's the truth."

"I don't know about that," said Lieutenant Charpentier. "I never thought much about fear and that sort of
thing—never tried to determine whether I was a coward
or a brave man; but the other night as we lay in the jungle there after poor D'Arnot was taken, and those jungle noises rose and fell around us, I began to think that I
was a coward indeed. It was not the roaring and growling of the big beasts that affected me so much as it was
the stealthy noises—the ones that you heard suddenly
close by and then listened vainly for a repetition of—the
unaccountable sounds as of a great body moving almost
noiselessly, and the knowledge that you didn't *know* how
close it was, or whether it were creeping closer after you
ceased to hear it? It was those noises—and the eyes.

"*Mon Dieu!* I shall see them in the dark forever—the
eyes that you see, and those that you don't see, but feel;
ah, they are the worst."

All were silent for a moment, and then Jane Porter
spoke.

"And he is out there," she said, in an awe-hushed whisper. "Those eyes will be glaring at him to-night, and at your comrade Lieutenant D'Arnot. Can you leave them, gentlemen, without at least rendering them the passive succor which remaining here a few days longer might insure them?"

"Tut, tut, child," said Professor Porter. "Captain Dufranne is willing to remain, and for my part I am perfectly willing, perfectly willing—as I always have been to humor your childish whims."

"We can utilize the morrow in recovering the chest, Professor," suggested Mr. Philander.

"Quite so, quite so, Mr. Philander, I had almost forgotten the treasure," exclaimed Professor Porter. "Possibly we can borrow some men from Captain Dufranne to assist us, and one of the prisoners to point out the location of the chest."

"Most assuredly, my dear Professor, we are all yours to command," said the captain.

And so it was arranged that on the next day Lieutenant Charpentier was to take a detail of ten men, and one of the mutineers of the *Arrow* as a guide, and unearth the treasure; and that the cruiser would remain for a full week in the little harbor. At the end of that time it was to be assumed that D'Arnot was truly dead, and that the forest man would not return while they remained. Then the two vessels were to leave with all the party.

Professor Porter did not accompany the treasure-seekers on the following day, but when he saw them returning empty-handed toward noon, he hastened forward to meet them—his usual preoccupied indifference entirely vanished, and in its place a nervous and excited manner.

"Where is the treasure?" he cried to Clayton, while yet a hundred feet separated them.

Clayton shook his head.

"Gone," he said, as he neared the professor.

"Gone! It cannot be. Who could have taken it?" cried Professor Porter.

"God only knows, Professor," replied Clayton. "We might have thought the fellow who guided us was lying about the location, but his surprise and consternation on finding no chest beneath the body of the murdered Snipes were too real to be feigned.

"And then our spades showed us that *something* had been buried beneath the corpse, for a hole had been there and it had been filled with loose earth."

"But who could have taken it?" repeated Professor Porter.

"Suspicion might naturally fall on the men of the cruiser," said Lieutenant Charpentier, "but for the fact that sub-lieutenant Janviers here assures me that no men have had shore leave—that none has been on shore since we anchored here except under command of an officer.

"I do not know that you would suspect our men, but I am glad that there is now no chance for suspicion to fall on them," he concluded.

"It would never have occurred to me to suspect the men to whom we owe so much," replied Professor Porter, graciously. "I would as soon suspect my dear Clayton here, or Mr. Philander."

The Frenchmen smiled, both officers and sailors. It was plain to see that a burden had been lifted from their minds.

"The treasure has been gone some time," continued Clayton. "In fact the body fell apart as we lifted it, which indicates that whoever removed the treasure did so while the corpse was still fresh, for it was intact when we first uncovered it."

"There must have been several in the party," said Jane Porter, who had joined them. "You remember that it took four men to carry it."

"By jove!" cried Clayton. "That's right. It must have been done by a party of blacks. Probably one of them saw the men bury the chest and then returned immediately after with a party of his friends, and carried it off."

"Speculation is futile," said Professor Porter, sadly.

"The chest is gone. We shall never see it more, nor the treasure that was in it."

Only Jane Porter knew what the loss meant to her father, and none there knew what it meant to her.

Six days later Captain Dufranne announced that they would sail early on the morrow.

Jane Porter would have begged for a further reprieve, had it not been that she too had begun to believe that her forest lover would return no more.

In spite of herself she began to entertain doubts and fears. The reasonableness of the arguments of these disinterested French officers commenced to convince her against her will.

That he was a cannibal she would not believe, but that he was an adopted member of some savage tribe at length seemed possible to her.

She would not admit that he could be dead. It was impossible to believe that that perfect body, so filled with triumphant life, could ever cease to harbor the vital spark—as soon believe that immortality were dust.

As Jane Porter permitted herself to harbor these thoughts, others equally unwelcome forced themselves upon her.

If he belonged to some savage tribe he had a savage wife—a dozen of them perhaps—and wild, half-caste children. The girl shuddered, and when they told her that the cruiser would sail on the morrow she was almost glad.

It was she, though, who suggested that arms, ammunition, supplies and comforts be left behind in the cabin, ostensibly for that intangible personality who had signed himself Tarzan of the Apes, and for D'Arnot should he still be living, but really, she hoped, for her forest god—even though his feet should prove of clay.

And at the last minute she left a message for him, to be transmitted by Tarzan of the Apes.

Jane Porter was the last to leave the cabin, returning on some trivial pretext, after the others had started for the boat.

She kneeled down beside the bed in which she had spent so many nights, and offered a prayer for the safety of her primeval man, and crushing his locket to her lips she murmured:

"I love you, and because I love you I believe in you. But if I did not believe, still should I love. May God have pity on my soul that I should acknowledge it. Had you come back for me, and there had been no other way, I would have gone into the jungle with you—forever."

CHAPTER XXV

The Outpost of the World

WITH the report of his gun D'Arnot saw the door fly open and the figure of a man pitch headlong within onto the cabin floor.

The Frenchman in his panic raised his gun to fire again into the prostrate form, but suddenly in the half dusk of the open door he saw that the man was white and in another instant realized that he had shot his friend and protector, Tarzan of the Apes.

With a cry of anguish D'Arnot sprang to the apeman's side, and, kneeling, lifted the black head in his arms—calling Tarzan's name aloud.

There was no response, and then D'Arnot placed his ear above the man's heart. To his joy he heard its steady beating beneath.

Carefully he lifted Tarzan to the cot, and then, after closing and bolting the door, he lighted one of the lamps and examined the wound.

The bullet had struck a glancing blow upon the skull. There was an ugly flesh wound, but no signs of a fracture of the skull.

D'Arnot breathed a sigh of relief, and went about bathing the blood from Tarzan's face.

Soon the cool water revived him, and presently he opened his eyes to look in questioning surprise at D'Arnot.

The latter had bound the wound with pieces of cloth, and as he saw that Tarzan had regained consciousness he arose and going to the table wrote a message, which he handed to the ape-man, explaining the terrible mistake he had made and how thankful he was that the wound was not more serious.

Tarzan, after reading the message, sat on the edge of the couch and laughed.

"It is nothing," he said in French, and then, his vocabulary failing him, he wrote:

> *You should have seen what Bolgani did to me, and Kerchak, and Terkoz, before I killed them— then you would laugh at such a little scratch.*

D'Arnot handed Tarzan the two messages that had been left for him.

Tarzan read the first one through with a look of sorrow on his face. The second one he turned over and over, searching for an opening—he had never seen a sealed envelope before. At length he handed it to D'Arnot.

The Frenchman had been watching him, and knew that Tarzan was puzzled over the envelope. How strange it seemed that to a full-grown white man an envelope was a mystery. D'Arnot opened it and handed the letter back to Tarzan. Sitting on a camp stool the ape-man spread the written sheet before him and read:

> To TARZAN OF THE APES:
>
> Before I leave let me add my thanks to those of Mr. Clayton for the kindness you have shown in permitting us the use of your cabin.
>
> That you never came to make friends with us had been a great regret to us. We should have liked so much to have seen and thanked our host.
>
> There is another I should like to thank also, but he did not come back, though I cannot believe that he is dead.

*I do not know his name. He is the great white
giant who wore the diamond locket upon his
breast.*

*If you know him and can speak his language
carry my thanks to him, and tell him that I waited
seven days for him to return.*

*Tell him, also, that in my home in America, in the
city of Baltimore, there will always be a welcome
for him if he cares to come.*

*I found a note you wrote me lying among the
leaves beneath a tree near the cabin. I do not know
how you learned to love me, who have never spoken to me, and I am very sorry if it is true, for I have
already given my heart to another.*

But know that I am always your friend,
JANE PORTER.

Tarzan sat with gaze fixed upon the floor for nearly
an hour. It was evident to him from the notes that they
did not know that he and Tarzan of the Apes were one
and the same.

"I have given my heart to another," he repeated over
and over again to himself.

Then she did not love him! How could she have pretended love, and raised him to such a pinnacle of hope
only to cast him down to such utter depths of despair!

Maybe her kisses were only signs of friendship. How
did he know, who knew nothing of the customs of
human beings?

Suddenly he arose, and, bidding D'Arnot good night
as he had learned to do, threw himself upon the couch
of ferns that had been Jane Porter's.

D'Arnot extinguished the lamp, and lay down upon
the cot.

For a week they did little but rest; D'Arnot coaching
Tarzan in French. At the end of that time the two men
could converse quite easily.

One night, as they were sitting within the cabin before retiring, Tarzan turned to D'Arnot.

"Where is America?" he said.

D'Arnot pointed toward the northwest.

"Many thousands of miles across the ocean," he replied. "Why?"

"I am going there."

D'Arnot shook his head.

"It is impossible, my friend," he said.

Tarzan rose, and, going to one of the cupboards, returned with a well-thumbed geography.

Turning to a map of the world, he said:

"I have never quite understood all this; explain it to me, please."

When D'Arnot had done so, showing him that the blue represented all the water on the earth, and the bits of other colors the continents and islands, Tarzan asked him to point out the spot where they now were.

D'Arnot did so.

"Now point out America," said Tarzan.

And as D'Arnot placed his finger upon North America, Tarzan smiled and laid his palm upon the page, spanning the great ocean that lay between the two continents.

"You see it is not so very far," he said; "scarce the width of my hand."

D'Arnot laughed. How could he make the man understand?

Then he took a pencil and made a tiny point upon the shore of Africa.

"This little mark," he said, "is many times larger upon this map than your cabin is upon the earth. Do you see now how very far it is?"

Tarzan thought for a long time.

"Do any white men live in Africa?" he asked.

"Yes."

"Where are the nearest?"

D'Arnot pointed out a spot on the shore just north of them.

"So close?" asked Tarzan, in surprise.

"Yes," said D'Arnot; "but it is not close."

"Have they big boats to cross the ocean?"

"Yes."

"We shall go there to-morrow," announced Tarzan.

Again D'Arnot smiled and shook his head.

"It is too far. We should die long before we reached them."

"Do you wish to stay here then forever?" asked Tarzan.

"No," said D'Arnot.

"Then we shall start to-morrow. I do not like it here longer. I should rather die than remain here."

"Well," answered D'Arnot, with a shrug, "I do not know, my friend, but that I also would rather die than remain here. If you go, I shall go with you."

"It is settled then," said Tarzan. "I shall start for America to-morrow."

"How will you get to America without money?" asked D'Arnot.

"What is money?" inquired Tarzan.

It took a long time to make him understand even imperfectly.

"How do men get money?" he asked at last.

"They work for it."

"Very well. I will work for it, then."

"No, my friend," returned D'Arnot, "you need not worry about money, nor need you work for it. I have enough for two—enough for twenty. Much more than is good for one man, and you shall have all you need if ever we reach civilization."

So on the following day they started north along the shore. Each man carrying a rifle and ammunition, besides bedding and some food and cooking utensils.

The latter seemed to Tarzan a most useless encumbrance, so he threw his away.

"But you must learn to eat cooked food, my friend," remonstrated D'Arnot. "No civilized men eat raw flesh."

"There will be time enough when I reach civilization," said Tarzan. "I do not like the things and they only spoil the taste of good meat."

For a month they traveled north. Sometimes finding food in plenty and again going hungry for days.

They saw no signs of natives nor were they molested by wild beasts. Their journey was a miracle of ease.

Tarzan asked questions and learned rapidly. D'Arnot taught him many of the refinements of civilization—even to the use of knife and fork; but sometimes Tarzan would drop them in disgust and grasp his food in his strong brown hands, tearing it with his molars like a wild beast.

Then D'Arnot would expostulate with him, saying:

"You must not eat like a brute, Tarzan, while I am trying to make a gentleman of you. *Mon Dieu!* Gentlemen do not thus—it is terrible."

Tarzan would grin sheepishly and pick up his knife and fork again, but at heart he hated them.

On the journey he told D'Arnot about the great chest he had seen the sailors bury; of how he had dug it up and carried it to the gathering place of the apes and buried it there.

"It must be the treasure chest of Professor Porter," said D'Arnot. "It is too bad, but of course you did not know."

Then Tarzan recalled the letter written by Jane Porter to her friend—the one he had stolen when they first came to his cabin, and now he knew what was in the chest and what it meant to Jane Porter.

"To-morrow we shall go back after it," he announced to D'Arnot.

"Go back?" exclaimed D'Arnot. "But, my dear fellow, we have now been three weeks upon the march. It would require three more to return to the treasure, and then, with that enormous weight which required, you say, four sailors to carry, it would be months before we had again reached this spot."

"It must be done, my friend," insisted Tarzan. "You may go on toward civilization, and I will return for the treasure. I can go very much faster alone."

"I have a better plan, Tarzan," exclaimed D'Arnot.

"We shall go on together to the nearest settlement, and there we will charter a boat and sail back down the coast for the treasure and so transport it easily.

"That will be safer and quicker and also not require us to be separated. What do you think of that plan?"

"Very well," said Tarzan. "The treasure will be there whenever we go for it; and while I could fetch it now, and catch up with you in a moon or two, I shall feel safer for you to know that you are not alone on the trail.

"When I see how helpless you are, D'Arnot, I often wonder how the human race has escaped annihilation all these ages which you tell me about. Why, Sabor, single-handed, could exterminate a thousand of you."

D'Arnot laughed.

"You will think more highly of your genus when you have seen its armies and navies, its great cities, and its mighty engineering works. Then you will realize that it is mind, and not muscle, that makes the human animal greater than the mighty beasts of your jungle.

"Alone and unarmed, a single man is no match for any of the larger beasts; but if ten men were together, they would combine their wits and their muscles against their savage enemies, while the beasts, being unable to reason, would never think of combining against the men.

"Otherwise, Tarzan of the Apes, how long would you have lasted in the savage wilderness?"

"You are right, D'Arnot," replied Tarzan, "for if Kerchak had come to Tublat's aid that night at the Dum-Dum, there would have been an end of me. But Kerchak could never think far enough ahead to take advantage of any such opportunity.

"Even Kala, my mother, could never plan ahead. She simply ate what she needed when she needed it, and if the supply was very scarce, even though she found plenty for several meals, she would never gather any ahead.

"I remember that she used to think it very silly of me to burden myself with extra food upon the march, though she was quite glad to eat it with me, if the way chanced to be barren of sustenance."

"Then you knew your mother, Tarzan?" asked D'Arnot, in surprise.

"Yes. She was a great, fine ape, larger than I, and weighing twice as much."

"And your father?" asked D'Arnot.

"I did not know him. Kala told me he was a white ape, and hairless like myself. I know now that he must have been a white man."

D'Arnot looked long and earnestly at his companion.

"Tarzan," he said at length, "it is impossible that the ape, Kala, was your mother. If such a thing can be, which I doubt, you would have inherited some of the characteristics of the ape, but you have not—you are pure man, and, I should say, the offspring of highly bred and intelligent parents."

"Have you not the slightest clue to your past?"

"Not the slightest," replied Tarzan.

"No writings in the cabin that might have told something of the lives of its original inmates?"

"I have read everything that was in the cabin with the exception of one book which I know now to be written in a language other than English. Possibly you can read it."

Tarzan fished the little black diary from the bottom of his quiver, and handed it to his companion.

D'Arnot glanced at the title page.

"It is the diary of John Clayton, Lord Greystoke, an English nobleman, and it is written in French," he said.

Then he proceeded to read the diary that had been written over twenty years before, and which recorded the details of the story which we already know—the story of adventure, hardships and sorrow of John Clayton and his wife Alice, from the day they left England until an hour before he was struck down by Kerchak.

D'Arnot read aloud. At times his voice broke, and he was forced to stop reading for the pitiful hopelessness that spoke between the lines.

Occasionally he glanced at Tarzan; but the ape-man sat upon his haunches, like a carven image, his eyes fixed upon the ground.

Only when the little babe was mentioned did the tone of the diary alter from the habitual note of despair which had crept into it by degrees after the first two months upon the shore.

Then the passages were tinged with a subdued happiness that was even sadder than the rest.

One entry showed an almost hopeful spirit.

> To-day our little boy is six months old. He is sitting in Alice's lap beside the table where I am writing—a happy, healthy, perfect child.
>
> Somehow, even against all reason, I seem to see him a grown man, taking his father's place in the world—the second John Clayton—and bringing added honors to the house of Greystoke.
>
> There—as though to give my prophecy the weight of his endorsement—he has grabbed my pen in his chubby fists and with his ink-begrimed little fingers has placed the seal of his tiny fingerprints upon the page.

And there, on the margin of the page, were the partially blurred imprints of four wee fingers and the outer half of the thumb.

When D'Arnot had finished the diary the two men sat in silence for some minutes.

"Well! Tarzan of the Apes, what think you?" asked D'Arnot. "Does not this little book clear up the mystery of your parentage?

"Why, man, you are Lord Greystoke."

Tarzan shook his head.

"The book speaks of but one child," he replied. "Its little skeleton lay in the crib, where it died crying for nourishment, from the first time I entered the cabin until Professor Porter's party buried it, with its father and mother, beside the cabin.

"No, that was the babe the book speaks of—and the mystery of my origin is deeper than before, for I have thought much of late of the possibility of that cabin having been my birthplace.

"I am afraid that Kala spoke the truth," he concluded sadly.

D'Arnot shook his head. He was unconvinced, and in his mind had sprung the determination to prove the correctness of his theory, for he had discovered the key which alone could unlock the mystery, or consign it forever to the realms of the unfathomable.

A week later the two men came suddenly upon a clearing in the forest.

In the distance were several buildings surrounded by a strong palisade. Between them and the enclosure stretched a cultivated field in which a number of negroes were working.

The two halted at the edge of the jungle.

Tarzan fitted his bow with a poisoned arrow, but D'Arnot placed a hand upon his arm.

"What would you do, Tarzan?" he asked.

"They will try to kill us if they see us," replied Tarzan. "I prefer to be the killer."

"Maybe they are friends," suggested D'Arnot.

"They are black," was Tarzan's only reply.

And again he drew back his shaft.

"You must not, Tarzan!" cried D'Arnot. "White men do not kill wantonly. *Mon Dieu!* but you have much to learn.

"I pity the ruffler who crosses you, my wild man, when I take you to Paris. I will have my hands full keeping your neck from beneath the guillotine."

Tarzan lowered his bow and smiled.

"I do not know why I should kill the blacks back there in my jungle, yet not kill them here. Suppose Numa, the lion, should spring out upon us, I should say, then, I presume: Good morning, Monsieur Numa, how is Madame Numa; eh?"

"Wait until the blacks spring upon you," replied D'Arnot, "then you may kill them. Do not assume that men are your enemies until they prove it."

"Come," said Tarzan, "let us go and present ourselves to be killed," and he started straight across the field, his head high held and the tropical sun beating upon his smooth, brown skin.

Behind him came D'Arnot, clothed in some garments which had been discarded at the cabin by Clayton when the officers of the French cruiser had fitted him out in more presentable fashion.

Presently one of the blacks looked up, and beholding Tarzan, turned, shrieking, toward the palisade.

In an instant the air was filled with cries of terror from the fleeing gardeners, but before any had reached the palisade a white man emerged from the enclosure, rifle in hand, to discover the cause of the commotion.

What he saw brought his rifle to his shoulder, and Tarzan of the Apes would have felt cold lead once again had not D'Arnot cried loudly to the man with the leveled gun:

"Do not fire! We are friends!"

"Halt, then!" was the reply.

"Stop, Tarzan!" cried D'Arnot. "He thinks we are enemies."

Tarzan dropped into a walk, and together he and D'Arnot advanced toward the white man by the gate.

The latter eyed them in puzzled bewilderment.

"What manner of men are you?" he asked, in French.

"White men," replied D'Arnot. "We have been lost in the jungle for a long time."

The man had lowered his rifle and now advanced with outstretched hand.

"I am Father Constantine of the French Mission here," he said, "and I am glad to welcome you."

"This is Monsieur Tarzan, Father Constantine," replied D'Arnot, indicating the ape-man; and as the priest extended his hand to Tarzan, D'Arnot added: "and I am Paul D'Arnot, of the French Navy."

Father Constantine took the hand which Tarzan extended in imitation of the priest's act, while the latter took in the superb physique and handsome face in one quick, keen glance.

And thus came Tarzan of the Apes to the first outpost of civilization.

For a week they remained there, and the ape-man, keenly observant, learned much of the ways of men; while black women sewed upon white duck garments for himself and D'Arnot that they might continue their journey properly clothed.

CHAPTER XXVI

The Height of Civilization

ANOTHER month brought them to a little group of buildings at the mouth of a wide river, and there Tarzan saw many boats, and was filled with the old timidity of the wild thing by the sight of many men.

Gradually he became accustomed to the strange noises and the odd ways of civilization, so that presently none might know that two short months before, this handsome Frenchman in immaculate white ducks, who laughed and chatted with the gayest of them, had been swinging naked through primeval forests to pounce upon some unwary victim, which, raw, was to fill his savage belly.

The knife and fork, so contemptuously flung aside a month before, Tarzan now manipulated as exquisitely as did the polished D'Arnot.

So apt a pupil had he been that the young Frenchman had labored assiduously to make of Tarzan of the Apes a polished gentleman in so far as nicety of manners and speech were concerned.

"God made you a gentleman at heart, my friend," D'Arnot had said; "but we want His works to show upon the exterior also."

As soon as they had reached the little port, D'Arnot had cabled his government of his safety, and requested a three-months' leave, which had been granted.

He had also cabled his bankers for funds, and the enforced wait of a month, under which both chafed, was due to their inability to charter a vessel for the return to Tarzan's jungle after the treasure.

During their stay at the coast town "Monsieur Tarzan" became the wonder of both whites and blacks because of several occurrences which to Tarzan seemed the merest of nothings.

Once a huge black, crazed by drink, had run amuck and terrorized the town, until his evil star had led him to where the black-haired French giant lolled upon the veranda of the hotel.

Mounting the broad steps, with brandishing knife, the negro made straight for a party of four men sitting at a table sipping the inevitable absinthe.

Shouting in alarm, the four took to their heels, and then the black spied Tarzan.

With a roar he charged the ape-man, while half a hundred heads peered from sheltering windows and doorways to witness the butchering of the poor Frenchman by the giant black.

Tarzan met the rush with the fighting smile that the joy of battle always brought to his lips.

As the negro closed upon him, steel muscles gripped the black wrist of the uplifted knife-hand, and a single swift wrench left the hand dangling below a broken bone.

With the pain and surprise, the madness left the black man, and as Tarzan dropped back into his chair the fellow turned, crying with agony, and dashed wildly toward the native village.

On another occasion as Tarzan and D'Arnot sat at dinner with a number of other whites, the talk fell upon lions and lion hunting.

Opinion was divided as to the bravery of the king of beasts—some maintaining that he was an arrant coward, but all agreeing that it was with a feeling of greater security that they gripped their express rifles when the monarch of the jungle roared about a camp at night.

D'Arnot and Tarzan had agreed that his past be kept secret, and so none other than the French officer knew of the ape-man's familiarity with the beasts of the jungle.

"Monsieur Tarzan has not expressed himself," said one of the party. "A man of his prowess who has spent some time in Africa, as I understand Monsieur Tarzan has, must have had experiences with lions—yes?"

"Some," replied Tarzan, dryly. "Enough to know that each of you are right in your judgment of the characteristics of the lions you have met. But one might as well judge all blacks by the fellow who ran amuck last week, or decide that all whites are cowards because one has met a cowardly white.

"There is as much individuality among the lower orders, gentlemen, as there is among ourselves.

"To-day we may go out and stumble upon a lion which is over-timid—he runs away from us. To-morrow we may meet his uncle or his twin-brother, and our friends wonder why we do not return from the jungle.

"For myself, I always assume that a lion is ferocious, and so I am never caught off my guard."

"There would be little pleasure in hunting," retorted the first speaker, "if one is afraid of the thing he hunts."

D'Arnot smiled. Tarzan afraid!

"I do not exactly understand what you mean by fear," said Tarzan. "Like lions, fear is a different thing in different men, but to me the only pleasure in the hunt is the knowledge that the hunted thing has power to harm me as much as I have to harm him.

"If I went out with a couple of rifles and a gun bearer, and twenty or thirty beaters, to hunt a lion, I should not feel that the lion had much chance, and so the pleasure of the hunt would be lessened in proportion to the increased safety which I felt."

"Then I am to take it that Monsieur Tarzan would prefer to go naked into the jungle, armed only with a jackknife, to kill the king of beasts," laughed the other, good naturedly, but with the merest touch of sarcasm in his tone.

"And a piece of rope," added Tarzan.

Just then the deep roar of a lion sounded from the distant jungle, as though to challenge whoever dared enter the lists with him.

"There is your opportunity, Monsieur Tarzan," bantered the Frenchman.

"I am not hungry," said Tarzan simply.

The men laughed, all but D'Arnot. He alone knew that a savage beast had spoken its simple reason through the lips of the ape-man.

"But you are afraid, just as any of us would be, to go out there naked, armed only with a knife and a piece of rope," said the banterer. "Is it not so?"

"No," replied Tarzan. "Only a fool performs any act without reason."

"Five thousand francs is a reason," said the other. "I wager you that amount you cannot bring back a lion from the jungle under the conditions we have named—naked and armed only with a knife and a piece of rope."

Tarzan glanced toward D'Arnot and nodded his head.

"Make it ten thousand," said D'Arnot.

"Done," replied the other.

Tarzan arose.

"I shall have to leave my clothes at the edge of the settlement, so that if I do not return before daylight I shall have something to wear through the streets."

"You are not going now," exclaimed the wagerer—"at night?"

"Why not?" asked Tarzan. "Numa walks abroad at night—it will be easier to find him."

"No," said the other, "I do not want your blood upon my hands. It will be foolhardy enough if you go forth by day."

"I shall go now," replied Tarzan, and went to his room for his knife and rope.

The men accompanied him to the edge of the jungle, where he left his clothes in a small storehouse.

But when he would have entered the blackness of the

undergrowth they tried to dissuade him; and the wagerer was most insistent of all that he abandon his foolhardy venture.

"I will accede that you have won," he said, "and the ten thousand francs are yours if you will but give up this foolish attempt, which can only end in your death."

Tarzan laughed, and in another moment the jungle had swallowed him.

The men stood silent for some moments and then slowly turned and walked back to the hotel veranda.

Tarzan had no sooner entered the jungle than he took to the trees, and it was with a feeling of exultant freedom that he swung once more through the forest branches.

This was life! ah, how he loved it! Civilization held nothing like this in its narrow and circumscribed sphere, hemmed in by restrictions and conventionalities. Even clothes were a hindrance and a nuisance.

At last he was free. He had not realized what a prisoner he had been.

How easy it would be to circle back to the coast, and then make toward the south and his own jungle and cabin.

Now he caught the scent of Numa, for he was traveling upwind. Presently his quick ears detected the familiar sound of padded feet and the brushing of a huge, fur-clad body through the undergrowth.

Tarzan came quietly above the unsuspecting beast and silently stalked him until he came into a little patch of moonlight.

Then the quick noose settled and tightened about the tawny throat, and, as he had done it a hundred times in the past, Tarzan made fast the end to a strong branch and, while the beast fought and clawed for freedom, dropped to the ground behind him, and leaping upon the great back, plunged his long thin blade a dozen times into the fierce heart.

Then with his foot upon the carcass of Numa, he raised his voice in the awesome victory cry of his savage tribe.

For a moment Tarzan stood irresolute, swayed by conflicting emotions of loyalty to D'Arnot and a mighty lust for the freedom of his own jungle. At last the vision of a beautiful face, and the memory of warm lips crushed to his dissolved the fascinating picture he had been drawing of his old life.

The ape-man threw the warm carcass of Numa across his shoulders and took to the trees once more.

The men upon the veranda had sat for an hour, almost in silence.

They had tried ineffectually to converse on various subjects, and always the thing uppermost in the mind of each had caused the conversation to lapse.

"Mon Dieu," said the wagerer at length, "I can endure it no longer. I am going into the jungle with my express and bring back that madman."

"I will go with you," said one.

"And I"—"And I"—"And I," chorused the others.

As though the suggestion had broken the spell of some horrid nightmare they hastened to their various quarters, and presently were headed toward the jungle—each man heavily armed.

"God! What was that?" suddenly cried one of the party, an Englishman, as Tarzan's savage cry came faintly to their ears.

"I heard the same thing once before," said a Belgian, "when I was in the gorilla country. My carriers said it was the cry of a great bull ape who has made a kill."

D'Arnot remembered Clayton's description of the awful roar with which Tarzan had announced his kills, and he half smiled in spite of the horror which filled him to think that the uncanny sound could have issued from a human throat—from the lips of his friend.

As the party stood finally near the edge of the jungle, debating as to the best distribution of their forces, they were startled by a low laugh near them, and turning, beheld advancing toward them a giant figure bearing a dead lion upon its broad shoulders.

Even D'Arnot was thunderstruck, for it seemed impossible that the man could have so quickly dispatched a lion with the pitiful weapons he had taken, or that alone he could have borne the huge carcass through the tangled jungle.

The men crowded about Tarzan with many questions, but his only answer was a laughing depreciation of his feat.

To Tarzan it was as though one should eulogize a butcher for his heroism in killing a cow, for Tarzan had killed so often for food and for self-preservation that the act seemed anything but remarkable to him. But he was indeed a hero in the eyes of these men—men accustomed to hunting big game.

Incidentally, he had won ten thousand francs, for D'Arnot insisted that he keep it all.

This was a very important item to Tarzan, who was just commencing to realize the power which lay behind the little pieces of metal and paper which always changed hands when human beings rode, or ate, or slept, or clothed themselves, or drank, or worked, or played, or sheltered themselves from the rain or cold or sun.

It had become evident to Tarzan that without money one must die. D'Arnot had told him not to worry, since he had more than enough for both, but the ape-man was learning many things and one of them was that people looked down upon one who accepted money from another without giving something of equal value in exchange.

Shortly after the episode of the lion hunt, D'Arnot succeeded in chartering an ancient tub for the coastwise trip to Tarzan's landlocked harbor.

It was a happy morning for them both when the little vessel weighed anchor and made for the open sea.

The trip to the beach was uneventful, and the morning after they dropped anchor before the cabin, Tarzan garbed once more in his jungle regalia, and carrying a spade, set out alone for the amphitheater of the apes where lay the treasure.

Late the next day he returned, bearing the great chest upon his shoulder, and at sunrise the little vessel was worked through the harbor's mouth and took up her northward journey.

Three weeks later Tarzan and D'Arnot were passengers on board a French steamer bound for Lyons, and after a few days in that city D'Arnot took Tarzan to Paris.

The ape-man was anxious to proceed to America, but D'Arnot insisted that he must accompany him to Paris first, nor would he divulge the nature of the urgent necessity upon which he based his demand.

One of the first things which D'Arnot accomplished after their arrival was to arrange to visit a high official of the police department, an old friend; and to take Tarzan with him.

Adroitly D'Arnot led the conversation from point to point until the policeman had explained to the interested Tarzan many of the methods in vogue for apprehending and identifying criminals.

Not the least interesting to Tarzan was the part played by fingerprints in this fascinating science.

"But of what value are these imprints," asked Tarzan, "when, after a few years the lines upon the fingers are entirely changed by the wearing out of the old tissue and the growth of new?"

"The lines never change," replied the official. "From infancy to senility the fingerprints of an individual change only in size, except as injuries alter the loops and whorls. But if imprints have been taken of the thumb and four fingers of both hands one must needs lose all entirely to escape identification."

"It is marvelous," exclaimed D'Arnot. "I wonder what the lines upon my own fingers may resemble."

"We can soon see," replied the police officer, and ringing a bell he summoned an assistant to whom he issued a few directions.

The man left the room, but presently returned with a little hardwood box which he placed on his superior's desk.

"Now," said the officer, "you shall have your finger-prints in a second."

He drew from the little case a square of plate glass, a little tube of thick ink, a rubber roller, and a few snowy-white cards.

Squeezing a drop of ink onto the glass, he spread it back and forth with the rubber roller until the entire surface of the glass was covered to his satisfaction with a very thin and uniform layer of ink.

"Place the four fingers of your right hand upon the glass, thus," he said to D'Arnot. "Now the thumb. That is right. Now place them in just the same position upon this card, here, no—a little to the right. We must leave room for the thumb and the fingers of the left hand. There, that's it. Now the same with the left."

"Come, Tarzan," cried D'Arnot, "let's see what your whorls look like."

Tarzan complied readily, asking many questions of the officer during the operation.

"Do fingerprints show racial characteristics?" he asked. "Could you determine, for example, solely from fingerprints whether the subject was Negro or Caucasian?"

"I think not," replied the officer, "although some claim that those of the negro are less complex."

"Could the fingerprints of an ape be detected from those of a man?"

"Probably, because the ape's would be far simpler than those of the higher organism."

"But a cross between an ape and a man might show the characteristics of either progenitor?" continued Tarzan.

"Yes, I should think likely," responded the official; "but the science has not progressed sufficiently to render it exact enough in such matters. I should hate to trust its findings further than to differentiate between individuals.

"There it is absolute. No two people born into the world probably have ever had identical lines upon all their digits. It is very doubtful if any single fingerprint will ever be exactly duplicated by any finger other than the one which originally made it."

"Does the comparison require much time or labor?" asked D'Arnot.

"Ordinarily but a few moments, if the impressions are distinct."

D'Arnot drew a little black book from his pocket and commenced turning the pages.

Tarzan looked at the book in surprise. How did D'Arnot come to have his book?

Presently D'Arnot stopped at a page on which were five tiny little smudges.

He handed the open book to the policeman.

"Are these imprints similar to mine or Monsieur Tarzan's or can you say that they are identical with either?"

The officer drew a powerful glass from his desk and examined all three specimens carefully, making notations meanwhile upon a pad of paper.

Tarzan realized now what was the meaning of their visit to the police officer.

The answer to his life's riddle lay in these tiny marks.

With tense nerves he sat leaning forward in his chair, but suddenly he relaxed and dropped back, smiling.

D'Arnot looked at him in surprise.

"You forget that for twenty years the dead body of the child who made those fingerprints lay in the cabin of his father, and that all my life I have seen it lying there," said Tarzan bitterly.

The policeman looked up in astonishment.

"Go ahead, Captain, with your examination," said D'Arnot, "we will tell you the story later—provided Monsieur Tarzan is agreeable."

Tarzan nodded his head.

"But you are mad, my dear D'Arnot," he insisted. "Those little fingers are buried on the west coast of Africa."

"I do not know as to that, Tarzan," replied D'Arnot. "It is possible, but if you are not the son of John Clayton then how in heaven's name did you come into that godforsaken jungle where no white man other than John Clayton had ever set foot?"

"You forget—Kala," said Tarzan.

"I do not even consider her," replied D'Arnot.

The friends had walked to the broad window overlooking the boulevard as they talked. For some time they stood there gazing out upon the busy throng beneath, each wrapped in his own thoughts.

"It takes some time to compare fingerprints," thought D'Arnot, turning to look at the police officer.

To his astonishment he saw the official leaning back in his chair hastily scanning the contents of the little black diary.

D'Arnot coughed. The policeman looked up, and, catching his eye, raised his finger to admonish silence.

D'Arnot turned back to the window, and presently the police officer spoke.

"Gentlemen," he said.

Both turned toward him.

"There is evidently a great deal at stake which must hinge to a greater or lesser extent upon the absolute correctness of this comparison. I therefore ask that you leave the entire matter in my hands until Monsieur Desquerc, our expert, returns. It will be but a matter of a few days."

"I had hoped to know at once," said D'Arnot. "Monsieur Tarzan sails for America to-morrow."

"I will promise that you can cable him a report within two weeks," replied the officer; "but what it will be I dare not say. There are resemblances, yet—well, we had better leave it for Monsieur Desquerc to solve."

CHAPTER XXVII

❧ ❧

The Giant Again

A TAXICAB drew up before an old-fashioned residence upon the outskirts of Baltimore.

A man of about forty, well built and with strong, regular features, stepped out, and paying the chauffeur, dismissed him.

A moment later the passenger was entering the library of the old home.

"Ah, Mr. Canler!" exclaimed an old man, rising to greet him.

"Good evening, my dear Professor," cried the man, extending a cordial hand.

"Who admitted you?" asked the professor.

"Esmeralda."

"Then she will acquaint Jane with the fact that you are here," said the old man.

"No, Professor," replied Canler, "for I came primarily to see you."

"Ah, I am honored," said Professor Porter.

"Professor," continued Robert Canler, with great deliberation, as though carefully weighing his words, "I have come this evening to speak with you about Jane.

"You know my aspirations, and you have been generous enough to approve my suit."

Professor Archimedes Q. Porter fidgeted in his arm-chair. The subject always made him uncomfortable. He could not understand why. Canler was a splendid match.

"But Jane," continued Canler, "I cannot understand her. She puts me off first on one ground and then another. I have always the feeling that she breathes a sigh of relief every time I bid her good-bye."

"Tut, tut," said Professor Porter. "Tut, tut, Mr. Canler. Jane is a most obedient daughter. She will do precisely as I tell her."

"Then I can still count on your support?" asked Canler, a tone of relief marking his voice.

"Certainly, sir; certainly, sir," exclaimed Professor Porter. "How could you doubt it?"

"There is young Clayton, you know," suggested Canler. "He has been hanging about for months."

"I don't know that Jane cares for him; but besides his title they say he has inherited a very considerable estate from his father, and it might not be strange—if he finally won her, unless—" and Canler paused.

"Tut, tut, Mr. Canler; unless—what?"

"Unless, you see fit to request that Jane and I be married at once," said Canler, slowly and distinctly.

"I have already suggested to Jane that it would be desirable," said Professor Porter sadly, "for we can no longer afford to keep up this house, and live as her associations demand."

"What was her reply?" asked Canler.

"She said she was not ready to marry anyone yet," replied Professor Porter, "and that we could go and live upon the farm in northern Wisconsin which her mother left her.

"It is a little more than self-supporting. The tenants have always made a living from it, and been able to send Jane a trifle besides, each year.

"She is planning on our going up there the first of the week. Philander and Mr. Clayton have already gone to get things in readiness for us."

"Clayton has gone there?" exclaimed Canler, visibly

chagrined. "Why was not I told? I would gladly have gone and seen that every comfort was provided."

"Jane feels that we are already too much in your debt, Mr. Canler," said Professor Porter.

Canler was about to reply, when the sound of footsteps came from the hall without, and Jane Porter entered the room.

"Oh, I beg your pardon!" she exclaimed, pausing on the threshold. "I thought you were alone, Papa."

"It is only I, Jane," said Canler, who had risen, "won't you come in and join the family group? We were just speaking of you."

"Thank you," said Jane Porter, entering and taking the chair Canler placed for her. "I only wanted to tell papa that Tobey is coming down from the college tomorrow to pack his books. I want you to be sure, Papa, to indicate all that you can do without until fall. Please don't carry this entire library to Wisconsin, as you would have carried it to Africa, if I had not put my foot down."

"Was Tobey here?" asked Professor Porter.

"Yes, I just left him. He and Esmeralda are exchanging religious experiences on the back porch now."

"Tut, tut, I must see him at once!" cried the professor. "Excuse me just a moment, children," and the old man hastened from the room.

As soon as he was out of earshot Canler turned to Jane Porter.

"See here, Jane," he said bluntly. "How long is this thing going on like this?

"You haven't refused to marry me, but you haven't promised either.

"I want to get the license to-morrow, so that we can be married quietly before you leave for Wisconsin. I don't care for any fuss or feathers, and I'm sure you don't either."

The girl turned cold, but she held her head bravely.

"Your father wishes it, you know," added Canler.

"Yes, I know."

She spoke scarcely above a whisper.

"Do you realize that you are buying me, Mr. Canler?" she said finally, and in a cold, level voice. "Buying me for a few paltry dollars? Of course you do, Robert Canler, and the hope of just such a contingency was in your mind when you loaned Papa the money for that harebrained escapade, which but for a most mysterious circumstance would have been surprisingly successful.

"But you, Mr. Canler, would have been the most surprised. You had no idea that the venture would succeed. You are too good a businessman for that. And you are too good a businessman to loan money for buried-treasure seeking, or to loan money without security—unless you had some special object in view.

"You knew that without security you had a greater hold on the honor of the Porters than with it. You knew the one best way to force me to marry you, without seeming to force me.

"You have never mentioned the loan. In any other man I should have thought that the prompting of a magnanimous and noble character. But you are deep, Mr. Robert Canler. I know you better than you think I know you.

"I shall certainly marry you if there is no other way, but let us understand each other once and for all."

While she spoke Robert Canler had alternately flushed and paled, and when she ceased speaking he arose, and with a cynical smile upon his strong face, said:

"You surprise me, Jane. I thought you had more self-control—more pride.

"Of course you are right. I am buying you, and I knew that you knew it, but I thought you would prefer to pretend that it was otherwise. I should have thought your self-respect and your Porter pride would have shrunk from admitting, even to yourself, that you were a bought woman.

"But have it your own way, dear girl," he added lightly. "I am going to have you, and that is all that interests me."

Without a word the girl turned and left the room.

Jane Porter was not married before she left with her father and Esmeralda for her little Wisconsin farm, and as she coldly bid Robert Canler good-bye as her train pulled out, he called to her that he would join them in a week or two.

At their destination they were met by Clayton and Mr. Philander in a huge touring car belonging to the former, and quickly whirled away through the dense northern woods toward the little farm which the girl had not visited before since childhood.

The farmhouse, which stood on a little elevation some hundred yards from the tenant house, had undergone a complete transformation during the three weeks that Clayton and Mr. Philander had been there.

The former had imported a small army of carpenters and plasterers, plumbers and painters from a distant city, and what had been but a dilapidated shell when they reached it was now a cozy little two-story house filled with every modern convenience procurable in so short a time.

"Why, Mr. Clayton, what have you done?" cried Jane Porter, her heart sinking within her as she realized the probable size of the expenditure that had been made.

"S-sh," cautioned Clayton. "Don't let your father guess. If you don't tell him he will never notice, and I simply couldn't think of him living in the terrible squalor and sordidness which Mr. Philander and I found. It was so little when I would do so much, Jane. For his sake, please, never mention it."

"But you know that we can't repay you," cried the girl. "Why do you want to put me under such terrible obligations?"

"Don't, Jane," said Clayton sadly. "If it had been just you, believe me, I wouldn't have done it, for I knew from the start that it would only hurt me in your eyes, but I couldn't think of that dear old man living in the hole we found here.

"Won't you please believe that I did it just for him and give me that little crumb of pleasure at least?"

"I do believe you, Mr. Clayton," said the girl, "because I know you are big enough and generous enough to have done it just for him—and, oh, Cecil, I wish I might repay you as you deserve—as you would wish."

"Why can't you, Jane?"

"Because I love another."

"Canler?"

"No."

"But you are going to marry him. He told me as much before I left Baltimore."

The girl winced.

"I do not love him," she said, almost proudly.

"It is because of the money, Jane?"

She nodded.

"Then am I so much less desirable than Canler? I have money enough, and far more, for every need," he said bitterly.

"I do not love you, Cecil," she said, "but I respect you. If I must disgrace myself by such a bargain with any man, I prefer that it be one I already despise. I should loathe the man to whom I sold myself without love, whomsoever he might be.

"You will be happier," she concluded, "alone—with my respect and friendship, than with me and my contempt."

He did not press the matter further, but if ever a man had murder in his heart it was William Cecil Clayton, Lord Greystoke, when, a week later, Robert Canler drew up before the farmhouse in his purring six-cylinder.

A week passed; a tense, uneventful, but uncomfortable week for all the inmates of the little Wisconsin farmhouse.

Canler was insistent that Jane marry him at once.

At length she gave in from sheer loathing of the continued and hateful importuning.

It was agreed that on the morrow Canler was to drive to town and bring back the license and a minister.

Clayton had wanted to leave as soon as the plan was

announced, but the girl's tired, hopeless look kept him. He could not desert her.

Something might happen yet, he tried to console himself by thinking. And in his heart, he knew that it would require but a tiny spark to turn his hatred for Canler into the blood lust of the killer. Early the next morning Canler set out for town. In the east smoke could be seen lying low over the forest, for a fire had been raging for a week not far from them, but the wind still lay in the west and no danger threatened them.

About noon Jane Porter started off for a walk. She would not let Clayton accompany her. She wanted to be alone, she said, and he respected her wishes.

In the house Professor Porter and Mr. Philander were immersed in an absorbing discussion of some weighty scientific problem. Esmeralda dozed in the kitchen, and Clayton, heavy-eyed after a sleepless night, threw himself down upon the couch in the living room and soon dropped into a fitful slumber.

To the east the black smoke clouds rose higher into the heavens, suddenly they eddied, and then commenced to drift rapidly toward the west.

On and on they came. The inmates of the tenant house were gone, for it was market day, and none there was to see the rapid approach of the fiery demon.

Soon the flames had spanned the road to the south and cut off Canler's return. A little fluctuation of the wind now carried the path of the forest fire to the north, then blew back and the flames nearly stood still as though held in leash by some master hand.

Suddenly, out of the northeast, a great black car came careening down the road.

With a jolt it stopped before the cottage, and a black-haired giant leaped out to run up onto the porch. Without a pause he rushed into the house. On the couch lay Clayton. The man started in surprise, but with a bound was at the side of the sleeping man.

Shaking him roughly by the shoulder, he cried:

"My God, Clayton, are you all mad here? Don't you

know you are nearly surrounded by fire? Where is Miss Porter?"

Clayton sprang to his feet. He did not recognize the man, but he understood the words and was upon the veranda in a bound.

"Scott!" he cried, and then, dashing back into the house, "Jane! Jane! where are you?"

In an instant Esmeralda, Professor Porter and Mr. Philander had joined the two men.

"Where is Miss Jane?" cried Clayton, seizing Esmeralda by the shoulders and shaking her roughly.

"Oh, Gaberelle, Marse Clayton, she done gone for a walk."

"Hasn't she come back yet?" and, without waiting for a reply, Clayton dashed out into the yard, followed by the others.

"Which way did she go?" cried the black-haired giant of Esmeralda.

"Down dat road," cried the frightened black, pointing toward the south where a mighty wall of roaring flames shut out the view.

"Put these people in the other car," shouted the stranger to Clayton. "I saw one as I drove up—and get them out of here by the north road.

"Leave my car here. If I find Miss Porter we shall need it. If I don't, no one will need it. Do as I say," as Clayton hesitated, and then they saw the lithe figure bound away cross the clearing toward the northwest where the forest still stood, untouched by flame.

In each rose the unaccountable feeling that a great responsibility had been raised from their shoulders; a kind of implicit confidence in the power of the stranger to save Jane Porter if she could be saved.

"Who was that?" asked Professor Porter.

"I do not know," replied Clayton. "He called me by name and he knew Jane, for he asked for her. And he called Esmeralda by name."

"There was something most startling familiar about

him," exclaimed Mr. Philander, "and yet, bless me, I know I never saw him before."

"Tut, tut!" cried Professor Porter. "Most remarkable! Who could it have been, and why do I feel that Jane is safe, now that he has set out in search of her?"

"I can't tell you, Professor," said Clayton soberly, "but I know I have the same uncanny feeling.

"But come," he cried, "we must get out of here ourselves, or we shall be shut off," and the party hastened toward Clayton's machine.

When Jane Porter turned to retrace her steps homeward, she was alarmed to note how near the smoke of the forest fire seemed, and as she hastened onward, her alarm became almost a panic when she perceived that the rushing flames were rapidly forcing their way between herself and the cottage.

At length she was compelled to turn into the dense thicket and attempt to force her way to the west in an effort to circle around the flames and regain her home.

In a short time the futility of her attempt became apparent and then her one hope lay in retracing her steps to the road and flying for her life to the south toward the town.

The twenty minutes that it took her to regain the road was all that had been needed to cut off her retreat as effectually as her advance had been cut off before.

A short run down the road brought her to a horrified stand, for there before her was another wall of flame. An arm of the parent conflagration had shot out a half mile south of its mate to embrace this tiny strip of road in its implacable clutches.

Jane Porter knew that it was useless again to attempt to force her way through the undergrowth.

She had tried it once, and failed. Now she realized that it would be but a matter of minutes ere the whole space between the enemy on the north and the enemy on the south would be a seething mass of billowing flames.

Calmly the girl kneeled down in the dust of the road-way and prayed to her Maker to give her strength to meet her fate bravely, and to deliver her father and her friends from death.

She did not think to pray for deliverance for herself; for she knew there was no hope—not even God could save her now.

Suddenly she heard her name being called aloud through the forest:

"Jane! Jane Porter!" It rang strong and clear, but in a strange voice.

"Here!" she called in reply. "Here! In the roadway!"

Then through the branches of the trees she saw a figure swinging with the speed of a squirrel.

A veering of the wind blew a cloud of smoke about them and she could no longer see the man who was speeding toward her, but suddenly she felt a great arm about her. Then she was lifted up, and she felt the rushing of the wind and the occasional brush of a branch as she was borne along.

She opened her eyes.

Far below her lay the undergrowth and the hard earth.

About her was the waving foliage of the forest.

From tree to tree swung the giant figure which bore her, and it seemed to Jane Porter that she was living over in a dream the experience that had been hers in that far African jungle.

Oh, if it were but the same man who had borne her so swiftly through the tangled verdure on that other day; but that were impossible. Yet who else in all the world was there with the strength and agility to do what this man was now doing?

She stole a sudden glance at the face close to hers, and then she gave a little frightened gasp—it was he!

"My man!" she murmured. "No, it is the delirium which precedes death."

She must have spoken aloud, for the eyes that bent occasionally to hers lighted with a smile.

"Yes, your man, Jane Porter—your savage, primeval man come out of the jungle to claim his mate—the woman who ran away from him," he added almost fiercely.

"I did not run away," she whispered. "I would only consent to leave when they had waited a week for you to return."

They had come to a point beyond the fire now, and he had turned back to the clearing.

Side by side they were walking toward the cottage. The wind had changed once more and the fire was burning back upon itself—another hour like that and it would be burned out.

"Why did you not return?" she asked.

"I was nursing D'Arnot. He was badly wounded."

"Ah, I knew it!" she exclaimed.

"They said you had gone to join the blacks—that they were your people."

He laughed.

"But you did not believe them, Jane?"

"No—what shall I call you?" she asked. "What is your name?"

"I was Tarzan of the Apes when you first knew me," he said.

"Tarzan of the Apes!" she cried—"and that was your note I answered when I left?"

"Yes, whose did you think it was?"

"I did not know; only that it could not be yours, for Tarzan of the Apes had written in English, and you could not understand a word of any language."

Again he laughed.

"It is a long story, but it was I who wrote what I could not speak—and now D'Arnot has made matters worse by teaching me to speak French instead of English."

"Come," he added, "jump into my car, we must overtake your father, they are only a little way ahead."

As they drove along, he said:

"Then when you said in your note to Tarzan of the Apes that you loved another—you might have meant me?"

"I might have," she answered, simply.

"But in Baltimore—oh, how I have searched for you—they told me you would possibly be married by now. That a man named Canler had come up here to wed you. Is that true?"

"Yes."

"Do you love him?"

"No."

"Do you love me?"

She buried her face in her hands.

"I am promised to another. I cannot answer you, Tarzan of the Apes," she cried.

"You have answered. Now, tell me why you would marry one you do not love."

"My father owes him money."

Suddenly there came back to Tarzan the memory of the letter he had read—and the name Robert Canler and the hinted trouble which he had been unable to understand then.

He smiled.

"If your father had not lost the treasure you would not feel forced to keep your promise to this man Canler?"

"I could ask him to release me."

"And if he refused?"

"I have given my promise."

He was silent for a moment. The car was plunging along the uneven road at a reckless pace, for the fire showed threateningly at their right, and another change of the wind might sweep it on with raging fury across this one avenue of escape.

Finally they passed the danger point, and Tarzan reduced their speed.

"Suppose I should ask him?" ventured Tarzan.

"He would scarely accede to the demand of a stranger," said the girl. "Especially one who wanted me himself."

"Terkoz did," said Tarzan, grimly.

Jane Porter shuddered and looked fearfully up at the giant figure beside her, for she knew that he meant the great anthropoid he had killed in her defense.

"This is not an African jungle," she said. "You are no

longer a savage beast. You are a gentleman, and gentlemen do not kill in cold blood."

"I am still a wild beast at heart," he said, in a low
voice, as though to himself.

Again they were silent for a time.

"Jane Porter," said the man, at length, "if you were
free, would you marry me?"

She did not reply at once, but he waited patiently.

The girl was trying to collect her thoughts.

What did she know of this strange creature at her
side? What did he know of himself? Who was he? Who,
his parents?

Why, his very name echoed his mysterious origin and
his savage life.

He had no name. Could she be happy with this jungle
waif? Could she find anything in common with a husband whose life had been spent in the tree tops of an
African wilderness, frolicking and fighting with fierce
anthropoids; tearing his food from the quivering flank
of fresh-killed prey, sinking his strong teeth into raw
flesh, and tearing away his portion while his mates
growled and fought about him for their share?

Could he ever rise to her social sphere? Could she
bear to think of sinking to his? Would either be happy
in such a horrible misalliance?

"You do not answer," he said. "Do you shrink from
wounding me?"

"I do not know what answer to make," said Jane
Porter sadly. "I do not know my own mind."

"You do not love me, then?" he asked, in a level tone.

"Do not ask me. You will be happier without me. You
were never meant for the formal restrictions and conventionalities of society—civilization would become
irksome to you, and in a little while you would long for
the freedom of your old life—a life to which I am as totally unfitted as you to mine."

"I think I understand you," he replied quietly. "I shall
not urge you, for I would rather see you happy than to
be happy myself.

"I see now that you could not be happy with—an ape."

There was just the faintest tinge of bitterness in his voice.

"Don't," she remonstrated. "Don't say that. You do not understand."

But before she could go on a sudden turn in the road brought them into the midst of a little hamlet.

Before them stood Clayton's car surrounded by the party he had brought from the cottage.

CHAPTER XXVIII

❧

Conclusion

A T the sight of Jane Porter, cries of relief and delight broke from every lip, and as Tarzan's car stopped beside the other, Professor Porter caught his daughter in his arms.

For a moment no one noticed Tarzan, sitting silently in his seat.

Clayton was the first to remember, and, turning, held out his hand.

"How can we ever thank you?" he exclaimed. "You have saved us all.

"You called me by name at the cottage, but I do not seem to recall yours, though there is something very familiar about you.

"It is as though I had known you well under very different conditions a long time ago."

Tarzan smiled as he took the proferred hand.

"You are quite right, Monsieur Clayton," he said, in French. "You will pardon me if I do not speak to you in English. I am just learning it, and while I understand it fairly well I speak it very poorly."

"But who are you?" insisted Clayton, speaking in French this time himself.

"Tarzan of the Apes."

Clayton started back in surprise.

"By Jove!" he exclaimed. "It is true."

And Professor Porter and Mr. Philander pressed forward to add their thanks to Clayton's, and to voice their surprise and pleasure at seeing their jungle friend so far from his savage home.

The party now entered the modest little hostelry, where Clayton soon made arrangements for their entertainment.

They were sitting in the little, stuffy parlor when the distant chugging of an approaching automobile caught their attention.

Mr. Philander, who was sitting near the window, looked out as the machine drew in sight, finally stopping beside the other cars.

"Bless me!" said Mr. Philander, a shade of annoyance in his tone. "It is Mr. Canler. I had hoped, er—I had thought or—er—how very happy we should be that he was not caught in the fire," he ended lamely.

"Tut, tut! Mr. Philander," said Professor Porter. "Tut, tut! I have often admonished my pupils to count ten before speaking. Were I you, Mr. Philander, I should count at least a thousand, and then maintain a discreet silence."

"Bless me, yes!" acquiesced Mr. Philander. "But who is the clerical-appearing gentleman with him?"

Jane Porter blanched.

Clayton moved uneasily in his chair.

Professor Porter removed his spectacles nervously, and breathed upon them, but replaced them on his nose without wiping.

The ubiquitous Esmeralda grunted.

Only Tarzan did not comprehend.

Presently Robert Canler burst into the room.

"Thank God!" he cried. "I feared the worst, until I saw your car, Clayton. I was cut off on the south road and had to go away back to town, and then strike east to this road. I thought we'd never reach the cottage."

No one seemed to enthuse much. Tarzan eyed Robert Canler as Sabor eyes her prey.

Jane Porter glanced at him and coughed nervously.

"Mr. Canler," she said, "this is Monsieur Tarzan, an old friend."

Canler turned and extended his hand. Tarzan rose and bowed as only D'Arnot could have taught a gentleman to do it, but he did not seem to see Canler's hand.

Nor did Canler appear to notice the oversight.

"This is the Reverend Mr. Tousley, Jane," said Canler, turning to the clerical party behind him. "Mr. Tousley, Miss Porter."

Mr. Tousley bowed and beamed.

Canler introduced him to the others.

"We can have the ceremony at once, Jane," said Canler. "Then you and I can catch the midnight train in town."

Tarzan understood the plan instantly. He glanced out of half-closed eyes at Jane Porter, but he did not move. The girl hesitated. The room was tense with the silence of taut nerves.

All eyes turned toward Jane Porter, awaiting her reply.

"Can't we wait a few days?" she asked. "I am all unstrung. I have been through so much to-day."

Canler felt the hostility that emanated from each member of the party. It made him angry.

"We have waited as long as I intend to wait," he said roughly. "You have promised to marry me. I shall be played with no longer. I have the license and here is the preacher. Come, Mr. Tousley; come, Jane. There are witnesses aplenty—more than enough," he added with a disagreeable inflection, and taking Jane Porter by the arm, he started to lead her toward the waiting minister.

But scarcely had he taken a single step ere a heavy hand closed upon his arm with a grip of steel.

Another hand shot to his throat and in a moment he was being shaken high above the floor, as a cat might shake a mouse.

Jane Porter turned in horrified surprise toward Tarzan.

And, as she looked into his face, she saw the crimson band upon his forehead that she had seen that other day in far-distant Africa, when Tarzan of the Apes had closed in mortal combat with the great anthropoid—Terkoz.

She knew that murder lay in that savage heart, and with a little cry of horror she sprang forward to plead with the ape-man. But her fears were more for Tarzan than for Canler. She realized the stern retribution which justice metes to the murderer.

Before she could reach them, however, Clayton had jumped to Tarzan's side and attempted to drag Canler from his grasp.

With a single sweep of one mighty arm the Englishman was hurled across the room, and then Jane Porter laid a firm white hand upon Tarzan's wrist, and looked up into his eyes.

"For my sake," she said.

The grasp upon Canler's throat relaxed.

Tarzan looked down into the beautiful face before him.

"Do you wish this to live?" he asked in surprise.

"I do not wish him to die at your hands, my friend," she replied. "I do not wish you to become a murderer."

Tarzan removed his hand from Canler's throat.

"Do you release her from her promise?" he asked. "It is the price of your life."

Canler, gasping for breath, nodded.

"Will you go away and never molest her further?"

Again the man nodded his head, his face distorted by fear of the death that had been so close.

Tarzan released him, and Canler staggered toward the door. In another moment he was gone, and the terror-stricken preacher with him.

Tarzan turned toward Jane Porter.

"May I speak with you for a moment, alone," he asked.

The girl nodded and started toward the door leading to the narrow veranda of the little hotel. She passed out to await Tarzan and so did not hear the conversation which followed.

"Wait," cried Professor Porter, as Tarzan was about to follow.

The professor had been stricken dumb with surprise by the rapid developments of the past few minutes.

"Before we go further, sir, I should like an explanation of the events which have just transpired.

"By what right, sir, did you interfere between my daughter and Mr. Canler?

"I had promised him her hand, sir, and regardless of our personal likes or dislikes, sir, that promise must be kept."

"I interfered, Professor Porter," replied Tarzan, "because your daughter does not love Mr. Canler—she does not wish to marry him. That is enough for me to know."

"You do not know what you have done," said Professor Porter. "Now he will doubtless refuse to marry her."

"He most certainly will," said Tarzan, emphatically.

"And further," added Tarzan, "you need not fear that your pride will suffer, Professor Porter, for you will be able to pay the Canler person what you owe him the moment you reach home."

"Tut, tut, sir!" exclaimed Professor Porter. "What do you mean, sir?"

"Your treasure has been found," said Tarzan.

"What—what is that you are saying?" cried the professor. "You are mad, man. It cannot be."

"It is, though. It was I who stole it, not knowing either its value or to whom it belonged. I saw the sailors bury it, and, apelike, I had to dig it up and bury it again elsewhere.

"When D'Arnot told me what it was and what it meant to you I returned to the jungle and recovered it. It had caused so much crime and suffering and sorrow that D'Arnot thought it best not to attempt to bring the treasure itself on here, as had been my intention, so I have brought a letter of credit instead.

"Here it is, Professor Porter," and Tarzan drew an envelope from his pocket and handed it to the astonished Professor, "two hundred and forty-one thousand dollars.

"The treasure was most carefully appraised by experts, but lest there should be any question in your mind, D'Arnot himself bought it and is holding it for you, should you prefer the treasure to the credit."

"To the already great burden of the obligations we owe you, sir," said Professor Porter, with trembling voice, "is now added this greatest of all services. You have given me the means to save my honor."

Clayton, who had left the room a moment after Canler, now returned.

"Pardon me," he said. "I think we had better try to reach town before dark and take the first train out of this forest. A native just rode by from the north, who reports that the fire is moving slowly in this direction."

This announcement broke up further conversation, and the entire party went out to the waiting machines.

Clayton, with Jane Porter, the professor and Esmeralda occupied Clayton's car, while Tarzan took Mr. Philander in with him.

"Bless me!" exclaimed Mr. Philander, as the car moved off after Clayton's machine. "Who would ever have thought it possible! The last time I saw you you were a veritable wild man, skipping about among the branches of a tropical African forest, and now you are driving me along a Wisconsin road in a French automobile. Bless me! But it is most remarkable."

"Yes," assented Tarzan, and then, after a pause; "Mr. Philander, do you recall any of the details of the finding and burying of three skeletons found in my cabin beside that African jungle?"

"Very distinctly, sir, very distinctly," replied Mr. Philander.

"Was there anything peculiar about any of those skeletons?"

Mr. Philander eyed Tarzan narrowly.

"Why do you ask?"

"It means a great deal to me to know," replied Tarzan.

"Your answer may clear up a mystery. It can do no worse, at any rate, than to leave it still a mystery.

"I have been entertaining a theory concerning those skeletons for the past two months, and I want you to answer my question to the best of your knowledge—were the three skeletons you buried all human skeletons?"

"No," said Mr. Philander, "the smallest one, the one found in the crib, was the skeleton of an anthropoid ape."

"Thank you," said Tarzan.

In the car ahead, Jane Porter was thinking fast and furiously. She had felt the purpose for which Tarzan had asked a few words with her, and she knew that she must be prepared to give him an answer in the very near future.

He was not the sort of person one could put off, and somehow that very thought made her wonder if she did not really fear him.

And could she love where she feared?

She realized the spell that had been upon her in the depths of that far-off jungle, but there was no spell of enchantment now in prosaic Wisconsin.

Nor did the immaculate young Frenchman appeal to the primal woman in her, as had the stalwart forest god.

Did she love him? She did not know—now.

She glanced at Clayton out of the corner of her eye. Was not here a man trained in the same school of environment in which she had been trained—a man with social position and culture such as she had been taught to consider as the prime essentials to congenial association?

Did not her best judgment point to this young English nobleman, whose love she knew to be of the sort a civilized woman should crave, as the logical mate for such as herself?

Could she love Clayton? She could see no reason why she could not. Jane Porter was not coldly calculating by nature, but training, environment and heredity had all combined to teach her to reason even in matters of the heart.

That she had been carried off her feet by the strength of the young giant when his great arms were about her in the distant African forest, and again to-day, in the Wisconsin woods, seemed to her only attributable to a temporary mental reversion to type on her part—to the psychological appeal of the primeval man to the primeval woman in her nature.

If he should never touch her again, she reasoned, she would never feel attracted toward him. She had not loved him, then. It had been nothing more than a passing hallucination, superinduced by excitement and by personal contact.

Excitement would not always mark their future relations, should she marry him, and the power of personal contact eventually would be dulled by familiarity.

Again she glanced at Clayton. He was very handsome and every inch a gentleman. She should be very proud of such a husband.

And then he spoke—a minute sooner or a minute later might have made all the difference in the world to three lives—but chance stepped in and pointed out to Clayton the psychological moment.

"You are free now, Jane," he said. "Won't you say yes—I will devote my life to making you very happy."

"Yes," she whispered.

That evening in the little waiting room at the station Tarzan caught Jane Porter alone for a moment.

"You are free now, Jane," he said, "and I have come across the ages out of the dim and distant past from the lair of the primeval man to claim you—for your sake I have become a civilized man—for your sake I have crossed oceans and continents—for your sake I will be whatever you will me to be. I can make you happy, Jane, in the life you know and love best. Will you marry me?"

For the first time she realized the depths of the man's love—all that he had accomplished in so short a time solely for love of her. Turning her head she buried her face in her arms.

What had she done? Because she had been afraid she

might succumb to the pleas of this giant, she had burned her bridges behind her—in her groundless apprehension that she might make a terrible mistake, she had made a worse one.

And then she told him all—told him the truth word by word, without attempting to shield herself or condone her error.

"What can we do?" he asked. "You have admitted that you love me. You know that I love you; but I do not know the ethics of society by which you are governed. I shall leave the decision to you, for you know best what will be for your eventual welfare."

"I cannot tell him, Tarzan," she said. "He too, loves me, and he is a good man. I could never face you nor any other honest person if I repudiated my promise to Mr. Clayton.

"I shall have to keep it—and you must help me bear the burden, though we may not see each other again after to-night."

The others were entering the room now and Tarzan turned toward the little window.

But he saw nothing without—within he saw a patch of greensward surrounded by a matted mass of gorgeous tropical plants and flowers, and, above, the waving foliage of mighty trees, and, over all, the blue of an equatorial sky.

In the center of the greensward a young woman sat upon a little mound of earth, and beside her sat a young giant. They ate pleasant fruit and looked into each other's eyes and smiled. They were very happy, and they were all alone.

His thoughts were broken in upon by the station agent who entered asking if there was a gentleman by the name of Tarzan in the party.

"I am Monsieur Tarzan," said the ape-man.

"Here is a message for you, forwarded from Baltimore; it is a cablegram from Paris."

Tarzan took the envelope and tore it open. The message was from D'Arnot.

It read:

> *Fingerprints prove you Greystoke. Congratulations.*
>
> D'ARNOT.

As Tarzan finished reading, Clayton entered and came toward him with extended hand.

Here was the man who had Tarzan's title, and Tarzan's estates, and was going to marry the woman whom Tarzan loved—the woman who loved Tarzan. A single word from Tarzan would make a great difference in this man's life.

It would take away his title and his lands and his castles, and—it would take them away from Jane Porter also.

"I say, old man," cried Clayton, "I haven't had a chance to thank you for all you've done for us. It seems as though you had your hands full saving our lives in Africa and here.

"I'm awfully glad you came on here. We must get better acquainted. I often thought about you, you know, and the remarkable circumstances of your environment.

"If it's any of my business, how the devil did you ever get into that bally jungle?"

"I was born there," said Tarzan, quietly. "My mother was an Ape, and of course she couldn't tell me much about it. I never knew who my father was."*

---

* The further adventures of Tarzan, and what came of his noble act of self-renunciation, will be told in the next book of Tarzan.

THE PRISONER
OF ZENDA

*Being the History of Three Months
in the Life of an English Gentleman*

Contents

Introduction

UNTIL he was about thirty, Anthony Hope Hawkins (1863–1933) practiced law in London and wrote moderately successful fiction on the side under his pen name, Anthony Hope. One day at the end of November 1893, while returning to his office after arguing a case before the Westminster County Court, he noticed two men, walking separately, who were so similar in appearance that each could have been mistaken for the other. He was to recall this random encounter as a turning point in his life. It sparked his notably active imagination and rapid pen and would soon give him a reason to abandon the law for literature.

Sometimes writing as many as two chapters a day, by the end of December, he had in hand the first draft of *The Prisoner of Zenda*, a brilliantly plotted novel of heroism, romance, chivalry, intrigue, skullduggery, and swordplay. He set his story in a moated castle that he named Zenda and in the imagined capital city, Strelsau, of a similarly imagined European monarchy that he named Ruritania. Only once in the course of his headlong composition was he seriously stuck with a plot problem, he wrote years later, and that was when "I seemed to have got 'The Prisoner' so tightly shut up in Zenda that it was impossible to get him out of it."[1] The prisoner of Zenda is the beleaguered king of Ruritania, Rudolf V.

Published in 1894 in both England and the United States, *The Prisoner of Zenda* was an immediate and lasting success. It went through more than two dozen printings its first year in print, was one of the bestsellers of the 1890s in both countries, and in addition to its commercial success won for its author literary praise from sources that he particularly cherished. "Allow me to congratulate you on your very spirited and gallant little book," his idol, Robert Louis Stevenson, wrote to him from Samoa. Andrew Lang, a prominent and versatile man of letters, singled it out for praise at a Royal Academy dinner in London. In 1894 *The Prisoner of Zenda* was by all accounts the book of the hour and its author a celebrity. Today, even after several revolutions in literary fashion and the passing of more than a century, Hope's novel retains its grip on the reader's imagination. It is, quite simply, a great adventure story written with verve and ingenuity. By latest count, there have been nine film or television versions of *The Prisoner of Zenda*, the most notable of which (1937) starred Ronald Colman, Douglas Fairbanks Jr., Madeleine Carroll, Raymond Massey, and one of the most spectacular sword fights ever seen on the screen.

When *The Prisoner of Zenda* first saw print, the Balkans, the generic locale of Hope's Ruritania, had an exotic and romantic appeal for British and American readers. The Balkans were Europe, but in many respects a premodern Europe that was mysterious and primitive. This was to be the locale of *Dracula*, Bram Stoker's tale of vampirism, published three years after Anthony Hope's novel. Since then, two world wars, decades of isolation behind the Iron Curtain, and recent episodes of savagery and ethnic cleansing have stripped the Balkans of whatever entertaining associations they may have had. Consequently, Hope's Ruritania is even more

---

[1]Anthony Hope, *Memories and Notes,* London: Hutchinson, 1927.

remote in spirit and circumstance than it was in the 1890s. But as an escapist fantasy for modern readers, a melodrama and mild political satire set in a realm of the imagination, it remains as delicious as ever. The vivacity, richness of incident, and pulsating emotionality of Hope's writing gallop over all the implausibilities and melodramatic perturbations of the Ruritanian state.

The instantaneous success of *The Prisoner of Zenda* confirmed its author in his decision to give up the law. He wrote letters of thanks and farewell to his colleagues and clients and closed his office door for good. He spent the rest of his life practicing his new profession. He was an acclaimed and prolific author of many more romances in addition to "serious" novels and short story collections, although nothing he wrote after 1893, with the exception of a sequel, *Rupert of Hentzau* (1898), came near to matching the triumph of *The Prisoner of Zenda*.

Illustrated in American editions by the fashionable Charles Dana Gibson, a specialist in depicting aristocratic-looking men and women, *The Prisoner of Zenda* inspired so many imitations and parodies that it practically created a subgenre of its own. Ruritania has had the staying power matched by few other purely invented places: Sir Thomas More's Utopia (meaning "not a place," 1516), Samuel Butler's Erewhon (an anagram of "nowhere," 1872), George Barr McCutcheon's Graustark (1901), or James Hilton's Shangri-La (1933). A Google search yields five towns in the United States named "Zenda" and a "Ruritania Street" in Raleigh, North Carolina.

Hope's imagined "Ruritania" may have had, and may still have, more reality for many readers than any of the Balkan countries of the Austro-Hungarian Empire on which it was based. The word "Ruritanian," suggesting an overripe, tragicomic kingdom of hereditary titles, contested succession, gorgeous uniforms, hugger-muggery, majestic mustaches, gloomy castles, and operetta ceremony and spectacle, has entered the lexicon (and Microsoft Spell-Checker) along with two other useful adjectives similarly derived from the names of countries that never existed, "Utopian" and "Lilliputian."

Inspired by his chance sighting of two apparently identical men on a London street, Hope's classic story revolves around a durable literary trope—mistaken and borrowed identity, twinship, the double—that may be ingrained in the binary habit of the Western mind. The Roman dramatist Plautus, for example, wrote a play about indistinguishable twins, *Menaechmi*, that Shakespeare adapted in *The Comedy of Errors*, elaborating the convolutions of Plautus' plot by adding a second set of indistinguishable twins. The root idea of *The Prisoner of Zenda*, Hope conceded, "was merely a variant on an old and widespread theme," mistaken identity, in this case involving an upper-class Englishman and a king of Ruritania, each of whom was named Rudolf and had red hair and a distinctive long nose. "It is indeed astonishing how many stories, novels, and plays may be reduced on analysis to this ancient plot and this elementary situation. . . . I think that the two variants which struck the popular fancy in my little book were royalty and red hair; the former is always a safe card to play and its combination with the latter had a touch of novelty."

Anthony Hope's contemporaries would have been familiar with mistaken, double, and appropriated identity as a basic plot device. It drove the action of stories like Charles Dickens' *A Tale of Two Cities*, Stevenson's *Dr. Jekyll and Mr. Hyde*, Mark Twain's *The Prince and the Pauper* and *Pudd'nhead Wilson*, and Alexandre Dumas' *The Man in the Iron Mask*, the last a romance about the supposed twin brother of Louis XIV, who for reasons of state had to be kept from view like Anthony Hope's King Rudolf V of Ruritania. Lurking in the Victorian memory was a celebrated and long-drawn-out episode of imposture and unmasking: a man named Arthur Orton, a butcher from Wagga Wagga, Australia, who put himself forward as the missing brother of Sir Roger Tichborne and heir to his baronetcy and estates.

The court convicted Orton of perjury and in 1874 sentenced him to fourteen years' penal servitude.

For Hope's readers, simply the name shared by two of his main characters, Rudolf, had a rich historical aura of tragedy and blighted romance. Five years before Hope sat down to write the novel that made him famous, Crown Prince Rudolf of Austria and his young lover, Baroness Marie Vetsera, committed suicide at the prince's hunting lodge at Mayerling. Their tryst, the tangled circumstances surrounding it, and its outcome could have been seen in retrospect as authentically Ruritanian.

The narrator and hero of *The Prisoner of Zenda*, Rudolf Rassendyll, is an idealized aristocratic Englishman. Younger brother of an earl, he is polished, gallant, high-minded, and courageous, a good shot, an accomplished horseman, and a skilled combatant with rapier and pistol. At least at the outset of his story, Rudolf hides his true nature under an unpromising, even deliberately exasperating mask of indolence and indulgence. Dickens' dissolute Sidney Carton (*A Tale of Two Cities*); Baroness Orczy's inane, bored, and flippant Sir Percy Blakeney (*The Scarlet Pimpernel*); and Arthur Conan Doyle's untidy and cocaine-habituated private detective Sherlock Holmes belong to the same breed of misleadingly unheroic heroes. But once Rassendyll springs into action, he demonstrates decisiveness, courage, and command appropriate to a subject of Queen Victoria at a time when the British Empire at high noon wielded dominion over one-quarter of the world's area and population. Hope's novel satisfied the same hunger of the reading public for imperialist adventure fiction that was fed by the novels of Rudyard Kipling, H. Rider Haggard, Thomas Mayne Reid, and the prolific G. A. Henty.

To scout a future diplomatic posting that his brother and sister-in-law, Lord and Lady Burlesdon, urge him to consider as a cure for idleness, Rudolf journeys across Europe by train to Ruritania, a monarchy racked, as he soon learns, by jealousy and inherent instability. He tells us at the outset of the story that a scandalous eighteenth-century liaison connects him by blood to the Ruritanian royal family of Elphberg. He has inherited the Elphberg hair and nose to such a pronounced degree that once he shaves off his beard and mustache he becomes a dead ringer for the about to be crowned King of Ruritania, Rudolf V.

A feckless and inoffensive fellow, a natural victim with a weak head for the bottle, royal Rudolf is no match in the arena of Ruritanian power politics for his jealous half brother, the Duke of Strelsau, known and feared as "Black Michael." The duke has been plotting to usurp the Ruritanian throne and claim as his queen the beauteous Princess Flavia. To this end, he has his confederates drug Rudolf V into insensibility, kidnap him, and lock him up deep within the walls of Zenda, Black Michael's fortress castle. (American editions of Hope's novel supplied a detailed map of the castle's labyrinthine interiors showing, among other crucial locations, "The King's Cell" and "Window from which Hentzau leaped into the Moat.")

Pressed into service by two highly placed subjects loyal to the rightful king, Rudolf Rassendyll agrees to stand in for him, go through with the coronation rites, accept the blessing of the archbishop and the cheers of the populace, and thereby keep the throne warm for Rudolf V, who remains snugly hidden away. Eventually, with the aid of an ingenious earthenware conduit that serves a function seemingly parallel to that of the birth canal, the king is extricated from his damp spider hole and returned to the royal palace at Strelsau. But in the course of the several months of what English Rudolf calls his "play-acting" as king, he and Princess Flavia have fallen in love with each other. She has recognized that he is an impostor, but she loves him for who he truly is, Rudolf Rassendyll of England. "It was always you," she says, "never the King!" But he knows, as Flavia does, that honor and duty prevent her from running away with him. For their final moments together, before Rassendyll leaves Ruritania, Hope turns up the heat in a scene of passionate avowal and equally passionate abnegation that must have drawn tears from even the most stonyhearted of his readers. "Your ring will always be on my finger," Flavia tells him as they part, "your heart in mine, the touch of your lips on mine. But you must go and I must stay. . . . Kiss me, my dear, and go!" In valor and nobility of character, Rudolf, although only an English gentleman, has proved himself to be more royal than the rightful king of Ruritania.

A second skein of action in Hope's tireless and intricate plot introduces a mysterious beauty named Antoinette de Mauban and her hot-blooded admirer, young Rupert of Hentzau, a relative newcomer to the story. Rupert is shown to be depraved enough to cast "lustful eyes" on Princess Flavia at the same time that he is lusting after Antoinette. "Wicked men I have known in plenty," Rassendyll declares, calling upon a hitherto unsuspected fund of worldly experience, "but Rupert Hentzau remains unique in my experience." Hope describes Rupert, Rassendyll's sworn enemy, in the most full-throated and implicitly admiring fashion as "reckless and wary, graceful and graceless, handsome, debonair, vile, and unconquered."

Rupert was altogether too attractive a villain for Hope to allow him to ride off into the forest gloom that surrounds Zenda. Rupert reappears in a sequel to *The Prisoner of Zenda,* in which, banished from Ruritania, he "wandered to and fro over Europe, making a living by his wits, and . . . adding to his resources by gallantries for which he did not refuse substantial recompense." (The contemporary novelist George MacDonald Fraser's equally unconquerable adventurer, Sir Harry Flashman, hero of a dozen volumes, may be Rupert's lineal descendant.) The sequel, *Rupert of Hentzau* (1898), is a much more somber tale than *Zenda* and ends with Rassendyll's death and his burial among the princes of the realm in the Cathedral of Strelsau.

"Many critics were found to suggest that *Rupert of Hentzau* was the better book," Sir Charles Mallet,

Hope's friend and biographer, wrote. "The workmanship was more experienced and finished. One or two of the scenes, towards the end especially, were stronger than anything in the earlier tale. And some reviewers, curiously enough, thought it a positive advantage that the main circumstances and setting of the story were familiar and not fresh. They liked to think they were coming back to places they knew, to friends they loved already: and, no doubt, that feeling appealed to the public also."[2]

In 1903 Hope married an American, Elizabeth Somerville, whom he had met on an author tour of the United States. During World War I, he worked in the field of counterpropaganda for what eventually became the Ministry of Information, published a tract about German militarism, and in 1918 was knighted for his services by King George. In London and at a country place in Surrey, Sir Anthony Hope Hawkins led the quiet life of a beloved man of letters much of whose work went out of fashion during the war years and after. He became increasingly dependent on income from reprints and film rights. But two of his books, *The Prisoner of Zenda* and, to a lesser extent for modern readers, *Rupert of Hentzau*, assure his standing as a master of romance, adventure, and escapist fiction. "He made more people happy," his friend and fellow author, J. M. Barrie, said after Hope's death in 1933, "than any other author of our time."[3]

—Justin Kaplan

[2]Sir Charles Mallet, *Anthony Hope and His Books,* London: Hutchinson, 1935.
[3]Mallet

CHAPTER I

The Rassendylls—with a Word on the Elphbergs

"I WONDER when in the world you're going to do anything, Rudolf?" said my brother's wife.

"My dear Rose," I answered, laying down my eggspoon, "why in the world should I do anything? My position is a comfortable one. I have an income nearly sufficient for my wants (no one's income is ever quite sufficient, you know): I enjoy an enviable social position: I am brother to Lord Burlesdon, and brother-in-law to that most charming lady, his countess. Behold, it is enough!"

"You are nine-and-twenty," she observed, "and you've done nothing but——"

"Knock about? It is true. Our family doesn't need to do things."

This remark of mine rather annoyed Rose, for everybody knows (and therefore there can be no harm in referring to the fact) that, pretty and accomplished as she herself is, her family is hardly of the same standing as the Rassendylls. Besides her attractions, she possessed a large fortune, and my brother Robert was wise enough not to mind about her ancestry. Ancestry is, in fact, a matter concerning which the next observation of Rose's has some truth.

"Good families are generally worse than any others," she said.

Upon this I stroked my hair: I knew quite well what she meant.

"I'm so glad Robert's is black!" she cried.

At this moment Robert (who rises at seven and works before breakfast) came in. He glanced at his wife: her cheek was slightly flushed; he patted it caressingly.

"What's the matter, my dear?" he asked.

"She objects to my doing nothing and having red hair," said I, in an injured tone.

"Oh! of course he can't help his hair," admitted Rose.

"It generally crops out once in a generation," said my brother. "So does the nose. Rudolf has got them both."

"I wish they didn't crop out," said Rose, still flushed.

"I rather like them myself," said I, and, rising, I bowed to the portrait of Countess Amelia.

My brother's wife uttered an exclamation of impatience.

"I wish you'd take that picture away, Robert," said she.

"My dear!" he cried.

"Good heavens!" I added.

"Then it might be forgotten," she continued.

"Hardly—with Rudolf about," said Robert, shaking his head.

"Why should it be forgotten?" I asked.

"Rudolf!" exclaimed my brother's wife, blushing very prettily.

I laughed, and went on with my egg. At least I had shelved the question of what (if anything) I ought to do. And, by way of closing the discussion—and also, I must admit, of exasperating my strict little sister-in-law a trifle more—I observed:

"I rather like being an Elphberg myself."

When I read a story, I skip the explanations; yet the moment I begin to write one, I find that I must have an explanation. For it is manifest that I must explain why my sister-in-law was vexed with my nose and hair, and why I ventured to call myself an Elphberg. For eminent as, I must protest, the Rassendylls have been for many generations, yet participation in their blood of course does not, at first sight, justify the boast of a connection with the grander stock of the Elphbergs or a claim to be one of that Royal House. For what relationship is there between Ruritania and Burlesdon, between the Palace at Strelsau or the Castle of Zenda and Number 305 Park Lane, W.?

Well then—and I must premise that I am going, perforce, to rake up the very scandal which my dear Lady Burlesdon wishes forgotten—in the year 1733, George II, sitting then on the throne, peace reigning for the moment, and the king and the Prince of Wales being not yet at loggerheads, there came on a visit to the English Court a certain prince, who was afterwards known to history as Rudolf the Third of Ruritania. The prince was a tall, handsome young fellow, marked (may be marred, it is not for me to say) by a somewhat unusually long, sharp and straight nose, and a mass of dark-red hair—in fact, the nose and the hair which have stamped the Elphbergs time out of mind. He stayed some months in England, where he was most courteously received; yet, in the end, he left rather under a cloud. For he fought a duel (it was considered highly well-bred of him to waive all question of his rank) with a nobleman, well known in the society of the day, not only for his own merits, but as the husband of a very beautiful wife. In that duel Prince Rudolf received a severe wound, and, recovering therefrom, was adroitly smuggled off by the Ruritanian ambassador, who had found him a pretty handful. The nobleman was not wounded in the duel; but the morning being raw and damp on the occasion of the meeting, he contracted a severe chill, and, failing to throw it off, he died some six months after the departure of Prince Rudolf, without having found leisure to adjust his relations with his wife—who, after another two months, bore an heir to the title and estates of the family of Burlesdon. This lady was the Countess Amelia, whose picture my sister-in-law wished to remove from the drawing-room in Park Lane; and her husband was

James, fifth Earl of Burlesdon and twenty-second Baron Rassendyll, both in the peerage of England, and a Knight of the Garter. As for Rudolf, he went back to Ruritania, married a wife, and ascended the throne, whereon his progeny in the direct line have sat from then till this very hour—with one short interval. And, finally, if you walk through the picture-galleries at Burlesdon, among the fifty portraits or so of the last century-and-a-half, you will find five or six, including that of the sixth earl, distinguished by long, sharp, straight noses and a quantity of dark-red hair; these five or six have also blue eyes, whereas among the Rassendylls dark eyes are the commoner.

That is the explanation, and I am glad to have finished it: the blemishes on honourable lineage are a delicate subject, and certainly this heredity we hear so much about is the finest scandalmonger in the world; it laughs at discretion, and writes strange entries between the lines of the "Peerages."

It will be observed that my sister-in-law, with a want of logic that must have been peculiar to herself (since we are no longer allowed to lay it to the charge of her sex), treated my complexion almost as an offence for which I was responsible, hastening to assume from that external sign inward qualities of which I protest my entire innocence; and this unjust inference she sought to buttress by pointing to the uselessness of the life I had led. Well, be that as it may, I had picked up a good deal of pleasure and a good deal of knowledge. I had been to a German school and a German University, and spoke German as readily and perfectly as English; I was thoroughly at home in French; I had a smattering of Italian and enough Spanish to swear by. I was, I believe, a strong, though hardly a fine, swordsman and a good shot. I could ride anything that had a back to sit on; and my head was as cool a one as you could find, for all its flaming cover. If you say that I ought to have spent my time in useful labour, I am out of Court and have nothing to say, save that my parents had no busi-

ness to leave me two thousand pounds a year and a rov-
ing disposition.

"The difference between you and Robert," said my
sister-in-law, who often (bless her!) speaks on a platform, and oftener still as if she were on one, "is that he
recognises the duties of his position, and you only see
the opportunities of yours."

"To a man of spirit, my dear Rose," I answered, "opportunities are duties."

"Nonsense!" said she, tossing her head; and after a
moment she went on: "Now, here's Sir Jacob Borrodaile
offering you exactly what you might be equal to."

"A thousand thanks!" I murmured.

"He's to have an Embassy in six months, and Robert
says he is sure that he'll take you as an *attaché*. Do take
it, Rudolf—to please me."

Now, when my sister-in-law puts the matter in that
way, wrinkling her pretty brows, twisting her little
hands, and growing wistful in the eyes, all on account of
an idle scamp like myself, for whom she has no natural
responsibility, I am visited with compunction. Moreover, I thought it possible that I could pass the time in
the position suggested with some tolerable amusement.
Therefore I said:

"My dear sister, if in six months' time no unforeseen
obstacle has arisen, and Sir Jacob invites me, hang me if
I don't go with Sir Jacob!"

"Oh, Rudolf, how good of you! I am glad!"

"Where's he going to?"

"He doesn't know yet; but it's sure to be a good Embassy."

"Madame," said I, "for your sake I'll go, if it's no more
than a beggarly Legation. When I do a thing, I don't do
it by halves."

My promise, then, was given; but six months are six
months, and seem an eternity, and, inasmuch as they
stretched between me and my prospective industry (I suppose *attachés* are industrious; but I know not, for I never
became *attaché* to Sir Jacob or to anybody else), I cast

about for some desirable mode of spending them. And it occurred to me suddenly that I would visit Ruritania. It may seem strange that I had never visited that country yet; but my father (in spite of a sneaking fondness for the Elphbergs, which led him to give me, his second son, the famous Elphberg name of Rudolf) had always been averse from my going, and, since his death, my brother, prompted by Rose, had accepted the family tradition which taught that a wide berth was to be given to that country. But the moment Ruritania had come into my head I was eaten up with curiosity to see it. After all, red hair and long noses are not confined to the House of Elphberg, and the old story seemed a preposterously insufficient reason for debarring myself from acquaintance with a highly interesting and important kingdom, one which had played no small part in European history, and might do the like again under the sway of a young and vigorous ruler, such as the new king was rumoured to be. My determination was clinched by reading in *The Times* that Rudolf the Fifth was to be crowned at Strelsau in the course of the next three weeks, and that great magnificence was to mark the occasion. At once I made up my mind to be present, and began my preparations. But, inasmuch as it has never been my practice to furnish my relatives with an itinerary of my journeys and in this case I anticipated opposition to my wishes, I gave out that I was going for a ramble in the Tyrol—an old haunt of mine—and propitiated Rose's wrath by declaring that I intended to study the political and social problems of the interesting community which dwells in that neighbourhood.

"Perhaps," I hinted darkly, "there may be an outcome of the expedition."

"What do you mean?" she asked.

"Well," said I, carelessly, "there seems a gap that might be filled by an exhaustive work on——"

"Oh! will you write a book?" she cried, clapping her hands. "That would be splendid, wouldn't it, Robert?"

"It's the best of introductions to political life nowadays," observed my brother, who has, by the way, introduced himself in this manner several times over. *Burlesdon on Ancient Theories and Modern Facts* and *The Ultimate Outcome, by a Political Student,* are both works of recognised eminence.

"I believe you are right, Bob, my boy," said I.

"Now promise you'll do it," said Rose earnestly.

"No, I won't promise; but if I find enough material, I will."

"That's fair enough," said Robert.

"Oh! material doesn't matter," she said, pouting.

But this time she could get no more than a qualified promise out of me. To tell the truth, I would have wagered a handsome sum that the story of my expedition that summer would stain no paper and spoil not a single pen. And that shows how little we know what the future holds; for here I am, fulfilling my qualified promise, and writing, as I never thought to write, a book—though it will hardly serve as an introduction to political life, and has not a jot to do with the Tyrol.

Neither would it, I fear, please Lady Burlesdon, if I were to submit it to her critical eye—a step which I have no intention of taking.

CHAPTER II

Concerning the
Colour of Men's Hair

IT was a maxim of my Uncle William's that no man should pass through Paris without spending four-and-twenty hours there. My uncle spoke out of a ripe experience of the world, and I honoured his advice by putting up for a day and a night at "The Continental" on my way to—the Tyrol. I called on George Featherly at the Embassy, and we had a bit of dinner together at Durand's, and afterwards dropped in to the Opera; and after that we had a little supper, and after that we called on Bertram Bertrand, a versifier of some repute and Paris correspondent to *The Critic*. He had a very comfortable little suite of rooms, and we found some pleasant fellows smoking and talking. It struck me, however, that Bertram himself was absent and in low spirits, and when everybody except ourselves had gone, I rallied him on his moping preoccupation. He fenced with me for a while, but at last, flinging himself on a sofa, he exclaimed:

"Very well; have it your own way. I am in love—infernally in love!"

"Oh, you'll write the better poetry," said I, by way of consolation.

He ruffled his hair with his hand and smoked furiously. George Featherly, standing with his back to the mantelpiece, smiled unkindly.

"If it's the old affair," said he, "you may as well throw it up, Bert. She's leaving Paris to-morrow."

"I know that," snapped Bertram.

"Not that it would make any difference if she stayed," pursued the relentless George. "She flies higher than the paper-trade, my boy!"

"Hang her!" said Bertram.

"It would make it more interesting for me," I ventured to observe, "if I knew who you were talking about."

"Antoinette Mauban," said George.

"De Mauban," growled Bertram.

"Oho!" said I, passing by the question of the *de*. "You don't mean to say, Bert——?"

"Can't you let me alone?"

"Where's she going to?" I asked, for the lady was something of a celebrity.

George jingled his money, smiled cruelly at poor Bertram, and answered pleasantly:

"Nobody knows. By the way, Bert, I met a great man at her house the other night—at least, about a month ago. Did you ever meet him—the Duke of Strelsau?"

"Yes, I did," growled Bertram.

"An extremely accomplished man, I thought him."

It was not hard to see that George's references to the duke were intended to aggravate poor Bertram's sufferings, so that I drew the inference that the duke had distinguished Madame de Mauban by his attentions. She was a widow, rich, handsome, and, according to repute, ambitious. It was quite possible that she, as George put it, was flying as high as a personage who was everything he could be, short of enjoying strictly royal rank: for the duke was the son of the late King of Ruritania by a second and morganatic marriage, and half-brother to the new king. He had been his father's favourite, and it had occasioned some unfavourable comment when he had been created a duke, with a title derived from no less a city than the capital itself. His mother had been of good, but not exalted, birth.

"He's not in Paris now, is he?" I asked.

"Oh no! He's gone back to be present at the king's coronation; a ceremony which, I should say, he'll not enjoy much. But, Bert, old man, don't despair! He won't marry the fair Antoinette—at least, not unless another plan comes to nothing. Still, perhaps, she——" He paused and added, with a laugh: "Royal attentions are hard to resist—you know that, don't you, Rudolf?"

"Confound you!" said I; and rising, I left the hapless Bertram in George's hands and went home to bed.

The next day George Featherly went with me to the station, where I took a ticket for Dresden.

"Going to see the pictures?" asked George, with a grin.

George is an inveterate gossip, and had I told him that I was off to Ruritania, the news would have been in London in three days and in Park Lane in a week. I was, therefore, about to return an evasive answer, when he saved my conscience by leaving me suddenly and darting across the platform. Following him with my eyes, I saw him lift his hat and accost a graceful, fashionably-dressed woman who had just appeared from the booking-office. She was, perhaps, a year or two over thirty, tall, dark, and of rather full figure. As George talked, I saw her glance at me, and my vanity was hurt by the thought that, muffled in a fur-coat and a neck-wrapper (for it was a chilly April day) and wearing a soft travelling-hat pulled down to my ears, I must be looking very far from my best. A moment later, George rejoined me.

"You've got a charming travelling companion," he said. "That's poor Bert Bertrand's goddess, Antoinette de Mauban, and, like you, she's going to Dresden—also, no doubt, to see the pictures. It's very queer, though, that she doesn't at present desire the honour of your acquaintance."

"I didn't ask to be introduced," I observed, a little annoyed.

"Well, I offered to bring you to her; but she said, 'Another time.' Never mind, old fellow, perhaps there'll be a smash, and you'll have a chance of rescuing her and cutting out the Duke of Strelsau!"

No smash, however, happened, either to me or to Madame de Mauban. I can speak for her as confidently as for myself; for when, after a night's rest in Dresden, I continued my journey, she got into the same train. Understanding that she wished to be let alone, I avoided her carefully, but I saw that she went the same way as I did to the very end of my journey, and I took opportunities of having a good look at her, when I could do so unobserved.

As soon as we reached the Ruritanian frontier (where the old officer who presided over the Custom House favoured me with such a stare that I felt surer than before of my Elphberg physiognomy), I bought the papers, and found in them news which affected my movements. For some reason, which was not clearly explained and seemed to be something of a mystery, the date of the coronation had been suddenly advanced, and the ceremony was to take place on the next day but one. The whole country seemed in a stir about it, and it was evident that Strelsau was thronged. Rooms were all let and hotels overflowing; there would be very little chance of my obtaining a lodging, and I should certainly have to pay an exorbitant charge for it. I made up my mind to stop at Zenda, a small town fifty miles short of the capital, and about ten from the frontier. My train reached there in the evening; I would spend the next day, Tuesday, in a wander over the hills, which were said to be very fine, and in taking a glance at the famous Castle, and go over by train to Strelsau on the Wednesday morning, returning at night to sleep at Zenda.

Accordingly at Zenda I got out, and as the train passed where I stood on the platform, I saw my friend Madame de Mauban in her place; clearly she was going through to Strelsau, having, with more providence than I could boast, secured apartments there. I smiled to think how surprised George Featherly would have been to know that she and I had been fellow-travellers for so long.

I was very kindly received at the hotel—it was really no more than an inn—kept by a fat old lady and her two daughters. They were good, quiet people, and seemed very little interested in the great doings at Strelsau. The old lady's hero was the duke, for he was now, under the late king's will, master of the Zenda estates and of the Castle, which rose grandly on its steep hill at the end of the valley, a mile or so from the inn. The old lady, indeed, did not hesitate to express regret that the duke was not on the throne, instead of his brother.

"We know Duke Michael," said she. "He has always lived among us; every Ruritanian knows Duke Michael. But the king is almost a stranger; he has been so much abroad, not one in ten knows him even by sight."

"And now," chimed in one of the young women, "they say he has shaved off his beard, so that no one at all knows him."

"Shaved his beard!" exclaimed her mother. "Who says so?"

"Johann, the duke's keeper. He has seen the king."

"Ah, yes. The king, sir, is now at the duke's shooting-lodge in the forest here; from here he goes to Strelsau to be crowned on Wednesday morning."

I was interested to hear this, and made up my mind to walk next day in the direction of the lodge, on the chance of coming across the king. The old lady ran on garrulously:

"Ah! and I wish he would stay at his shooting—that and wine (and one thing more) are all he loves, they say—and suffer our duke to be crowned on Wednesday. That I wish, and I don't care who knows it."

"Hush, mother!" urged the daughters.

"Oh, there's many to think as I do!" cried the old woman stubbornly.

I threw myself back in my deep arm-chair, and laughed at her zeal.

"For my part," said the younger and prettier of the

two daughters, a fair, buxom, smiling wench, "I hate Black Michael! A red Elphberg for me, mother! The king, they say, is as red as a fox or as——"

And she laughed mischievously as she cast a glance at me, and tossed her head at her sister's reproving face.

"Many a man has cursed their red hair before now," muttered the old lady—and I remembered James, fifth Earl of Burlesdon.

"But never a woman!" cried the girl.

"Ay, and women, when it was too late," was the stern answer, reducing the girl to silence and blushes.

"How comes the king here?" I asked, to break an embarrassed silence. "It is the duke's land here, you say."

"The duke invited him, sir, to rest here till Wednesday. The duke is at Strelsau, preparing the king's reception."

"Then they're friends?"

"None better," said the old lady.

But my rosy damsel tossed her head again; she was not to be repressed for long, and she broke out again:

"Ay, they love one another as men do who want the same place and the same wife!"

The old woman glowered; but the last words pricked my curiosity, and I interposed before she could begin scolding:

"What, the same wife, too! How's that, young lady?"

"All the world knows that Black Michael—well then, mother, the duke—would give his soul to marry his cousin, the Princess Flavia, and that she is to be the queen."

"Upon my word," said I, "I begin to be sorry for your duke. But if a man will be a younger son, why he must take what the elder leaves, and be as thankful to God as he can;" and, thinking of myself, I shrugged my shoulders and laughed. And then I thought also of Antoinette de Mauban and her journey to Strelsau.

"It's little dealing Black Michael has with——" began the girl, braving her mother's anger; but as she spoke a heavy step sounded on the floor, and a gruff voice asked in a threatening tone:

"Who talks of 'Black Michael' in his Highness's own burgh?"

The girl gave a little shriek, half of fright—half, I think, of amusement.

"You'll not tell of me, Johann?" she said.

"See where your chatter leads," said the old lady.

The man who had spoken came forward.

"We have company, Johann," said my hostess, and the fellow plucked off his cap. A moment later he saw me, and, to my amazement, he started back a step, as though he had seen something wonderful.

"What ails you, Johann?" asked the elder girl. "This is a gentleman on his travels, come to see the coronation."

The man had recovered himself, but he was staring at me with an intense, searching, almost fierce glance.

"Good-evening to you," said I.

"Good-evening, sir," he muttered, still scrutinising me, and the merry girl began to laugh as she called:

"See, Johann, it is the colour you love! He started to see your hair, sir. It's not the colour we see most of here in Zenda."

"I crave your pardon, sir," stammered the fellow, with puzzled eyes. "I expected to see no one."

"Give him a glass to drink my health in; and I'll bid you good-night, and thanks to you, ladies, for your courtesy and pleasant conversation."

So speaking, I rose to my feet, and with a slight bow turned to the door. The young girl ran to light me on the way, and the man fell back to let me pass, his eyes still fixed on me. The moment I was by, he started a step forward, asking:

"Pray, sir, do you know our king?"

"I never saw him," said I. "I hope to do so on Wednesday."

He said no more, but I felt his eyes following me till the door closed behind me. My saucy conductor, looking over her shoulder at me as she preceded me upstairs, said:

"There's no pleasing Master Johann for one of your colour, sir."

"He prefers yours, may be?" I suggested.

"I meant, sir, in a man," she answered, with a coquettish glance.

"What," asked I, taking hold of the other side of the candlestick, "does colour matter in a man?"

"Nay, but I love yours—it's the Elphberg red."

"Colour in a man," said I, "is a matter of no more moment than that!"—and I gave her something of no value.

"God send the kitchen-door be shut!" said she.

"Amen!" said I, and left her.

In fact, however, as I now know, colour is sometimes of considerable moment to a man.

CHAPTER III

❦

A Merry Evening
with a Distant Relative

I WAS not so unreasonable as to be prejudiced against
the duke's keeper because he disliked my complexion; and if I had been, his most civil and obliging conduct (as it seemed to me to be) next morning would
have disarmed me. Hearing that I was bound for Strelsau, he came to see me while I was breakfasting, and
told me that a sister of his, who had married a well-to-
do tradesman and lived in the capital, had invited him
to occupy a room in her house. He had gladly accepted,
but now found that his duties would not permit of his
absence. He begged therefore that, if such humble
(though, as he added, clean and comfortable) lodgings
would satisfy me, I would take his place. He pledged his
sister's acquiescence, and urged the inconvenience and
crowding to which I should be subject in my journeys to
and from Strelsau the next day. I accepted his offer
without a moment's hesitation, and he went off to tele-
graph to his sister, while I packed up and prepared to
take the next train. But I still hankered after the forest
and the shooting-lodge, and when my little maid told
me that I could, by walking ten miles or so through the
forest, hit the railway at a roadside station, I decided to
send my luggage direct to the address which Johann had
given, take my walk, and follow to Strelsau myself. Jo-

hann had gone off and was not aware of the change in
my plans; but, as its only effect was to delay my arrival
at his sister's for a few hours, there was no reason for
troubling to inform him of it. Doubtless the good lady
would waste no anxiety on my account.

I took an early luncheon, and, having bidden my kind
entertainers farewell, promising to return to them on
my way home, I set out to climb the hill that led to the
Castle, and thence to the forest of Zenda. Half-an-
hour's leisurely walking brought me to the Castle. It had
been a fortress in old days, and the ancient keep was still
in good preservation and very imposing. Behind it stood
another portion of the original castle, and behind that
again, and separated from it by a deep and broad moat,
which ran all round the old buildings, was a handsome
modern *château,* erected by the last king, and now form-
ing the country residence of the Duke of Strelsau. The
old and the new portions were connected by a drawbridge, and this indirect mode of access formed the only
passage between the old building and the outer world;
but leading to the modern *château* there was a broad
and handsome avenue. It was an ideal residence: when
"Black Michael" desired company, he could dwell in his
château; if a fit of misanthropy seized him, he had
merely to cross the bridge and draw it up after him (it
ran on rollers), and nothing short of a regiment and a
train of artillery could fetch him out. I went on my way,
glad that poor Black Michael, though he could not have
the throne or the princess, had, at least, as fine a residence as any prince in Europe.

Soon I entered the forest, and walked on for an hour
or more in its cool sombre shade. The great trees en-
laced with one another over my head, and the sunshine
stole through in patches as bright as diamonds, and
hardly bigger. I was enchanted with the place, and, finding a felled tree-trunk, propped my back against it, and
stretching my legs out gave myself up to undisturbed
contemplation of the solemn beauty of the woods and
to the comfort of a good cigar. And when the cigar was

finished and I had (I suppose) inhaled as much beauty as I could, I went off into the most delightful sleep, regardless of my train to Strelsau and of the fast-waning afternoon. To remember a train in such a spot would have been rank sacrilege. Instead of that, I fell to dreaming that I was married to the Princess Flavia and dwelt in the Castle of Zenda, and beguiled whole days with my love in the glades of the forest—which made a very pleasant dream. In fact, I was just impressing a fervent kiss on the charming lips of the princess, when I heard (and the voice seemed at first a part of the dream) someone exclaim, in rough strident tones:

"Why, the devil's in it! Shave him, and he'd be the king!"

The idea seemed whimsical enough for a dream: by the sacrifice of my heavy moustache and carefully pointed imperial, I was to be transformed into a monarch! I was about to kiss the princess again, when I arrived (very reluctantly) at the conclusion that I was awake.

I opened my eyes, and found two men regarding me with much curiosity. Both wore shooting costumes and carried guns. One was rather short and very stoutly built, with a big bullet-shaped head, a bristly grey moustache, and small pale-blue eyes, a trifle bloodshot. The other was a slender young fellow, of middle height, dark in complexion, and bearing himself with grace and distinction. I set the one down as an old soldier; the other for a gentleman accustomed to move in good society, but not unused to military life either. It turned out afterwards that my guess was a good one.

The elder man approached me, beckoning the younger to follow. He did so, courteously raising his hat. I rose slowly to my feet.

"He's the height, too!" I heard the elder murmur, as he surveyed my six feet two inches of stature. Then, with a cavalier touch of the cap, he addressed me:

"May I ask your name?"

"As you have taken the first step in the acquaintance,

gentlemen," said I, with a smile, "suppose you give me a lead in the matter of names."

The young man stepped forward with a pleasant smile.

"This," said he, "is Colonel Sapt, and I am called Fritz von Tarlenheim: we are both in the service of the King of Ruritania."

I bowed and, baring my head, answered:

"I am Rudolf Rassendyll. I am a traveller from England; and once for a year or two I held a commission from Her Majesty the Queen."

"Then we are all brethren of the sword," answered Tarlenheim, holding out his hand, which I took readily.

"Rassendyll, Rassendyll!" muttered Colonel Sapt; then a gleam of intelligence flitted across his face.

"By Heaven!" he cried, "you're of the Burlesdons?"

"My brother is now Lord Burlesdon," said I.

"Thy head bewrayeth thee," he chuckled, pointing to my uncovered poll.—"Why, Fritz, you know the story?"

The young man glanced apologetically at me. He felt a delicacy which my sister-in-law would have admired. To put him at his ease, I remarked, with a smile:

"Ah! the story is known here as well as among us, it seems."

"Known!" cried Sapt. "If you stay here, the deuce a man in all Ruritania will doubt of it—or a woman either."

I began to feel uncomfortable. Had I realised what a very plainly-written pedigree I carried about with me, I should have thought long before I visited Ruritania. However, I was in for it now.

At this moment a ringing voice sounded from the wood behind us:

"Fritz, Fritz! where are you, man?"

Tarlenheim started, and said hastily:

"It's the king!"

Old Sapt chuckled again.

Then a young man jumped out from behind the trunk of a tree and stood beside us. As I looked on him, I uttered an astonished cry; and he, seeing me, drew back in sudden wonder. Saving the hair on my face and a manner of conscious dignity which his position gave him, saving also that he lacked perhaps half-an-inch—nay, less than that, but still something—of my height, the King of Ruritania might have been Rudolf Rassendyll, and I, Rudolf, the King.

For an instant we stood motionless, looking at one another. Then I bared my head again and bowed respectfully. The king found his voice, and asked in bewilderment:

"Colonel—Fritz—who is this gentleman?"

I was about to answer, when Colonel Sapt stepped between the king and me, and began to talk to his Majesty in a low growl. The king towered over Sapt, and, as he listened, his eyes now and again sought mine. I looked at him long and carefully. The likeness was certainly astonishing, though I saw the points of difference also. The king's face was slightly more fleshy than mine, the oval of its contour the least trifle more pronounced, and, as I fancied, his mouth lacking something of the firmness (or obstinacy) which was to be gathered from my close-shutting lips. But, for all that, and above all minor distinctions, the likeness rose striking, salient, wonderful.

Sapt ceased speaking, and the king still frowned. Then, gradually, the corners of his mouth began to twitch, his nose came down (as mine does when I laugh), his eyes twinkled, and, behold! he burst into the merriest fit of irrepressible laughter, which rang through the woods and proclaimed him a jovial soul.

"Well met, cousin!" he cried, stepping up to me, clapping me on the back, and laughing still. "You must forgive me if I was taken aback. A man doesn't expect to see double at this time of day, eh, Fritz?"

"I must pray pardon, sire, for my presumption," said I. "I trust it will not forfeit your Majesty's favour."

"By Heaven! you'll always enjoy the king's countenance," he laughed, "whether I like it or not; and, sir, I shall very gladly add to it what services I can. Where are you travelling to?"

"To Strelsau, sire—to the coronation."

The king looked at his friends: he still smiled, though his expression hinted some uneasiness. But the humorous side of the matter caught him again.

"Fritz, Fritz!" he cried, "a thousand crowns for a sight of brother Michael's face when he sees a pair of us!" and the merry laugh rang out again.

"Seriously," observed Fritz von Tarlenheim, "I question Mr. Rassendyll's wisdom in visiting Strelsau just now."

The king lit a cigarette.

"Well, Sapt?" said he, questioningly.

"He mustn't go," growled the old fellow.

"Come, colonel, you mean that I should be in Mr. Rassendyll's debt, if——"

"Oh, ay! wrap it up in the right way," said Sapt, hauling a great pipe out of his pocket.

"Enough, sire," said I. "I'll leave Ruritania to-day."

"Now, by thunder, you shan't—and that's *sans phrase,* as Sapt likes it. For you shall dine with me to-night, happen what will afterwards. Come, man, you don't meet a new relation every day!"

"We dine sparingly to-night," said Fritz von Tarlenheim.

"Not we—with our new cousin for a guest!" cried the king; and, as Fritz shrugged his shoulders, he added: "Oh! I'll remember our early start, Fritz."

"So will I—to-morrow morning," said old Sapt, pulling at his pipe.

"O wise old Sapt!" cried the king. "Come, Mr. Rassendyll—by the way, what name did they give you?"

"Your Majesty's," I answered, bowing.

"Well, that shows they weren't ashamed of us," he laughed. "Come, then, cousin Rudolf; I've got no house of my own here, but my dear brother Michael lends us a place of his, and we'll make shift to entertain you there;" and he put his arm through mine and, signing to the others to accompany us, walked me off, westerly, through the forest.

We walked for more than half-an-hour, and the king smoked cigarettes and chattered incessantly. He was full of interest in my family, laughed heartily when I told him of the portraits with Elphberg hair in our galleries, and yet more heartily when he heard that my expedition to Ruritania was a secret one.

"You have to visit your disreputable cousin on the sly, have you?" said he.

Suddenly emerging from the wood, we came on a small and rude shooting-lodge. It was a one-story building, a sort of bungalow, built entirely of wood. As we approached it, a little man in a plain livery came out to meet us. The only other person I saw about the place was a fat elderly woman, whom I afterwards discovered to be the mother of Johann, the duke's keeper.

"Well, is dinner ready, Josef?" asked the king.

The little servant informed us that it was, and we soon sat down to a plentiful meal. The fare was plain enough: the king ate heartily, Fritz von Tarlenheim delicately, old Sapt voraciously. I played a good knife and fork, as my custom is; the king noticed my performance with approval.

"We're all good trenchermen, we Elphbergs," said he. "But what?—we're eating dry! Wine, Josef! wine, man! Are we beasts, to eat without drinking? Are we cattle, Josef?"

At this reproof Josef hastened to load the table with bottles.

"Remember to-morrow!" said Fritz.

"Ay—to-morrow!" said old Sapt.

The king drained a bumper to his "Cousin Rudolf," as he was gracious—or merry—enough to call me; and I drank its fellow to the "Elphberg Red," whereat he laughed loudly.

Now, be the meat what it might, the wine we drank was beyond all price or praise, and we did it justice. Fritz ventured once to stay the king's hand.

"What?" cried the king. "Remember you start before I do, Master Fritz—you must be more sparing by two hours than I."

Fritz saw that I did not understand.

"The colonel and I," he explained, "leave here at six: we ride down to Zenda and return with the guard of honour to fetch the king at eight, and then we all ride together to the station."

"Hang that same guard!" growled Sapt.

"Oh! it's very civil of my brother to ask the honour for his regiment," said the king. "Come, cousin, you need not start early. Another bottle, man!"

I had another bottle—or, rather, a part of one, for the larger half travelled quickly down his Majesty's throat. Fritz gave up his attempts at persuasion: from persuading, he fell to being persuaded, and soon we were all of us as full of wine as we had any right to be. The king began talking of what he would do in the future, old Sapt of what he had done in the past, Fritz of some beautiful girl or other, and I of the wonderful merits of the Elphberg dynasty. We all talked at once, and followed to the letter Sapt's exhortation to let the morrow take care of itself.

At last the king set down his glass and leant back in his chair.

"I have drunk enough," said he.

"Far be it from me to contradict the king," said I.

Indeed, his remark was most absolutely true—so far as it went.

While I yet spoke, Josef came and set before the king a marvellous old wicker-covered flagon. It had lain so long in some darkened cellar that it seemed to blink in the candlelight.

"His Highness the Duke of Strelsau bade me set this wine before the king, when the king was weary of all other wines, and pray the king to drink, for the love that he bears his brother."

"Well done, Black Michael!" said the king. "Out with the cork, Josef. Hang him! Did he think I'd flinch from his bottle?"

The bottle was opened, and Josef filled the king's glass. The king tasted it. Then, with a solemnity born of the hour and his own condition, he looked round on us:

"Gentlemen, my friends—Rudolf, my cousin ('tis a scandalous story, Rudolf, on my honour!), everything is yours to the half of Ruritania. But ask me not for a single drop of this divine bottle, which I will drink to the health of that—that sly knave, my brother, Black Michael."

And the king seized the bottle and turned it over his mouth, and drained it and flung it from him, and laid his head on his arms on the table.

And we drank pleasant dreams to his Majesty—and that is all I remember of the evening. Perhaps it is enough.

CHAPTER IV

The King Keeps His Appointment

WHETHER I had slept a minute or a year I knew not. I awoke with a start and a shiver; my face, hair, and clothes dripped water, and opposite me stood old Sapt, a sneering smile on his face and an empty bucket in his hand. On the table by him sat Fritz von Tarlenheim, pale as a ghost and black as a crow under the eyes.

I leapt to my feet in anger.

"Your joke goes too far, sir!" I cried.

"Tut, man, we've no time for quarrelling. Nothing else would rouse you. It's five o'clock."

"I'll thank you, Colonel Sapt——" I began again, hot in spirit, though I was uncommonly cold in body.

"Rassendyll," interrupted Fritz, getting down from the table and taking my arm, "look here."

The king lay full length on the floor. His face was red as his hair, and he breathed heavily. Sapt, the disrespectful old dog, kicked him sharply. He did not stir, nor was there any break in his breathing. I saw that his face and head were wet with water, as were mine.

"We've spent half an hour on him," said Fritz.

"He drank three times what either of you did," growled Sapt.

I knelt down and felt his pulse. It was alarmingly languid and slow. We three looked at one another.

341

"Was it drugged—that last bottle?" I asked in a whisper.

"I don't know," said Sapt.

"We must get a doctor."

"There's none within ten miles, and a thousand doctors wouldn't take him to Strelsau to-day. I know the look of it. He'll not move for six or seven hours yet."

"But the coronation!" I cried in horror.

Fritz shrugged his shoulders, as I began to see was his habit on most occasions.

"We must send word that he's ill," he said.

"I suppose so," said I.

Old Sapt, who seemed as fresh as a daisy, had lit his pipe and was puffing hard at it.

"If he's not crowned to-day," said he, "I'll lay a crown he's never crowned."

"But, heavens, why?"

"The whole nation's there to meet him; half the army—ay, and Black Michael at the head. Shall we send word that the king's drunk?"

"That he's ill," said I, in correction.

"Ill!" echoed Sapt, with a scornful laugh. "They know his illnesses too well. He's been 'ill' before!"

"Well, we must chance what they think," said Fritz helplessly. "I'll carry the news and make the best of it."

Sapt raised his hand.

"Tell me," said he. "Do you think the king was drugged?"

"I do," said I.

"And who drugged him?"

"That damned hound, Black Michael," said Fritz between his teeth.

"Ay," said Sapt, "that he might not come to be crowned. Rassendyll here doesn't know our pretty Michael. What think you, Fritz, has Michael no king ready? Has half Strelsau no other candidate? As God's alive, man, the throne's lost if the king show himself not in Strelsau to-day. I know Black Michael."

"We could carry him there," said I.

"And a very pretty picture he makes," sneered Sapt.

Fritz von Tarlenheim buried his face in his hands. The king breathed loudly and heavily. Sapt stirred him again with his foot.

"The drunken dog!" he said; "but he's an Elphberg and the son of his father, and may I rot in hell before Black Michael sits in his place!"

For a moment or two we were all silent; then Sapt, knitting his bushy grey brows, took his pipe from his mouth and said to me:

"As a man grows old he believes in Fate. Fate sent you here. Fate sends you now to Strelsau."

I staggered back, murmuring "Good God!"

Fritz looked up with an eager, bewildered gaze.

"Impossible!" I muttered. "I should be known."

"It's a risk—against a certainty," said Sapt. "If you shave, I'll wager you'll not be known. Are you afraid?"

"Sir!"

"Come, lad, there, there; but it's your life, you know, if you're known—and mine—and Fritz's here. But, if you don't go, I swear to you Black Michael will sit to-night on the throne, and the king lie in prison or his grave."

"The king would never forgive it," I stammered.

"Are we women? Who cares for his forgiveness?"

The clock ticked fifty times, and sixty and seventy times, as I stood in thought. Then I suppose a look came over my face, for old Sapt caught me by the hand, crying:

"You'll go?"

"Yes, I'll go," said I, and I turned my eyes on the prostrate figure of the king on the floor.

"To-night," Sapt went on in a hasty whisper, "we are to lodge in the Palace. The moment they leave us you and I will mount our horses—Fritz must stay there and guard the king's room—and ride here at a gallop. The king will be ready—Josef will tell him—and he must ride back with me to Strelsau, and you ride as if the devil were behind you to the frontier."

I took it all in in a second, and nodded my head.

"There's a chance," said Fritz, with his first sign of hopefulness.

"If I escape detection," said I.

"If we're detected," said Sapt, "I'll send Black Michael down below before I go myself, so help me heaven! Sit in that chair, man."

I obeyed him.

He darted from the room, calling, "Josef! Josef!" In three minutes he was back, and Josef with him. The latter carried a jug of hot water, soap, and razors. He was trembling as Sapt told him how the land lay, and bade him shave me.

Suddenly Fritz smote on his thigh:

"But the guard! They'll know! they'll know!"

"Pooh! We shan't wait for the guard. We'll ride to Hofbau and catch a train there. When they come, the bird'll be flown."

"But the king?"

"The king will be in the wine-cellar. I'm going to carry him there now."

"If they find him?"

"They won't. How should they? Josef will put them off."

"But——"

Sapt stamped his foot.

"We're not playing," he roared. "My God! don't I know the risk? If they do find him, he's no worse off than if he isn't crowned to-day in Strelsau."

So speaking, he flung the door open and, stooping, put forth a strength I did not dream he had, and lifted the king in his hands. And as he did so, the old woman, Johann the keeper's mother, stood in the doorway. For a moment she stood, then she turned on her heel, without a sign of surprise, and clattered down the passage.

"Has she heard?" cried Fritz.

"I'll shut her mouth!" said Sapt grimly, and he bore off the king in his arms.

For me, I sat down in an arm-chair, and as I sat there, half-dazed, Josef clipped and scraped me till my moustache and imperial were things of the past and my face was as bare as the king's. And when Fritz saw me thus he drew a long breath and exclaimed:

"By Jove, we shall do it!"

It was six o'clock now, and we had no time to lose. Sapt hurried me into the king's room, and I dressed myself in the uniform of a colonel of the Guard, finding time as I slipped on the king's boots to ask Sapt what he had done with the old woman.

"She swore she'd heard nothing," said he; "but to make sure I tied her legs together and put a handkerchief in her mouth and bound her hands, and locked her up in the coal-cellar, next door to the king. Josef'll look after them both later on."

Then I burst out laughing, and even old Sapt grimly smiled.

"I fancy," said he, "that when Josef tells them the king is gone they'll think it is because we smelt a rat. For you may swear Black Michael doesn't expect to see him in Strelsau to-day."

I put the king's helmet on my head. Old Sapt handed me the king's sword, looking at me long and carefully.

"Thank God, he shaved his beard!" he exclaimed.

"Why did he?" I asked.

"Because Princess Flavia said he grazed her cheek when he was graciously pleased to give her a cousinly kiss. Come though, we must ride."

"Is all safe here?"

"Nothing's safe anywhere," said Sapt, "but we can make it no safer."

Fritz now rejoined us in the uniform of a captain in the same regiment as that to which my dress belonged. In four minutes Sapt had arrayed himself in his uniform. Josef called that the horses were ready. We jumped on their backs and started at a rapid trot. The game had begun. What would the issue of it be?

The cool morning air cleared my head, and I was able to take in all Sapt said to me. He was wonderful. Fritz hardly spoke, riding like a man asleep, but Sapt, without another word for the king, began at once to instruct me most minutely in the history of my past life, of my family, of my tastes, pursuits, weaknesses, friends, companions, and servants. He told me the etiquette of the Ruritanian Court, promising to be constantly at my elbow to point out everybody whom I ought to know, and give me hints with what degree of favour to greet them.

"By the way," he said, "you're a Catholic, I suppose?"

"Not I," I answered.

"Lord, he's a heretic!" groaned Sapt, and forthwith he fell to a rudimentary lesson in the practices and observances of the Romish faith.

"Luckily," said he, "you won't be expected to know much, for the king's notoriously lax and careless about such matters. But you must be as civil as butter to the Cardinal. We hope to win him over, because he and Michael have a standing quarrel about their precedence."

We were by now at the station. Fritz had recovered nerve enough to explain to the astonished stationmaster that the king had changed his plans. The train steamed up. We got into a first-class carriage, and Sapt, leaning back on the cushions, went on with his lesson. I looked at my watch—the king's watch it was, of course. It was just eight.

"I wonder if they've gone to look for us," I said.

"I hope they won't find the king," said Fritz nervously, and this time it was Sapt who shrugged his shoulders.

The train travelled well, and at half-past nine, looking out of the window, I saw the towers and spires of a great city.

"Your capital, my liege," grinned old Sapt, with a wave of his hand, and, leaning forward, he laid his finger on my pulse. "A little too quick," said he, in his grumbling tone.

"I'm not made of stone!" I exclaimed.

"You'll do," said he, with a nod. "We must say Fritz here has caught the ague. Drain your flask, Fritz, for heaven's sake, boy!"

Fritz did as he was bid.

"We're an hour early," said Sapt. "We'll send word

forward of your Majesty's arrival, for there'll be no one here to meet us yet. And meanwhile——"

"Meanwhile," said I, "the king'll be hanged if he doesn't have some breakfast."

Old Sapt chuckled, and held out his hand.

"You're an Elphberg, every inch of you," said he. Then he paused, and looking at us, said quietly, "God send we may be alive to-night!"

"Amen!" said Fritz von Tarlenheim.

The train stopped. Fritz and Sapt leapt out, uncovered, and held the door for me. I choked down a lump that rose in my throat, settled my helmet firmly on my head, and (I'm not ashamed to say it) breathed a short prayer to God. Then I stepped on the platform of the station at Strelsau.

A moment later, all was bustle and confusion: men hurrying up, hats in hand, and hurrying off again; men conducting me to the *buffet;* men mounting and riding in hot haste to the quarters of the troops, to the Cathedral, to the residence of Duke Michael. Even as I swallowed the last drop of my cup of coffee, the bells throughout all the city broke out into a joyful peal, and the sound of a military band and of men cheering smote upon my ear.

King Rudolf the Fifth was in his good city of Strelsau! And they shouted outside:

"God save the King!"

Old Sapt's mouth wrinkled into a smile.

"God save 'em both!" he whispered. "Courage, lad!" and I felt his hand press my knee.

CHAPTER V

The Adventures of an Understudy

WITH Fritz von Tarlenheim and Colonel Sapt close behind me, I stepped out of the *buffet* on to the platform. The last thing I did was to feel if my revolver were handy and my sword loose in the scabbard. A gay group of officers and high dignitaries stood waiting me, at their head a tall old man, covered with medals, and of military bearing. He wore the yellow-and-red ribbon of the Red Rose of Ruritania—which, by the way, decorated my unworthy breast also.

"Marshal Strakencz," whispered Sapt, and I knew that I was in the presence of the most famous veteran of the Ruritanian army.

Just behind the Marshal stood a short spare man, in flowing robes of black and crimson.

"The Chancellor of the Kingdom," whispered Sapt.

The Marshal greeted me in a few loyal words, and proceeded to deliver an apology from the Duke of Strelsau. The duke, it seemed, had been afflicted with a sudden indisposition which made it impossible for him to come to the station, but he craved leave to await his Majesty at the Cathedral. I expressed my concern, accepted the Marshal's excuses very suavely, and received the compliments of a large number of distinguished personages. No one betrayed the least suspicion, and I felt my nerve returning and the agitated beating of my heart subsiding. But Fritz was still pale, and his hand shook like a leaf as he extended it to the Marshal.

Presently we formed procession and took our way to the door of the station. Here I mounted my horse, the Marshal holding my stirrup. The civil dignitaries went off to their carriages, and I started to ride through the streets with the Marshal on my right and Sapt (who, as my chief *aide-de-camp*, was entitled to the place) on my left. The city of Strelsau is partly old and partly new. Spacious modern boulevards and residential quarters surround and embrace the narrow, tortuous and picturesque streets of the original town. In the outer circles the upper classes live; in the inner the shops are situated; and, behind their prosperous fronts, lie hidden populous but wretched lanes and alleys, filled with a poverty-stricken, turbulent, and (in large measure) criminal class. These social and local divisions corresponded, as I knew from Sapt's information, to another division more important to me. The New Town was for the king; but to the Old Town Michael of Strelsau was a hope, a hero, and a darling.

The scene was very brilliant as we passed along the Grand Boulevard and on to the great square where the Royal Palace stood. Here I was in the midst of my devoted adherents. Every house was hung with red and bedecked with flags and mottoes. The streets were lined with raised seats on each side, and I passed along, bowing this way and that, under a shower of cheers, blessings, and waving handkerchiefs. The balconies were full of gaily-dressed ladies, who clapped their hands and curtsied and threw their brightest glances at me. A torrent of red roses fell on me; one bloom lodged in my horse's mane, and I took it and stuck it in my coat. The Marshal smiled grimly. I had stolen some glances at his face, but he was too impassive to show me whether his sympathies were with me or not.

"The red rose for the Elphbergs, Marshal," said I gaily, and he nodded.

I have written "gaily," and a strange word it must

seem. But the truth is, that I was drunk with excitement. At that moment I believed—I almost believed—that I was in very truth the king; and, with a look of laughing triumph, I raised my eyes to the beauty-laden balconies again . . . and then I started. For, looking down on me, with her handsome face and proud smile, was the lady who had been my fellow-traveller—Antoinette de Mauban; and I saw her also start, and her lips moved, and she leant forward and gazed at me. And I, collecting myself, met her eyes full and square, while again I felt my revolver. Suppose she had cried aloud, "That's not the king!"

Well, we went by; and then the Marshal, turning round in his saddle, waved his hand, and the Cuirassiers closed round us, so that the crowd could not come near me. We were leaving my quarter and entering Duke Michael's, and this action of the Marshal's showed me more clearly than words what the state of feeling in the town must be. But if Fate made me a king, the least I could do was to play the part handsomely.

"Why this change in our order, Marshal?" said I.

The Marshal bit his white moustache.

"It is more prudent, sire," he murmured.

I drew rein.

"Let those in front ride on," said I, "till they are fifty yards ahead. But do you, Marshal, and Colonel Sapt and my friends, wait here till I have ridden fifty yards. And see that no one is nearer to me. I will have my people see that their king trusts them."

Sapt laid his hand on my arm. I shook him off. The Marshal hesitated.

"Am I not understood?" said I; and, biting his moustache again, he gave the orders. I saw old Sapt smiling into his beard, but he shook his head at me. If I had been killed in open day in the streets of Strelsau, Sapt's position would have been a difficult one.

Perhaps I ought to say that I was dressed all in white, except my boots. I wore a silver helmet with gilt ornaments, and the broad ribbon of the Rose looked well across my chest. I should be paying a poor compliment to the king if I did not set modesty aside and admit that I made a very fine figure. So the people thought; for when I, riding alone, entered the dingy, sparsely-decorated, sombre streets of the Old Town, there was first a murmur, then a cheer, and a woman, from a window above a cookshop, cried the old local saying:

"If he's red, he's right!" whereat I laughed and took off my helmet that she might see that I was of the right colour, and they cheered me again at that.

It was more interesting riding thus alone, for I heard the comments of the crowd.

"He looks paler than his wont," said one.

"You'd look pale if you lived as he does," was the highly disrespectful retort.

"He's a bigger man than I thought," said another.

"So he had a good jaw under that beard after all," commented a third.

"The pictures of him aren't handsome enough," declared a pretty girl, taking great care that I should hear. No doubt it was mere flattery.

But, in spite of these signs of approval and interest, the mass of the people received me in silence and with sullen looks, and my dear brother's portrait ornamented most of the windows—which was an ironical sort of greeting to the king. I was quite glad that he had been spared the unpleasant sight. He was a man of quick temper, and perhaps he would not have taken it so placidly as I did.

At last we were at the Cathedral. Its great grey front, embellished with hundreds of statues and boasting a pair of the finest oak doors in Europe, rose for the first time before me, and the sudden sense of my audacity almost overcame me. Everything was in a mist as I dismounted, I saw the Marshal and Sapt dimly, and dimly the throng of gorgeously-robed priests who awaited me. And my eyes were still dim as I walked up the great nave, with the pealing of the organ in my ears. I saw nothing of the brilliant throng that filled it, I hardly dis-

tinguished the stately figure of the Cardinal as he rose
from the archiepiscopal throne to greet me. Two faces
only stood out side by side clearly before my eyes—the
face of a girl, pale and lovely, surmounted by a crown of
the glorious Elphberg hair (for in a woman it is glorious), and the face of a man, whose full-blooded red
cheeks, black hair, and dark deep eyes told me that at
last I was in presence of my brother, Black Michael.
And when he saw me his red cheeks went pale all in a
moment, and his helmet fell with a clatter on the floor.
Till that moment, I believe that he had not realised that
the king was in very truth come to Strelsau.

Of what followed next I remember nothing. I knelt
before the altar and the Cardinal anointed my head.
Then I rose to my feet, and stretched out my hand and
took from him the crown of Ruritania and set it on my
head, and I swore the old oath of the king; and (if it
were a sin, may it be forgiven me) I received the Holy
Sacrament there before them all. Then the great organ
pealed out again, the Marshal bade the heralds proclaim me, and Rudolf the Fifth was crowned king; of
which imposing ceremony an excellent picture hangs
now in my dining-room. The portrait of the king is
very good.

Then the lady with the pale face and the glorious hair,
her train held by two pages, stepped from her place and
came to where I stood. And a herald cried:

"Her Royal Highness the Princess Flavia!"

She curtsied low, and put her hand under mine and
raised my hand and kissed it. And for an instant I
thought what I had best do. Then I drew her to me and
kissed her twice on the cheek, and she blushed red,
and—why, then his Eminence the Cardinal Archbishop
slipped in front of Black Michael, and kissed my hand
and presented me with a letter from the Pope—the first
and last which I have ever received from that exalted
quarter!

And then came the Duke of Strelsau. His step trembled, I swear, and he looked to the right and to the left,

as a man looks who thinks on flight; and his face was patched with red and white, and his hand shook so that it jumped under mine, and I felt his lips dry and parched. And I glanced at Sapt, who was smiling again into his beard, and, resolutely doing my duty in that station of life to which I had been marvellously called, I took my dear Michael by both hands and kissed him on the cheek. I think we were both glad when that was over!

But neither in the face of the princess nor in that of any other did I see the least doubt or questioning. Yet, had I and the king stood side by side, she could have told us in an instant, or, at least, on a little consideration. But neither she nor anyone else dreamed or imagined that I could be other than the king. So the likeness served, and for an hour I stood there, feeling as weary and *blasé* as though I had been a king all my life; and everybody kissed my hand, and the ambassadors paid me their respects, among them old Lord Topham, at whose house in Grosvenor Square I had danced a score of times. Thank heaven, the old man was as blind as a bat, and did not claim my acquaintance.

Then back we went through the streets to the Palace, and I heard them cheering Black Michael; but he, Fritz told me, sat biting his nails like a man in a reverie, and even his own friends said that he should have made a braver show. I was in a carriage now, side by side with the Princess Flavia, and a rough fellow cried out:

"And when's the wedding?" and as he spoke another struck him in the face, crying, "Long live Duke Michael!" and the princess coloured—it was an admirable tint—and looked straight in front of her.

Now I felt in a difficulty, because I had forgotten to ask Sapt the state of my affections, or how far matters had gone between the princess and myself. Frankly, had I been the king, the further they had gone the better should I have been pleased. For I am not a slow-blooded man, and I had not kissed Princess Flavia's cheek for nothing. These thoughts passed through my head, but, not being sure of my ground, I said nothing; and in a moment or two the princess, recovering her equanimity, turned to me.

"Do you know, Rudolf," said she, "you look somehow different to-day?"

The fact was not surprising, but the remark was disquieting.

"You look," she went on, "more sober, more sedate; you're almost careworn, and I declare you're thinner. Surely it's not possible that you've begun to take anything seriously?"

The princess seemed to hold of the king much the same opinion that Lady Burlesdon held of me.

I braced myself up to the conversation.

"Would that please you?" I asked softly.

"Oh, you know my views," said she, turning her eyes away.

"Whatever pleases you I try to do," I said; and, as I saw her smile and blush, I thought that I was playing the king's hand very well for him. So I continued, and what I said was perfectly true:

"I assure you, my dear cousin, that nothing in my life has affected me more than the reception I've been greeted with to-day."

She smiled brightly, but in an instant grew grave again, and whispered:

"Did you notice Michael?"

"Yes," said I, adding, "He wasn't enjoying himself."

"Do be careful!" she went on. "You don't—indeed you don't—keep enough watch on him. You know——"

"I know," said I, "that he wants what I've got."

"Yes. Hush!"

Then—and I can't justify it, for I committed the king far beyond what I had a right to do—I suppose she carried me off my feet—I went on:

"And perhaps also something which I haven't got yet, but hope to win some day."

This was my answer. Had I been the king, I should have thought it encouraging:

"Haven't you enough responsibilities on you for one day, cousin?"

Bang, bang! Blare, blare! We were at the Palace. Guns were firing and trumpets blowing. Rows of lackeys stood waiting, and, handing the princess up the broad marble staircase, I took formal possession, as a crowned king, of the House of my ancestors, and sat down at my own table, with my cousin on my right hand, on her other side Black Michael, and on my left his Eminence the Cardinal. Behind my chair stood Sapt; and at the end of the table, I saw Fritz von Tarlenheim drain to the bottom his glass of champagne rather sooner than he decently should.

I wondered what the King of Ruritania was doing.

CHAPTER VI

The Secret of a Cellar

WE were in the king's dressing-room—Fritz von Tarlenheim, Sapt, and I. I flung myself exhausted into an arm-chair. Sapt lit his pipe. He uttered no congratulations on the marvellous success of our wild risk, but his whole bearing was eloquent of satisfaction. The triumph, aided perhaps by good wine, had made a new man of Fritz.

"What a day for you to remember!" he cried. "Gad, I'd like to be a king for twelve hours myself! But, Rassendyll, you mustn't throw your heart too much into the part. I don't wonder Black Michael looked blacker than ever—you and the princess had so much to say to one another."

"How beautiful she is!" I exclaimed.

"Never mind the women," growled Sapt. "Are you ready to start?"

"Yes," said I, with a sigh.

It was five o'clock, and at twelve I should be no more than Rudolf Rassendyll. I remarked on it in a joking tone.

"You'll be lucky," observed Sapt grimly, "if you're not the late Rudolf Rassendyll. By Heaven! I feel my head wobbling on my shoulders every minute you're in the city. Do you know, friend, that Michael has had news

356

from Zenda? He went into a room alone to read it—
and he came out looking like a man dazed."

"I'm ready," said I, this news making me none the
more eager to linger.

Sapt sat down.

"I must write us an order to leave the city. Michael's
Governor, you know, and we must be prepared for hin-
drances. You must sign the order."

"My dear colonel, I've not been bred a forger!"

Out of his pocket Sapt produced a piece of paper.

"There's the king's signature," he said, "and here," he
went on, after another search in his pocket, "is some
tracing paper. If you can't manage a 'Rudolf' in ten minutes, why—I can."

"Your education has been more comprehensive than
mine," said I. "You write it."

And a very tolerable forgery did this versatile hero
produce.

"Now, Fritz," said he, "the king goes to bed. He is
upset. No one is to see him till nine o'clock to-morrow.
You understand—no one?"

"I understand," answered Fritz.

"Michael may come, and claim immediate audience.
You'll answer that only princes of the blood are entitled
to it."

"That'll annoy Michael," laughed Fritz.

"You quite understand?" asked Sapt again. "If the
door of this room is opened while we're away, you're
not to be alive to tell us about it."

"I need no schooling, Colonel," said Fritz, a trifle
haughtily.

"Here, wrap yourself in this big cloak," Sapt continued to me, "and put on this flat cap. My orderly rides
with me to the shooting-lodge to-night."

"There's an obstacle," I observed. "The horse doesn't
live that can carry me forty miles."

"Oh, yes, he does—two of him: one here—one at the
lodge. Now, are you ready?"

"I'm ready," said I.

Fritz held out his hand.

"In case," said he; and we shook hands heartily.

"Damn your sentiment!" growled Sapt. "Come along."

He went, not to the door, but to a panel in the wall.

"In the old king's time," said he, "I knew this way well."

I followed him, and we walked, as I should estimate, near two hundred yards along a narrow passage. Then we came to a stout oak door. Sapt unlocked it. We passed through, and found ourselves in a quiet street that ran along the back of the Palace gardens. A man was waiting for us with two horses. One was a magnificent bay, up to any weight; the other a sturdy brown. Sapt signed to me to mount the bay. Without a word to the man, we mounted and rode away. The town was full of noise and merriment, but we took secluded ways. My cloak was wrapped over half my face; the capacious flat cap hid every lock of my tell-tale hair. By Sapt's directions, I crouched on my saddle, and rode with such a round back as I hope never to exhibit on a horse again. Down a long narrow lane we went, meeting some wanderers and some roisterers; and, as we rode, we heard the Cathedral bells still clanging out their welcome to the king. It was half-past six, and still light. At last we came to the city wall and to a gate.

"Have your weapon ready," whispered Sapt. "We must stop his mouth, if he talks."

I put my hand on my revolver. Sapt hailed the door-keeper. The stars fought for us! A little girl of fourteen tripped out.

"Please, sir, father's gone to see the king."

"He'd better have stayed here," said Sapt to me, grinning.

"But he said I wasn't to open the gate, sir."

"Did he, my dear?" said Sapt, dismounting. "Then give me the key."

The key was in the child's hand. Sapt gave her a crown.

"Here's an order from the king. Show it to your father. Orderly, open the gate!"

I leapt down. Between us we rolled back the great gate, led our horses out, and closed it again.

"I shall be sorry for the doorkeeper, if Michael finds out that he wasn't there. Now then, lad, for a canter. We mustn't go too fast while we're near the town."

Once, however, outside the city, we ran little danger, for everybody else was inside, merry-making; and as the evening fell we quickened our pace, my splendid horse bounding along under me as though I had been a feather. It was a fine night, and presently the moon appeared. We talked little on the way, and chiefly about the progress we were making.

"I wonder what the duke's despatches told him!" said I, once.

"Ay, I wonder!" responded Sapt.

We stopped for a draught of wine and to bait our horses, losing half-an-hour thus. I dared not go into the inn, and stayed with the horses in the stable. Then we went ahead again, and had covered some five-and-twenty miles, when Sapt abruptly stopped.

"Hark!" he cried.

I listened. Away, far behind us, in the still of the evening—it was just half-past nine—we heard the beat of horses' hoofs. The wind blowing strong behind us, carried the sound. I glanced at Sapt.

"Come on!" he cried, and spurred his horse into a gallop. When we next paused to listen, the hoof-beats were not audible, and we relaxed our pace. Then we heard them again. Sapt jumped down and laid his ear to the ground.

"There are two," he said. "They're only a mile behind. Thank God the road curves in and out, and the wind's our way."

We galloped on. We seemed to be holding our own. We had entered the outskirts of the forest of Zenda, and the trees, closing in behind us as the track zigged and zagged, prevented us seeing our pursuers, and them from seeing us.

Another half-hour brought us to a divide of the road. Sapt drew rein.

"To the right is our road," he said. "To the left, to the Castle. Each about eight miles. Get down."

"But they'll be on us!" I cried.

"Get down!" he repeated, brusquely; and I obeyed.

The wood was dense up to the very edge of the road. We led our horses into the covert, bound handkerchiefs over their eyes, and stood beside them.

"You want to see who they are?" I whispered.

"Ay, and where they're going," he answered.

I saw that his revolver was in his hand.

Nearer and nearer came the hoofs. The moon shone out now clear and full, so that the road was white with it. The ground was hard, and we had left no traces.

"Here they come!" whispered Sapt.

"It's the duke!"

"I thought so!" he answered.

It was the duke; and with him a burly fellow whom I knew well, and who had cause to know me afterwards—Max Holf, brother to Johann the keeper, and body-servant to his Highness. They were up to us: the duke reined up. I saw Sapt's finger curl lovingly towards the trigger. I believe he would have given ten years of his life for a shot; and he could have picked off Black Michael as easily as I could a barn-door fowl in a farmyard. I laid my hand on his arm. He nodded reassuringly: he was always ready to sacrifice inclination to duty.

"Which way?" asked Black Michael.

"To the Castle, your Highness," urged his companion. "There we shall learn the truth."

For an instant the duke hesitated.

"I thought I heard hoofs," said he.

"I think not, your Highness."

"Why shouldn't we go to the lodge?"

"I fear a trap. If all is well, why go to the lodge? If not, it's a snare to trap us."

Suddenly the duke's horse neighed. In an instant we folded our cloaks close round our horses' heads, and, holding them thus, covered the duke and his attendant with our revolvers. If they had found us, they had been dead men, or our prisoners.

Michael waited a moment longer. Then he cried:

"To Zenda, then!" and setting spurs to his horse, galloped on.

Sapt raised his weapon after him, and there was such an expression of wistful regret on his face that I had much ado not to burst out laughing.

For ten minutes we stayed where we were.

"You see," said Sapt, "they've sent him news that all is well."

"What does that mean?" I asked.

"God knows," said Sapt, frowning heavily. "But it's brought him from Strelsau in a rare puzzle."

Then we mounted, and rode fast as our weary horses could lay their feet to the ground. For those last eight miles we spoke no more. Our minds were full of apprehension. "All is well." What did it mean? Was all well with the king?

At last the lodge came in sight. Spurring our horses to a last gallop, we rode up to the gate. All was still and quiet. Not a soul came to meet us. We dismounted in haste. Suddenly Sapt caught me by the arm.

"Look there!" he said, pointing to the ground.

I looked down. At my feet lay five or six silk handkerchiefs, torn and slashed and rent. I turned to him questioningly.

"They're what I tied the old woman up with," said he. "Fasten the horses, and come along."

The handle of the door turned without resistance. We passed into the room which had been the scene of last night's bout. It was still strewn with the remnants of our meal and with empty bottles.

"Come on," cried Sapt, whose marvellous composure had at last almost given way.

We rushed down the passage towards the cellars. The door of the coal-cellar stood wide open.

"They found the old woman," said I.

"You might have known that from the handker-chiefs," he said.

Then we came opposite the door of the wine-cellar. It was shut. It looked in all respects as it had looked when we left it that morning.

"Come, it's all right," said I.

A loud oath from Sapt rang out. His face turned pale, and he pointed again at the floor. From under the door a red stain had spread over the floor of the passage and dried there. Sapt sank against the opposite wall. I tried the door. It was locked.

"Where's Josef?" muttered Sapt.

"Where's the king?" I responded.

Sapt took out a flask and put it to his lips. I ran back to the dining-room, and seized a heavy poker from the fireplace. In my terror and excitement I rained blows on the lock of the door, and I fired a cartridge into it. It gave way, and the door swung open.

"Give me a light," said I; but Sapt still leant against the wall.

He was, of course, more moved than I, for he loved his master. Afraid for himself he was not—no man ever saw him that; but to think what might lie in that dark cellar was enough to turn any man's face pale. I went myself, and took a silver candle-stick from the dining-table and struck a light, and, as I returned, I felt the hot wax drip on my naked hand as the candle swayed to and fro; so that I cannot afford to despise Colonel Sapt for his agitation.

I came to the door of the cellar. The red stain, turning more and more to a dull brown, stretched inside. I walked two yards into the cellar, and held the candle high above my head. I saw the full bins of wine; I saw spiders crawling on the walls; I saw, too, a couple of empty bottles lying on the floor; and then, away in the corner, I saw the body of a man, lying flat on his back, with his arms stretched wide, and a crimson gash across his throat. I walked to him and knelt down beside him, and commended to God the soul of a faithful man. For it was the body of Josef, the little servant, slain in guarding the king.

I felt a hand on my shoulders, and, turning, saw Sapt's eyes, glaring and terror-struck, beside me.

"The king? My God! the king?" he whispered hoarsely.

I threw the candle's gleam over every inch of the cellar.

"The king is not here," said I.

CHAPTER VII

His Majesty Sleeps in Strelsau

I PUT my arm round Sapt's waist and supported him out of the cellar, drawing the battered door close after me. For ten minutes or more we sat silent in the dining-room. Then old Sapt rubbed his knuckles into his eyes, gave one great gasp, and was himself again. As the clock on the mantelpiece struck one he stamped his foot on the floor, saying:

"They've got the king!"

"Yes," said I, " 'all's well!' as Black Michael's despatch said. What a moment it must have been for him when the royal salutes fired at Strelsau this morning! I wonder when he got the message!"

"It must have been sent in the morning," said Sapt. "They must have sent it before news of your arrival at Strelsau reached Zenda—I suppose it came from Zenda."

"And he's carried it about all day!" I exclaimed. "Upon my honour, I'm not the only man who's had a trying day! What did he think, Sapt?"

"What does that matter? What does he think, lad, now?"

I rose to my feet.

"We must get back," I said, "and rouse every soldier

in Strelsau. We ought to be in pursuit of Michael before mid-day."

Old Sapt pulled out his pipe and carefully lit it from the candle which guttered on the table.

"The king may be murdered while we sit here!" I urged.

Sapt smoked on for a moment in silence.

"That cursed old woman!" he broke out. "She must have attracted their attention somehow. I see the game. They came up to kidnap the king, and—as I say—somehow they found him. If you hadn't gone to Strelsau, you and I and Fritz had been in heaven by now!"

"And the king?"

"Who knows where the king is now?" he asked.

"Come, let's be off!" said I; but he sat still. And suddenly he burst into one of his grating chuckles:

"By Jove, we've shaken up Black Michael!"

"Come, come!" I repeated impatiently.

"And we'll shake him up a bit more," he added, a cunning smile broadening on his wrinkled, weather-beaten face and his teeth working on an end of his grizzled moustache. "Ay, lad, we'll go back to Strelsau. The king shall be in his capital again to-morrow."

"The king?"

"The crowned king!"

"You're mad!" I cried.

"If we go back and tell the trick we played, what would you give for our lives?"

"Just what they're worth," said I.

"And for the king's throne? Do you think that the nobles and the people will enjoy being fooled as you've fooled them? Do you think they'll love a king who was too drunk to be crowned, and sent a servant to personate him?"

"He was drugged—and I'm no servant."

"Mine will be Black Michael's version."

He rose, came to me, and laid his hand on my shoulder.

"Lad," he said, "if you play the man, you may save the king yet. Go back and keep his throne warm for him."

"But the duke knows—the villains he has employed know——"

"Ay, but they can't speak!" roared Sapt, in grim triumph. "We've got 'em! How can they denounce you without denouncing themselves? 'This is not the king, because we kidnapped the king and murdered his servant.' Can they say that?"

The position flashed on me. Whether Michael knew me or not, he could not speak. Unless he produced the king, what could he do? And if he produced the king, where was he? For a moment I was carried away headlong; but in an instant the difficulties came strong upon me.

"I must be found out," I urged.

"Perhaps; but every hour's something. Above all, we must have a king in Strelsau, or the city will be Michael's in four-and-twenty hours, and what would the king's life be worth then—or his throne? Lad, you must do it!"

"Suppose they kill the king?"

"They'll kill him, if you don't."

"Sapt, suppose they have killed the king?"

"Then, by heaven, you're as good an Elphberg as Black Michael, and you shall reign in Ruritania! But I don't believe they have; nor will they kill him if you're on the throne. Will they kill him, to put you in?"

It was a wild plan—wilder even and more hopeless than the trick we had already carried through; but as I listened to Sapt I saw the strong points in our game. And then I was a young man and I loved action, and I was offered such a hand in such a game as perhaps never man played yet.

"I shall be found out," I said.

"Perhaps," said Sapt. "Come! to Strelsau! We shall be caught like rats in a trap if we stay here."

"Sapt," I cried, "I'll try it!"

"Well played!" said he. "I hope they've left us the horses. I'll go and see."

"We must bury that poor fellow," said I.

"No time," said Sapt.

"I'll do it."

"Hang you!" he grinned. "I make you a king, and—— Well, do it. Go and fetch him, while I look to the horses. He can't lie very deep, but I doubt if he'll care about that. Poor little Josef! He was an honest bit of a man."

He went out, and I went to the cellar. I raised poor Josef in my arms and bore him into the passage and thence towards the door of the house. Just inside I laid him down, remembering that I must find spades for our task. At this instant Sapt came up.

"The horses are all right; there's the own brother to the one that brought you here. But you may save yourself that job."

"I'll not go before he's buried."

"Yes, you will."

"Not I, Colonel Sapt; not for all Ruritania."

"You fool!" said he. "Come here."

He drew me to the door. The moon was sinking, but about three hundred yards away, coming along the road from Zenda, I made out a party of men. There were seven or eight of them; four were on horseback and the rest were walking, and I saw that they carried long implements, which I guessed to be spades and mattocks, on their shoulders.

"They'll save you the trouble," said Sapt. "Come along."

He was right. The approaching party must, beyond doubt, be Duke Michael's men, come to remove the traces of their evil work. I hesitated no longer, but an irresistible desire seized me. Pointing to the corpse of poor little Josef, I said to Sapt:

"Colonel, we ought to strike a blow for him!"

"You'd like to give him some company, eh? But it's too risky work, your Majesty."

"I must have a slap at 'em," said I.

Sapt wavered.

"Well," said he, "it's not business, you know; but

you've been a good boy—and if we come to grief, why, hang me, it'll save us a lot of thinking! I'll show you how to touch them."

He cautiously closed the open chink of the door. Then we retreated through the house and made our way to the back entrance. Here our horses were standing. A carriage-drive swept all round the lodge.

"Revolver ready?" asked Sapt.

"No; steel for me," said I.

"Gad, you're thirsty to-night," chuckled Sapt. "So be it."

We mounted, drawing our swords, and waited silently for a minute or two. Then we heard the tramp of men on the drive the other side of the house. They came to a stand, and one cried:

"Now then, fetch him out!"

"Now!" whispered Sapt.

Driving the spurs into our horses, we rushed at a gallop round the house, and in a moment we were among the ruffians. Sapt told me afterwards that he killed a man, and I believe him; but I saw no more of him. With a cut, I split the head of a fellow on a brown horse, and he fell to the ground. Then I found myself opposite a big man, and I was half-conscious of another to my right. It was too warm to stay, and with a simultaneous action I drove my spurs into my horse again and my sword full into the big man's breast. His bullet whizzed past my ear—I could almost swear it touched it. I wrenched at the sword, but it would not come, and I dropped it and galloped after Sapt, whom I now saw about twenty yards ahead. I waved my hand in farewell, and dropped it a second later with a yell, for a bullet had grazed my finger and I felt the blood. Old Sapt turned round in the saddle. Someone fired again, but they had no rifles, and we were out of range. Sapt fell to laughing.

"That's one to me and two to you, with decent luck," said he. "Little Josef will have company."

"Ay, they'll be a *partie carrée*," said I. My blood was up, and I rejoiced to have killed them.

"Well, a pleasant night's work to the rest!" said he. "I wonder if they noticed you!"

"The big fellow did; as I stuck him I heard him cry, 'The king!' "

"Good! good! Oh, we'll give Black Michael some work before we've done!"

Pausing an instant, we made a bandage for my wounded finger, which was bleeding freely and ached severely, the bone being much bruised. Then we rode on, asking of our good horses all that was in them. The excitement of the fight and of our great resolve died away, and we rode in gloomy silence. Day broke clear and cold. We found a farmer just up, and made him give us sustenance for ourselves and our horses. I, feigning a toothache, muffled my face closely. Then ahead again, till Strelsau lay before us. It was eight o'clock or nearing nine, and the gates were all open, as they always were save when the duke's caprice or intrigues shut them. We rode in by the same way as we had come out the evening before, all four of us—the men and the horses—wearied and jaded. The streets were even quieter than when we had gone: everyone was sleeping off last night's revelry, and we met hardly a soul till we reached the little gate of the Palace. There Sapt's old groom was waiting for us.

"Is all well, sir?" he asked.

"All's well," said Sapt, and the man, coming to me, took my hand to kiss.

"The king's hurt!" he cried.

"It's nothing," said I, as I dismounted; "I caught my finger in the door."

"Remember—silence!" said Sapt. "Ah! but, my good Freyler, I do not need to tell you that!"

The old fellow shrugged his shoulders.

"All young men like to ride abroad now and again, why not the king?" said he; and Sapt's laugh left his opinion of my motives undisturbed.

"You should always trust a man," observed Sapt, fitting the key in the lock—"just as far as you must."

We went in and reached the dressing-room. Flinging

open the door, we saw Fritz von Tarlenheim stretched, fully dressed, on the sofa. He seemed to have been sleeping, but our entry woke him. He leapt to his feet, gave one glance at me, and with a joyful cry, threw himself on his knees before me.

"Thank God, sire! thank God, you're safe!" he cried, stretching his hand up to catch hold of mine.

I confess that I was moved. This king, whatever his faults, made people love him. For a moment I could not bear to speak or break the poor fellow's illusion. But tough old Sapt had no such feeling. He slapped his hand on his thigh delightedly.

"Bravo, lad!" cried he. "We shall do!"

Fritz looked up in bewilderment. I held out my hand.

"You're wounded, sire!" he exclaimed.

"It's only a scratch," said I, "but——" I paused.

He rose to his feet with a bewildered air. Holding my hand, he looked me up and down, and down and up. Then suddenly he dropped my hand and reeled back.

"Where's the king? Where's the king?" he cried.

"Hush, you fool!" hissed Sapt. "Not so loud! Here's the king!"

A knock sounded at the door. Sapt seized me by the hand.

"Here, quick, to the bedroom! Off with your cap and your boots. Get into bed. Cover everything up."

I did as I was bid. A moment later Sapt looked in, nodded, grinned, and introduced an extremely smart and deferential young gentleman, who came up to my bedside, bowing again and again, and informed me that he was of the household of the Princess Flavia, and that her Royal Highness had sent him especially to inquire how the king's health was after the fatigues which his Majesty had undergone yesterday.

"My best thanks, sir, to my cousin," said I; "and tell her Royal Highness that I was never better in my life."

"The king," added old Sapt (who, I began to find, loved a good lie for its own sake), "has slept without a break all night."

The young gentleman (he reminded me of "Osric" in *Hamlet*) bowed himself out again. The farce was over, and Fritz von Tarlenheim's pale face recalled us to reality—though, in faith, the farce had to be reality for us now.

"Is the king dead?" he whispered.

"Please God, no," said I. "But he's in the hands of Black Michael!"

CHAPTER VIII

❧❧

A Fair Cousin and a Dark Brother

A REAL king's life is perhaps a hard one; but a pretended king's is, I warrant, much harder. On the next day, Sapt instructed me in my duties—what I ought to do and what I ought to know—for three hours; then I snatched breakfast, with Sapt still opposite me, telling me that the king always took white wine in the morning and was known to detest all highly-seasoned dishes. Then came the Chancellor, for another three hours; and to him I had to explain that the hurt to my finger (we turned that bullet to happy account) prevented me from writing—whence arose great to-do, hunting of precedents and so forth, ending in my "making my mark," and the Chancellor attesting it with a superfluity of solemn oaths. Then the French ambassador was introduced, to present his credentials; here my ignorance was of no importance, as the king would have been equally raw to the business (we worked through the whole *corps diplomatique* in the next few days, a demise of the Crown necessitating all this pother).

Then, at last, I was left alone. I called my new servant (we had chosen, to succeed poor Josef, a young man who had never known the king), had a brandy-and-soda brought to me, and observed to Sapt that I trusted that I might now have a rest.

Fritz von Tarlenheim was standing by.

"By Heaven!" he cried, "we waste time. Aren't we going to throw Black Michael by the heels?"

"Gently, my son, gently," said Sapt, knitting his brows. "It would be a pleasure, but it might cost us dear. Would Michael fall and leave the king alive?"

"And," I suggested, "while the king is here in Strelsau, on his throne, what grievance has he against his dear brother Michael?"

"Are we to do nothing, then?"

"We're to do nothing stupid," growled Sapt.

"In fact, Fritz," said I, "I am reminded of a situation in one of our English plays—*The Critic*—have you heard of it? Or, if you like, of two men, each covering the other with a revolver. For I can't expose Michael without exposing myself——"

"And the king," put in Sapt.

"And, hang me if Michael won't expose himself, if he tries to expose me!"

"It's very pretty," said old Sapt.

"If I'm found out," I pursued, "I will make a clean breast of it, and fight it out with the duke; but at present I'm waiting for a move from him."

"He'll kill the king," said Fritz.

"Not he," said Sapt.

"Half of the Six are in Strelsau," said Fritz.

"Only half? You're sure?" asked Sapt eagerly.

"Yes—only half."

"Then the king's alive, for the other three are guarding him!" cried Sapt.

"Yes—you're right!" exclaimed Fritz, his face brightening. "If the king were dead and buried, they'd all be here with Michael. You know Michael's back, Colonel?"

"I know, curse him!"

"Gentlemen, gentlemen," said I, "who are the Six?"

"I think you'll make their acquaintance soon," said Sapt. "They are six gentlemen whom Michael maintains in his household: they belong to him body and soul.

There are three Ruritanians; then there's a Frenchman, a Belgian, and one of your countrymen."

"They'd all cut a throat if Michael told them," said Fritz.

"Perhaps they'll cut mine," I suggested.

"Nothing more likely," agreed Sapt. "Who are here, Fritz?"

"De Gautet, Bersonin, and Detchard."

"The foreigners! It's as plain as a pikestaff. He's brought them, and left the Ruritanians with the king; that's because he wants to commit the Ruritanians as deep as he can."

"They were none of them among our friends at the lodge, then?" I asked.

"I wish they had been," said Sapt, wistfully. "They had been, not Six, but Four, by now."

I had already developed one attribute of royalty—a feeling that I need not reveal all my mind or my secret designs even to my intimate friends. I had fully resolved on my course of action. I meant to make myself as popular as I could, and at the same time to show no disfavour to Michael. By these means I hoped to allay the hostility of his adherents, and make it appear, if an open conflict came about, that he was ungrateful and not oppressed.

Yet an open conflict was not what I hoped for.

The king's interest demanded secrecy; and while secrecy lasted, I had a fine game to play in Strelsau. Michael should not grow stronger for delay!

I ordered my horse, and, attended by Fritz von Tarlenheim, rode in the grand new avenue of the Royal Park, returning all the salutes which I received with punctilious politeness. Then I rode through a few of the streets, stopped and bought flowers of a pretty girl, paying her with a piece of gold; and then, having attracted the desired amount of attention (for I had a trail of half-a-thousand people after me), I rode to the residence of the Princess Flavia, and asked if she would receive me. This step created much interest, and was met with shouts of approval. The princess was very popular, and the Chancellor himself had not scrupled to hint to me that the more I pressed my suit, and the more rapidly I brought it to a prosperous conclusion, the stronger should I be in the affection of my subjects. The Chancellor, of course, did not understand the difficulties which lay in the way of following his loyal and excellent advice. However, I thought I could do no harm by calling; and in this view Fritz supported me with a cordiality that surprised me, until he confessed that he also had his motives for liking a visit to the princess's house, which motive was no other than a great desire to see the princess's lady-in-waiting and bosom friend, the Countess Helga von Strofzin.

Etiquette seconded Fritz's hopes. While I was ushered into the princess's room, he remained with the countess in the ante-chamber: in spite of the people and servants who were hanging about, I doubt not that they managed a *tête-à-tête;* but I had no leisure to think of them, for I was playing the most delicate move in all my difficult game. I had to keep the princess devoted to me—and yet indifferent to me: I had to show affection for her—and not feel it. I had to make love for another, and that to a girl who—princess or no princess—was the most beautiful I had ever seen. Well, I braced myself to the task, made no easier by the charming embarrassment with which I was received. How I succeeded in carrying out my programme will appear hereafter.

"You are gaining golden laurels," she said. "You are like the prince in Shakespeare who was transformed by becoming king. But I'm forgetting you are king, sire."

"I ask you to speak nothing but what your heart tells you—and to call me nothing but my name."

She looked at me for a moment.

"Then I'm glad and proud, Rudolf," said she. "Why, as I told you, your very face is changed."

I acknowledged the compliment, but I disliked the topic; so I said:

"My brother is back, I hear. He made an excursion, didn't he?"

"Yes, he is here," she said, frowning a little.

"He can't stay long from Strelsau, it seems," I observed, smiling. "Well, we are all glad to see him. The nearer he is, the better."

The princess glanced at me with a gleam of amusement in her eyes.

"Why, cousin? Is it that you can——?"

"See better what he's doing? Perhaps," said I. "And why are you glad?"

"I didn't say I was glad," she answered.

"Some people say so for you."

"There are many insolent people," she said, with delightful haughtiness.

"Possibly you mean that I am one?"

"Your Majesty could not be," she said, curtseying in feigned deference, but adding, mischievously, after a pause: "Unless, that is——"

"Well, unless what?"

"Unless you tell me that I mind a snap of my fingers where the Duke of Strelsau is."

Really, I wished that I had been the king.

"You don't care where cousin Michael——"

"Ah, cousin Michael! I call him the Duke of Strelsau."

"You call him Michael when you meet him?"

"Yes—by the orders of your father."

"I see. And now by mine?"

"If those are your orders."

"Oh, decidedly! We must all be pleasant to our dear Michael."

"You order me to receive his friends, too, I suppose?"

"The Six?"

"You call them that, too?"

"To be in the fashion, I do. But I order you to receive no one unless you like."

"Except yourself?"

"I pray for myself. I could not order."

As I spoke, there came a cheer from the street. The princess ran to the window.

"It is he!" she cried. "It is—the Duke of Strelsau!"

I smiled, but said nothing. She returned to her seat. For a few moments we sat in silence. The noise outside subsided, but I heard the tread of feet in the ante-room. I began to talk on general subjects. This went on for some minutes. I wondered what had become of Michael, but it did not seem to be for me to interfere. All at once, to my great surprise, Flavia, clasping her hands, asked in an agitated voice:

"Are you wise to make him angry?"

"What? Who? How am I making him angry?"

"Why, by keeping him waiting."

"My dear cousin, I don't want to keep him——"

"Well, then, is he to come in?"

"Of course, if you wish it."

She looked at me curiously.

"How funny you are," she said. "Of course no one could be announced while I was with you."

Here was a charming attribute of royalty!

"An excellent etiquette!" I cried. "But I had clean forgotten it; and if I were alone with someone else, couldn't you be announced?"

"You know as well as I do. I could be, because I am of the Blood;" and she still looked puzzled.

"I never could remember all these silly rules," said I, rather feebly, as I inwardly cursed Fritz for not posting me up. "But I'll repair my fault."

I jumped up, flung open the door, and advanced into the ante-room. Michael was sitting at a table, a heavy frown on his face. Everyone else was standing, save that impudent young dog Fritz, who was lounging easily in an arm-chair, and flirting with the Countess Helga. He leapt up as I entered, with a deferential alacrity that lent point to his former nonchalance. I had no difficulty in understanding that the duke might not like young Fritz.

I held out my hand, Michael took it, and I embraced him. Then I drew him with me into the inner room.

"Brother," I said, "if I had known you were here, you should not have waited a moment before I asked the princess to permit me to bring you to her."

He thanked me, but coldly. The man had many qualities, but he could not hide his feelings. A mere stranger could have seen that he hated me, and hated worse to see me with Princess Flavia; yet I am persuaded that he tried to conceal both feelings, and, further, that he tried to persuade me that he believed I was verily the king. I did not know, of course; but, unless the king were an imposter, at once cleverer and more audacious than I (and I began to think something of myself in that *rôle*), Michael could not believe that. And, if he didn't, how he must have loathed paying me deference, and hearing my "Michael" and my "Flavia"!

"Your hand is hurt, sire," he observed, with concern.

"Yes; I was playing a game with a mongrel dog" (I meant to stir him), "and you know, brother, such have uncertain tempers."

He smiled sourly, and his dark eyes rested on me for a moment.

"But is there no danger from the bite?" cried Flavia, anxiously.

"None from this," said I. "If I gave him a chance to bite deeper, it would be different, cousin."

"But surely he has been destroyed?" said she.

"Not yet. We're waiting to see if his bite is harmful."

"And if it is?" asked Michael, with his sour smile.

"He'll be knocked on the head, brother," said I.

"You won't play with him any more?" urged Flavia.

"Perhaps I shall."

"He might bite again."

"Doubtless he'll try," said I, smiling.

Then, fearing Michael would say something which I must appear to resent (for, though I might show him my hate, I must seem to be full of favour), I began to compliment him on the magnificent condition of his regiment, and of their loyal greeting to me on the day of my coronation. Thence I passed to a rapturous description of the shooting-lodge which he had lent me. But he rose suddenly to his feet. His temper was failing him, and, with an excuse, he said farewell. However, as he reached the door he stopped, saying:

"Three friends of mine are very anxious to have the honour of being presented to you, sire. They are here in the ante-chamber."

I joined him directly, passing my arm through his. The look on his face was honey to me. We entered the ante-chamber in fraternal fashion. Michael beckoned, and three men came forward.

"These gentlemen," said Michael, with a stately courtesy which, to do him justice, he could assume with perfect grace and ease, "are the loyalest and most devoted of your Majesty's servants, and are my very faithful and attached friends."

"On the last ground as much as the first," said I, "I am very pleased to see them."

They came one by one and kissed my hand—De Gautet, a tall lean fellow, with hair standing straight up and waxed moustache; Bersonin, the Belgian, a portly man of middle height with a bald head (though he was not far past thirty); and, last, the Englishman, Detchard, a narrow-faced fellow, with close-cut fair hair and a bronzed complexion. He was a finely-made man, broad in the shoulders and slender in the hips. A good fighter, but a crooked customer, I put him down for. I spoke to him in English, with a slight foreign accent, and I swear the fellow smiled, though he hid the smile in an instant.

"So Mr. Detchard is in the secret," thought I.

Having got rid of my dear brother and his friends, I returned to make my adieu to my cousin. She was standing at the door. I bade her farewell, taking her hand in mine.

"Rudolf," she said, very low, "be careful, won't you?"

"Of what?"

"You know—I can't say. But think what your life is to——"

"Well, to——?"

"To Ruritania."

Was I right to play the part, or wrong to play the part? I know not: evil lay both ways, and I dared not tell her the truth.

"Only to Ruritania?" I asked softly.

A sudden flush spread over her incomparable face.

"To your friends, too," she said.

"Friends?"

"And to your cousin," she whispered, "and loving servant."

I could not speak. I kissed her hand, and went out cursing myself.

Outside I found Master Fritz, quite reckless of the footmen, playing at cat's-cradle with the Countess Helga.

"Hang it!" said he, "we can't always be plotting. Love claims his share."

"I'm inclined to think he does," said I; and Fritz, who had been by my side, dropped respectfully behind.

CHAPTER IX

A New Use for a Tea-Table

IF I were to detail the ordinary events of my daily life at this time, they might prove instructive to people who are not familiar with the insides of palaces; if I revealed some of the secrets I learnt, they might prove of interest to the statesmen of Europe. I intend to do neither of these things. I should be between the Scylla of dulness and the Charybdis of indiscretion, and I feel that I had far better confine myself strictly to the underground drama which was being played beneath the surface of Ruritanian politics. I need only say that the secret of my imposture defied detection. I made mistakes. I had bad minutes: it needed all the tact and graciousness whereof I was master to smooth over some apparent lapses of memory and unmindfulness of old acquaintances of which I was guilty. But I escaped, and I attribute my escape, as I have said before, most of all, to the very audacity of the enterprise. It is my belief that, given the necessary physical likeness, it was far easier to pretend to be King of Ruritania than it would have been to personate my next-door neighbour.

One day Sapt came into my room. He threw me a letter, saying:

"That's for you—a woman's hand, I think. But I've some news for you first."

"What's that?"

"The king's at the Castle of Zenda," said he.

"How do you know?"

"Because the other half of Michael's Six are there. I had enquiries made, and they're all there—Lauengram, Krafstein, and young Rupert Hentzau; three rogues, too, on my honour, as fine as live in Ruritania."

"Well?"

"Well, Fritz wants you to march to the Castle with horse, foot, and artillery."

"And drag the moat?" I asked.

"That would be about it," grinned Sapt; "and we shouldn't find the king's body then."

"You think it's certain he's there?"

"Very probable. Besides the fact of those three being there, the drawbridge is kept up, and no one goes in without an order from young Hentzau or Black Michael himself. We must tie Fritz up."

"I'll go to Zenda," said I.

"You're mad."

"Some day."

"Oh, perhaps. You'll very likely stay there though, if you do."

"That may be, my friend," said I carelessly.

"His Majesty looks sulky," observed Sapt. "How's the love affair?"

"Damn you, hold your tongue!" I said.

He looked at me for a moment, then he lit his pipe. It was quite true that I was in a bad temper, and I went on perversely:

"Wherever I go, I'm dodged by half-a-dozen fellows."

"I know you are; I send 'em," he replied composedly.

"What for?"

"Well," said Sapt, puffing away, "it wouldn't be exactly inconvenient for Black Michael if you disappeared. With you gone, the old game that we stopped would be played—or he'd have a shot at it."

"I can take care of myself."

"De Gautet, Bersonin, and Detchard are in Strelsau;

and any one of them, lad, would cut your throat as readily—as readily as I would Black Michael's, and a deal more treacherously. What's the letter?"

I opened it and read it aloud:

"If the king desires to know what it deeply concerns the king to know, let him do as this letter bids him. At the cud of the New Avenue there stands a house in large grounds. The house has a portico, with a statue of a nymph on it. A wall encloses the garden; there is a gate in the wall at the back. At twelve o'clock to-night, if the king enters alone by that gate, turns to the right, and walks twenty yards, he will find a summer-house, approached by a flight of six steps. If he mounts and enters, he will find someone who will tell him what touches most dearly his life and his throne. This is written by a faithful friend. He must be alone. If he neglects the invitation his life will be in danger. Let him show this to no one, or he will ruin a woman who loves him: Black Michael does not pardon."

"No," observed Sapt, as I ended, "but he can dictate a very pretty letter."

I had arrived at the same conclusion, and was about to throw the letter away, when I saw there was more writing on the other side.

"Hallo! there's some more."

"If you hesitate," the writer continued, *"consult Colonel Sapt——"*

"Eh!" exclaimed that gentleman, genuinely astonished. "Does she take me for a greater fool than you?"

I waved to him to be silent.

"Ask him what woman would do most to prevent the duke from marrying his cousin, and therefore most to prevent him becoming king? And ask if her name begins with—A?"

I sprang to my feet. Sapt laid down his pipe.

"Antoinette de Mauban, by heaven!" I cried.

"How do you know?" asked Sapt.

I told him what I knew of the lady, and how I knew it. He nodded.

"It's so far true that she's had a great row with Michael," said he, thoughtfully.

"If she would, she could be useful," I said.

"I believe, though, that Michael wrote that letter."

"So do I, but I mean to know for certain. I shall go, Sapt."

"No, I shall go," said he.

"You may go as far as the gate."

"I shall go to the summer-house."

"I'm hanged if you shall!"

I rose and leant my back against the mantelpiece.

"Sapt, I believe in that woman, and I shall go."

"I don't believe in any woman," said Sapt, "and you shan't go."

"I either go to the summer-house or back to England," said I.

Sapt began to know exactly how far he could lead or drive, and when he must follow.

"We're playing against time," I added. "Every day we leave the king where he is there is fresh risk. Every day I masquerade like this, there is fresh risk. Sapt, we must play high; we must force the game."

"So be it," he said, with a sigh.

To cut the story short, at half-past eleven that night Sapt and I mounted our horses. Fritz was again left on guard, our destination not being revealed to him. It was a very dark night. I wore no sword, but I carried a revolver, a long knife, and a bull's-eye lantern. We arrived outside the gate. I dismounted. Sapt held out his hand.

"I shall wait here," he said. "If I hear a shot, I'll——"

"Stay where you are; it's the king's only chance. You mustn't come to grief too."

"You're right, lad. Good luck!"

I pressed the little gate. It yielded, and I found myself in a wild sort of shrubbery. There was a grass-grown path and, turning to the right as I had been bidden, I followed it cautiously. My lantern was closed, the revolver was in my hand. I heard not a sound. Presently a large dark object loomed out of the gloom ahead of me. It was the summer-house. Reaching the steps, I mounted them and found myself confronted by a weak, rickety wooden door, which hung upon the latch. I pushed it open and walked in. A woman flew to me and seized my hand.

"Shut the door," she whispered.

I obeyed, and turned the light of my lantern on her. She was in evening dress, arrayed very sumptuously, and her dark striking beauty was marvellously displayed in the glare of the bull's-eye. The summer-house was a bare little room, furnished only with a couple of chairs and a small iron table, such as one sees in a tea-garden or an open-air café.

"Don't talk," she said. "We've no time. Listen! I know you, Mr. Rassendyll. I wrote that letter at the duke's orders."

"So I thought," said I.

"In twenty minutes three men will be here to kill you."

"Three—the three?"

"Yes. You must be gone by then. If not, to-night you'll be killed——"

"Or they will."

"Listen, listen! When you're killed, your body will be taken to a low quarter of the town. It will be found there. Michael will at once arrest all your friends—Colonel Sapt and Captain von Tarlenheim first—proclaim a state of siege in Strèlsau, and send a messenger to Zenda. The other three will murder the king in the Castle, and the duke will proclaim either himself or the princess—himself, if he is strong enough. Anyhow, he'll marry her, and become king in fact, and soon in name. Do you see?"

"It's a pretty plot. But why, madame, do you——?"

"Say I'm a Christian—or say I'm jealous. My God! shall I see him marry her? Now go; but remember—this is what I have to tell you—that never, by night or by day, are you safe. Three men follow you as a guard. Is it not so? Well, three follow them; Michael's three are never two hundred yards from you. Your life is not worth a moment if ever they find you alone. Now go. Stay, the gate will be guarded by now. Go down softly, go past the summer-house, on for a hundred yards, and you'll find a ladder against the wall. Get over it, and fly for your life."

"And you?" I asked.

"I have my game to play too. If he finds out what I have done, we shall not meet again. If not, I may yet—— But never mind. Go at once."

"But what will you tell him?"

"That you never came—that you saw through the trick."

I took her hand and kissed it.

"Madame," said I, "you have served the king well to-night. Where is he in the Castle?"

She sank her voice to a fearful whisper. I listened eagerly.

"Across the drawbridge you come to a heavy door; behind that lies—— Hark! What's that?"

There were steps outside.

"They're coming! They're too soon! Heavens! they're too soon!" and she turned pale as death.

"They seem to me," said I, "to be in the nick of time."

"Close your lantern. See, there's a chink in the door. Can you see them?"

I put my eye to the chink. On the lowest step I saw three dim figures. I cocked my revolver. Antoinette hastily laid her hand on mine.

"You may kill one," said she. "But what then?"

A voice came from outside—a voice that spoke perfect English.

"Mr. Rassendyll," it said.

I made no answer.

"We want to talk to you. Will you promise not to shoot till we've done?"

"Have I the pleasure of addressing Mr. Detchard?" I said.

"Never mind names."

"Then let mine alone."

"All right, *sire*. I've an offer for you."

I still had my eye to the chink. The three had mounted two steps more; three revolvers pointed full at the door.

"Will you let us in? We pledge our honour to observe the truce."

"Don't trust them," whispered Antoinette.

"We can speak through the door," said I.

"But you might open it and fire," objected Detchard; "and though we should finish you, you might finish one of us. Will you give your honour not to fire while we talk?"

"Don't trust them," whispered Antoinette again.

A sudden idea struck me. I considered it for a moment. It seemed feasible.

"I give my honour not to fire before you do," said I; "but I won't let you in. Stand outside and talk."

"That's sensible," he said.

The three mounted the last step, and stood just outside the door. I laid my ear to the chink. I could hear no words, but Detchard's head was close to that of the taller of his companions (De Gautet, I guessed).

"H'm! Private communications," thought I. Then I said aloud:

"Well, gentlemen, what's the offer?"

"A safe-conduct to the frontier, and fifty thousand pounds English."

"No, no," whispered Antoinette in the lowest of whispers. "They are treacherous."

"That seems handsome," said I, reconnoitring through the chink. They were all close together, just outside the door now.

I had probed the hearts of the ruffians, and I did not need Antoinette's warning. They meant to "rush" me as soon as I was engaged in talk.

"Give me a minute to consider," said I; and I thought I heard a laugh outside.

I turned to Antoinette.

"Stand up close to the wall, out of the line of fire from the door," I whispered.

"What are you going to do?" she asked in fright.

"You'll see," said I.

I took up the little iron table. It was not very heavy for a man of my strength, and I held it by the legs. The top, protruding in front of me, made a complete screen for my head and body. I fastened my closed lantern to my belt and put my revolver in a handy pocket. Suddenly I saw the door move ever so slightly—perhaps it was the wind, perhaps it was a hand trying it outside.

I drew back as far as I could from the door, holding the table in the position that I have described. Then I called out:

"Gentlemen, I accept your offer, relying on your honour. If you will open the door——"

"Open it yourself," said Detchard.

"It opens outwards," said I. "Stand back a little, gentlemen, or I shall hit you when I open it."

I went and fumbled with the latch. Then I stole back to my place on tiptoe.

"I can't open it!" I cried. "The latch has caught."

"Tut! I'll open it!" cried Detchard. "Nonsense, Bersonin, why not? Are you afraid of one man?"

I smiled to myself. An instant later the door was flung back. The gleam of a lantern showed me the three close together outside, their revolvers levelled. With a shout, I charged at my utmost pace across the summer-house and through the doorway. Three shots rang out and battered into my shield. Another moment, and I leapt out and the table caught them full and square, and in a tumbling, swearing, struggling mass they and I and that brave table rolled down the steps of the summer-house to the ground below. Antoinette de Mauban shrieked, but I rose to my feet, laughing aloud.

De Gautet and Bersonin lay like men stunned. Detchard was under the table, but, as I rose, he pushed it from him and fired again. I raised my revolver and took a snap shot; I heard him curse, and then I ran like a hare, laughing as I went, past the summer-house and along by the wall. I heard steps behind me, and turning round I fired again for luck. The steps ceased.

"Please God," said I, "she told me the truth about the ladder!" for the wall was high and topped with iron spikes.

Yes, there it was. I was up and over in a minute. Doubling back, I saw the horses; then I heard a shot. It was Sapt. He had heard us, and was battling and raging with the locked gate, hammering it and firing into the key-hole, like a man possessed. He had quite forgotten that he was not to take part in the fight. Whereat I laughed again, and said, as I clapped him on the shoulder:

"Come home to bed, old chap. I've got the finest tea-table story that ever you heard!"

He started and cried: "You're safe!" and wrung my hand. But a moment later he added:

"And what the devil are you laughing at?"

"Four gentlemen round a tea-table," said I, laughing still, for it had been uncommonly ludicrous to see the formidable three altogether routed and scattered with no more deadly weapon than an ordinary tea-table.

Moreover, you will observe that I had honourably kept my word, and not fired till they did.

CHAPTER X

A Great Chance for a Villain

IT was the custom that the Prefect of Police should send every afternoon a report to me on the condition of the capital and the feeling of the people: the document included also an account of the movements of any persons whom the police had received instructions to watch. Since I had been in Strelsau, Sapt had been in the habit of reading the report and telling me any items of interest which it might contain. On the day after my adventure in the summer-house, he came in as I was playing a hand of *écarté* with Fritz von Tarlenheim.

"The report is rather full of interest this afternoon," he observed, sitting down.

"Do you find," I asked, "any mention of a certain *fraças?*"

He shook his head with a smile.

"I find this first," he said: " 'His Highness the Duke of Strelsau left the city (so far as it appears, suddenly), accompanied by several of his household. His destination is believed to be the Castle of Zenda, but the party travelled by road and not by train. MM. De Gautet, Bersonin and Detchard followed an hour later, the last-named carrying his arm in a sling. The cause of his wound is not known, but it is suspected that he has fought a duel, probably incidental to a love affair.' "

"That is remotely true," I observed, very well pleased to find that I had left my mark on the fellow.

"Then we come to this," pursued Sapt: " 'Madame de Mauban, whose movements have been watched according to instructions, left by train at midday. She took a ticket for Dresden——' "

"It's an old habit of hers," said I.

" 'The Dresden trains stop at Zenda.' An acute fellow, this. And finally listen to this: 'The state of feeling in the city is not satisfactory. The king is much criticised' (you know, he's told to be quite frank) 'for taking no steps about his marriage. From enquiries among the *entourage* of the Princess Flavia, her Royal Highness is believed to be deeply offended by the remissness of his Majesty. The common people are coupling her name with that of the Duke of Strelsau, and the duke gains much popularity from the suggestion. I have caused the announcement that the king gives a ball to-night in honour of the princess to be widely diffused, and the effect is good.' "

"That is news to me," said I.

"Oh, the preparations are all made!" laughed Fritz. "I've seen to that."

Sapt turned to me and said, in a sharp, decisive voice: "You must make love to her to-night, you know."

"I think it very likely I shall, if I see her alone," said I. "Hang it, Sapt, you don't suppose I find it difficult?"

Fritz whistled a bar or two; then he said:

"You'll find it only too easy. Look here, I hate telling you this, but I must. The Countess Helga told me that the princess had become most attached to the king. Since the coronation, her feelings have undergone a marked development. It's quite true that she is deeply wounded by the king's apparent neglect."

"Here's a kettle of fish!" I groaned.

"Tut, tut!" said Sapt. "I suppose you've made pretty speeches to a girl before now? That's all she wants."

Fritz, himself a lover, understood better my distress. He laid his hand on my shoulder, but said nothing.

"I think, though," pursued that cold-blooded old Sapt, "that you'd better make your offer to-night."

"Good heavens!"

"Or, at any rate, go near it: and I shall send a 'semi-official' to the papers."

"I'll do nothing of the sort—no more will you!" said I. "I utterly refuse to take part in making a fool of the princess."

Sapt looked at me with his small keen eyes. A slow cunning smile passed over his face.

"All right, lad, all right," said he. "We mustn't press you too hard. Soothe her down a bit, if you can, you know. Now for Michael!"

"Oh, damn Michael!" said I. "He'll do to-morrow. Here, Fritz, come for a stroll in the garden."

Sapt at once yielded. His rough manner covered a wonderful tact—and, as I came to recognise more and more, a remarkable knowledge of human nature. Why did he urge me so little about the princess? Because he knew that her beauty and my ardour would carry me further than all his arguments—and that the less I thought about the thing, the more likely was I to do it. He must have seen the unhappiness he might bring on the princess; but that went for nothing with him. Can I say, confidently, that he was wrong? If the king were re-stored, the princess must turn to him, either knowing or not knowing the change. And if the king were not re-stored to us? It was a subject that we had never yet spo-ken of. But I had an idea that, in such a case, Sapt meant to seat me on the throne of Ruritania for the term of my life. He would have set Satan himself there sooner than that pupil of his, Black Michael.

The ball was a sumptuous affair. I opened it by danc-ing a quadrille with Flavia: then I waltzed with her. Cu-rious eyes and eager whispers attended us. We went in to supper; and, half-way through, I, half-mad by then, for her glance had answered mine, and her quick breathing met my stammered sentences—I rose in my place before all the brilliant crowd, and taking the Red

Rose that I wore, flung the ribbon with its jewelled badge round her neck. In a tumult of applause I sat down: I saw Sapt smiling over his wine, and Fritz frowning. The rest of the meal passed in silence; neither Flavia nor I could speak. Fritz touched me on the shoulder, and I rose, gave her my arm, and walked down the hall into a little room, where coffee was served to us. The gentlemen and ladies in attendance withdrew, and we were alone.

The little room had French windows opening on the gardens. The night was fine, cool, and fragrant. Flavia sat down, and I stood opposite her. I was struggling with myself: if she had not looked at me, I believe that even then I should have won my fight. But suddenly, involuntarily, she gave me one brief glance—a glance of question, hurriedly turned aside; a blush that the question had ever come spread over her cheek, and she caught her breath. Ah, if you had seen her! I forgot the king in Zenda. I forgot the king in Strelsau. She was a princess—and I an impostor. Do you think I remembered that? I threw myself on my knee and seized her hands in mine. I said nothing. Why should I? The soft sounds of the night set my wooing to a wordless melody, as I pressed my kisses on her lips.

She pushed me from her, crying suddenly:

"Ah! is it true? or is it only because you must?"

"It's true!" I said, in low smothered tones—"true that I love you more than life—or truth—or honour!"

She set no meaning to my words, treating them as one of love's sweet extravagances. She came close to me, and whispered:

"Oh, if you were not the king! Then I could show you how I love you! How is it that I love you now, Rudolf?"

"Now?"

"Yes—just lately. I—I never did before."

Pure triumph filled me. It was I—Rudolf Rassendyll—who had won her! I caught her round the waist.

"You didn't love me before?" I asked.

She looked up into my face, smiling, as she whispered:

"It must have been your Crown. I felt it first on the Coronation Day."

"Never before?" I asked eagerly.

She laughed low.

"You speak as if you would be pleased to hear me say 'Yes' to that," she said.

"Would 'Yes' be true?"

"Yes," I just heard her breathe, and she went on in an instant: "Be careful, Rudolf; be careful, dear. He will be mad now."

"What, Michael? If Michael were the worst——"

"What worse is there?"

There was yet a chance for me. Controlling myself with a mighty effort, I took my hands off her and stood a yard or two away. I remember now the note of the wind in the elm-trees outside.

"If I were not the king," I began, "if I were only a private gentleman——"

Before I could finish, her hand was in mine.

"If you were a convict in the prison of Strelsau, you would be my king," she said.

And under my breath I groaned, "God forgive me!" and, holding her hand in mine, I said again:

"If I were not the king——"

"Hush, hush!" she whispered. "I don't deserve it—I don't deserve to be doubted. Ah, Rudolf! does a woman who marries without love look on the man as I look on you?"

And she hid her face from me.

For more than a minute we stood there together; and I, even with my arm about her, summoned up what honour and conscience her beauty and the toils that I was in had left me.

"Flavia," I said, in a strange dry voice that seemed not my own, "I am not——"

As I spoke—as she raised her eyes to me—there was a heavy step on the gravel outside, and a man appeared at the window. A little cry burst from Flavia, as she sprang back from me. My half-finished sentence died on my lips. Sapt stood there, bowing low, but with a stern frown on his face.

"A thousand pardons, sire," said he, "but his Eminence the Cardinal has waited this quarter of an hour to offer his respectful adieu to your Majesty."

I met his eye full and square; and I read in it an angry warning. How long he had been a listener I knew not, but he had come in upon us in the nick of time.

"We must not keep his Eminence waiting," said I.

But Flavia, in whose love there lay no shame, with radiant eyes and blushing face, held out her hand to Sapt. She said nothing, but no man could have missed her meaning who had ever seen a woman in the exultation of love. A sour, yet sad, smile passed over the old soldier's face, and there was tenderness in his voice as, bending to kiss her hand, he said:

"In joy and sorrow, in good times and bad, God save your Royal Highness!"

He paused and added, glancing at me and drawing himself up to military erectness:

"But, before all comes the king—God save the King!"

And Flavia caught at my hand and kissed it, murmuring:

"Amen! Good God, Amen!"

We went into the ball-room again. Forced to receive adieus, I was separated from Flavia: everyone, when they left me, went to her. Sapt was out and in of the throng, and where he had been, glances, smiles, and whispers were rife. I doubted not that, true to his relentless purpose, he was spreading the news that he had learnt. To uphold the Crown and beat Black Michael— that was his one resolve. Flavia, myself—ay, and the real king in Zenda, were pieces in his game; and pawns have no business with passions. Not even at the walls of the Palace did he stop; for when at last I handed Flavia down the broad marble steps and into her carriage, there was a great crowd awaiting us, and we were wel-

comed with deafening cheers. What could I do? Had I
spoken then, they would have refused to believe that I
was not the king; they might have believed that the king
had run mad. By Sapt's devices and my own un-
governed passion I had been forced on, and the way
back had closed behind me; and the passion still drove
me in the same direction as the devices seduced me. I
faced all Strelsau that night as the king and the accepted
suitor of the Princess Flavia.

At last, at three in the morning, when the cold light of
dawning day began to steal in, I was in my dressing-room,
and Sapt alone was with me. I sat like a man dazed, staring into the fire; he puffed at his pipe; Fritz was gone to
bed, having almost refused to speak to me. On the table
by me lay a rose; it had been in Flavia's dress, and, as we
parted, she had kissed it and given it to me.

Sapt advanced his hand towards the rose, but, with a
quick movement, I shut mine down upon it.

"That's mine," I said, "not yours—nor the king's either."

"We struck a good blow for the king to-night," said he.

I turned on him fiercely.

"What's to prevent me striking a blow for myself?" I
said.

He nodded his head.

"I know what's in your mind," he said. "Yes, lad; but
you're bound in honour."

"Have you left me any honour?"

"Oh, come, to play a little trick on a girl——"

"You can spare me that. Colonel Sapt, if you would
not have me utterly a villain—if you would not have
your king rot in Zenda, while Michael and I play for the
great stake outside——You follow me?"

"Ay, I follow you."

"We must act, and quickly! You saw to-night—you
heard to-night——"

"I did," said he.

"Your cursed acuteness told you what I should do.
Well, leave me here a week—and there's another problem for you. Do you find the answer?"

"Yes, I find it," he answered, frowning heavily. "But if you did that, you'd have to fight me first—and kill me."

"Well, and if I had—or a score of men? I tell you, I could raise all Strelsau on you in an hour, and choke you with your lies—yes, your mad lies—in your mouth."

"It's gospel truth," he said—"thanks to my advice, you could."

"I could marry the princess, and send Michael and his brother together to——"

"I'm not denying it, lad," said he.

"Then, in God's name," I cried, stretching out my hands to him, "let us go to Zenda and crush this Michael, and bring the king back to his own again."

The old fellow stood and looked at me for full a minute.

"And the princess?" he said.

I bowed my head to meet my hands, and crushed the rose between my fingers and my lips.

I felt his hand on my shoulder, and his voice sounded husky as he whispered low in my ear:

"Before God, you're the finest Elphberg of them all. But I have eaten of the king's bread, and I am the king's servant. Come, we will go to Zenda!"

And I looked up and caught him by the hand. And the eyes of both of us were wet.

CHAPTER XI

Hunting a Very Big Boar

THE terrible temptation which was assailing me will now be understood. I could so force Michael's hand that he must kill the king. I was in a position to bid him defiance and tighten my grasp on the crown—not for its own sake, but because the King of Ruritania was to wed the Princess Flavia. What of Sapt and Fritz? Ah! but a man cannot be held to write down in cold blood the wild and black thoughts that storm his brain when an uncontrolled passion has battered a breach for them. Yet, unless he sets up as a saint, he need not hate himself for them. He is better employed, as it humbly seems to me, in giving thanks that power to resist was vouchsafed to him, than in fretting over wicked impulses which come unsought and extort an unwilling hospitality from the weakness of our nature.

It was a fine bright morning when I walked, unattended, to the princess's house, carrying a nosegay in my hand. Policy made excuses for love, and every attention that I paid her, while it riveted my own chains, bound closer to me the people of the great city, who worshipped her. I found Fritz's *inamorata*, the Countess Helga, gathering blooms in the garden for her mistress's wear, and prevailed on her to take mine in their place. The girl was rosy with happiness, for Fritz, in his turn, had not wasted his evening, and no dark shadow hung over his wooing, save the hatred which the Duke of Strelsau was known to bear him.

"And that," she said, with a mischievous smile, "your Majesty has made of no moment. Yes, I will take the flowers; shall I tell you, sire, what is the first thing the princess does with them?"

We were talking on a broad terrace that ran along the back of the house, and a window above our heads stood open.

"Madame!" cried the countess merrily, and Flavia herself looked out. I bared my head and bowed. She wore a white gown, and her hair was loosely gathered in a knot. She kissed her hand to me, crying:

"Bring the king up, Helga; I'll give him some coffee."

The countess, with a gay glance, led the way, and took me into Flavia's morning-room. And, left alone, we greeted one another as lovers are wont. Then the princess laid two letters before me. One was from Black Michael— a most courteous request that she would honour him by spending a day at his Castle of Zenda, as had been her custom once a year in the summer, when the place and its gardens were in the height of their great beauty. I threw the letter down in disgust, and Flavia laughed at me. Then, growing grave again, she pointed to the other sheet.

"I don't know who that comes from," she said. "Read it."

I knew in a moment. There was no signature at all this time, but the handwriting was the same as that which had told me of the snare in the summer-house; it was Antoinette de Mauban's.

"I have no cause to love you," it ran, *"but God forbid that you should fall into the power of the duke. Accept no invitations of his. Go nowhere without a large guard—a regiment is not too much to make you safe. Show this, if you can, to him who reigns in Strelsau."*

"Why doesn't it say 'the king'?" asked Flavia, leaning over my shoulder, so that the ripple of her hair played on my cheek. "Is it a hoax?"

"As you value life, and more than life, my queen," I said, "obey it to the very letter. A regiment shall camp round your house to-day. See that you do not go out unless well guarded."

"An order, sire?" she asked, a little rebellious.

"Yes, an order, madame—if you love me."

"Ah!" she cried; and I could not but kiss her.

"You know who sent it?" she asked.

"I guess," said I. "It is from a good friend—and, I fear, an unhappy woman. You must be ill, Flavia, and unable to go to Zenda. Make your excuses as cold and formal as you like."

"So you feel strong enough to anger Michael?" she said, with a proud smile.

"I'm strong enough for anything, while you are safe," said I.

Soon I tore myself away from her, and then, without consulting Sapt, I took my way to the house of Marshal Strakencz. I had seen something of the old general, and I liked and trusted him. Sapt was less enthusiastic, but I had learnt by now that Sapt was best pleased when he could do everything, and jealousy played some part in his views. As things were now, I had more work than Sapt and Fritz could manage, for they must come with me to Zenda, and I wanted a man to guard what I loved most in all the world, and suffer me to set about my task of releasing the king with a quiet mind.

The Marshal received me with most loyal kindness. To some extent, I took him into my confidence. I charged him with the care of the princess, looking him full and significantly in the face as I bade him let no one from her cousin the duke approach her, unless he himself were there and a dozen of his men with him.

"You may be right, sire," said he, shaking his grey head sadly. "I have known better men than the duke do worse things than that for love."

I could quite appreciate the remark, but I said:

"There's something beside love, Marshal. Love's for

the heart; is there nothing my brother might like for his head?"

"I pray that you wrong him, sire."

"Marshal, I'm leaving Strelsau for a few days. Every evening I will send a courier to you. If for three days none comes, you will publish an order which I will give you, depriving Duke Michael of the governorship of Strelsau and appointing you in his place. You will declare a state of siege. Then you will send word to Michael that you demand an audience of the king—— You follow me?"

"Ay, sire."

"—In twenty-four hours. If he does not produce the king" (I laid my hand on his knee), "then the king is dead, and you will proclaim the next heir. You know who that is?"

"The Princess Flavia."

"And swear to me, on your faith and honour and by the fear of the living God, that you will stand by her to your death, and kill that reptile, and seat her where I sit now."

"On my faith and honour, and by the fear of God, I swear it! And may Almighty God preserve your Majesty, for I think that you go on an errand of danger."

"I hope that no life more precious than mine may be demanded," said I, rising. Then I held out my hand to him.

"Marshal," I said, "in days to come, it may be—I know not—that you will hear strange things of the man who speaks to you now. Let him be what he may, and who he may, what say you of the manner in which he has borne himself as king in Strelsau?"

The old man, holding my hand, spoke to me, man to man.

"I have known many of the Elphbergs," said he, "and I have seen you. And, happen what may, you have borne yourself as a wise king and a brave man; ay, and you have proved as courteous a gentleman and as gallant a lover as any that have been of the House."

"Be that my epitaph," said I, "when the time comes that another sits on the throne of Ruritania."

"God send a far day, and may I not see it!" said he.

I was much moved, and the Marshal's worn face twitched. I sat down and wrote my order.

"I can hardly yet write," said I; "my finger is stiff still."

It was, in fact, the first time that I had ventured to write more than a signature; and in spite of the pains I had taken to learn the king's hand, I was not yet perfect in it.

"Indeed, sire," he said, "it differs a little from your ordinary handwriting. It is unfortunate, for it may lead to a suspicion of forgery."

"Marshal," said I, with a laugh, "what use are the guns of Strelsau, if they can't assuage a little suspicion?"

He smiled grimly, and took the paper.

"Colonel Sapt and Fritz von Tarlenheim go with me," I continued.

"You go to seek the duke?" he asked in a low tone.

"Yes, the duke, and someone else of whom I have need, and who is at Zenda," I replied.

"I wish I could go with you," he cried, tugging at his white moustache. "I'd like to strike a blow for you and your crown."

"I leave you what is more than my life and more than my crown," said I, "because you are the man I trust more than all others in Ruritania."

"I will deliver her to you safe and sound," said he, "and, failing that, I will make her queen."

We parted, and I returned to the Palace and told Sapt and Fritz what I had done. Sapt had a few faults to find and a few grumbles to utter. This was merely what I expected, for Sapt liked to be consulted beforehand, not informed afterwards; but on the whole he approved of my plans, and his spirits rose high as the hour of action drew nearer and nearer. Fritz, too, was ready; though he, poor fellow, risked more than Sapt did, for he was a lover, and his happiness hung in the scale. Yet how I envied him! For the triumphant issue which would crown him with happiness and unite him to his mistress, the success for which we were bound to hope and strive and struggle, meant to me sorrow more certain and greater than if I were doomed to fail. He understood something of this, for when we were alone (save for old Sapt, who was smoking at the other end of the room) he passed his arm through mine, saying:

"It's hard for you. Don't think I don't trust you; I know you have nothing but true thoughts in your heart."

But I turned away from him, thankful that he could not see what my heart held, but only be witness to the deeds that my hands were to do.

Yet even he did not understand, for he had not dared to lift his eyes to the Princess Flavia, as I had lifted mine.

Our plans were now all made, even as we proceeded to carry them out, and as they will hereafter appear. The next morning we were to start on the hunting excursion. I had made all arrangements for being absent, and now there was only one thing left to do—the hardest, the most heart-breaking. As evening fell, I drove through the busy streets to Flavia's residence. I was recognised as I went and heartily cheered. I played my part, and made shift to look the happy lover. In spite of my depression, I was almost amused at the coolness and delicate *hauteur* with which my sweet lover received me. She had heard that the king was leaving Strelsau on a hunting expedition.

"I regret that we cannot amuse your Majesty here in Strelsau," she said, tapping her foot lightly on the floor. "I would have offered you more entertainment, but I was foolish enough to think——"

"Well, what?" I asked, leaning over her.

"That for just a day or two, after—after last night— you might be happy without much gaiety;" and she turned pettishly from me, as she added, "I hope the boars will be more engrossing."

"I'm going after a very big boar," said I; and, because

I could not help it, I began to play with her hair, but she moved her head away.

"Are you offended with me?" I asked, in feigned surprise, for I could not resist tormenting her a little. I had never seen her angry, and every fresh aspect of her was a delight to me.

"What right have I to be offended? True, you said last night that every hour away from me was wasted. But a very big boar! that's a different thing."

"Perhaps the boar will hunt me," I suggested. "Perhaps, Flavia, he'll catch me."

She made no answer.

"You are not touched even by that danger?"

Still she said nothing; and I, stealing round, found her eyes full of tears.

"You weep for my danger?"

Then she spoke very low:

"This is like what you used to be; but not like the king—the king I—I have come to love!"

With a sudden great groan, I caught her to my heart.

"My darling!" I cried, forgetting everything but her, "did you dream that I left you to go hunting?"

"What then, Rudolf? Ah! you're not going——?"

"Well, it is hunting. I go to seek Michael in his lair."

She had turned very pale.

"So you see, sweet, I was not so poor a lover as you thought me. I shall not be long gone."

"You will write to me, Rudolf?"

I was weak, but I could not say a word to stir suspicion in her.

"I'll send you all my heart every day," said I.

"And you'll run no danger?"

"None that I need not."

"And when will you be back? Ah, how long it will be!"

"When shall I be back?" I repeated.

"Yes, yes! Don't be long, dear, don't be long. I shan't sleep while you're away."

"I don't know when I shall be back," said I.

"Soon, Rudolf, soon?"

"God knows, my darling. But, if never——"

"Hush, hush!" and she pressed her lips to mine.

"If never," I whispered, "you must take my place; you'll be the only one of the House then. You must reign, and not weep for me."

For a moment she drew herself up like a very queen.

"Yes, I will!" she said. "I will reign. I will do my part, though all my life will be empty and my heart dead; yet I'll do it!"

She paused, and sinking against me again, wailed softly:

"Come soon! come soon!"

Carried away, I cried loudly:

"As God lives, I—yes, I myself—will see you once more before I die!"

"What do you mean?" she exclaimed, with wondering eyes; but I had no answer for her, and she gazed at me with her wondering eyes.

I dared not ask her to forget, she would have found it an insult. I could not tell her then who and what I was. She was weeping, and I had but to dry her tears.

"Shall a man not come back to the loveliest lady in all the wide world?" said I. "A thousand Michaels should not keep me from you!"

She clung to me, a little comforted.

"You won't let Michael hurt you?"

"No, sweetheart."

"Or keep you from me?"

"No, sweetheart."

"Nor anyone else?"

And again I answered:

"No, sweetheart."

Yet there was one—not Michael—who, if he lived, must keep me from her; and for whose life I was going forth to stake my own. And his figure—the lithe, buoyant figure I had met in the woods of Zenda—the dull, inert mass I had left in the cellar of the shooting-lodge—seemed to rise, double-shaped, before me, and to come between us, thrusting itself in even where she lay, pale, exhausted, fainting, in my arms, and yet looking up at me with those eyes that bore such love as I have never seen, and haunt me now, and will till the ground closes over me—and (who knows?) perhaps beyond.

CHAPTER XII

❧❧

I Receive a Visitor and Bait a Hook

A BOUT five miles from Zenda—on the opposite side from that on which the Castle is situated, there lies a large tract of wood. It is rising ground, and in the centre of the demesne, on the top of the hill, stands a fine modern *château,* the property of a distant kinsman of Fritz's, the Count Stanislas von Tarlenheim. Count Stanislas himself was a student and a recluse. He seldom visited the house, and had, on Fritz's request, very readily and courteously offered me its hospitality for myself and my party. This, then, was our destination; chosen ostensibly for the sake of the boar-hunting (for the wood was carefully preserved, and boars, once common all over Ruritania, were still to be found there in considerable numbers), really because it brought us within striking distance of the Duke of Strelsau's more magnificent dwelling on the other side of the town. A large party of servants, with horses and luggage, started early in the morning; we followed at midday, travelling by train for thirty miles, and then mounting our horses to ride the remaining distance to the *château.*

We were a gallant party. Besides Sapt and Fritz, I was accompanied by ten gentlemen: every one of them had been carefully chosen, and no less carefully sounded, by my two friends, and all were devotedly attached to the

407

person of the king. They were told a part of the truth: the attempt on my life in the summer-house was revealed to them, as a spur to their loyalty and an incitement against Michael. They were also informed that a friend of the king's was suspected to be forcibly confined within the Castle of Zenda. His rescue was one of the objects of the expedition; but, it was added, the king's main desire was to carry into effect certain steps against his treacherous brother, as to the precise nature of which they could not at present be further enlightened. Enough that the king commanded their services, and would rely on their devotion when occasion arose to call for it. Young, well-bred, brave, and loyal, they asked no more: they were ready to prove their dutiful obedience, and prayed for a fight as the best and most exhilarating mode of showing it.

Thus the scene was shifted from Strelsau to the *château* of Tarlenheim and Castle of Zenda, which frowned at us across the valley. I tried to shift my thoughts also, to forget my love, and to bend all my energies to the task before me. It was to get the king out of the Castle alive. Force was useless: in some trick lay the chance; and I had already an inkling of what we must do. But I was terribly hampered by the publicity which attended my movements. Michael must know by now of my expedition; and I knew Michael too well to suppose that his eyes would be blinded by the feint of the boar-hunt. He would understand very well what the real quarry was. That, however, must be risked—that and all it might mean; for Sapt, no less than myself, recognised that the present state of things had become unendurable. And there was one thing that I dared to calculate on—not, as I now know, without warrant. It was this—that Black Michael would not believe that I meant well by the king. He could not appreciate—I will not say an honest man, for the thoughts of my own heart have been revealed—but a man acting honestly. He saw my opportunity as I had seen it, as Sapt had seen it; he knew the princess—nay (and I declare that a sneaking sort of pity for him invaded me), in his way he loved her; he would think that Sapt and Fritz could be bribed, so the bribe were large enough. Thinking thus, would he kill the king, my rival and my danger? Ay, verily, that he would, with as little compunction as he would kill a rat. But he would kill Rudolf Rassendyll first, if he could; and nothing but the certainty of being utterly damned by the release of the king alive and his restoration to the throne would drive him to throw away the trump card which he held in reserve to baulk the supposed game of the impudent impostor Rassendyll. Musing on all this as I rode along, I took courage.

Michael knew of my coming, sure enough. I had not been in the house an hour, when an imposing Embassy arrived from him. He did not quite reach the impudence of sending my would-be assassins, but he sent the other three of his famous Six—the three Ruritanian gentlemen—Lauengram, Krafstein, and Rupert Hentzau. A fine, strapping trio they were, splendidly horsed and admirably equipped. Young Rupert, who looked a dare-devil, and could not have been more than twenty-two or twenty-three, took the lead, and made us the neatest speech, wherein my devoted subject and loving brother, Michael of Strelsau, prayed me to pardon him for not paying his addresses in person, and, further, for not putting his Castle at my disposal; the reason for both of these apparent derelictions being that he and several of his servants lay sick of scarlet fever, and were in a very sad, and also a very infectious, state. So declared young Rupert with an insolent smile on his curling upper-lip and a toss of his thick hair—he was a handsome villain, and the gossip ran that many a lady had troubled her heart for him already.

"If my brother has scarlet fever," said I, "he is nearer my complexion than he is wont to be, my lord. I trust he does not suffer?"

"He is able to attend to his affairs, sire."

"I hope all beneath your roof are not sick. What of my good friends, De Gautet, Bersonin, and Detchard? I heard the last had suffered a hurt."

Lauengram and Krafstein looked glum and uneasy, but young Rupert's smile grew broader.

"He hopes soon to find a medicine for it, sire," he answered.

And I burst out laughing, for I knew what medicine Detchard longed for—it is called Revenge.

"You will dine with us, gentlemen?" I asked.

Young Rupert was profuse in apologies. They had urgent duties at the Castle.

"Then," said I, with a wave of my hand, "to our next meeting, gentlemen. May it make us better acquainted."

"We will pray your Majesty for an early opportunity," quoth Rupert airily; and he strode past Sapt with such jeering scorn on his face that I saw the old fellow clench his fist and scowl black as night.

For my part, if a man must needs be a knave, I would have him a debonair knave, and I liked Rupert Hentzau better than his long-faced, close-eyed companions. It makes your sin no worse, as I conceive, to do it *à la mode* and stylishly.

Now it was a curious thing that on this first night, instead of eating the excellent dinner my cooks had prepared for me, I must needs leave my gentlemen to eat it alone, under Sapt's presiding care, and ride myself with Fritz to the town of Zenda and a certain little inn that I knew of. There was little danger in the excursion; the evenings were long and light, and the road this side of Zenda well frequented. So off we rode, with a groom behind us. I muffled myself up in a big cloak.

"Fritz," said I, as we entered the town, "there's an uncommonly pretty girl at this inn."

"How do you know?" he asked.

"Because I've been there," said I.

"Since——?" he began.

"No. Before," said I.

"But they'll recognise you?"

"Well, of course they will. Now, don't argue, my good fellow, but listen to me. We're two gentlemen of the king's household, and one of us has a toothache. The other will order a private room and dinner, and, further, a bottle of the best wine for the sufferer. And if he be as clever a fellow as I take him for, the pretty girl and no other will wait on us."

"What if she won't?" objected Fritz.

"My dear Fritz," said I, "if she won't for you, she will for me."

We were at the inn. Nothing of me but my eyes was visible as I walked in. The landlady received us; two minutes later, my little friend (ever, I fear me, on the look out for such guests as might prove amusing) made her appearance. Dinner and the wine were ordered. I sat down in the private room. A minute later Fritz came in.

"She's coming," he said.

"If she were not, I should have to doubt the Countess Helga's taste."

She came in. I gave her time to set the wine down—I didn't want it dropped. Fritz poured out a glass and gave it to me.

"Is the gentleman in great pain?" the girl asked, sympathetically.

"The gentleman is no worse than when he saw you last," said I, throwing away my cloak.

She started, with a little shriek. Then she cried:

"It was the king, then! I told mother so the moment I saw his picture. Oh, sir, forgive me!"

"Faith, you gave me nothing that hurt much," said I.

"But the things we said!"

"I forgive them for the thing you did."

"I must go and tell mother."

"Stop," said I, assuming a graver air. "We are not here for sport to-night. Go and bring dinner, and not a word of the king being here."

She came back in a few minutes, looking grave, yet very curious.

"Well, how is Johann?" I asked, beginning my dinner.

"Oh, that fellow, sir—my lord king, I mean!"

" 'Sir' will do, please. How is he?"

"We hardly see him now, sir."

"And why not?"

"I told him he came too often, sir," said she, tossing her head.

"So he sulks and stays away?"

"Yes, sir."

"But you could bring him back?" I suggested, with a smile.

"Perhaps I could," said she.

"I know your powers, you see," said I, and she blushed with pleasure.

"It's not only that, sir, that keeps him away. He's very busy at the Castle."

"But there's no shooting on now."

"No, sir; but he's in charge of the house."

"Johann turned housemaid?"

The little girl was brimming over with gossip.

"Well, there are no others," said she. "There's not a woman there—not as a servant, I mean. They do say— but perhaps it's false, sir."

"Let's have it for what it's worth," said I.

"Indeed, I'm ashamed to tell you, sir."

"Oh, see, I'm looking at the ceiling."

"They do say there is a lady there, sir; but, except for her, there's not a woman in the place. And Johann has to wait on the gentlemen."

"Poor Johann! He must be overworked. Yet I'm sure he could find half-an-hour to come and see you."

"It would depend on the time, sir, perhaps."

"Do you love him?" I asked.

"Not I, sir."

"And you wish to serve the king?"

"Yes, sir."

"Then tell him to meet you at the second milestone out of Zenda to-morrow evening at ten o'clock. Say you'll be there and will walk home with him."

"Do you mean him harm, sir?"

"Not if he will do as I bid him. But I think I've told you enough, my pretty maid. See that you do as I bid you. And, mind, no one is to know that the king has been here."

I spoke a little sternly, for there is seldom harm in infusing a little fear into a woman's liking for you, and I softened the effect by giving her a handsome present. Then we dined, and, wrapping my cloak about my face, with Fritz leading the way, we went downstairs to our horses again.

It was but half-past eight, and hardly yet dark; the streets were full for such a quiet little place, and I could see that gossip was all agog. With the king on one side and the duke on the other, Zenda felt itself the centre of all Ruritania. We jogged gently through the town, but set our horses to a sharper pace when we reached the open country.

"You want to catch this fellow Johann?" asked Fritz.

"Ay, and I fancy I've baited the hook right. Our little Delilah will bring our Samson. It is not enough, Fritz, to have no women in a house, though brother Michael shows some wisdom there. If you want safety, you must have none within fifty miles."

"None nearer than Strelsau, for instance," said poor Fritz, with a lovelorn sigh.

We reached the avenue of the *château,* and were soon at the house. As the hoofs of our horses sounded on the gravel, Sapt rushed out to meet us.

"Thank God, you're safe!" he cried. "Have you seen anything of them?"

"Of whom?" I asked, dismounting.

He drew us aside, that the grooms might not hear.

"Lad," he said to me, "you must not ride about here, unless with half-a-dozen of us. You know among our men a tall young fellow, Bernenstein by name?"

I knew him. He was a fine strapping young man, almost of my height and of light complexion.

"He lies in his room upstairs, with a bullet through his arm."

"The deuce he does!"

"After dinner he strolled out alone, and went a mile

or so into the wood; and as he walked, he thought he
saw three men among the trees; and one levelled a gun
at him. He had no weapon, and he started at a run back
towards the house. But one of them fired, and he was
hit, and had much ado to reach here before he fainted.
By good luck, they feared to pursue him nearer the
house."

He paused, and added:

"Lad, the bullet was meant for you."

"It is very likely," said I, "and it's first blood to
brother Michael."

"I wonder which three it was," said Fritz.

"Well, Sapt," I said, "I went out to-night for no idle
purpose, as you shall hear. But there's one thing in my
mind."

"What's that?" he asked.

"Why this," I answered. "That I shall ill requite the
very great honours Ruritania has done me if I depart
from it, leaving one of those Six alive—neither, with the
help of God, will I."

And Sapt shook my hand on that.

CHAPTER XIII

❦

An Improvement on Jacob's Ladder

IN the morning of the day after that on which I swore my oath against the Six, I gave certain orders, and then rested in greater contentment than I had known for some time. I was at work; and work, though it cannot cure love, is yet a narcotic to it; so that Sapt, who grew feverish, marvelled to see me sprawling in an armchair in the sunshine, listening to one of my friends who sang me amorous songs in a mellow voice and induced in me a pleasing melancholy. Thus was I engaged when young Rupert Hentzau, who feared neither man nor devil, and rode through the demesne—where every tree might hide a marksman, for all he knew—as though it had been the park at Strelsau, cantered up to where I lay, bowing with burlesque deference, and craving private speech with me in order to deliver a message from the Duke of Strelsau. I made all withdraw, and then he said, seating himself by me:

"The king is in love, it seems?"

"Not with life, my lord," said I, smiling.

"It is well," he rejoined. "Come, we are alone. Rassendyll——"

I rose to a sitting posture.

"What's the matter?" he asked.

"I was about to call one of my gentlemen to bring

your horse, my lord. If you do not know how to address the king, my brother must find another messenger."

"Why keep up the farce?" he asked, negligently dusting his boot with his glove.

"Because it is not finished yet; and meanwhile I'll choose my own name."

"Oh, so be it! Yet I spoke in love for you; for indeed you are a man after my own heart."

"Saving my poor honesty," said I, "maybe I am. But that I keep faith with men, and honour with women, maybe I am, my lord."

He darted a glance at me—a glance of anger.

"Is your mother dead?" said I.

"Ay, she's dead."

"She may thank God," said I, and I heard him curse me softly. "Well, what's the message?" I continued.

I had touched him on the raw, for all the world knew he had broken his mother's heart and flaunted his mistresses in her house; and his airy manner was gone for the moment.

"The duke offers you more than I would," he growled. "A halter for you, *sire,* was my suggestion. But he offers you safe-conduct across the frontier and a million crowns."

"I prefer your offer, my lord, if I am bound to one."

"You refuse?"

"Of course."

"I told Michael you would;" and the villain, his temper restored, gave me the sunniest of smiles. "The fact is, between ourselves," he continued, "Michael doesn't understand a gentleman."

I began to laugh.

"And you?" I asked.

"I do," he said. "Well, well, the halter be it."

"I'm sorry you won't live to see it," I observed.

"Has his Majesty done me the honour to fasten a particular quarrel on me?"

"I would you were a few years older, though."

"Oh, God gives years, but the devil gives increase," laughed he. "I can hold my own."

"How is your prisoner?" I asked.

"The k——?"

"Your prisoner."

"I forgot your wishes, sire. Well, he is alive."

He rose to his feet; I imitated him. Then, with a smile, he said:

"And the pretty princess? Faith, I'll wager the next Elphberg will be red enough, for all that Black Michael will be called his father."

I sprang a step towards him, clenching my hand. He did not move an inch, and his lip curled in insolent amusement.

"Go, while your skin's whole!" I muttered. He had repaid me with interest my hit about his mother.

Then came the most audacious thing I have known in my life. My friends were some thirty yards away. Rupert called to a groom to bring him his horse, and dismissed the fellow with a crown. The horse stood near. I stood still, suspecting nothing. Rupert made as though to mount; then he suddenly turned to me, his left hand resting in his belt, his right outstretched:

"Shake hands," he said.

I bowed, and did as he had foreseen—I put my hands behind me. Quicker than thought, his left hand darted out at me, and a small dagger flashed in the air; he struck me in the left shoulder—had I not swerved, it had been my heart. With a cry, I staggered back. Without touching the stirrup, he leapt upon his horse and was off like an arrow, pursued by cries and revolver-shots—the last as useless as the first—and I sank into my chair, bleeding profusely, as I watched the devil's brat disappear down the long avenue. My friends surrounded me, and then I fainted.

I suppose that I was put to bed, and there lay, unconscious, or half-conscious, for many hours; for it was night when I awoke to my full mind, and found Fritz beside me. I was weak and weary, but he bade me be of good cheer, saying that my wound would soon heal, and that meanwhile all had gone well, for Johann, the keeper, had fallen into the snare we had laid for him, and was even now in the house.

"And the queer thing is," pursued Fritz, "that I fancy he's not altogether sorry to find himself here. He seems to think that when Black Michael has brought off his *coup,* witnesses of how it was effected—saving, of course, the Six themselves—will not be at a premium."

This idea argued a shrewdness in our captive which led me to build hopes on his assistance. I ordered him to be brought in at once. Sapt conducted him, and set him in a chair by my bedside. He was sullen and afraid; but, to say truth, after young Rupert's exploit, we also had our fears, and, if he got as far as possible from Sapt's formidable six-shooter, Sapt kept him as far as he could from me. Moreover, when he came in his hands were bound but that I would not suffer.

I need not stay to recount the safeguards and rewards we promised the fellow—all of which were honourably observed and paid, so that he lives now in prosperity (though where I may not mention); and we were the more free inasmuch as we soon learnt that he was rather a weak man than a wicked, and had acted throughout this matter more from fear of the duke and of his own brother Max than for any love of what was done. But he had persuaded all of his loyalty; and though not in their secret counsels, was yet, by his knowledge of their dispositions within the Castle, able to lay bare before us the very heart of their devices. And here, in brief, is his story:

Below the level of the ground in the Castle, approached by a flight of stone steps which abutted on the end of the drawbridge, were situate two small rooms, cut out of the rock itself. The outer of the two had no windows, but was always lighted with candles; the inner had one square window, which gave upon the moat. In the outer room there lay always, day and night, three of the Six; and the instructions of Duke Michael were, that on any attack being made on the outer room, the three were to defend the door of it so long as they could with-

out risk to themselves. But, so soon as the door should
be in danger of being forced, then Rupert Hentzau or
Detchard (for one of these two was always there)
should leave the others to hold it as long as they could,
and himself pass into the inner room, and, without more
ado, kill the king who lay there, well-treated indeed, but
without weapons, and with his arms confined in fine
steel chains, which did not allow him to move his elbow
more than three inches from his side. Thus, before the
outer door were stormed, the king would be dead. And
his body? For his body would be evidence as damning
as himself.

"Nay, sir," said Johann, "his Highness has thought of
that. While the two hold the outer room, the one who
has killed the king unlocks the bars in the square window (they turn on a hinge). The window now gives no
light, for its mouth is choked by a great pipe of earthenware; and this pipe, which is large enough to let pass
through it the body of a man, passes into the moat, coming to an end immediately above the surface of the
water, so that there is no perceptible interval between
water and pipe. The king being dead, his murderer
swiftly ties a weight to the body, and, dragging it to the
window, raises it by a pulley (for, lest the weight should
prove too great, Detchard has provided one) till it is
level with the mouth of the pipe. He inserts the feet in
the pipe, and pushes the body down. Silently, without
splash or sound, it falls into the water and thence to the
bottom of the moat, which is twenty feet deep there-
abouts. This done, the murderer cries loudly, 'All's well!'
and himself slides down the pipe; and the others, if they
can and the attack is not too hot, run to the inner room
and, seeking a moment's delay, bar the door, and in their
turn slide down. And though the king rises not from the
bottom, they rise and swim round to the other side,
where the orders are for men to wait them with ropes,
to haul them out, and horses. And here, if things go ill,
the duke will join them and seek safety by riding; but if
all goes well, they will return to the Castle and have

their enemies in a trap. That, sir, is the plan of his Highness for the disposal of the king in case of need. But it is not to be used till the last; for, as we all know, he is not minded to kill the king unless he can, before or soon after, kill you also, sir. Now, sir, I have spoken the truth, as God is my witness, and I pray you to shield me from the vengeance of Duke Michael; for if, after he knows what I have done, I fall into his hands, I shall pray for one thing out of all the world—a speedy death, and that I shall not obtain from him!"

The fellow's story was rudely told, but our questions supplemented his narrative. What he had told us applied to an armed attack; but if suspicions were aroused, and there came overwhelming force—such, for instance, as I, the king, could bring—the idea of resistance would be abandoned; the king would be quietly murdered and slid down the pipe. And—here comes an ingenious touch—one of the Six would take his place in the cell, and, on the entrance of the searchers, loudly demand release and redress; and Michael, being summoned, would confess to hasty action, but he would say the man had angered him by seeking the favour of a lady in the Castle (this was Antoinette de Mauban), and he had confined him there, as he conceived he, as Lord of Zenda, had right to do. But he was now, on receiving his apology, content to let him go, and so end the gossip which, to his Highness's annoyance, had arisen concerning a prisoner in Zenda, and had given his visitors the trouble of this inquiry. The visitors, baffled, would retire, and Michael could, at his leisure, dispose of the body of the king.

Sapt, Fritz, and I in my bed, looked round on one another in horror and bewilderment at the cruelty and cunning of the plan. Whether I went in peace or in war, openly at the head of a *corps,* or secretly by a stealthy assault, the king would be dead before I could come near him. If Michael were stronger and overcame my party, there would be an end. But if I were stronger, I should have no way to punish him, no means of proving any guilt in him without proving my own guilt also. On the other hand, I should be left as king (ah! for a moment my pulse quickened), and it would be for the future to witness the final struggle between him and me. He seemed to have made triumph possible and ruin impossible. At the worst, he would stand as well as he had stood before I crossed his path—with but one man between him and the throne, and that man an impostor; at best, there would be none left to stand against him. I had begun to think that Black Michael was over fond of leaving the fighting to his friends; but now I acknowledged that the brains, if not the arms, of the conspiracy were his.

"Does the king know this?" I asked.

"I and my brother," answered Johann, "put up the pipe, under the orders of my Lord of Hentzau. He was on guard that day, and the king asked my lord what it meant. 'Faith,' he answered, with his airy laugh, 'it's a new improvement on the ladder of Jacob, whereby, as you have read, sire, men pass from earth to heaven. We thought it not meet that your Majesty should go, in case, sire, you must go, by the common route. So we have made you a pretty private passage, where the vulgar cannot stare at you or incommode your passage. That, sire, is the meaning of that pipe.' And he laughed and bowed, and prayed the king's leave to replenish the king's glass—for the king was at supper. And the king, though he is a brave man, as are all of his House, grew red and then white as he looked on the pipe and at the merry devil who mocked him. Ah, sir," (and the fellow shuddered) "it is not easy to sleep quiet in the Castle of Zenda, for all of them would as soon cut a man's throat as play a game at cards; and my Lord Rupert would choose it sooner for a pastime than any other—ay, sooner than he would ruin a woman, though that he loves also."

The man ceased, and I bade Fritz take him away and have him carefully guarded; and, turning to him, I added:

"If anyone asks you if there is a prisoner in Zenda, you may answer 'Yes.' But if any asks who the prisoner is, do not answer. For all my promises will not save you if any man here learns from you the truth as to the prisoner in Zenda. I'll kill you like a dog if the thing be so much as breathed within the house!"

Then, when he was gone, I looked at Sapt.

"It is a hard nut!" said I.

"So hard," said he, shaking his grizzled head, "that, as I think, this time next year is like to find you still king of Ruritania!" and he broke out into curses on Michael's cunning.

I lay back on my pillows.

"There seem to me," I observed, "to be two ways by which the king can come out of Zenda alive. One is by treachery in the duke's followers."

"You can leave that out," said Sapt.

"I hope not," I rejoined, "because the other I was about to mention is—by a miracle from heaven!"

CHAPTER XIV

❧❧

A Night Outside the Castle

IT would have surprised the good people of Ruritania
to know of the foregoing talk; for, according to the official reports, I had suffered a grievous and dangerous
hurt from an accidental spear-thrust, received in the
course of my sport. I caused the bulletins to be of a very
serious character, and created great public excitement,
whereby three things occurred: first, I gravely offended
the medical faculty of Strelsau by refusing to summon
to my bedside any of them, save a young man, a friend
of Fritz's, whom we could trust; secondly, I received
word from Marshal Strakencz that my orders seemed to
have no more weight than his, and that the Princess
Flavia was leaving for Tarlenheim under his unwilling
escort (news whereat I strove not to be glad and proud);
and thirdly, my brother, the Duke of Strelsau, although
too well informed to believe the account of the origin of
my sickness, was yet persuaded by the reports and by
my seeming inactivity that I was in truth incapable of
action, and that my life was in some danger. This I learnt
from the man Johann, whom I was compelled to trust
and send back to Zenda, where, by the way, Rupert
Hentzau had him soundly flogged for daring to smirch
the morals of Zenda by staying out all night in the pursuits of love. This, from Rupert, Johann deeply resented,

and the duke's approval of it did more to bind the keeper to my side than all my promises.

On Flavia's arrival I cannot dwell. Her joy at finding me up and well, instead of on my back and fighting with death, makes a picture that even now dances before my eyes till they grow too dim to see it; and her reproaches that I had not trusted even her, must excuse the means I took to quiet them. In truth, to have her with me once more was like a taste of heaven to a damned soul, the sweeter for the inevitable doom that was to follow; and I rejoiced in being able to waste two whole days with her. And when I had wasted two days, the Duke of Strelsau arranged a hunting-party.

The stroke was near now. For Sapt and I, after anxious consultations, had resolved that we must risk a blow, our resolution being clinched by Johann's news that the king grew peaked, pale, and ill, and that his health was breaking down under his rigorous confinement. Now a man—be he king or no king—may as well die swiftly and as becomes a gentleman, from bullet or thrust, as rot his life out in a cellar! That thought made prompt action advisable in the interests of the king; from my own point of view, it grew more and more necessary. For Strakencz urged on me the need of a speedy marriage, and my own inclinations seconded him with such terrible insistence that I feared for my resolution. I do not believe that I should have done the deed I dreamt of; but I might have come to flight, and my flight would have ruined the cause. And—yes, I am no saint (ask my little sister-in-law), and worse still might have happened.

It is perhaps as strange a thing as has ever been in the history of a country that the king's brother and the king's personator, in a time of profound outward peace, near a placid undisturbed country town, under semblance of amity, should wage a desperate war for the person and life of the king. Yet such was the struggle that began now between Zenda and Tarlenheim. When I look back on the time, I seem to myself to have been half-mad. Sapt has told me that I suffered no interference and listened to no remonstrances; and if ever a King of Ruritania ruled like a despot, I was, in those days, the man. Look where I would, I saw nothing that made life sweet to me, and I took my life in my hand and carried it carelessly as a man dangles an old glove. At first they strove to guard me, to keep me safe, to persuade me not to expose myself; but when they saw how I was set, there grew up among them—whether they knew the truth or not—a feeling that Fate ruled the issue, and that I must be left to play my game with Michael my own way.

Late next night I rose from table, where Flavia had sat by me, and conducted her to the door of her apartments. There I kissed her hand, and bade her sleep sound and wake to happy days. Then I changed my clothes and went out. Sapt and Fritz were waiting for me with six men and the horses. Over his saddle Sapt carried a long coil of rope, and both were heavily armed. I had with me a short stout cudgel and a long knife. Making a circuit, we avoided the town, and in an hour found ourselves slowly mounting the hill that led to the Castle of Zenda. The night was dark and very stormy; gusts of wind and spits of rain caught us as we breasted the incline, and the great trees moaned and sighed. When we came to a thick clump, about a quarter of a mile from the Castle, we bade our six friends hide there with the horses. Sapt had a whistle, and they could rejoin us in a few moments, if danger came: but, up till now, we had met no one. I hoped that Michael was still off his guard, believing me to be safe in bed. However that might be, we gained the top of the hill without accident, and found ourselves on the edge of the moat where it sweeps under the road, separating the old Castle from it. A tree stood on the edge of the bank, and Sapt, silently and diligently, set to make fast the rope. I stripped off my boots, took a pull at a flask of brandy, loosened the knife in its sheath, and took the cudgel between my teeth. Then I shook hands with my friends, not heeding a last look of entreaty from Fritz, and laid hold of the rope. I was going to have a look at Jacob's Ladder.

Gently I lowered myself into the water. Though the night was wild, the day had been warm and bright, and the water was not cold. I struck out, and began to swim round the great walls which frowned above me. I could see only three yards ahead; I had then good hopes of not being seen, as I crept along close under the damp, moss-grown masonry. There were lights from the new part of the Castle on the other side, and now and again I heard laughter and merry shouts. I fancied I recognised young Rupert Hentzau's ringing tones, and pictured him flushed with wine. Recalling my thoughts to the business in hand, I rested a moment. If Johann's description were right, I must be near the window now. Very slowly I moved; and, out of the darkness ahead, loomed a shape. It was the pipe, curving from the window to the water: about four feet of its surface were displayed; it was as big round as two men. I was about to approach it, when I saw something else, and my heart stood still. The nose of a boat protruded beyond the pipe on the other side; and listening intently, I heard a slight shuffle—as of a man shifting his position. Who was the man who guarded Michael's invention? Was he awake or was he asleep? I felt if my knife were ready, and trod water; as I did so, I found bottom under my feet. The foundations of the Castle extended some fifteen inches, making a ledge; and I stood on it, out of water from my armpits upwards. Then I crouched and peered through the darkness under the pipe, where, curving, it left a space.

There was a man in the boat. A rifle lay by him—I saw the gleam of the barrel. Here was the sentinel! He sat very still. I listened: he breathed heavily, regularly, monotonously. By Heaven, he slept! Kneeling on the shelf, I drew forward under the pipe till my face was within two feet of his. He was a big man, I saw. It was Max Holf, the brother of Johann. My hand stole to my belt, and I drew out my knife. Of all the deeds of my life, I love the least to think of this, and whether it were the act of a man or a traitor I will not ask. I said to myself: "It is war—and the king's life is the stake." And I raised myself from beneath the pipe and stood up by the boat, which lay moored by the ledge. Holding my breath, I marked the spot and raised my arm. The great fellow stirred. He opened his eyes—wide, wider. He gasped in terror at my face and clutched at his rifle. I struck home. And I heard the chorus of a love-song from the opposite bank.

Leaving him where he lay, a huddled mass, I turned to "Jacob's Ladder." My time was short. This fellow's turn of watching might be over directly, and relief would come. Leaning over the pipe, I examined it, from the end near the water to the topmost extremity where it passed, or seemed to pass, through the masonry of the wall. There was no break in it, no chink. Dropping on my knees, I tested the under side. And my breath went quick and fast, for on this lower side, where the pipe should have clung close to the masonry, there was a gleam of light! That light must come from the cell of the king! I set my shoulder against the pipe and exerted my strength. The chink widened a very, very little, and hastily I desisted; I had done enough to show that the pipe was not fixed in the masonry at the lower side.

Then I heard a voice—a harsh, grating voice:

"Well, sire, if you have had enough of my society, I will leave you to repose; but I must fasten the little ornaments first."

It was Detchard! I caught the English accent in a moment.

"Have you anything to ask, sire, before we part?"

The king's voice followed. It was his, though it was faint and hollow—different from the merry tones I had heard in the glades of the forest.

"Pray my brother," said the king, "to kill me. I am dying by inches here."

"The duke does not desire your death, sire—yet,"

sneered Detchard; "when he does, behold your path to heaven!"

The king answered:

"So be it! And now, if your orders allow it, pray leave me."

"May you dream of paradise!" said the ruffian.

The light disappeared. I heard the bolts of the door run home. And then I heard the sobs of the king. He was alone, as he thought. Who dares mock at him?

I did not venture to speak to him. The risk of some exclamation escaping him in surprise was too great. I dared do nothing that night; and my task now was to get myself away in safety, and to carry off the carcase of the dead man. To leave him there would tell too much. Casting loose the boat, I got in. The wind was blowing a gale now, and there was little danger of oars being heard. I rowed swiftly round to where my friends waited. I had just reached the spot, when a loud whistle sounded over the moat behind me.

"Hullo, Max!" I heard shouted.

I hailed Sapt in a low tone. The rope came down. I tied it round the corpse, and then went up it myself.

"Whistle you too," I whispered, "for our men, and haul in the line. No talk now."

They hauled up the body. Just as it reached the road, three men on horseback swept round from the front of the Castle. We saw them; but, being on foot ourselves, we escaped their notice. But we heard our men coming up with a shout.

"The devil, but it's dark!" cried a ringing voice.

It was young Rupert. A moment later, shots rang out. Our people had met them. I started forward at a run, Sapt and Fritz following me.

"Thrust, thrust!" cried Rupert again, and a loud groan following told that he himself was not behindhand.

"I'm done, Rupert!" cried a voice. "They're two to one. Save yourself!"

I ran on, holding my cudgel in my hand. Suddenly a

horse came towards me. A man was on it, leaning over his shoulder.

"Are you cooked too, Krafstein?" he cried.

There was no answer.

I sprang to the horse's head. It was Rupert Hentzau.

"At last!" I cried.

For we seemed to have him. He had only his sword in his hand. My men were hot upon him; Sapt and Fritz were running up. I had outstripped them; but if they got close enough to fire, he must die or surrender.

"At last!" I cried.

"It's the play-actor!" cried he, slashing at my cudgel. He cut it clean in two; and, judging discretion better than death, I ducked my head and (I blush to tell it) scampered for my life. The devil was in Rupert Hentzau; for he put spurs to his horse, and I, turning to look, saw him ride, full gallop, to the edge of the moat and leap in, while the shots of our party fell thick round him like hail. With one gleam of moonlight we should have riddled him with balls; but, in the darkness, he won to the corner of the Castle, and vanished from our sight.

"The deuce take him!" grinned Sapt.

"It's a pity," said I, "that he's a villain. Whom have we got?"

We had Lauengram and Krafstein: they lay dead; and, concealment being no longer possible, we flung them, with Max, into the moat; and, drawing together in a compact body, rode off down the hill. And, in our midst, went the bodies of three gallant gentlemen. Thus we travelled home, heavy at heart for the death of our friends, sore uneasy concerning the king, and cut to the quick that young Rupert had played yet another winning hand with us.

For my own part, I was vexed and angry that I had killed no man in open fight, but only stabbed a knave in his sleep. And I did not love to hear Rupert call me a play-actor.

CHAPTER XV

❦

I Talk with a Tempter

RURITANIA is not England, or the quarrel between
Duke Michael and myself could not have gone on,
with the remarkable incidents which marked it, without
more public notice being directed to it. Duels were fre-
quent among all the upper classes, and private quarrels
between great men kept the old habit of spreading to
their friends and dependents. Nevertheless, after the affray which I have just related, such reports began to cir-
culate that I felt it necessary to be on my guard. The
death of the gentlemen involved could not be hidden
from their relatives. I issued a stern order, declaring that
duelling had attained unprecedented licence (the Chancellor drew up the document for me, and very well he
did it), and forbidding it save in the gravest cases. I sent
a public and stately apology to Michael, and he returned
a deferential and courteous reply to me; for our one
point of union was—and it underlay all our differences
and induced an unwilling harmony between our actions—that we could neither of us afford to throw our
cards on the table. He, as well as I, was a "play-actor,"
and, hating one another, we combined to dupe public
opinion. Unfortunately, however, the necessity for concealment involved the necessity of delay: the king might
die in his prison, or even be spirited off somewhere else;

it could not be helped. For a little while I was compelled to observe a truce, and my only consolation was that Flavia most warmly approved of my edict against duelling; and, when I expressed delight at having won her favour, prayed me, if her favour were any motive to me, to prohibit the practice altogether.

"Wait till we are married," said I, smiling.

Not the least peculiar result of the truce and of the secrecy which dictated it was that the town of Zenda became in the daytime—I would not have trusted far to its protection by night—a sort of neutral zone, where both parties could safely go; and I, riding down one day with Flavia and Sapt, had an encounter with an acquaintance, which presented a ludicrous side, but was at the same time embarrassing. As I rode along, I met a dignified-looking person driving in a two-horsed carriage. He stopped his horses, got out, and approached me, bowing low. I recognised the Head of the Strelsau Police.

"Your Majesty's ordinance as to duelling is receiving our best attention," he assured me.

If the best attention involved his presence in Zenda, I determined at once to dispense with it.

"Is that what brings you to Zenda, Prefect?" I asked.

"Why no, sire; I am here because I desired to oblige the British Ambassador."

"What's the British Ambassador doing *dans cette galère?*" said I, carelessly.

"A young countryman of his, sire—a man of some position—is missing. His friends have not heard from him for two months, and there is reason to believe that he was last seen in Zenda."

Flavia was paying little attention. I dared not look at Sapt.

"What reason?"

"A friend of his in Paris—a certain M. Featherly—has given us information which makes it possible that he came here, and the officials of the railway recollect his name on some luggage."

"What was his name?"

"Rassendyll, sire," he answered; and I saw that the name meant nothing to him. But, glancing at Flavia, he lowered his voice as he went on: "It is thought that he may have followed a lady here. Has your Majesty heard of a certain Madame de Mauban?"

"Why, yes," said I, my eye involuntarily travelling towards the Castle.

"She arrived in Ruritania about the same time as this Rassendyll."

I caught the Prefect's glance; he was regarding me with inquiry writ large on his face.

"Sapt," said I, "I must speak a word to the Prefect. Will you ride on a few paces with the princess?" And I added to the Prefect: "Come, sir, what do you mean?"

He drew close to me, and I bent in the saddle.

"If he were in love with the lady?" he whispered. "Nothing has been heard of him for two months;" and this time it was the eye of the Prefect which travelled towards the Castle.

"Yes, the lady is there," I said quietly. "But I don't suppose Mr. Rassendyll—is that the name?—is."

"The duke," he whispered, "does not like rivals, sire."

"You're right there," said I, with all sincerity. "But surely you hint at a very grave charge?"

He spread his hands out in apology. I whispered in his ear:

"This is a grave matter. Go back to Strelsau——"

"But, sire, if I have a clue here?"

"Go back to Strelsau," I repeated. "Tell the Ambassador that you have a clue, but that you must be left alone for a week or two. Meanwhile, I'll charge myself with looking into the matter."

"The Ambassador is very pressing, sire."

"You must quiet him. Come, sir; you see that if your suspicions are correct, it is an affair in which we must move with caution. We can have no scandal. Mind you return to-night."

He promised to obey me, and I rode on to rejoin my companions, a little easier in my mind. Inquiries after me must be stopped at all hazards for a week or two; and this clever official had come surprisingly near the truth. His impression might be useful some day, but if he acted on it now it might mean the worst to the king. Heartily did I curse George Featherly for not holding his tongue.

"Well," asked Flavia, "have you finished your business?"

"Most satisfactorily," said I. "Come, shall we turn round? We are almost trenching on my brother's territory."

We were, in fact, at the extreme end of the town, just where the hill begins to mount towards the Castle. We cast our eyes up, admiring the massive beauty of the old walls, and we saw a *cortège* winding slowly down the hill. On it came.

"Let us go back," said Sapt.

"I should like to stay," said Flavia; and I reined my horse beside hers.

We could distinguish the approaching party now. There came first two mounted servants in black uniforms, relieved only by a silver badge. These were followed by a car drawn by four horses: on it, under a heavy pall, lay a coffin; behind it rode a man in plain black clothes, carrying his hat in his hand. Sapt uncovered, and we stood waiting, Flavia keeping by me and laying her hand on my arm.

"It is one of the gentlemen killed in the quarrel, I expect," she said.

I beckoned to a groom.

"Ride and ask whom they escort," I ordered.

He rode up to the servants, and I saw him pass on to the gentleman who rode behind.

"It's Rupert of Hentzau," whispered Sapt.

Rupert it was, and directly afterwards, waving to the procession to stand still, Rupert trotted up to me. He was in a frock-coat, tightly buttoned, and trousers. He wore an aspect of sadness, and he bowed with profound respect. Yet suddenly he smiled, and I smiled too, for old Sapt's hand lay in his left breast-pocket, and Rupert and I both guessed what lay in the hand inside the pocket.

"Your Majesty asks whom we escort," said Rupert. "It is my dear friend, Albert of Lauengram."

"Sir," said I, "no one regrets the unfortunate affair more than I. My ordinance, which I mean to have obeyed, is witness to it."

"Poor fellow!" said Flavia softly, and I saw Rupert's eyes flash at her. Whereat I grew red; for, if I had my way, Rupert Hentzau should not have defiled her by so much as a glance. Yet he did it and dared to let admiration be seen in his look.

"Your Majesty's words are gracious," he said. "I grieve for my friend. Yet, sire, others must soon lie as he lies now."

"It is a thing we all do well to remember, my lord," I rejoined.

"Even kings, sire," said Rupert, in a moralising tone; and old Sapt swore softly by my side.

"It is true," said I. "How fares my brother, my lord?"

"He is better, sire."

"I am rejoiced."

"He hopes soon to leave for Strelsau, when his health is secured."

"He is only convalescent, then?"

"There remain one or two small troubles," answered the insolent fellow, in the mildest tone in the world.

"Express my earnest hope," said Flavia, "that they may soon cease to trouble him."

"Your Royal Highness's wish is, humbly, my own," said Rupert, with a bold glance that brought a blush to Flavia's cheek.

I bowed; and Rupert, bowing lower, backed his horse and signed to his party to proceed. With a sudden impulse, I rode after him. He turned swiftly, fearing that, even in the presence of the dead and before a lady's eyes, I meant him mischief.

"You fought as a brave man the other night," I said.

"Come, you are young, sir. If you will deliver your prisoner alive to me, you shall come to no hurt."

He looked at me with a mocking smile; but suddenly he rode nearer to me.

"I'm unarmed," he said; "and our old Sapt there could pick me off in a minute."

"I'm not afraid," said I.

"No, curse you!" he answered. "Look here, I made you a proposal from the duke once."

"I'll hear nothing from Black Michael," said I.

"Then hear one from me." He lowered his voice to a whisper. "Attack the Castle boldly. Let Sapt and Tarlenheim lead."

"Go on," said I.

"Arrange the time with me."

"I have such confidence in you, my lord!"

"Tut! I'm talking business now. Sapt there and Fritz will fall; Black Michael will fall——"

"What!"

"—Black Michael will fall, like the dog he is; the prisoner, as you call him, will go by Jacob's Ladder—ah, you know that!—to hell! Two men will be left—I, Rupert Hentzau, and you, the King of Ruritania."

He paused, and then, in a voice that quivered with eagerness, added:

"Isn't that a hand to play?—a throne and your princess! And for me, say a competence and your Majesty's gratitude."

"Surely," I exclaimed, "while you're above ground, hell wants its master!"

"Well, think it over," he said. "And, look you, it would take more than a scruple or two to keep me from yonder girl," and his evil eye flashed again at her I loved.

"Get out of my reach!" said I; and yet in a moment I began to laugh for the very audacity of it.

"Would you turn against your master?" I asked.

He swore at Michael for being what the offspring of a legal, though morganatic, union should not be called, and said to me, in an almost confidential and apparently friendly tone:

"He gets in my way, you know. He's a jealous brute! Faith, I nearly stuck a knife into him last night; he came most cursedly *mal à propos!*"

My temper was well under control now: I was learning something.

"A lady?" I asked negligently.

"Ay, and a beauty," he nodded. "But you've seen her."

"Ah! was it at a tea-party, when some of your friends got on the wrong side of the table?"

"What can you expect of fools like Detchard and De Gautet? I wish I'd been there."

"And the duke interferes?"

"Well," said Rupert meditatively, "that's hardly a fair way of putting it, perhaps. I want to interfere."

"And she prefers the duke?"

"Ay, the silly creature! Ah, well, you think about my plan;" and, with a bow, he pricked his horse and trotted after the body of his friend.

I went back to Flavia and Sapt, pondering on the strangeness of the man. Wicked men I have known in plenty, but Rupert Hentzau remains unique in my experience. And if there be another anywhere, let him be caught and hanged out of hand. So say I!

"He's very handsome, isn't he?" said Flavia.

Well, of course she didn't know him as I did; yet I was put out, for I thought his bold glances would have made her angry. But my dear Flavia was a woman, and so— she was not put out. On the contrary, she thought young Rupert very handsome—as, beyond question, the ruffian was.

"And how sad he looked at his friend's death!" said she.

"He'll have better reason to be sad at his own," observed Sapt, with a grim smile.

As for me, I grew sulky; unreasonable it was perhaps, for what better business had I to look at her with love than had even Rupert's lustful eyes? And sulky I remained till, as evening fell and we rode up to Tarlenheim, Sapt having fallen behind in case anyone should be following us, Flavia, riding close beside me, said softly, with a little half-ashamed laugh:

"Unless you smile, Rudolf, I cry. Why are you angry?"

"It was something that fellow said to me," said I; but I was smiling as we reached the doors and dismounted.

There a servant handed me a note; it was unaddressed.

"Is it for me?" I asked.

"Yes, sire; a boy brought it."

I tore it open:

"Johann carries this for me. I warned you once. In the name of God, and if you are a man, rescue me from this den of murderers!—A. de M."

I handed it to Sapt; but all that the tough old soul said in reply to this piteous appeal was:

"Whose fault brought her there?"

Nevertheless, not being faultless myself, I took leave to pity Antoinette de Mauban.

CHAPTER XVI

❧❧

A Desperate Plan

AS I had ridden publicly in Zenda, and had talked there with Rupert Hentzau, of course all pretence of illness was at an end. I marked the effect on the garrison of Zenda: they ceased to be seen abroad; and any of my men who went near the Castle reported that the utmost vigilance prevailed there. Touched as I was by Madame de Mauban's appeal, I seemed as powerless to befriend her as I had proved to help the king. Michael bade me defiance; and—although he too had been seen outside the walls—with more disregard for appearances than he had hitherto shown, he did not take the trouble to send any excuse for his failure to wait on the king. Time ran on in inactivity, when every moment was pressing; for not only was I faced with the new danger which the stir about my own disappearance brought on me, but great murmurs had arisen in Strelsau at my continued absence from the city. They had been greater, but for the knowledge that Flavia was with me; and for this reason I suffered her to stay, though I hated to have her where danger was, and though every day of our present sweet intercourse strained my endurance almost to breaking. As a final blow, nothing would content my advisers, Strakencz and the Chancellor (who came out from Strelsau to make an urgent representation to me),

save that I should appoint a day for the public solemni-
sation of my betrothal, a ceremony which in Ruritania
is well-nigh as binding and great a thing as the marriage
itself. And this—with Flavia sitting by me—I was forced
to do, setting a date a fortnight ahead, and appointing
the Cathedral in Strelsau as the place. And this formal
act being published far and wide, caused great joy
throughout the kingdom, and was the talk of all
tongues: so that I reckoned there were but two men who
chafed at it—I mean Black Michael and myself; and but
one who did not know of it—that one the man whose
name I bore, the King of Ruritania.

In truth, I heard something of the way the news was
received in the Castle; for after an interval of three
days, the man Johann, greedy for more money, though
fearful for his life, again found means to visit us. He had
been waiting on the duke when the tidings came. Black
Michael's face had grown blacker still, and he had
sworn savagely; nor was he better pleased when young
Rupert took oath that I meant to do as I said, and turning to Madame de Mauban, wished her joy on a rival
gone. Michael's hand stole towards his sword (said Johann), but not a bit did Rupert care; for he rallied the
duke on having made a better king than had reigned for
years past in Ruritania. "And," said he, with a meaning
bow to his exasperated master, "the devil sends the
princess a finer man than heaven had marked out for
her, by my soul, it does!" Then Michael harshly bade
him hold his tongue, and leave them; but Rupert must
needs first kiss madame's hand, which he did as though
he loved her, while Michael glared at him.

This was the lighter side of the fellow's news; but
more serious came behind, and it was plain that if time
pressed at Tarlenheim, it pressed none the less fiercely
at Zenda. For the king was very sick: Johann had seen
him, and he was wasted and hardly able to move. "There
could be no thought of taking another for him now." So
alarmed were they, that they had sent for a physician
from Strelsau; and the physician having been intro-

duced into the king's cell, had come forth pale and
trembling, and urgently prayed the duke to let him go
back and meddle no more in the affair; but the duke
would not, and held him there a prisoner, telling him his
life was safe if the king lived while the duke desired and
died when the duke desired—not otherwise. And, persuaded by the physician, they had allowed Madame de
Mauban to visit the king and give him such attendance
as his state needed, and as only a woman can give. Yet
his life hung in the balance; and I was still strong and
whole and free. Wherefore great gloom reigned at
Zenda; and save when they quarrelled, to which they
were very prone, they hardly spoke. But the deeper the
depression of the rest, young Rupert went about Satan's
work with a smile in his eye and a song on his lip; and
laughed "fit to burst" (said Johann) because the duke
always set Detchard to guard the king when Madame
de Mauban was in the cell—which precaution was, indeed, not unwise in my careful brother. Thus Johann
told his tale and seized his crowns. Yet he besought us to
allow him to stay with us in Tarlenheim, and not venture
his head again in the lion's den; but we had need of him
there, and, although I refused to constrain him, I prevailed on him by increased rewards to go back and to
carry tidings to Madame de Mauban that I was working
for her, and that, if she could, she should speak one
word of comfort to the king. For while suspense is bad
for the sick, yet despair is worse still, and it might be
that the king lay dying of mere hopelessness, for I could
learn of no definite disease that afflicted him.

"And how do they guard the king now?" I asked, remembering that two of the Six were dead, and Max Holf
also.

"Detchard and Bersonin watch by night, Rupert
Hentzau and De Gautet by day, sir," he answered.

"Only two at a time?"

"Ay, sir; but the others rest in a room just above, and
are within sound of a cry or a whistle."

"A room just above? I didn't know of that. Is there

any communication between it and the room where they watch?"

"No, sir. You must go down a few stairs and through the door by the drawbridge, and so to where the king is lodged."

"And that door is locked?"

"Only the four lords have keys, sir."

I drew nearer to him.

"And have they keys of the grating?" I asked in a low whisper.

"I think, sir, only Detchard and Rupert."

"Where does the duke lodge?"

"In the *château*, on the first floor. His apartments are on the right as you go towards the drawbridge."

"And Madame de Mauban?"

"Just opposite, on the left. But her door is locked after she has entered."

"To keep her in?"

"Doubtless, sir."

"Perhaps for another reason?"

"It is possible."

"And the duke, I suppose, has the key?"

"Yes. And the drawbridge is drawn back at night, and of that too the duke holds the key, so that it cannot be run across the moat without application to him."

"And where do you sleep?"

"In the entrance-hall of the *château*, with five servants."

"Armed?"

"They have pikes, sir, but no firearms. The duke will not trust them with firearms."

Then at last I took the matter boldly in my hands. I had failed once at Jacob's Ladder; I should fail again there. I must make the attack from the other side.

"I have promised you twenty thousand crowns," said I. "You shall have fifty thousand if you will do what I ask of you to-morrow night. But, first, do those servants know who your prisoner is?"

"No, sir. They believe him to be some private enemy of the duke's."

"And they would not doubt that I am the king?"

"How should they?" he asked.

"Look to this, then. To-morrow, at two in the morning exactly, fling open the front door of the *château*. Don't fail by an instant."

"Shall you be there, sir?"

"Ask no questions. Do what I tell you. Say the hall is close, or what you will. That is all I ask of you."

"And may I escape by the door, sir, when I have opened it?"

"Yes, as quick as your legs will carry you. One thing more. Carry this note to madame—oh, it's in French, you can't read it—and charge her, for the sake of all our lives, not to fail in what it orders."

The man was trembling, but I had to trust to what he had of courage and to what he had of honesty. I dared not wait, for I feared that the king would die.

When the fellow was gone, I called Sapt and Fritz to me, and unfolded the plan that I had formed. Sapt shook his head over it.

"Why can't you wait?" he asked.

"The king may die."

"Michael will be forced to act before that."

"Then," said I, "the king may live."

"Well, and if he does?"

"For a fortnight?" I asked simply.

And Sapt bit his moustache.

Suddenly Fritz von Tarlenheim laid his hand on my shoulder.

"Let us go and make the attempt," said he.

"I mean you to go—don't be afraid," said I.

"Ay, but do you stay here, and take care of the princess."

A gleam came into old Sapt's eye.

"We should have Michael one way or the other then," he chuckled; "whereas if you go, and are killed with the king, what will become of those of us who are left?"

"They will serve Queen Flavia," said I, "and I would to God I could be one of them."

A pause followed. Old Sapt broke it by saying sadly, yet with an unmeant drollery that set Fritz and me laughing:

"Why didn't old Rudolf the Third marry your—great-grandmother, was it?"

"Come," said I, "it is the king we are thinking about."

"It is true," said Fritz.

"Moreover," I went on, "I have been an impostor for the profit of another, but I will not be one for my own; and if the king is not alive and on his throne before the day of betrothal comes, I will tell the truth, come what may."

"You shall go, lad," said Sapt.

Here is the plan I had made. A strong party under Sapt's command was to steal up to the door of the *château*. If discovered prematurely, they were to kill anyone who found them—with their swords, for I wanted no noise of firing. If all went well, they would be at the door when Johann opened it. They were to rush in and secure the servants if their mere presence and the use of the king's name were not enough. At the same moment—and on this hinged the plan—a woman's cry was to ring out loud and shrill from Antoinette de Mauban's chamber. Again and again she was to cry: "Help, help! Michael, help!" and then to utter the name of young Rupert Hentzau. Then, as we hoped, Michael, in fury, would rush out of his apartments opposite, and fall alive into the hands of Sapt. Still the cries would go on; my men would let down the drawbridge; and it would be strange if Rupert, hearing his name thus taken in vain, did not descend from where he slept and seek to cross. De Gautet might or might not come with him: that must be left to chance.

And when Rupert set his foot on the drawbridge? There was my part: for I was minded for another swim in the moat; and, lest I should grow weary, I had resolved to take with me a small wooden ladder, on which I could rest my arms in the water—and my feet when I left it. I would rear it against the wall just by the bridge;

and when the bridge was across, I would stealthily creep on to it—and then if Rupert or De Gautet crossed in safety, it would be my misfortune, not my fault. They dead, two men only would remain; and for them we must trust to the confusion we had created and to a sudden rush. We should have the keys of the door that led to the all-important rooms. Perhaps they would rush out. If they stood by their orders, then the king's life hung on the swiftness with which we could force the outer door; and I thanked God that not Rupert Hentzau watched, but Detchard. For though Detchard was a cool man, relentless, and no coward, he had neither the dash nor the recklessness of Rupert. Moreover, he, if any one of them, really loved Black Michael, and it might be that he would leave Bersonin to guard the king and rush across the bridge to take part in the affray on the other side.

So I planned—desperately. And, that our enemy might be the better lulled to security, I gave orders that our residence should be brilliantly lighted from top to bottom, as though we were engaged in revelry; and should so be kept all night, with music playing and people moving to and fro. Strakencz would be there, and he was to conceal our departure, if he could, from Flavia. And if we came not again by the morning, he was to march, openly and in force, to the Castle, and demand the person of the king: if Black Michael were not there, as I did not think he would be, the marshal would take Flavia with him, as swiftly as he could, to Strelsau, and there proclaim Black Michael's treachery and the probable death of the king, and rally all that there was honest and true round the banner of the princess. And, to say truth, this was what I thought most likely to happen. For I had great doubts whether either the king or Black Michael or I had more than a day to live. Well, if Black Michael died, and if I, the play-actor, slew Rupert Hentzau with my own hand, and then died myself, it might be that Fate would deal as lightly with Ruritania as could be hoped, notwithstanding that she demanded the life of the king—and to her dealing thus with me, I was in no temper to make objection.

It was late when we rose from conference, and I betook me to the princess's apartments. She was pensive that evening; yet, when I left her, she flung her arms about me and grew, for an instant, bashfully radiant as she slipped a ring on my finger. I was wearing the king's ring; but I had also on my little finger a plain band of gold engraved with the motto of our family, "*Nil Quae Feci.*" This I took off and put on her, and signed to her to let me go. And she, understanding, stood away and watched me with dimmed eyes.

"Wear that ring, even though you wear another when you are queen," I said.

"Whatever else I wear, this I will wear till I die and after," said she, as she kissed the ring.

CHAPTER XVII

Young Rupert's Midnight
Diversions

THE night came fine and clear. I had prayed for dirty weather, such as had favoured my previous voyage in the moat, but Fortune was this time against me. Still I reckoned that by keeping close under the wall and in the shadow I could escape detection from the windows of the *château* that looked out on the scene of my efforts. If they searched the moat, indeed, my scheme must fail; but I did not think they would. They had made Jacob's Ladder secure against attack. Johann had himself helped to fix it closely to the masonry on the under side, so that it could not now be moved from below any more than from above. An assault with explosives or a long battering with picks alone could displace it, and the noise involved in either of these operations put them out of the question. What harm, then, could a man do in the moat? I trusted that Black Michael, putting this query to himself, would answer confidently, "None"; while, even if Johann meant treachery, he did not know my scheme, and would doubtless expect to see me, at the head of my friends, before the front entrance to the *château.* There, I said to Sapt, was the real danger.

"And there," I added, "you shall be. Doesn't that content you?"

But it did not. Dearly would he have liked to come

with me, had I not utterly refused to take him. One man might escape notice, to double the party more than doubled the risk; and when he ventured to hint once again that my life was too valuable, I, knowing the secret thought he clung to, sternly bade him be silent, assuring him that unless the king lived through the night, I would not live through it either.

At twelve o'clock, Sapt's command left the *château* of Tarlenheim and struck off to the right, riding by unfrequented roads, and avoiding the town of Zenda. If all went well, they would be in front of the Castle by about a quarter to two. Leaving their horses half a mile off, they were to steal up to the entrance and hold themselves in readiness for the opening of the door. If the door were not opened by two, they were to send Fritz von Tarlenheim round to the other side of the Castle. I would meet him there if I were alive, and we would consult whether to storm the Castle or not. If I were not there, they were to return with all speed to Tarlenheim, rouse the Marshal, and march in force on Zenda. For if not there, I should be dead; and I knew that the king would not be alive five minutes after I had ceased to breathe.

I must now leave Sapt and his friends, and relate how I myself proceeded on this eventful night. I went out on the good horse which had carried me, on the night of the coronation, back from the shooting-lodge to Strelsau. I carried a revolver in the saddle and my sword. I was covered with a large cloak, and under this I wore a warm, tight-fitting woollen jersey, a pair of knickerbockers, thick stockings, and light canvas shoes. I had rubbed myself thoroughly with oil, and I carried a large flask of whisky. The night was warm, but I might probably be immersed a long while, and it was necessary to take every precaution against cold: for cold not only saps a man's courage if he has to die, but impairs his energy if others have to die, and, finally, gives him rheumatics, if it be God's will that he live. Also I tied round my body a length of thin but stout cord, and I did not forget my ladder. I, starting after Sapt, took a shorter route, skirting the town to the left, and found myself in the outskirts of the forest at about half-past twelve. I tied my horse up in a thick clump of trees, leaving the revolver in its pocket in the saddle—it would be no use to me—and, ladder in hand, made my way to the edge of the moat. Here I unwound my rope from about my waist, bound it securely round the trunk of a tree on the bank, and let myself down. The Castle clock struck a quarter to one as I felt the water under me and began to swim round the keep, pushing the ladder before me, and hugging the Castle wall. Thus voyaging, I came to my old friend, "Jacob's Ladder," and felt the ledge of masonry under me. I crouched down in the shadow of the great pipe—I tried to stir it, but it was quite immovable—and waited. I remember that my predominant feeling was, neither anxiety for the king nor longing for Flavia, but an intense desire to smoke; and this craving, of course, I could not gratify.

The drawbridge was still in its place. I saw its airy, slight framework above me, some ten yards to my right, as I crouched with my back against the wall of the king's cell. I made out a window two yards my side of it and nearly on the same level. That, if Johann spoke true, must belong to the duke's apartments; and on the other side, in about the same relative position, must be Madame de Mauban's window. Women are careless, forgetful creatures. I prayed that she might not forget that she was to be the victim of a brutal attempt at two o'clock precisely. I was rather amused at the part I had assigned to my young friend Rupert Hentzau; but I owed him a stroke—for, even as I sat, my shoulder ached where he had, with an audacity that seemed half to hide his treachery, struck at me, in sight of all my friends, on the terrace at Tarlenheim.

Suddenly the duke's window grew bright. The shutters were not closed, and the interior became partially visible to me as I cautiously raised myself till I stood on tiptoe. Thus placed, my range of sight embraced a yard or more inside the window, while the radius of light did not reach me. The window was flung open and someone looked out. I marked Antoinette de Mauban's graceful figure, and, though her face was in shadow, the fine outline of her head was revealed against the light behind. I longed to cry softly, "Remember!" but I dared not—and happily, for a moment later a man came up and stood by her. He tried to put his arm round her waist, but with a swift motion she sprang away and leant against the shutter, her profile towards me. I made out who the new-comer was: it was young Rupert. A low laugh from him made me sure, as he leant forwards, stretching out his hand towards her.

"Gently, gently!" I murmured. "You're too soon, my boy!"

His head was close to hers. I suppose he whispered to her, for I saw her point to the moat, and I heard her say, in slow and distinct tones:

"I had rather throw myself out of this window!"

He came close up to the window and looked out.

"It looks cold," said he. "Come, Antoinette, are you serious?"

She made no answer, so far as I heard; and he, smiting his hand petulantly on the window-sill, went on, in the voice of some spoilt child:

"Hang Black Michael! Isn't the princess enough for him? Is he to have everything? What the devil do you see in Black Michael?"

"If I told him what you say——" she began.

"Well, tell him," said Rupert, carelessly; and, catching her off her guard, he sprang forward and kissed her, laughing, and crying, "There's something to tell him!"

If I had kept my revolver with me, I should have been very sorely tempted. Being spared the temptation, I merely added this new score to his account.

"Though, faith," said Rupert, "it's little he cares. He's mad about the princess, you know. He talks of nothing but cutting the play-actor's throat."

Didn't he, indeed?

"And if I do it for him, what do you think he's promised me?"

The unhappy woman raised her hands above her head, in prayer or in despair.

"But I detest waiting," said Rupert; and I saw that he was about to lay his hand on her again, when there was a noise of a door in the room opening, and a harsh voice cried:

"What are you doing here, sir?"

Rupert turned his back to the window, bowed low, and said, in his loud, merry tones:

"Apologising for your absence, sir. Could I leave the lady alone?"

The new-comer must be Black Michael. I saw him directly, as he advanced towards the window. He caught young Rupert by the arm.

"The moat would hold more than the king!" said he, with a significant gesture.

"Does your Highness threaten me?" asked Rupert.

"A threat is more warning than most men get from me."

"Yet," observed Rupert, "Rudolf Rassendyll has been much threatened, and yet lives!"

"Am I in fault because my servants bungle?" asked Michael scornfully.

"Your Highness has run no risk of bungling!" sneered Rupert.

It was telling the duke that he shirked danger as plain as ever I have heard a man told. Black Michael had self-control. I daresay he scowled—it was a great regret to me that I could not see their faces better—but his voice was even and calm, as he answered:

"Enough, enough! We mustn't quarrel, Rupert. Are Detchard and Bersonin at their posts?"

"They are, sir."

"I need you no more."

"Nay, I'm not oppressed with fatigue," said Rupert.

"Pray, sir, leave us," said Michael, more impatiently. "In ten minutes the drawbridge will be drawn back, and I presume you have no wish to swim to your bed."

Rupert's figure disappeared. I heard the door open and shut again. Michael and Antoinette de Mauban were left together. To my chagrin, the duke laid his hand on the window and closed it. He stood talking to Antoinette for a moment or two. She shook her head, and he turned impatiently away. She left the window. The door sounded again, and Black Michael closed the shutters.

"De Gautet, De Gautet, man!" sounded from the drawbridge. "Unless you want a bath before your bed, come along!"

It was Rupert's voice, coming from the end of the drawbridge. A moment later he and De Gautet stepped out on the bridge. Rupert's arm was through De Gautet's, and in the middle of the bridge he detained his companion and leant over. I dropped beside the shelter of "Jacob's Ladder."

Then Master Rupert had a little sport. He took from De Gautet a bottle which he carried, and put it to his lips.

"Hardly a drop!" he cried discontentedly, and flung it in the moat.

It fell, as I judged from the sound and the circles on the water, within a yard of the pipe. And Rupert, taking out his revolver, began to shoot at it. The first two shots missed the bottle, but hit the pipe. The third shattered the bottle. I hoped that the young ruffian would be content; but he emptied the other barrels at the pipe, and one, skimming over the pipe, whistled through my hair as I crouched on the other side.

" 'Ware bridge!" a voice cried, to my relief.

Rupert and De Gautet cried, "A moment!" and ran across. The bridge was drawn back, and all became still. The clock struck a quarter-past one. I rose and stretched myself and yawned.

I think some ten minutes had passed when I heard a slight noise to my right. I peered over the pipe, and saw a dark figure standing in the gateway that led to the bridge. It was a man. By the careless, graceful poise, I guessed it to be Rupert again. He held a sword in his hand, and he stood motionless for a minute or two. Wild thoughts ran through me. On what mischief was the young fiend bent now? Then he laughed low to himself; then he turned his face to the wall, took a step in my direction, and, to my surprise, began to climb down the wall. In an instant I saw that there must be steps in the wall; it was plain. They were cut into or affixed to the wall, at intervals of about eighteen inches. Rupert set his foot on the lower one. Then he placed his sword between his teeth, turned round, and noiselessly let himself down into the water. Had it been a matter of my life only, I would have swum to meet him. Dearly would I have loved to fight it out with him then and there—with steel, on a fine night and none to come between us. But there was the king! I restrained myself, but I could not bridle my swift breathing, and I watched him with the intensest eagerness.

He swam leisurely and quietly across. There were more foot-steps up on the other side, and he climbed them. When he set foot in the gateway, standing on the drawn-back bridge, he felt in his pocket and took something out. I heard him unlock the door. I could hear no noise of its closing behind him. He vanished from my sight.

Abandoning my ladder—I saw I did not need it now—I swam to the side of the bridge, and climbed half-way up the steps. There I hung, with my sword in my hand, listening eagerly. The duke's room was shuttered and dark. There was a light in the window on the opposite side of the bridge. Not a sound broke the silence, till half-past one chimed from the great clock in the tower of the *château*.

There were other plots than mine afoot in the Castle that night.

CHAPTER XVIII

The Forcing of the Trap

THE position wherein I stood does not appear very favourable to thought; yet for the next moment or two I thought profoundly. I had, I told myself, scored one point. Be Rupert Hentzau's errand what it might, and the villainy he was engaged on what it would, I had scored one point. He was on the other side of the moat from the king, and it would be by no fault of mine if ever he set foot on the same side again. I had three left to deal with: two on guard and De Gautet in his bed. Ah, if I had the keys! I would have risked everything and attacked Detchard and Bersonin before their friends could join them. But I was powerless. I must wait till the coming of my friends enticed someone to cross the bridge—someone with the keys. And I waited, as it seemed, for half-an-hour, really for about five minutes, before the next act in the rapid drama began.

All was still on the other side. The duke's room remained inscrutable behind its shutters. The light burnt steadily in Madame de Mauban's window. Then I heard the faintest, faintest sound: it came from behind the door which led to the drawbridge on the other side of the moat. It but just reached my ear, yet I could not be mistaken as to what it was. It was made by a key being turned very carefully and slowly. Who was turning it?

And of what room was it the key? There leapt before my eyes the picture of young Rupert, with the key in one hand, his sword in the other, and an evil smile on his face. But I did not know what door it was, nor on which of his favourite pursuits young Rupert was spending the hours of that night.

I was soon to be enlightened, for the next moment—before my friends could be near the *château* door—before Johann the keeper would have thought to nerve himself for his task—there was a sudden crash from the room with the lighted window. It sounded as though someone had flung down a lamp; and the window went dark and black. At the same instant a cry rang out, shrill in the night: "Help, help! Michael, help!" and was followed by a shriek of utter terror.

I was tingling in every nerve. I stood on the topmost step, clinging to the threshold of the gate with my right hand and holding my sword in my left. Suddenly I perceived that the gateway was broader than the bridge; there was a dark corner on the opposite side where a man could stand. I darted across and stood there. Thus placed, I commanded the path, and no man could pass between the *château* and the old Castle till he had tried conclusions with me.

There was another shriek. Then a door was flung open and clanged against the wall, and I heard the handle of a door savagely twisted.

"Open the door! In God's name, what's the matter?" cried a voice—the voice of Black Michael himself.

He was answered by the very words I had written in my letter:

"Help, Michael—Hentzau!"

A fierce oath rang out from the duke, and with a loud thud he threw himself against the door. At the same moment I heard a window above my head open, and a voice cried: "What's the matter?" and I heard a man's hasty footsteps. I grasped my sword. If De Gautet came my way, the Six would be less by one more.

Then I heard the clash of crossed swords and a tramp

of feet, and—I cannot tell the thing so quickly as it happened, for all seemed to come at once. There was an angry cry from madame's room, the cry of a wounded man; the window was flung open; young Rupert stood there sword in hand. He turned his back, and I saw his body go forward to the lunge.

"Ah, Johann, there's one for you! Come on, Michael!"

Johann was there, then—come to the rescue of the duke! How would he open the door for me? For I feared that Rupert had slain him.

"Help!" cried the duke's voice, faint and husky.

I heard a step on the stairs above me; and I heard a stir down to my right, in the direction of the king's cell. But, before anything happened on my side of the moat, I saw five or six men round young Rupert in the embrasure of madame's window. Three or four times he lunged with incomparable dash and dexterity. For an instant they fell back, leaving a ring round him. He leapt on the parapet of the window, laughing as he leapt, and waving his sword in his hand. He was drunk with blood, and he laughed again wildly as he flung himself headlong into the moat.

What became of him then? I did not see: for as he leapt, De Gautet's lean face looked out through the door by me, and, without a second's hesitation, I struck at him with all the strength God had given me, and he fell dead in the doorway without a word or a groan. I dropped on my knees by him. Where were the keys? I found myself muttering: "The keys, man, the keys?" as though he had been yet alive and could listen; and when I could not find them, I—God forgive me!—I believe I struck a dead man's face.

At last I had them. There were but three. Seizing the largest, I felt the lock of the door that led to the cell. I fitted in the key. It was right! The lock turned. I drew the door close behind me and locked it as noiselessly as I could, putting the key in my pocket.

I found myself at the top of a flight of steep stone

stairs. An oil-lamp burnt dimly in the bracket. I took it down and held it in my hand; and I stood and listened.

"What in the devil can it be?" I heard a voice say.

It came from behind a door that faced me at the bottom of the stairs.

And another answered:

"Shall we kill him?"

I strained to hear the answer, and could have sobbed with relief when Detchard's voice came grating and cold:

"Wait a bit. There'll be trouble if we strike too soon."

There was a moment's silence. Then I heard the bolt of the door cautiously drawn back. Instantly I put out the light I held, replacing the lamp in the bracket.

"It's dark—the lamp's out. Have you a light?" said the other voice—Bersonin's.

No doubt they had a light, but they should not use it. It was come to the crisis now, and I rushed down the steps and flung myself against the door. Bersonin had unbolted it and it gave way before me. The Belgian stood there sword in hand, and Detchard was sitting on a couch at the side of the room. In astonishment at seeing me, Bersonin recoiled; Detchard jumped to his sword. I rushed madly at the Belgian: he gave way before me, and I drove him up against the wall. He was no swordsman, though he fought bravely, and in a moment he lay on the floor before me. I turned—Detchard was not there. Faithful to his orders, he had not risked a fight with me, but had rushed straight to the door of the king's room, opened it and slammed it behind him. Even now he was at his work inside.

And surely he would have killed the king, and perhaps me also, had it not been for one devoted man who gave his life for the king. For when I forced the door, the sight I saw was this. The king stood in the corner of the room: broken by his sickness, he could do nothing; his fettered hands moved uselessly up and down, and he was laughing horribly in half-mad delirium. Detchard and the doctor were together in the middle of the room;

and the doctor had flung himself on the murderer, pinning his hands to his sides for an instant. Then Detchard wrenched himself free from the feeble grip and, as I entered, drove his sword through the hapless man.

Then he turned on me, crying:

"At last!"

We were sword to sword. By blessed chance, neither he nor Bersonin had been wearing their revolvers. I found them afterwards, ready loaded, on the mantelpiece of the outer room: it was hard by the door, ready to their hands, but my sudden rush in had cut off access to them. Yes, we were man to man: and we began to fight, silently, sternly, and hard. Yet I remember little of it, save that the man was my match with the sword— nay, and more, for he knew more tricks than I; and that he forced me back against the bars that guarded the entrance to "Jacob's Ladder." And I saw a smile on his face, and he wounded me in the left arm.

No glory do I take for that contest. I believe that the man would have mastered me and slain me, and then done his butcher's work, for he was the most skilful swordsman I have ever met; but even as he pressed me hard, the half-mad, wasted, wan creature in the corner leapt high in lunatic mirth, shrieking:

"It's cousin Rudolf! Cousin Rudolf! I'll help you, cousin Rudolf!" and catching up a chair in his hands (he could but just lift it from the ground and hold it uselessly before him) he came towards us. Hope came to me.

"Come on!" I cried. "Come on! Drive it against his legs."

Detchard replied with a savage thrust. He all but had me.

"Come on! Come on, man!" I cried. "Come and share the fun!"

And the king laughed gleefully, and came on, pushing his chair before him.

With an oath Detchard skipped back, and, before I knew what he was doing, had turned his sword against the king. He made one fierce cut at the king, and the king, with a piteous cry, dropped where he stood. The stout ruffian turned to face me again. But his own hand had prepared his destruction: for in turning, he trod in the pool of blood that flowed from the dead physician. He slipped; he fell. Like a dart I was upon him. I caught him by the throat, and before he could recover himself I drove my point through his neck, and with a stifled curse he fell across the body of his victim.

Was the king dead? It was my first thought. I rushed to where he lay. Ay, it seemed as if he were dead, for he had a great gash across the forehead, and he lay still in a huddled heap on the floor. I dropped on my knees beside him, and leant my ear down to hear if he breathed. But before I could, there was a loud rattle from the outside. I knew the sound: the drawbridge was being pushed out. A moment later it rang home against the wall on my side of the moat. I should be caught in a trap and the king with me, if he yet lived. He must take his chance, to live or to die. I took my sword, and passed into the outer room. Who were pushing the drawbridge out—my men? If so, all was well. My eye fell on the revolvers, and I seized one; and paused to listen in the doorway of the outer room. To listen, say I? Yes, and to get my breath: and I tore my shirt and twisted a strip of it round my bleeding arm; and stood listening again. I would have given the world to hear Sapt's voice. For I was faint, spent, and weary. And that wild-cat Rupert Hentzau was yet at large in the Castle. Yet, because I could better defend the narrow door at the top of the stairs than the wider entrance to the room, I dragged myself up the steps, and stood behind it listening.

What was the sound? Again a strange one for the place and the time. An easy, scornful, merry laugh—the laugh of young Rupert Hentzau! I could scarcely believe that a sane man would laugh. Yet the laugh told me that my men had not come; for they must have shot Rupert ere now, if they had come. And the clock struck half-past two! My God! The door had not been opened!

They had gone to the bank! They had not found me! They had gone by now back to Tarlenheim, with the news of the king's death—and mine. Well, it would be true before they got there. Was not Rupert laughing in triumph?

For a moment I sank, unnerved, against the door. Then I started up alert again, for Rupert cried scornfully:

"Well, the bridge is there! Come over it! And in God's name, let's see Black Michael. Keep back, you curs! Michael, come and fight for her!"

If it were a three-cornered fight, I might yet bear my part. I turned the key in the door and looked out.

CHAPTER XIX

Face to Face in the Forest

FOR a moment I could see nothing, for the glare of lanterns and torches caught me full in the eyes from the other side of the bridge. But soon the scene grew clear: and it was a strange scene. The bridge was in its place. At the far end of it stood a group of the duke's servants; two or three carried the lights which had dazzled me, three or four held pikes in rest. They were huddled together; their weapons were protruded before them; their faces were pale and agitated. To put it plainly, they looked in as arrant a fright as I have seen men look, and they gazed apprehensively at a man who stood in the middle of the bridge, sword in hand. Rupert Hentzau was in his trousers and shirt; the white linen was stained with blood, but his easy, buoyant pose told me that he was himself either not touched at all or merely scratched. There he stood, holding the bridge against them, and daring them to come on; or, rather, bidding them send Black Michael to him; and they, having no firearms, cowered before the desperate man and dared not attack him. They whispered to one another; and, in the backmost rank, I saw my friend Johann, leaning against the portal of the door and stanching with a handkerchief the blood which flowed from a wound in his cheek.

By marvellous chance, I was master. The cravens would oppose me no more than they dared attack Rupert. I had but to raise my revolver, and I sent him to his account with his sins on his head. He did not so much as know that I was there. I did nothing—why I hardly know to this day. I had killed one man stealthily that night, and another by luck rather than skill—perhaps it was that. Again, villain as the man was, I did not relish being one of a crowd against him—perhaps it was that. But stronger than either of these restraining feelings came a curiosity and a fascination which held me spellbound, watching for the outcome of the scene.

"Michael, you dog! Michael! If you can stand, come on!" cried Rupert; and he advanced a step, the group shrinking back a little before him. "Michael, you bastard! come on!"

The answer to his taunts came in the wild cry of a woman:

"He's dead! My God, he's dead!"

"Dead!" shouted Rupert. "I struck better than I knew!" and he laughed triumphantly. Then he went on: "Down with your weapons there! I'm your master now! Down with them, I say!"

I believe they would have obeyed, but as he spoke came new things. First, there arose a distant sound, as of shouts and knockings from the other side of the *château*. My heart leapt. It must be my men, come by a happy disobedience to seek me. The noise continued, but none of the rest seemed to heed it. Their attention was chained by what now happened before their eyes. The group of servants parted and a woman staggered on to the bridge. Antoinette de Mauban was in a loose white robe, her dark hair streamed over her shoulders, her face was ghastly pale, and her eyes gleamed wildly in the light of the torches. In her shaking hand she held a revolver, and, as she tottered forward, she fired it at Rupert Hentzau. The ball missed him, and struck the woodwork over my head.

"Faith, madame," laughed Rupert, "had your eyes

been no more deadly than your shooting, I had not been in this scrape—nor Black Michael in hell—to-night!"

She took no notice of his words. With a wonderful effort, she calmed herself till she stood still and rigid. Then very slowly and deliberately she began to raise her arm again, taking most careful aim.

He would be mad to risk it. He must rush on her, chancing the bullet, or retreat towards me. I covered him with my weapon.

He did neither. Before she had got her aim, he bowed in his most graceful fashion, cried, "I can't kill where I've kissed," and before she or I could stop him, laid his hand on the parapet of the bridge, and lightly leapt into the moat.

At the very moment I heard a rush of feet, and a voice I knew—Sapt's—cry: "God! it's the duke—dead!" Then I knew that the king needed me no more, and, throwing down my revolver, I sprang out on the bridge. There was a cry of wild wonder, "The king!" and then I, like Rupert Hentzau, sword in hand, vaulted over the parapet, intent on finishing my quarrel with him where I saw his curly head fifteen yards off in the water of the moat.

He swam swiftly and easily. I was weary and half-crippled with my wounded arm. I could not gain on him. For a time I made no sound, but as we rounded the corner of the old keep I cried:

"Stop, Rupert, stop!"

I saw him look over his shoulder, but he swam on. He was under the bank now, searching, as I guessed, for a spot that he could climb. I knew there to be none—but there was my rope, which would still be hanging where I had left it. He would come to where it was before I could. Perhaps he would miss it—perhaps he would find it; and if he drew it up after him, he would get a good start of me. I put forth all my remaining strength and pressed on. At last I began to gain on him; for he, occupied with his search, unconsciously slackened his pace.

Ah, he had found it! A low shout of triumph came

from him. He laid hold of it and began to haul himself up. I was near enough to hear him mutter: "How the devil comes this here?" I was at the rope, and he, hanging in mid-air, saw me; but I could not reach him.

"Hullo! who's here?" he cried in startled tones.

For a moment, I believe, he took me for the king—I daresay I was pale enough to lend colour to the thought; but an instant later he cried:

"Why, it's the play-actor! How came you here, man?"

And so saying, he gained the bank.

I laid hold of the rope, but I paused. He stood on the bank, sword in hand, and he could cut my head open or spit me through the heart as I came up. I let go the rope.

"Never mind," said I; "but as I am here, I think I'll stay."

He smiled down on me.

"These women are the deuce——" he began; when suddenly the great bell of the Castle started to ring furiously, and a loud shout reached us from the moat.

Rupert smiled again, and waved his hand to me.

"I should like a turn with you, but it's a little too hot!" said he, and he disappeared from above me.

In an instant, without thinking of danger, I laid my hand to the rope. I was up. I saw him thirty yards off, running like a deer towards the shelter of the forest. For once Rupert Hentzau had chosen discretion for his part. I laid my feet to the ground and rushed after him, calling to him to stand. He would not. Unwounded and vigorous, he gained on me at every step; but, forgetting everything in the world except him and my thirst for his blood, I pressed on, and soon the deep shades of the forest of Zenda engulfed us both, pursued and pursuer.

It was three o'clock now, and day was dawning. I was on a long straight grass avenue, and a hundred yards ahead ran young Rupert, his curls waving in the fresh breeze. I was weary and panting; he looked over his shoulder and waved his hand again to me. He was mocking me, for he saw he had the pace of me. I was forced to pause for breath. A moment later, Rupert turned sharply to the right and was lost from my sight.

I thought all was over, and in deep vexation sank on the ground. But I was up again directly, for a scream rang through the forest—a woman's scream. Putting forth the last of my strength, I ran on to the place where he had turned out of my sight, and, turning also, I saw him again. But alas! I could not touch him. He was in the act of lifting a girl down from her horse; doubtless it was her scream that I heard. She looked like a small farmer's or a peasant's daughter, and she carried a basket on her arm. Probably she was on her way to the early market at Zenda. Her horse was a stout, well-shaped animal. Master Rupert lifted her down amid her shrieks—the sight of him frightened her; but he treated her gently, laughed, kissed her, and gave her money. Then he jumped on the horse, sitting sideways like a woman; and then he waited for me. I, on my part, waited for him.

Presently he rode towards me, keeping his distance however. He lifted up his hand, saying:

"What did you in the Castle?"

"I killed three of your friends," said I.

"What! You got to the cells?"

"Yes."

"And the king?"

"He was hurt by Detchard before I killed Detchard, but I pray that he lives."

"You fool!" said Rupert, pleasantly.

"One thing more I did."

"And what's that?"

"I spared your life. I was behind you on the bridge, with a revolver in my hand."

"No? Faith, I was between two fires!"

"Get off your horse," I cried, "and fight like a man."

"Before a lady!" said he, pointing to the girl. "Fie, your Majesty!"

Then in my rage, hardly knowing what I did, I rushed at him. For a moment he seemed to waver. Then he reined his horse in and stood waiting for me. On I went in my folly. I seized the bridle and I struck at him. He parried and thrust at me. I fell back a pace and rushed in at him again; and this time I reached his face and laid his cheek open, and darted back before he could strike me. He seemed almost mazed at the fierceness of my attack; otherwise I think he must have killed me. I sank on my knee panting, expecting him to ride at me. And so he would have done, and then and there, I doubt not, one or both of us would have died; but at the moment there came a shout from behind us, and, looking round, I saw, just at the turn of the avenue, a man on a horse. He was riding hard, and he carried a revolver in his hand. It was Fritz von Tarlenheim, my faithful friend. Rupert saw him, and knew that the game was up. He checked his rush at me and flung his leg over the saddle, but yet for just a moment he waited. Leaning forward, he tossed his hair off his forehead and smiled, and said:

"*Au revoir,* Rudolf Rassendyll!"

Then, with his cheek streaming blood, but his lips laughing and his body swaying with ease and grace, he bowed to me; and he bowed to the farm-girl, who had drawn near in trembling fascination, and he waved his hand to Fritz, who was just within range and let fly a shot at him. The ball came nigh doing its work, for it struck the sword he held, and he dropped the sword with an oath, wringing his fingers, and clapped his heels hard on his horse's belly, and rode away at a gallop.

And I watched him go down the long avenue, riding as though he rode for his pleasure and singing as he went, for all there was that gash in his cheek.

Once again he turned to wave his hand, and then the gloom of the thickets swallowed him and he was lost from our sight. Thus he vanished—reckless and wary, graceful and graceless, handsome, debonair, vile, and unconquered. And I flung my sword passionately on the ground and cried to Fritz to ride after him. But Fritz stopped his horse, and leapt down and ran to me, and knelt, putting his arm about me. And indeed it was time, for the wound that Detchard had given me was broken forth afresh, and my blood was staining the ground.

"Then give me the horse!" I cried, staggering to my feet and throwing his arms off me. And the strength of my rage carried me so far as where the horse stood, and then I fell prone beside it. And Fritz knelt by me again.

"Fritz!" I said.

"Ay, friend—dear friend!" said he, tender as a woman.

"Is the king alive?"

He took his handkerchief and wiped my lips, and bent and kissed me on the forehead.

"Thanks to the most gallant gentleman that lives," said he softly, "the king is alive!"

The little farm-girl stood by us, weeping for fright and wide-eyed for wonder; for she had seen me at Zenda: and was not I, pallid, dripping, foul, and bloody as I was—yet was not I the king?

And when I heard that the king was alive, I strove to cry "Hurrah!" But I could not speak, and I laid my head back in Fritz's arms and closed my eyes, and I groaned; and then, lest Fritz should do me wrong in his thoughts, I opened my eyes and tried to say "Hurrah!" again. But I could not. And being very tired, and now very cold, I huddled myself close up to Fritz, to get the warmth of him, and shut my eyes again and went to sleep.

CHAPTER XX

The Prisoner and the King

IN order to gain a full understanding of what had occurred in the Castle of Zenda, it is necessary to sup-
plement my account of what I myself saw and did on
that night by relating briefly what I afterwards learnt
from Fritz and from Madame de Mauban. The story told
by the latter explained clearly how it happened that the
cry which I had arranged as a stratagem and a sham had
come, in dreadful reality, before its time, and had thus,
as it seemed at the moment, ruined our hopes, while in
the end it had favoured them. The unhappy woman,
fired, I believe, by a genuine attachment to the Duke of
Strelsau, no less than by the dazzling prospects which a
dominion over him opened before her eyes, had followed him at his request from Paris to Ruritania. He
was a man of strong passions, but of stronger will, and
his cool head ruled both. He was content to take all and
give nothing. When she arrived, she was not long in finding that she had a rival in the Princess Flavia; rendered
desperate, she stood at nothing which might give, or
keep for her, her power over the duke. As I say, he took
and gave not. Simultaneously, Antoinette found herself
entangled in his audacious schemes. Unwilling to abandon him, bound to him by the chains of shame and
hope, yet she would not be a decoy, nor, at his bidding,

lure me to death. Hence the letters of warning she had
written. Whether the lines she sent to Flavia were inspired by good or bad feeling, by jealousy or by pity, I
do not know; but here also she served us well. When the
duke went to Zenda, she accompanied him; and here for
the first time she learnt the full measure of his cruelty,
and was touched with compassion for the unfortunate
king. From this time she was with us; yet, from what she
told me, I know that she still (as women will) loved
Michael, and trusted to gain his life, if not his pardon,
from the king, as the reward for her assistance. His triumph she did not desire, for she loathed his crime, and
loathed yet more fiercely what would be the prize of
it—his marriage with his cousin, Princess Flavia.

At Zenda new forces came into play—the lust and
daring of young Rupert. He was caught by her beauty,
perhaps; perhaps it was enough for him that she belonged to another man, and that she hated him. For
many days there had been quarrels and ill-will between
him and the duke, and the scene which I had witnessed
in the duke's room was but one of many. Rupert's pro-
posals to me, of which she had, of course, been ignorant,
in no way surprised her when I related them; she had
herself warned Michael against Rupert, even when she
was calling on me to deliver her from both of them. On
this night, then, Rupert had determined to have his will.
When she had gone to her room, he, having furnished
himself with a key to it, had made his entrance. Her
cries had brought the duke, and there in the dark
room, while she screamed, the men had fought; and
Rupert, having wounded his master with a mortal
blow, had, on the servants rushing in, escaped through
the window as I have described. The duke's blood,
spurting out, had stained his opponent's shirt; but Rupert, not knowing that he had dealt Michael his death,
was eager to finish the encounter. How he meant to
deal with the other three of the band, I know not. I daresay he did not think, for the killing of Michael was not
premeditated. Antoinette, left alone with the duke, had

tried to stanch his wound, and thus was she busied till he died; and then, hearing Rupert's taunts, she had come forth to avenge him. Me she had not seen, nor did she till I darted out of my ambush, and leapt after Rupert into the moat.

The same moment found my friends on the scene. They had reached the *château* in due time, and waited ready by the door. But Johann, swept with the rest to the rescue of the duke, did not open it; nay, he took a part against Rupert, putting himself forward more bravely than any in his anxiety to avert suspicion; and he had received a wound, in the embrasure of the window. Till nearly half-past two Sapt waited; then, following my orders, he had sent Fritz to search the banks of the moat. I was not there. Hastening back, Fritz told Sapt; and Sapt was for following orders still, and riding at full speed back to Tarlenheim; while Fritz would not hear of abandoning me, let me have ordered what I would. On this they disputed some few minutes; then Sapt, persuaded by Fritz, detached a party under Bernenstein to gallop back to Tarlenheim and bring up the marshal, while the rest fell to on the great door of the *château*. For several minutes it resisted them; then, just as Antoinette de Mauban fired at Rupert Hentzau on the bridge, they broke in, eight of them in all: and the first door they came to was the door of Michael's room; and Michael lay dead across the threshold, with a sword-thrust through his breast. Sapt cried out at his death, as I had heard, and they rushed on the servants; but these, in fear, dropped their weapons, and Antoinette flung herself weeping at Sapt's feet. And all she cried was, that I had been at the end of the bridge and had leapt off. "What of the prisoner?" asked Sapt; but she shook her head. Then Sapt and Fritz, with the gentlemen behind them, crossed the bridge, slowly, warily, and without noise; and Fritz stumbled over the body of De Gautet in the way of the door. They felt him and found him dead.

Then they consulted, listening eagerly for any sound

from the cells below; but there came none, and they were greatly afraid that the king's guards had killed him, and having pushed his body through the great pipe, had escaped the same way themselves. Yet, because I had been seen here, they had still some hope (thus indeed Fritz, in his friendship, told me); and going back to Michael's body, pushing aside Antoinette, who prayed by it, they found a key to the door which I had locked, and opened the door. The staircase was dark, and they would not use a torch at first, lest they should be the more exposed to fire. But soon Fritz cried: "The door down there is open! See, there is light!" So they went on boldly, and found none to oppose them. And when they came to the outer room and saw the Belgian, Bersonin, lying dead, they thanked God, Sapt saying: "Ay, he has been here." Then rushing into the king's cell, they found Detchard lying dead across the dead physician, and the king on his back with his chair by him. And Fritz cried: "He's dead!" and Sapt drove all out of the room except Fritz, and knelt down by the king; and, having learnt more of wounds and the signs of death than I, he soon knew that the king was not dead, nor, if properly attended, would die. And they covered his face and carried him to Duke Michael's room, and laid him there; and Antoinette rose from praying by the body of the duke and went to bathe the king's head and dress his wounds, till a doctor came. And Sapt, seeing I had been there, and having heard Antoinette's story, sent Fritz to search the moat and then the forest. He dared send no one else. And Fritz found my horse, and feared the worst. Then, as I have told, he found me, guided by the shout with which I had called on Rupert to stop and face me. And I think a man has never been more glad to find his own brother alive than was Fritz to come on me; so that, in love and anxiety for me, he thought nothing of a thing so great as would have been the death of Rupert Hentzau. Yet, had Fritz killed him, I should have grudged it.

The enterprise of the king's rescue being thus prosperously concluded, it lay on Colonel Sapt to secure secrecy as to the king ever having been in need of rescue. Antoinette de Mauban and Johann the keeper (who, indeed, was too much hurt to be wagging his tongue just now) were sworn to reveal nothing; and Fritz went forth to find—not the king, but the unnamed friend of the king, who had lain in Zenda and flashed for a moment before the dazed eyes of Duke Michael's servants on the drawbridge. The metamorphosis had happened; and the king, wounded almost to death by the attacks of the gaolers who guarded his friend, had at last overcome them, and rested now, wounded but alive, in Black Michael's own room in the Castle. There he had been carried, his face covered with a cloak, from the cell; and thence orders issued, that if his friend were found, he should be brought directly and privately to the king, and that meanwhile messengers should ride at full speed to Tarlenheim, to tell Marshal Strakencz to assure the princess of the king's safety, and to come himself with all speed to greet the king. The princess was enjoined to remain at Tarlenheim, and there await her cousin's coming or his further injunctions. Thus the king would come to his own again, having wrought brave deeds, and escaped, almost by a miracle, the treacherous assault of his unnatural brother.

This ingenious arrangement of my long-headed old friend prospered in every way, save where it encountered a force that often defeats the most cunning schemes. I mean nothing else than the pleasure of a woman. For, let her cousin and sovereign send what command he chose (or Colonel Sapt chose for him), and let Marshal Strakencz insist as he would, the Princess Flavia was in no way minded to rest at Tarlenheim while her lover lay wounded at Zenda; and when the marshal, with a small *suite,* rode forth from Tarlenheim on the way to Zenda, the princess's carriage followed immediately behind, and in this order they passed through the town, where the report was already rife that the king, going the night before to remonstrate with his brother, in all friendliness, for that he held one of the king's friends in confinement in the Castle, had been most traitorously set upon; that there had been a desperate conflict; that the duke was slain with several of his gentlemen; and that the king, wounded as he was, had seized and held the Castle of Zenda. All of which talk made, as may be supposed, a mighty excitement; and the wires were set in motion, and the tidings came to Strelsau only just after orders had been sent thither to parade the troops and overawe the dissatisfied quarters of the town with a display of force.

Thus the Princess Flavia came to Zenda. And as she drove up the hill, with the marshal riding by the wheel and still imploring her to return in obedience to the king's orders, Fritz von Tarlenheim, with the prisoner of Zenda, came to the edge of the forest. I had revived from my swoon, and walked, resting on Fritz's arm; and looking out from the cover of the trees, I saw the princess. Suddenly understanding from a glance at my companion's face that we must not meet her, I sank on my knees behind a clump of bushes. But there was one whom we had forgotten, but who followed us, and was not disposed to let slip the chance of earning a smile and maybe a crown or two; and, while we lay hidden, the little farm-girl came by us and ran to the princess, curtseying and crying:

"Madame, the king is here—in the bushes! May I guide you to him, Madame?"

"Nonsense, child!" said old Strakencz; "the king lies wounded in the Castle."

"Yes, sir, he's wounded, I know; but he's there—with Count Fritz—and not at the Castle," she persisted.

"Is he in two places, or are there two kings?" asked Flavia, bewildered. "And how should he be here?"

"He pursued a gentleman, Madame, and they fought till Count Fritz came; and the other gentleman took my father's horse from me and rode away; but the king is here with Count Fritz. Why, Madame, is there another man in Ruritania like the king?"

"No, my child," said Flavia softly (I was told it afterwards), and she smiled and gave the girl money. "I will
go and see this gentleman," and she rose to alight from
the carriage.

But at this moment Sapt came riding from the Castle,
and, seeing the princess, made the best of a bad job, and
cried to her that the king was well tended and in no
danger.

"In the Castle?" she asked.

"Where else, Madame?" said he, bowing.

"But this girl says he is yonder—with Count Fritz."

Sapt turned his eyes on the child with an incredulous
smile.

"Every fine gentleman is a king to such," said he.

"Why, he's as like the king as one pea to another,
Madame!" cried the girl, a little shaken but still obstinate.

Sapt started round. The old marshal's face asked un-
spoken questions. Flavia's glance was no less eloquent.
Suspicion spreads quick.

"I'll ride myself and see this man," said Sapt, hastily.

"Nay, I'll come myself," said the princess.

"Then come alone," he whispered.

And she, obedient to the strange hinting in his face,
prayed the marshal and the rest to wait; and she and
Sapt came on foot towards where we lay, Sapt waving to
the farm-girl to keep at a distance. And when I saw
them coming, I sat in a sad heap on the ground, and
buried my face in my hands. I could not look at her. Fritz
knelt by me, laying his hand on my shoulder.

"Speak low, whatever you say," I heard Sapt whisper
as they came up; and the next thing I heard was a low
cry—half of joy, half of fear—from the princess:

"It is he! Are you hurt?"

And she fell on the ground by me, and gently pulled
my hands away; but I kept my eyes to the ground.

"It is the king!" she said. "Pray, Colonel Sapt, tell me
where lay the wit of the joke you played on me?"

We answered, none of us: we three were silent before

her. Regardless of them, she threw her arms round my neck and kissed me. Then Sapt spoke in a low hoarse whisper:

"It is not the king. Don't kiss him; he's not the king."

She drew back for a moment; then, with an arm still round my neck, she asked, in superb indignation:

"Do I not know my love? Rudolf, my love!"

"It is not the king," said old Sapt again; and a sudden sob broke from tender-hearted Fritz.

It was the sob that told her no comedy was afoot.

"He is the king!" she cried. "It is the king's face—the king's ring—my ring! It is my love!"

"Your love, madame," said old Sapt, "but not the king. The king is there in the Castle. This gentleman——"

"Look at me, Rudolf! look at me!" she cried, taking my face between her hands. "Why do you let them torment me? Tell me what it means!"

Then I spoke, gazing into her eyes.

"God forgive me, Madame!" I said. "I am not the king!"

I felt her hands clutch my cheeks. She gazed at me as never man's face was scanned yet. And I, silent again, saw wonder born, and doubt grow, and terror spring to life as she looked. And very gradually the grasp of her hands slackened: she turned to Sapt, to Fritz, and back to me: then suddenly she reeled forward and fell in my arms; and with a great cry of pain I gathered her to me and kissed her lips. Sapt laid his hand on my arm. I looked up in his face. And I laid her softly on the ground, and stood up, looking on her, cursing heaven that young Rupert's sword had spared me for this sharper pang.

CHAPTER XXI

If Love Were All!

IT was night, and I was in the cell wherein the king had lain in the Castle of Zenda. The great pipe that Rupert of Hentzau had nicknamed "Jacob's Ladder" was gone, and the lights in the room across the moat twinkled in the darkness. All was still; the din and clash of strife were gone. I had spent the day hidden in the forest, from the time when Fritz had led me off, leaving Sapt with the princess. Under cover of dusk, muffled up, I had been brought to the Castle and lodged where I now lay. Though three men had died there—two of them by my hand,—I was not troubled by ghosts. I had thrown myself on a pallet by the window, and was looking out on the black water; Johann the keeper, still pale from his wound, but not much hurt besides, had brought me supper. He told me that the king was doing well, that he had seen the princess; that she and he, Sapt and Fritz, had been long together. Marshal Strakencz was gone to Strelsau: Black Michael lay in his coffin, and Antoinette de Mauban watched by him; had I not heard, from the chapel, priests singing mass for him?

Outside there were strange rumours afloat. Some said that the prisoner of Zenda was dead; some, that he had vanished yet alive; some, that he was a friend who had served the king well in some adventure in England;

others, that he had discovered the duke's plots, and had therefore been kidnapped by him. One or two shrewd fellows shook their heads and said only that they would say nothing, but they had suspicions that more was to be known than was known, if Colonel Sapt would tell all he knew.

Thus Johann chattered till I sent him away and lay there alone, thinking, not of the future, but—as a man is wont to do when stirring things have happened to him—rehearsing the events of the past weeks, and wondering how strangely they had fallen out. And above me, in the stillness of the night, I heard the standards flapping against their poles, for Black Michael's banner hung there half-mast high, and above it the royal flag of Ruritania, floating for one night more over my head. Habit grows so quick, that only by an effort did I recollect that it floated no longer for me.

Presently Fritz von Tarlenheim came into the room. I was standing then by the window; the glass was opened, and I was idly fingering the cement which clung to the masonry where "Jacob's Ladder" had been. He told me briefly that the king wanted me, and together we crossed the drawbridge and entered the room that had been Black Michael's.

The king was lying there in bed; our doctor from Tarlenheim was in attendance on him, and whispered to me that my visit must be brief. The king held out his hand and shook mine. Fritz and the doctor withdrew to the window.

I took the king's ring from my finger and placed it on his.

"I have tried not to dishonour it, sire," said I.

"I can't talk much to you," he said, in a weak voice. "I have had a great fight with Sapt and the marshal—for we have told the marshal everything. I wanted to take you to Strelsau and keep you with me, and tell everyone of what you had done; and you would have been my best and nearest friend, Cousin Rudolf. But they tell me I must not, and that the secret must be kept—if kept it can be."

"They are right, sire. Let me go. My work here is done."

"Yes, it is done, as no man but you could have done it. When they see me again, I shall have my beard on; I shall—yes, faith, I shall be wasted with sickness. They will not wonder that the king looks changed in face. Cousin, I shall try to let them find him changed in nothing else. You have shown me how to play the king."

"Sire," said I, "I can take no praise from you. It is by the narrowest grace of God that I was not a worse traitor than your brother."

He turned inquiring eyes on me; but a sick man shrinks from puzzles, and he had no strength to question me. His glance fell on Flavia's ring, which I wore. I thought he would question me about it; but, after fingering it idly, he let his head fall on his pillow.

"I don't know when I shall see you again," he said faintly, almost listlessly.

"If I can ever serve you again, sire," I answered.

His eyelids closed. Fritz came with the doctor. I kissed the king's hand, and let Fritz lead me away. I have never seen the king since.

Outside, Fritz turned, not to the right, back towards the drawbridge, but to the left, and, without speaking, led me upstairs, through a handsome corridor in the *château*.

"Where are we going?" I asked.

Looking away from me, Fritz answered:

"She has sent for you. When it is over, come back to the bridge. I'll wait for you there."

"What does she want?" said I, breathing quickly.

He shook his head.

"Does she know everything?"

"Yes, everything."

He opened a door, and gently pushing me in, closed it behind me. I found myself in a drawing-room, small and richly furnished. At first I thought that I was alone, for the light that came from a pair of shaded candles on the mantelpiece was very dim. But presently I discerned a woman's figure standing by the window. I knew it was the princess, and I walked up to her, fell on one knee, and carried the hand that hung by her side to my lips. She neither moved nor spoke. I rose to my feet, and, piercing the gloom with my eager eyes, saw her pale face and the gleam of her hair, and before I knew, I spoke softly:

"Flavia!"

She trembled a little, and looked round. Then she darted to me, taking hold of me.

"Don't stand, don't stand! No, you mustn't! You're hurt! Sit down—here, here!"

She made me sit on a sofa, and put her hand on my forehead.

"How hot your head is," she said, sinking on her knees by me. Then she laid her head against me, and I heard her murmur: "My darling, how hot your head is!"

Somehow love gives even to a dull man the knowledge of his lover's heart. I had come to humble myself and pray pardon for my presumption; but what I said now was:

"I love you with all my heart and soul!"

For what troubled and shamed her? Not her love for me, but the fear that I had counterfeited the lover as I had acted the king, and taken her kisses with a smothered smile.

"With all my life and heart!" said I, as she clung to me. "Always, from the first moment I saw you in the Cathedral! There has been but one woman in the world to me—and there will be no other. But God forgive me the wrong I've done you!"

"They made you do it!" she said quickly; and she added, raising her head and looking in my eyes: "It might have made no difference if I'd known it. It was always you, never the king!" and she raised herself and kissed me.

"I meant to tell you," said I. "I was going to on the night of the ball in Strelsau, when Sapt interrupted me. After that, I couldn't—I couldn't risk losing you before—

before—I must! My darling, for you I nearly left the king to die!"

"I know, I know! What are we to do now, Rudolf?"

I put my arm round her and held her up while I said:

"I am going away to-night."

"Ah, no, no!" she cried. "Not to-night!"

"I must go to-night, before more people have seen me. And how would you have me stay, sweetheart, except——?"

"If I could come with you!" she whispered very low.

"My God!" said I roughly, "don't talk about that!" and I thrust her a little back from me.

"Why not? I love you. You are as good a gentleman as the king!"

Then I was false to all that I should have held by. For I caught her in my arms and prayed her, in words that I will not write, to come with me, daring all Ruritania to take her from me. And for a while she listened, with wondering, dazzled eyes. But as her eyes looked on me, I grew ashamed, and my voice died away in broken murmurs and stammerings, and at last I was silent.

She drew herself away from me and stood against the wall, while I sat on the edge of the sofa, trembling in every limb, knowing what I had done—loathing it, obstinate not to undo it. So we rested a long time.

"I am mad!" I said sullenly.

"I love your madness, dear," she answered.

Her face was away from me, but I caught the sparkle of a tear on her cheek. I clutched the sofa with my hand and held myself there.

"Is love the only thing?" she asked, in low, sweet tones that seemed to bring a calm even to my wrung heart. "If love were the only thing, I would follow you—in rags, if need be—to the world's end; for you hold my heart in the hollow of your hand! But is love the only thing?"

I made her no answer. It gives me shame now to think that I would not help her.

She came near me and laid her hand on my shoulder. I put my hand up and held hers.

"I know people write and talk as if it were. Perhaps, for some, Fate lets it be. Ah, if I were one of them! But if love had been the only thing, you would have let the king die in his cell."

I kissed her hand.

"Honour binds a woman too, Rudolf. My honour lies in being true to my country and my House. I don't know why God has let me love you; but I know that I must stay."

Still I said nothing; and she, pausing a while, then went on:

"Your ring will always be on my finger, your heart in my heart, the touch of your lips on mine. But you must go, and I must stay. Perhaps I must do what it kills me to think of doing."

I knew what she meant, and a shiver ran through me. But I could not utterly fail beside her. I rose and took her hand.

"Do what you will, or what you must," I said. "I think God shows his purposes to such as you. My part is lighter; for your ring shall be on my finger and your heart in mine, and no touch save of your lips will ever be on mine. So, may God comfort you, my darling!"

There struck on our ears the sound of singing. The priests in the chapel were singing masses for the souls of those who lay dead. They seemed to chant a requiem over our buried joy, to pray forgiveness for our love that would not die. The soft, sweet, pitiful music rose and fell as we stood opposite one another, her hands in mine.

"My queen and my beauty!" said I.

"My lover and true knight!" she said. "Perhaps we shall never see one another again. Kiss me, my dear, and go!"

I kissed her as she bade me; but at the last she clung to me, whispering nothing but my name, and that over and over again—and again—and again; and then I left her.

Rapidly I walked down to the bridge. Sapt and Fritz were waiting for me. Under their directions I changed

my dress, and muffling my face, as I had done more than
once before, I mounted with them at the door of the
Castle, and we three rode through the night and on to
the breaking of day, and found ourselves at a little roadside station just over the border of Ruritania. The train
was not quite due, and I walked with them in a meadow
by a little brook while we waited for it. They promised to
send me all news; they overwhelmed me with kindness—
even old Sapt was touched to gentleness, while Fritz was
half-unmanned. I listened in a kind of dream to all they
said. "Rudolf! Rudolf! Rudolf!" still rang in my ears—a
burden of sorrow and of love. At last they saw that I
could not heed them, and we walked up and down in silence, till Fritz touched me on the arm, and I saw, a mile
or more away, the blue smoke of the train. Then I held
out a hand to each of them.

"We are all but half-men this morning," said I, smiling. "But we have been men, eh, Sapt and Fritz, old
friends? We have run a good course between us."

"We have defeated traitors and set the king firm on
his throne," said Sapt.

Then Fritz von Tarlenheim suddenly, before I could
discern his purpose or stay him, uncovered his head and
bent as he used to do, and kissed my hand; and, as I
snatched it away, he said, trying to laugh:

"Heaven doesn't always make the right men kings!"

Old Sapt twisted his mouth as he wrung my hand.

"The devil has his share in most things," said he.

The people at the station looked curiously at the tall
man with the muffled face, but we took no notice of
their glances. I stood with my two friends, and waited till
the train came up to us. Then we shook hands again, saying nothing; and both this time—and, indeed, from old
Sapt it seemed strange—bared their heads, and so stood
still till the train bore me away from their sight. So that
it was thought some great man travelled privately for
his pleasure from the little station that morning;
whereas, in truth, it was only I, Rudolf Rassendyll, an
English gentleman, a cadet of a good House, but a man

of no wealth nor position, nor of much rank. They would have been disappointed to know that. Yet had they known all, they would have looked more curiously still. For, be I what I might now, I had been for three months a king; which, if not a thing to be proud of, is at least an experience to have undergone. Doubtless I should have thought more of it, had there not echoed through the air, from the towers of Zenda that we were leaving far away, into my ears and into my heart the cry of a woman's love—"Rudolf! Rudolf! Rudolf!"

Hark! I hear it now!

CHAPTER XXII

Present, Past—and Future?

THE details of my return home can have but little interest. I went straight to the Tyrol and spent a quiet fortnight—mostly on my back, for a severe chill developed itself; and I was also the victim of a nervous reaction, which made me weak as a baby. As soon as I had reached my quarters, I sent an apparently careless postcard to my brother, announcing my good health and prospective return. That would serve to satisfy the enquiries as to my whereabouts, which were probably still vexing the Prefect of the Police of Strelsau. I let my moustache and imperial grow again; and as hair comes quickly on my face, they were respectable, though not luxuriant, by the time that I landed myself in Paris and called on my friend George Featherly. My interview with him was chiefly remarkable for the number of unwilling but necessary falsehoods that I told; and I rallied him unmercifully when he told me that he had made up his mind that I had gone in the track of Madame de Mauban to Strelsau. The lady, it appeared, was back in Paris but was living in great seclusion—a fact for which gossip found no difficulty in accounting. Did not all the world know of the treachery and death of Duke Michael? Nevertheless, George bade Bertram Bertrand be of good cheer, "for," said he flippantly, "a live poet is better than a dead duke." Then he turned on me and asked:

"What have you been doing to your moustache?"

"To tell the truth," I answered, assuming a sly air, "a man now and then has reasons for wishing to alter his appearance. But it's coming on very well again."

"What? Then I wasn't so far out! If not the fair Antoinette, there was a charmer?"

"There is always a charmer," said I, sententiously.

But George would not be satisfied till he had wormed out of me (he took much pride in his ingenuity) an absolutely imaginary love-affair, attended with the proper *soupçon* of scandal, which had kept me all this time in the peaceful regions of the Tyrol. In return for this narrative, George regaled me with a great deal of what he called "inside information" (known only to diplomatists), as to the true course of events in Ruritania, the plots and counter-plots. In his opinion, he told me, with a significant nod, there was more to be said for Black Michael than the public supposed; and he hinted at a well-founded suspicion that the mysterious prisoner of Zenda, concerning whom a good many paragraphs had appeared, was not a man at all, but (here I had some ado not to smile) a woman disguised as a man; and that strife between the king and his brother for this imaginary lady's favour was at the bottom of their quarrel.

"Perhaps it was Madame de Mauban herself," I suggested.

"No!" said George decisively. "Antoinette de Mauban was jealous of her, and betrayed the duke to the king for that reason. And, to confirm what I say, it's well known that the Princess Flavia is now extremely cold to the king, after having been most affectionate."

At this point I changed the subject, and escaped from George's "inspired" delusions. But if diplomatists never know anything more than they had succeeded in finding out in this instance, they appear to me to be somewhat expensive luxuries.

While in Paris I wrote to Antoinette, though I did not

venture to call upon her. I received in return a very affecting letter, in which she assured me that the king's generosity and kindness, no less than her regard for me, bound her conscience to absolute secrecy. She expressed the intention of settling in the country, and withdrawing herself entirely from society. Whether she carried out her designs, I have never heard; but as I have not met her, or heard news of her up to this time, it is probable that she did. There is no doubt that she was deeply attached to the Duke of Strelsau; and her conduct at the time of his death proved that no knowledge of the man's real character was enough to root her regard for him out of her heart.

I had one more battle left to fight—a battle that would, I knew, be severe, and was bound to end in my complete defeat. Was I not back from the Tyrol, without having made any study of its inhabitants, institutions, scenery, fauna, flora, or other features? Had I not simply wasted my time in my usual frivolous, good-for-nothing way? That was the aspect of the matter which, I was obliged to admit, would present itself to my sister-in-law; and against a verdict based on such evidence, I had really no defence to offer. It may be supposed, then, that I presented myself in Park Lane in a shame-faced, sheepish fashion. On the whole, my reception was not so alarming as I had feared. It turned out that I had done, not what Rose wished, but—the next best thing—what she prophesied. She had declared that I should make no notes, record no observations, gather no materials. My brother, on the other hand, had been weak enough to maintain that a really serious resolve had at length animated me.

When I returned empty-handed, Rose was so occupied in triumphing over Burlesdon that she let me down quite easily, devoting the greater part of her reproaches to my failure to advertise my friends of my whereabouts.

"We've wasted a lot of time trying to find you," she said.

"I know you have," said I. "Half our ambassadors have led weary lives on my account. George Featherly told me so. But why should you have been anxious? I can take care of myself."

"Oh, it wasn't that," she cried scornfully; "but I wanted to tell you about Sir Jacob Borrodaile. You know, he's got an Embassy—at least, he will have in a month—and he wrote to say he hoped you would go with him."

"Where's he going to?"

"He's going to succeed Lord Topham at Strelsau," said she. "You couldn't have a nicer place, short of Paris."

"Strelsau! H'm!" said I, glancing at my brother.

"Oh, *that* doesn't matter!" exclaimed Rose, impatiently. "Now, you will go, won't you?"

"I don't know that I care about it!"

"Oh, you're too exasperating!"

"And I don't think I can go to Strelsau. My dear Rose, would it be—suitable?"

"Oh, nobody remembers that horrid old story now."

Upon this, I took out of my pocket a portrait of the King of Ruritania. It had been taken a month or two before he ascended the throne. She could not miss my point when I said, putting it into her hands:

"In case you've not seen, or not noticed, a picture of Rudolf V., there he is. Don't you think they might recall the story, if I appeared at the Court of Ruritania?"

My sister-in-law looked at the portrait, and then at me.

"Good gracious!" she said, and flung the photograph down on the table.

"What do you say, Bob?" I asked.

Burlesdon got up, went to a corner of the room, and searched in a heap of newspapers. Presently he came back with a copy of the *Illustrated London News*. Opening the paper, he displayed a double-page engraving of the Coronation of Rudolf V. at Strelsau. The photograph and the picture he laid side by side. I sat at the table fronting them; and, as I looked, I grew absorbed. My eye travelled from my own portrait to Sapt, to Strakencz, to the rich robes of the Cardinal, to Black Michael's face, to the stately figure of the princess by his side. Long I looked and eagerly. I was roused by my brother's hand on my shoulder. He was gazing down at me with a puzzled expression.

"It's a remarkable likeness, you see," said I. "I really think I had better not go to Ruritania."

Rose, though half convinced, would not abandon her position.

"It's just an excuse," she said pettishly. "You don't want to do anything. Why, you might become an ambassador!"

"I don't think I want to be an ambassador," said I.

"It's more than you ever will be," she retorted.

That is very likely true, but it is not more than I have been. The idea of being an ambassador could scarcely dazzle me. I had been a king!

So pretty Rose left us in dudgeon; and Burlesdon, lighting a cigarette, looked at me still with that curious gaze.

"That picture in the paper——" he said.

"Well, what of it? It shows that the King of Ruritania and your humble servant are as like as two peas."

My brother shook his head.

"I suppose so," he said. "But I should know you from the man in the photograph."

"And not from the picture in the paper?"

"I should know the photograph from the picture: the picture's very like the photograph, but——"

"Well?"

"It's more like you," said my brother.

My brother is a good man and true—so that, for all that he is a married man and mighty fond of his wife, he should know any secret of mine. But this secret was not mine, and I could not tell it to him.

"I don't think it's so much like me as the photograph," said I boldly. "But, anyhow, Bob, I won't go to Strelsau."

"No, don't go to Strelsau, Rudolf," said he.

And whether he suspects anything, or has a glimmer of the truth, I do not know. If he has, he keeps it to himself, and he and I never refer to it. And we let Sir Jacob Borrodaile find another *attaché.*

Since all these events whose history I have set down happened, I have lived a very quiet life at a small house which I have taken in the country. The ordinary ambitions and aims of men in my position seem to me dull and unattractive. I have little fancy for the whirl of society, and none for the jostle of politics. Lady Burlesdon utterly despairs of me; my neighbours think me an indolent, dreamy, unsociable fellow. Yet I am a young man; and sometimes I have a fancy—the superstitious would call it a presentiment—that my part in life is not yet altogether played; that, somehow and some day, I shall mix again in great affairs, I shall again spin policies in a busy brain, match my wits against my enemies', brace my muscles to fight a good fight and strike stout blows. Such is the tissue of my thoughts as, with gun or rod in hand, I wander through the woods or by the side of the stream. Whether the fancy will be fulfilled, I cannot tell—still less whether the scene that, led by memory, I lay for my new exploits will be the true one—for I love to see myself once again in the crowded streets of Strelsau, or beneath the frowning keep of the Castle of Zenda.

Thus led, my broodings leave the future, and turn back on the past. Shapes rise before me in long array—the wild first revel with the king, the rush with my brave tea-table, the night in the moat, the pursuit in the forest: my friends and my foes, the people who learnt to love and honour me, the desperate men who tried to kill me. And, from amidst these last, comes one who alone of all of them yet moves on earth, though where I know not, yet plans (as I do not doubt) wickedness, yet turns women's hearts to softness and men's to fear and hate.

Where is young Rupert of Hentzau—the boy who came so nigh to beating me? When his name comes into my head, I feel my hand grip and the blood move quicker through my veins: and the hint of Fate—the presentiment—seems to grow stronger and more definite, and to whisper insistently in my ear that I have yet a hand to play with young Rupert; therefore I exercise myself in arms, and seek to put off the day when the vigour of youth must leave me.

One break comes every year in my quiet life. Then I go to Dresden, and there I am met by my dear friend and companion, Fritz von Tarlenheim. Last time, his pretty wife Helga came, and a lusty crowing baby with her. And for a week Fritz and I are together, and I hear all of what falls out in Strelsau; and in the evenings, as we walk and smoke together, we talk of Sapt, and of the king, and often of young Rupert; and, as the hours grow small, at last we speak of Flavia. For every year Fritz carries with him to Dresden a little box; in it lies a red rose, and round the stalk of the rose is a slip of paper with the words written: "Rudolf—Flavia—always." And the like I send back by him. That message, and the wearing of the rings, are all that now bind me and the Queen of Ruritania. For—nobler, as I hold her, for the act—she has followed where her duty to her country and her House led her, and is the wife of the king, uniting his subjects to him by the love they bear to her, giving peace and quiet days to thousands by her self-sacrifice. There are moments when I dare not think of it, but there are others when I rise in spirit to where she ever dwells; then I can thank God that I love the noblest lady in the world, the most gracious and beautiful, and that there was nothing in my love that made her fall short in her high duty.

Shall I see her face again—the pale face and the glorious hair? Of that I know nothing; Fate has no hint, my heart no presentiment. I do not know. In this world, perhaps—nay, it is likely—never. And can it be that somewhere, in a manner whereof our flesh-bound minds have no apprehension, she and I will be together again, with nothing to come between us, nothing to forbid our love? That I know not, nor wiser heads than mine. But if it be never—if I can never hold sweet converse again with her, or look upon her face, or know from her her love; why, then, this side the grave, I will live as becomes the man whom she loves; and, for the other side, I must pray a dreamless sleep.

READ THE TOP 20
SIGNET CLASSICS

1984 BY GEORGE ORWELL

ANIMAL FARM BY GEORGE ORWELL

NARRATIVE OF THE LIFE OF FREDERICK DOUGLASS
   BY FREDERICK DOUGLASS

THE INFERNO BY DANTE

ROMEO AND JULIET BY WILLIAM SHAKESPEARE

WHY WE CAN'T WAIT BY DR. MARTIN LUTHER KING, JR.

NECTAR IN A SIEVE BY KAMALA MARKANDAYA

FRANKENSTEIN BY MARY SHELLEY

BEOWULF TRANSLATED BY BURTON RAFFEL

HAMLET BY WILLIAM SHAKESPEARE

THE FEDERALIST PAPERS BY ALEXANDER HAMILTON

THE ODYSSEY BY HOMER

MACBETH BY WILLIAM SHAKESPEARE

CRIME AND PUNISHMENT BY FYODOR DOSTOYEVSKY

THE HOUND OF THE BASKERVILLES
   BY SIR ARTHUR CONAN DOYLE

THE SCARLET LETTER BY NATHANIEL HAWTHORNE

DR. JEKYLL AND MR. HYDE BY ROBERT L. STEVENSON

A MIDSUMMER NIGHT'S DREAM BY WILLIAM SHAKESPEARE

THE CLASSIC SLAVE NARRATIVES BY HENRY L. GATES

A TALE OF TWO CITIES BY CHARLES DICKENS

PENGUIN.COM
FACEBOOK.COM/SIGNETCLASSIC